More praise for Barbara Victor and FRIENDS, LOVERS, ENEMIES

''Barbara Victor skillfully develops the romantic relation between Beale and Aviram but also provides an insight into the feelings, beliefs and lives of Karami and his wife.''
The Pittsburgh Press

''The love story behind the headlines. One of the most realistic and passionate accounts of the Arab-Israeli conflict ever told in fiction. FRIENDS, LOVERS, ENEMIES captures the pain and tragedy of a century-old war and the love of a man and a woman tangled up in the violence. Terrific—a compelling read. You'll be hooked from the first page.''
LINDA SCHERZER
CNN Jerusalem Correspondent

Friends, Lovers, Enemies

Barbara Victor

BALLANTINE BOOKS • NEW YORK

Copyright © 1991 by Barbara Victor

All rights reserved under International and Pan-American Copyright Conventions, including the right of reproduction in whole or in part in any form. Published in the United States of America by Ballantine Books, a division of Random House, Inc., New York, and simultaneously in Canada by Random House of Canada Limited, Toronto.

This novel is a work of fiction. Names, characters, places and incidents are either the product of the author's imagination or are used fictitiously. Any resemblance to actual events, locales, organizations or persons, living or dead, is entirely coincidental and beyond the intent of either the author or publisher.

Library of Congress Catalog Card Number: 90-56048

ISBN 0-345-37720-6

This edition published by arrangement with Donald I. Fine, Inc.

Manufactured in the United States of America

First Ballantine Books Edition: January 1993

In loving memory of another Gideon who remains the inspiration of all things past and present.

And for the women in my life: Barbara Taylor Bradford, whose gift for words is only exceeded by her gift of friendship. Susan Watt for her steadfast belief and support. Lynn Nesbit whose sense of morality and loyalty is unique in any time, place, or profession.

Acknowledgments

The good-guy list is a list of people without whose talent, guidance, generosity, and wisdom, the author would be unable to write a grocery list let alone a book. The good-guy list is also a list of those same people without whose love and encouragement the author would be unable to walk, talk, have a laugh once in a while or make a sandwich while grocery lists and books are being written.

As all lists have beginnings, middles, and ends, it would be easy to claim that the order of names on this good-guy list is purely haphazard and has nothing to do with emotional preference. That is not the case. The order of names on this list has everything to do with emotional preference. But that is not to say that to be listed at the beginning of this list is better than being listed at the end or somewhere in the middle. For what do any of us really have that is ours alone except a secret order of emotional preference in our heads? And, if we're very lucky, a good-guy list of people without whom our lives would be less full.

Amelia de Marcos, who doesn't realize how much she is appreciated and needed. And for José de Marcos, thank you.

Sabine Boulongne for knowing when to keep my words and when to throw them away.

Jean Rosenthal, again, for the very beginning.

Michel Alexandre for his continued friendship.

Brigitte Jessen, my very best friend on two continents.

Mark Schiffer, a new face in an old crowd.

Roz Scott because she takes everything to heart and makes us all so secure.

Lisa Healy, a find as a friend, a gift as an editor.

Tom Wallace for his astounding faith.

Robert Solomon for all the years of patience.

Beth Tedesco for her unfailing dependability in a sometimes chaotic world.

Jeff Thau for all his optimism.

Alain Carrière, the Gérard Depardieu of French publishing; my hardest, toughest and most favorite editor.

Sally and Erich Heinemann for their generosity and love.

Cathy Nolan for being present and accounted for during all the ups, downs, and sideways of life.

Lisa Berkowitz, my very best friend on three continents; for her support, belief, loyalty and loads of laughs from New York to Florida—the fourth continent.

David, Ellie, and Benjamin Schiffer with loads of love and kisses.

Lennart Sane, my worldwide and moonwide agent, for his tireless effort and devotion.

Dmitri Nabokov, with affection and love, my still-best friend.

Herzog.

And for Stephanie Schiffer who gets the sister of the decade award. Here's to another five or so decades.

And for the good guys on both sides of the struggle, a special thanks for all the help and a profound wish for a lasting peace.

Chapter One

WHEN THE BOMB exploded in front of the Alitalia office on the Via Veneto, Sasha Beale had just pulled on one thigh-high beige suede boot and was about to pull on the other. Had she paused several seconds longer outside Giovanni's Bootery to decide whether or not to spend money on this latest fad, she would have undoubtedly lost a leg. Or, had she accepted the offer of a second espresso at Harry's American Bar from the man who smelled as if he had toppled into a vat of Giorgio cologne, she might have found herself crossing the street just as the bomb detonated and would have surely lost her life.

In either case, had she dawdled, she might have noticed the chocolate brown Mercedes as it pulled up in front of Alitalia, and the short, muscular man step out. But then again, she might not have paid any attention since he was typical of so many Italian males who dressed all in black, adorned by gold chains, watches, and rings. Still, if questioned, she might have described him as a "bodybuilder" type, distracted perhaps, even rude, obviously in a big hurry but certainly not someone who would have caused her any alarm. Or, if really pressed, she might have said that he looked like any one of those sleazy natives who hung around hotel lobbies hawking his wares and hoping for a taker in the body of a lonely tourist. What Sasha wouldn't have done was to describe the man as a terrorist. She wouldn't

1

have known that he was actually a Palestinian carrying
a false Libyan passport. Nor could she have known
about the false bottom in the pigskin briefcase that he
left just inside the double glass entrance door of the
Alitalia office.

The blast knocked Sasha to the floor of Giovanni's
when it blew out a portion of the plate window. Despite
what felt like a twisted back and bruised elbow, she
was far luckier than some of the others who were thrown
sideways instead of down and who, as a result, suffered
cuts, concussions and one partially severed leg.

From the instant of the explosion—and it wasn't impossible that Sasha lost consciousness for several minutes—everything seemed to happen in slow motion. The
traffic outside seemed to coast to a halt, the light seemed
to change from *avanti* to *stop* at least four times before
anybody moved, the bodies seemed to float through the
air like so many pieces of fluff from a hundred dande-
lions. Yet, when she managed to crawl toward what was
left of the door, she had the distinct impression that an
unseen hand had turned on klieg lights and pumped up
the speed from thirty-three to seventy-eight while an
unheard voice had yelled, ''Action.'' For within seconds of the time that it took her to stand up and step
into the glorious Rome sunlight, sirens were blasting
and people were screaming and running in all directions. And what struck her then and what she would
never forget was that everywhere she looked, all she
saw was a carnage of humanity, a grotesque stew of the
dead and dying.

Wandering through the rubble, the only rational
thought she had was of the indignity of such violent
death. She was acutely aware of the contents of briefcases and purses and shopping bags that were scattered
everywhere, papers blowing in the gentle spring breeze,
lipsticks and pens rolling around in the gutter, bread

and eggs crushed under the feet of those who had managed to run away. Her movements were on automatic as she stopped to talk to or touch the injured who were moaning in fear and pain.

In numbed silence, she watched as a man picked his way through the flesh and dust, his arms outstretched, tears rolling down his cheeks. She waited with a woman whose body was bent into a seated position like one of those plastic figures that fit into one of those plastic cars, until several medics lifted the woman onto a stretcher. Backing away, she turned her head, her eyes focusing on fragments of a red jacket that was strewn over a car and partially hooked over its radio antenna. Moving forward, she looked down to notice the small boy lying facedown in the gutter, his arms somehow still in the jacket's sleeves. Through more bits of clothing and rubble, she reached him, kneeling down to stroke his hair. He was barely alive, making gurgling and rasping noises as he labored to breathe through a hole in his chest. Eight or nine years old, she judged; mortally wounded, the words bounced around inside her head. Cheek nearly touching his, she soothed him with lies, whispered words that were useless as he slipped away. "Mummy!" he whimpered only once before there was silence. Several policemen gently removed her. "Where are you taking him?" she heard herself asking, unable to wipe away the tears fast enough. Eight or nine years old. It was questionable how long she could remain standing.

"*Morto,*" one of the policemen tried to explain.

"Yes," she wept, "*morto*. But where, *dove*, where?"

"*Morto,*" someone else added as if she might have still been unsure.

She wept softly as she watched someone cover the child with a blanket that someone else had pulled from the trunk of a car. It was then that she turned her head to notice the body of a woman—a piece of that same

fabric clutched in one of her hands—trapped under the
wheels of a car that had obviously screeched out of
control, but not before its front axle had rolled over her
broken body. Sasha rushed up to the medic who at-
tended the woman and again tried to make herself understood. "The boy, *bambino*," she pointed to the
small covered figure being slid into the back of an ambulance. "Red jacket, look," she cried. As if it mattered. "*Morto*," the man repeated gently before he said
it all in English. "They are both dead, *Signorina*, both
of them."

In every direction that Sasha turned, there was nothing left. Each way that she looked, the street was blan-
keted with shards of glass, twisted metal and the leaves
from magnolia trees that had been shaken loose in the
explosion, a bizarre mosaic of what would be called
debris in tomorrow's newspapers.

She would never be able to explain why at that moment all her instincts surged to the surface to overcome
the shock. Suddenly she felt herself gathering every last
ounce of strength that she had to race toward the Flora
Hotel on the corner. Running inside and up to the front
desk, she searched around for a telephone until she
spotted a row of them on the opposite wall. There was
the usual slot for a five- ten- or thirty-lira piece. After
spending two weeks in Rome, Sasha knew enough to
put the proper coin in the slot so her call would go
through to the Federated Broadcast Network's Rome
Bureau. This inexplicable ability to think clearly in a
disaster was something she would either regret later or
congratulate herself on. Technically, she was on vacation from her job as a crime reporter for the local nightly
news, on leave to recover from a divorce that had sapped
every bit of humor and pragmatism she possessed, on
holiday before taping would begin for a brand-new documentary that she was slated to host. After witnessing
what she had just witnessed, however, recovering from

a divorce seemed insignificant. Suddenly Carl Feldhammer, esteemed member of the American Psychiatric Association, witty, charming, handsome and able to make love all night every night—although not necessarily always to her—just didn't seem paramount to her very survival.

It wasn't the first time that Sasha called the Rome Bureau since arriving there. Either loneliness or duty or respect had prompted her to check in with Bernie Hernandez, the Rome Bureau chief, shortly after checking into the hotel. Hello, this is Sasha Beale and I just wanted to let you know that I was here in case you needed anything or wanted me to take anything back to the States for you. A family of sorts, she reasoned, a home away from home, or as it turned out, a canteen in a war zone.

Bernie had invited her to the office, complimented her on her cheekbones and legs, offered her the predictable Cinzano from the usual refrigerator in the corner of the office, and settled back to recount his experiences as a foreign correspondent, or as Bernie put it, the man who single-handedly covered every rotten, lousy piece of news that ever broke in Western Europe. Bernie wore tough, crusty, almost vulgar skin, was built like a Mayan Indian, had apparently slept through integration and feminism in the United States, and generally loved every minute of who he was and what he did. He'd seen it all, he bragged shamelessly, done it all, he winked, so that now he only stepped in to help the regular reporters cover the really big stories. Only Bernie called them events.

Sasha wasn't impressed. At thirty-four, after a six-year marriage to a Freudian psychiatrist and a ten-year career in the news business, she found it difficult to relate to a man whose walls were covered with membership certificates to various airline clubs and whose desk was cluttered with photographs of himself in a belted trenchcoat posing with famous people.

But she was polite, even charming. Bernie Hernandez wasn't her problem, she reasoned, and the possibility of ever having to work with him was remote. She was only passing through, consider this a courtesy call, and she hoped she hadn't disturbed him, but no, she wasn't able to see Rome nightlife on this trip, but how nice of him to ask. They parted after only half an hour, he with the expectation of dinner before she left, she with the intention of never seeing him again. And here she was now, standing in the lobby of the Flora Hotel and calling him because they both happened to be in the business of catastrophes and what just happened certainly qualified as one of the bigger ones.

"Bernie Hernandez," Sasha said into the receiver.

"Who's calling him?"

"Sasha Beale."

The bored tone, "I'll see if he's in," didn't exactly make her calmer.

But Bernie was on the line instantly. "Sasha, you got my message."

"What message?"

"I left a message at your hotel because there's been a terrorist attack."

"I know, I was there when it happened. I mean, I'm here now."

"Holy shit! That's fantastic!"

She shut her eyes. It didn't compute.

"What're you doing there?" he went on excitedly.

"I'm not sure," she replied, her voice unsteady.

"Are you hurt?"

"No, I'm all right," she said softly, the image of that child before her eyes.

"Look, Sasha," he began urgently, "don't go getting hysterical on me because I need you."

"Bernie, I can't," she started to say but he was still talking.

"Just stay calm, do you hear me?"

Calm wasn't the solution in her mind right then. What she wanted was to find out about that little boy.

"I need you, Sasha," he repeated.

"Me?" she managed, "why me?"

He cleared his throat. "That's why I called you. I just got off the phone with New York and they, uh, they want you to . . ."

"They what?"

"They want you to cover it."

"Me? Why me?"

"Hey, don't think I didn't ask them that."

But she was far away. "Ask them what?"

"Why they wanted you to cover it." His tone was calmer still. "Look, Sasha, I don't badger New York. I just push the buttons to make it all happen so everybody's happy."

She was back with them then. "Where's your regular reporter?"

He cleared his throat again. "On maternity leave."

Another spear through her heart, that child, that little boy with that baby-smooth cheek. "Why can't you do this? You can't get a story much bigger than this."

"They want you," he said dully.

"But I've been covering street crime," she said wearily, already aware of how ridiculous and lame and dumb it sounded.

"And what do you think that is—a bake-off in Secaucus?"

She leaned her head against the wall and closed her eyes. "No, Bernie, it's no bake-off."

"This is heaven-fucking sent," he whispered with an intensity that made Sasha hold the receiver slightly away from her ear. "Just when New York was thinking about closing the Rome Bureau, we're going to scoop the other

networks right up their asses! So don't fold on me, Sasha Beale, just stay calm and cool and position yourself
in the best spot you can find with the sun behind you
so when the crew gets there, all they have to do is hand
you the microphone and we're in business. Are you
with me?''

And she was busy right then, trying to remember all
the answers and questions and excuses and smart retorts
she might possibly need to find out about that child. To
find out if the woman under that car was his mother or
at least someone who was in charge of his safety for the
afternoon.

''Are you with me?''

She felt herself nodding before realizing that Bernie
couldn't see her or the tears that streaked her face or
the fear in her eyes. ''I'm with you,'' she mumbled.
And she was, ''with him,'' that is. After all, she was
the one who had made the phone call in the first place.
What did she expect, she wondered, that he'd thank her
and tell her to go some place and relax until everything
blew over?

''Do you have a white handkerchief?''

''A what?''

''A white handkerchief?'' he repeated impatiently.

''Why?''

''Don't ask questions, just answer.''

''No,'' she said, looking down at the crumpled pink
tissue clutched in one hand.

''Then go out and find one,'' Bernie spoke slowly as
if to an idiot.

''Where am I supposed to find a white handkerchief?''

''Then go find a white Kleenex,'' he snapped. ''And
when you do, hold it in your right hand, up high, so
the crew recognizes you when they get there.'' He
chuckled. ''The best part about this is those clowns
from the other networks won't even know who you are

until it's all over. Now go find a white Kleenex. Do you hear me?''

Again, she nodded, forgetting that he wasn't actually standing right on top of her with his finger pointed in her face. "Bernie, I can't."

"Yes, you can, Sasha, and you will because I'm going to be right with you, feeding while you report."

It wasn't really happening, she considered until she realized that it had already happened and whether she reported it or not wasn't going to change anything. At least that's what Carl would have told her, that whether or not she had come to Rome in the first place or wandered into that bootery or agreed to cover this catastrophe, she simply didn't have the power to alter other people's fate. So, how come he did? How come Carl Feldhammer managed to change the direction of her entire life by walking out one day? Not that any of this made a difference to that little boy who once wore a red jacket.

Bernie's tone was vaguely patronizing when he inquired, "Is your face all blotchy?"

The questions didn't make sense. "Probably," she answered distractedly.

"Then go wash it and comb your hair and put on some makeup—not too much, but just enough to look appealingly wan. Got that?"

A rage was choking her, struggling to the surface and caught somewhere in her throat. "I don't think so, Bernie."

"What does that mean?"

But she had already reached the limit. Every part of her mind and body had gone to war with every other part and it was a draw. "It means we're going to cover this as if it were radio. No props or glamour or makeup or lights, nothing except what's already out there on the street." She wanted to throw up. "And if your crew goes in for a close-up that invades anybody's privacy, I walk.'' She blew her nose.

''So,'' he said slowly, ''you're giving me conditions.''

She shook her head. ''No, I'm just telling you that what happened is horrible enough without turning it into a circus.''

''Have it your way,'' he said after several seconds of silence.

''I'll do a good job,'' she added, remembering that in this business *A* was for *ambition* and not *anguish*.

''I hope so, because you really fell into it this time.''

In all fairness, not that she was obliged to be fair, Bernie hadn't been there when it happened. He hadn't seen what was left or what wasn't from one minute to the next. She hung up the phone, determined to find a white Kleenex and the best possible spot with the sun behind her to do the stand-up. Which was when she glanced down and noticed that she had on only one thigh-high beige suede boot. The other foot was bare.

Chapter Two

THE SEASIDE COMMUNITY of Herziliah Petuah had all
the charm of the Côte d'Azur with its sprawling white
stucco houses and sweeping palm trees that lined the
coast of the blue waters of the Mediterranean. Unlike
the coast of the Riviera, however, the beaches were
relatively unspoiled—wide expanses of white sand that
stretched as far north as the less chic city of Natanya,
and south toward the urban chaos of Tel Aviv.

The city itself was European in atmosphere, French
in style, and famous for the boutiques and bistros along
the corniche, some selling designer clothes, others nou-
velle cuisine, but all at prices rivaling those in Paris.

The majority of people who lived there were of Bel-
gian or French descent and their financial ties remained
in the diamond center of Antwerp, the arms market of
Brussels, or the stock exchange of Paris. Yet, if there
was a facade of luxury and complacency, it was just
that—a facade—as everybody knew only too well that
their insulated community was nothing more than a
bourgeois oasis set in the middle of literal and figurative
land mines.

The last house at the end of the cul de sac on Mevo
Yoram Street was slightly less grand than the others,
although some said its charm was in its unpainted stone
exterior and rustic overgrowth of ivy that nearly covered the first-floor windows. Others in the neighborhood took exception to the untended grass and cluster

11

of tall and ragged flowers that were planted in what was a rather unsuccessful attempt at an "English" garden. But what evoked the most conflict and discussion were the large sculptures that were scattered about the lawn, abstract works of art to the more cultivated eyes, scraps of twisted metal to the less imaginative.

Toward the back of the property, the door to a shed was ajar so that through it could be seen other works of art in various stages of completion, a disarray of paint bottles, brushes, canvasses and cracked pottery. But the disorder inside the house was of another variety, more eclectic than messy, a conscious effort to defy convention, to display the dusty past in what was clearly a stark and modern setting.

Glass and chrome and raw wood were mixed in with shabby antiques, Hebraic artifacts and tattered leather photograph albums. Stacks of new books and current magazines were piled on frayed Oriental rugs while pictures of people from another era stared out from tarnished silver frames. Yet, there was a definite thread that linked each room with its high ceilings and white walls. Black and white lithographs of scenes from the Holocaust hung in layers all over the house, one on top of the other and all signed with the same signature.

Gideon Aviram sat in what had once been the library when his father was alive, and what had become known as "off limits" after he and Miriam and their only child, Avi, lived there alone. Not only was the room "off limits" as a rule, but also as a necessity as it was filled with possessions that belonged only to Gideon. Tennis equipment, old records and tapes, beat-up running shoes, torn socks, piles of books and dozens of files and papers were strewn all over the floor and tables. Displayed on the bookshelves were archeological finds that Gideon had dug up in Egypt during the 1973 Yom Kippur War, memorabilia collected during a career that spanned four continents and two decades. The room was "off limits" for another reason—it was the only room in the house that had been spared a tribute to the dead while they were barely alive. One side of the argument was that Gideon wasn't supportive of Miriam's career, especially since she had gained all her success and recognition as a "Holocaust" artist, acclaimed for bringing life to a period when there was none. On the other side, the argument was that Gideon resented living each day infused by his wife's perpetual sadness, swept along by her obsessive preparation for an event that had already happened.

He was handsome, Gideon, in a classic way with an aristocratic ruggedness: the jaw square, the nose masculine although perfectly refined and chiseled, the mouth sensuous, the bottom lip slightly fuller than the top, a cleft in the chin, the complexion olive, hair dark and somewhat longer than might be expected given the flecks of gray in the sideburns. Still, he was in tremendous shape for a man who had recently celebrated his forty-fifth birthday, even if he could occasionally look older than his years given the number of fine lines when he frowned or the two creases on either side of his mouth when he smiled. The most startling feature, however, were his eyes, clear blue. They stood out more for their unusual color than for the appearance in such an otherwise brooding face. Now they were red-rimmed and puffy as he squinted through a haze of smoke, letting one cigarette after the other burn down between his fingers until nothing remained but an ash which he let fall into a ceramic bowl.

He had been in this uncombed, unshaved, and numbed state for nearly two weeks now, ever since Miriam gave him the ultimatum to give up Yael or the marriage was over. And what had been different that time from all the others was that his wife hadn't gotten hysterical when she demanded her husband back, nor had

Gideon retreated within himself as a response. Instead, he absorbed her words the way a prize fighter absorbs a punch on slow-motion film—an imperceptible twinge of the jaw, blinks of the eye and what might have been interpreted as apathy had both of them not known better. The truth was that while Gideon appeared unfeeling on the surface, underneath he carried his own guilt so close to his heart that every weakness or fault or mistake became a silent but all-consuming crusade. And he hadn't changed since he was a young man studying Arab Affairs at the Hebrew University in Jerusalem, which was where the Mossad had found him and recruited him.

Given his training and old habits, Gideon's first reaction to Miriam was predictable when he neither admitted nor denied his involvement with another woman. Yet, as the days passed and discussions intensified, he found himself more willing to talk about it. Perhaps it was because a tacit agreement of sorts had been reached where each was prepared to relinquish certain patterns, pleasure and obsessions. In a rare instance when there was no barrage of tears, Miriam claimed her ultimatum had less to do with her pride than it had with her work. She announced that the forms had become flat, the images lifeless, the subject tired. And in an even rarer instance of self-deprecating humor, she added that maybe the moment had come to move on to other atrocities.

For Gideon, the desire to stop leading a double life had been occurring to him for some time. Gradually, he had begun to consider another career as well as another way of living. Perhaps the time had come to get into something that he could share with his family, especially with his son who was getting old enough to ask questions. There was no doubt that Gideon had become disillusioned with his life, with all the lies and excuses and sacrifices that somehow didn't quite justify the results either for the State or for his marriage. Still, it was easier to rectify the problem when it came to his personal life, which was why he decided to end the affair. He also decided he needed time alone with Yael to explain that everything was over, that he had changed, that they could never be again.

He thought it a good idea, therefore, to appeal to the artist in his wife when he suggested that instead of being so conventional to patch up a marriage with a discussion, or worse, an intention, that she might want to take the boy to Rome, go visit the museums and the ruins. He would join them in a few days, he promised, after he tended to some unfinished business in Israel. And if Miriam chose to accept the lie and not make an issue, it was because she saw the trapped look on Gideon's face and recognized his sense of decency in an otherwise indecent situation. And if Gideon intended absolutely to keep his word, it was because he saw how ravaged Miriam looked, something he attributed to all those weeks and months and years of deception . . .

When the bomb exploded in front of the Alitalia office on the Via Veneto, Miriam and Avi had just arrived and were waiting in line for a map of Rome. The impact of the blast had thrown Miriam through the plate-glass window and into the street, where any doubt or hope or chance that she had survived was eliminated when a car lurched out of control and ran over her body. Avi had been hurled face down in the gutter, the explosion not only ripping off his brand-new red jacket but also tearing a hole clear through his chest. The best estimate after the autopsy was that he had taken twenty-two minutes to die.

Even before the identities of the victims were officially released, Gideon knew. But it wasn't until several agonizing hours later when the names came over the fax machine in his office that he read that his wife and son were among those blown to bits by a bomb carrying the usual demand for justice and land. His reaction was so violent that the head of the Mossad instructed everyone to withhold further information from him and deny him access to the photographs that were beginning to filter out of Rome.

Gideon's grief came over him in waves, like labor pains that intensified with each stage yet couldn't be delayed while reserves of strength were summoned. At first he sat in his office and contemplated suicide, murder and then several ironies that hadn't yet escaped him. He wondered if Miriam, in those infinitesimal seconds before she died, had realized that she had been killed by a second-generation enemy of mankind, her parents having survived the prototype. Or, had she realized that she had been the victim of what she had jokingly referred to as one of those "other" atrocities? It occurred to Gideon that she would never know that whatever he had ever found difficult about her had vanished with that bomb. As a penance, he was doomed to live with only the good memories; as a punishment, he was destined to feel only love for the woman he had married when they were both so young and hopeful.

Avi was another story. The loss was intolerable, with the boy's face assaulting his mind until Gideon became demented with grief. All the clichés he had ever heard or read or rejected he found himself experiencing as real symptoms in relentless succession. He had a lump in his throat, wooden limbs, a heavy heart and tears that flowed without warning as if someone had turned on a faucet. And sometimes, he would just sit back and wait for the heart attack to come, when the cramps in his left arm would persist, or the dull ache in his jaw and neck wouldn't let up, or the searing pain through his chest overcame his sense of reason.

The least complicated chore became an insurmountable effort, whether it was washing his face or walking from room to room or making a cup of coffee. What was ironic was that if either Miriam or Avi had ever accused him of being withdrawn and undemonstrative, withholding and incapable of showing emotion, he exhibited none of those failings in his anguish. Gideon wept and mourned with an abandon that sapped every last ounce of strength from his body and which, had his family been forced to live through it with him, they would have found impossible to bear.

In defense of what little sanity remained, he closed the door to Avi's room without entering, unable to touch or look at the boy's things without collapsing. The stockings and bras that Miriam had left drying in the bathroom he took down and folded away in her drawer, the lingering scent of her perfume wafting over him until he felt as if he would faint.

The news was recounted in several different versions, all sensational, although some were more accurate and up-to-date than others. Several German chains reported that a right-wing pro-Nazi group had taken credit for the bombing in retaliation for the Vatican's refusal to receive Kurt Waldheim, while one of the privately owned English stations claimed that it was the IRA who had committed the "heinous act," an attempt to secure the release of one of their members from a Sicilian jail. But that theory fell apart when it was learned that the IRA member in question had been released on drunk-driving charges one week earlier. And through it all, one of the American networks kept blasting its scoop of the attack across international air waves, boasting that not only had one of its journalists been on the scene when it happened, but had also sustained minor injuries.

The first few days when those images were being flashed across television screens every few hours, Gideon took to answering the phone when it rang—which was incessantly—and saying nothing. Holding the receiver to his ear, he would listen while the caller sputtered his or her condolences before hanging up soundlessly. Even when the big boss, the head of the Mossad, called, Gideon said nothing, just listened to the words, knowing that whenever he was ready to talk—anytime, anywhere—the boss was available. Yael telephoned as well, three, six, sometimes ten times a day in the beginning. She would plead with Gideon to say something, anything, just so she could hear his voice. After a while, when it was obvious that he had no intention of satisfying her pleas, she would call and hang up when he picked up the receiver. But he never doubted who it was as the click was always preceded by a sigh that he recognized as hers.

Neighbors came by as well, knocked on the door or rang the bell, and left baskets of food and flowers or notes expressing their shock and sorrow. And even when they wouldn't knock or ring, Gideon could feel their presence as they lingered outside, too tactful to intrude, too horrified to stay away.

Dusk was settling over Herziliah one evening when the doorbell rang for the first time in days. It was a long and steady ring that somehow sounded different than the others, more confident, as if the person belonging to the finger poised on the bell had no intention of going away. And as Gideon moved slowly through the house toward the entrance foyer, he had no doubt who the visitor was and even less doubt that he would let him in. One hand on the knob, he flung it open, stepping aside so that Rafi Unger could enter.

"It's enough," the older man announced, clutching Gideon's shoulders and drawing him close. "You need me here," he added before releasing him.

There was no argument as Gideon stood there, looking at the man through his tears. Glancing away self-consciously, he answered, "You look worse than I do."

"I wouldn't be so sure," Rafi answered in his raspy voice. "And anyway, you haven't stayed with me for twenty years because of my looks." He ran a hand through his white hair, the only feature about him that had changed over the years. Everything else had stayed the same: the trim physique, the energy, the intense dark eyes, and the commitment to the job as head of the Mossad.

Gideon turned to lead the way into the library. Rafi followed and when both men were seated, announced, "You're smoking too much."

Exhaling, Gideon shut his eyes, leaned his head back against the chair, and stretched out his legs, the cigarette dangling at his side. "How would you know? You just got here."

"I can smell it."

Gazing off in the distance somewhere, Gideon's tone was bitter when he finally spoke. "I used to make Avi take vitamins every day and eat properly so he wouldn't get sick and run down. For what?"

"Gideon, it's impossible to know what to say."

But all the frustration and anger were suddenly on the surface. "Don't say anything about my smoking and don't say anything comforting because I've had enough words and flowers and notes to last me—"

"People don't know any other way to express their sympathy."

Gideon turned to look at a grouping of photographs on a bookshelf. "You know," he began almost to himself, "for the first time in all the years we were married, she talked to me." He didn't wait for a response because his words weren't meant as an invitation to a dialogue. "Right before she left, she talked to me for the first time." He shook his head. "She told me I was the only person who never expected explanations or asked questions. And the horrible part is that the reason I never invaded her life was only because I never wanted mine invaded, and it wasn't because of the work." He rubbed his eyes. "My whole life was a series of compartments that had to be kept secret so I spent most of my time making sure nothing ever overlapped." He inhaled. "What I should have been doing was trying to understand how much my wife was suffering."

"In what way?"

"In *every* way. From the beginning, from the time she was a child and her family saw her as the first generation of hope who was born in Israel and who was supposed to do great things just for that reason alone."

"Out of the ashes," Rafi murmured.

"So common, so understandable," Gideon said, "except when you're living with it every day."

"How could you understand in the beginning, you were both so young."

Still, it wasn't a discussion and still there was little continuity in Gideon's words or thoughts. He was suddenly far away, back in the beginning of their lives together. "Every night there was a fight. She'd wait until I was already in bed before she'd come into the bedroom. And then she'd stand there to make sure that I was asleep and if I moved or tossed or said something to her, she'd stall, folding her clothes over and over again." He took a drag on his cigarette. "Then she'd crouch down in the dark at the foot of the bed and pull on a nightgown that looked like it belonged to her grandmother. I'd yell at her and she'd cry and if I tried to touch her when she finally got into bed, it was as if I was trying to kill her. Until one day I just stopped trying and yelling but I never bothered to understand why.''

''Nothing happens without reasons.''

''I'm not trying to justify anything.''

''But you had no choice.''

''That's a bad excuse.''

''What should you have done?''

''Tried to understand why she was so cold and withdrawn, so frightened . . .''

''You were her husband, Gideon, not her doctor.''

Gideon stood to walk over to the window. ''We stayed up most of that last night talking about Yael, and about all the others.'' He smiled vaguely. ''Her reaction was so incredible to me, so unbelievable, coming from her. She said it wasn't the sex that bothered her, it was the lunches and the dinners and the walks by the sea or the movies or the phone conversations.'' He turned his head toward a photograph of his wife taken on their wedding day. ''She was jealous of the intimacy, not the act. And do you know what she did then?'' But he didn't wait for an answer. ''She took my hands and told me about . . . the women in her life. My wife, she told me about her women.'' He paused to wipe his eyes. ''Women were always the problem, she said, always the issue between us.'' He sank down into the chair, a movement that put years on his life. ''It was just a question of whose women and which one of us had our priorities straight.'' He looked at Rafi. ''So you see, all these years, with my monumental ego, I never believed for a minute that my wife had a lover.'' He stood again to lean against the window and when he held the cigarette to his lips, his hand trembled. ''And now,'' he shook his head, ''I don't even know what I'm mourning, her death or our life together.''

Rafi's tone was impassive. ''And so she didn't have a lover, at least not the way you imagined.''

''No, I guess she didn't,'' Gideon said softly, ''because men to her were black boots and torture chambers and concentration camps. But with me, she claimed she felt safe." His eyes filled with tears. "So, I sent her to Rome to die."

"You're not responsible."

"Don't be a fool, of course I'm responsible."

"Why, because you couldn't predict the future?"

But he was beyond cynicism or even reason, for that matter. "No, because of all the things I did or didn't do or couldn't be for her."

"The Messiah in the body of a Mossadnik."

His voice was husky. "Because I created the reason that Rome became a choice in our lives. Me, I created that option."

"No, you have no part in it except what you insist on making. You're not guilty."

"There are degrees of guilt. And my son . . ."

"I have facts," Rafi said without warning.

Turning, Gideon walked slowly back to the chair. "That doesn't surprise me," he said wearily, "since you run an efficient organization."

"Do you want to know?"

How simply the question was posed, how casually, although the reaction it evoked inside Gideon's head was a series of explosions that filled every chamber with images that had already become part of his past. "And what do you propose I do with that information?" he inquired, the accent suddenly more British than Israeli, although fatigue caused traces of the French from his childhood to emerge as well. "Will it change my part in it? Or theirs?"

"You're playing God and it's not fair to yourself or even to them. They wouldn't want you taking the blame for what happened."

"Who's playing God now? Or is speaking for the dead a human trait, or maybe that particular facility comes with the job of running that super-human organization of yours.''

"So now it's mine," the man mumbled before rubbing his eyes. "No, Gideon, no, but how I wish I could have played God, since God was the only one who could have known how to stop what happened."

It was the first time he felt relief, hearing about someone else's failure, someone else's culpability.

"Even our own sources in the PLO didn't know anything until after it was all over. This was one time when only the people directly involved knew dates and places and equipment and delivery. This one was absolutely contained."

Still, Gideon wouldn't permit himself to abandon the basic premise. "My family didn't have to be there," he said, and then repeated, "They didn't have to be in Rome, *goddamnit*."

"But they were and nothing can ever change that." He stared at his hands a moment, clasping them on his lap. "All I can offer you now is information so we can act."

"So it won't happen again. Tell me, do you really think it makes a difference to me whether or not something like this ever happens again?" Head back, he closed his eyes for a moment before opening them to squint through the smoke. "I don't care," he said, separating the words precisely. And he didn't, because he simply didn't know how. For all the horrors he had ever witnessed in what was considered to be a dangerous career, there had never been anything to prepare him for this. "The rest of it is your reality, not mine."

"My only reality is to satisfy a sense of justice."

"How the hell can you use the word *justice* to me? Or maybe that's one of your euphemisms and what you really mean to say is *revenge*. Only I'm not up for that either right now—"

"You never were, Gideon," Rafi said with a tinge of regret, "so what's changed?"

"What's changed is that this time the bomb fell on my house."

"As if your way could have stopped it from falling anywhere."

"There was a chance in the beginning."

"You can't even define the beginning."

But Gideon could define it, Lebanon in 1982, which was when he first began agonizing over motives and methods of defending his country. It was then that he started reading certain Russian writers, some from before the revolution, and others who had emerged after the Gulag, but who all made him ponder the dilemma of negotiation, of compromise, of murder.

In the age of the locomotive, he told Rafi one night, it was absurd to imagine two men facing each other with pistols drawn as a way of settling a dispute. It struck him as equally barbaric that in the age of space travel, enemies should face each other through the sight of a missile. In other words, it was no longer solely a case of survival since there were other options. A divorce, he announced quite seriously, he wanted a divorce, and when Rafi appeared confused by the word he explained, "For years we've been sleeping in the same bed with the Arabs and not making love. It's time to separate."

"So even now, it gets back to the same argument."

"Do you remember what you once said?" Gideon asked.

Rafi shook his head.

"If we give them Nablus and Gaza, the next thing they'd want would be Haifa and Tel Aviv." Gideon waited. "Do you remember?"

Rafi nodded.

"Tell me, if we don't give them Nablus and Gaza, will they stop wanting Haifa and Tel Aviv?"

"It's gone beyond territory."

"Which is why my wife and son died on the streets of Rome," he said angrily, feeling a bizarre sense of triumph when he watched the other man pale.

"I need you, Gideon."

"Are you drafting me as your resident rabid dog?"

"Not a rabid dog."

"Then what do you prefer calling it?"

"A man with a sense of duty."

He laughed.

"A victim," Rafi tried.

How he wished he was the victim instead of the malefactor charged with the responsibility of taking revenge. Yet, somehow he saw himself as neither victim nor malefactor, but rather as accomplice—by omission, benign neglect, or sheer stupidity. "You're right about one thing, Rafi, without a personal stake in it, there's always the possibility of distraction." His voice was steady. "But with one, there's this thing about guilt." He clasped his hands on his knees and sat forward. "And there's something else," he added, just as calmly, "I'm not particularly interested in who lives or who dies right now."

"Of course you're not," Rafi said quickly. "But you will be again because it's not possible to survive this kind of tragedy without thinking about the future."

"And what makes you think I intend to survive?"

"What does that mean?"

"Something like this never heals."

"Everything heals, Gideon, that's part of the problem."

Gideon stood then, his six-foot frame looking not so robust as usual, his broad shoulders slumped. "I appreciate everything you're trying to do," he began, "but do me a favor now and go away."

"They died instantly," Rafi lied.

He started, a million angry words suppressed as fast as they entered his head.

And as if to make amends, Rafi explained, "I was in Rome the other day and went over forensic reports." He cleared his throat. "I also went to the hospital to see the survivors and most of them would have been better off if they hadn't."

The unmentionable had been addressed, the wound opened.

"We know exactly who did this."

Gideon said nothing, counting the seconds before the rest would follow.

"Let me show you some pictures."

Gideon put up a hand. "No, please."

"Of someone who's in a position to help."

Relieved, he lowered it. "My judgment is shot."

"Let me decide."

"It's not up to you."

"This isn't a contest," Gideon hedged, aware that the dossier was already on the table, the photographs half out of the folder.

"It's a question of time before your judgment comes back, so it might as well be sooner instead of later. At least then you won't have any regrets."

"There's only one regret." But he was already sitting back in the chair, his hands no longer clutching the sides in resistance.

A stroke of good luck was the way Rafi put it, an unexpected bonus that would confirm everything they picked up from other sources, as well as supply them with daily information they would ordinarily never know. The girl happened to be very good at what she did and what she did was television; drawing out the most intimate facts from people, getting emotionally involved with her subjects, bringing out the same feel-

ings in them, making them relax, and laugh and forget
they were being interviewed. But most of all, she had
this uncanny ability to absorb the most minute detail.
And she was good-looking, recently divorced, vulnerable, a sucker for the underdog and had questionable
judgment when it came to men. Gideon didn't react as
he took the half-dozen photographs from Rafi's outstretched hand and began studying them one at a time.

"There's a man in New York who works for the Federated Broadcast Network. His name is Maury Glick
and he's in charge of the news division for all FBN-
owned-and-operated stations. Glick has helped us out
before by turning over some of his reporters' tapes of
interviews done in Arab countries. And sometimes he's
even tagged along himself when one of his people did
a particularly interesting interview of an Arab head-of-
state. He's supplied us with very useful information
about food lines, attitudes, active and inactive construction sites, missile clusters, all kinds of facts that are fed
into the computers to evaluate small to medium to large
threats." Rafi coughed. "But always on a need-to-know
basis, which means that he never knows how his information is being used. He's just a good Jew who likes
the excitement of even a small connection to the Mossad." Rafi smiled. "It's romantic, they tell me, heroic,
brave, even sexy." He shrugged.

"Who is she?" Gideon asked, looking at a shot of a
woman jogging around the perimeter of the Coliseum
in Rome in the pouring rain, wisps of her thick, dark
hair sticking to her heart-shaped face, her clothes
streaked with mud.

"Who she is happens to be the whole point. She's
the television reporter from New York who got herself
caught up in the middle of the attack."

Gideon glanced up.

"And she even has a name. Would you like to know it?"

But he had already lapsed into one of his typical silences.

"Since you seem so anxious, I won't keep you waiting. It's Sasha Beale."

Still, Gideon had no comment as he studied another photograph of the woman, this time in a short skirt as she exited her Rome hotel. Tall and slim and attractive, her arms were filled with files and newspapers.

Rafi reached for one of Gideon's cigarettes, searched in his pockets for a match, lit it, inhaled and settled back to blow out some smoke. "Two months ago," he began, "Glick came up with an idea for a documentary series that was eventually called 'Family.' Each program focuses on a particular family somewhere in the world. The one for the fall premiere was supposed to be a snap-bean farmer, his wife and eight children from Appalachia."

Gideon said nothing as he studied the last picture in the group, Sasha coming out of a restaurant with a man, the wind tugging at the hem of her trenchcoat, a kerchief tied around her head.

Rafi's tone dimmed. "As of two weeks ago, the format for the show changed slightly so the family from Appalachia was postponed to air as the second episode."

"Why?" Gideon asked cautiously.

"Someone suggested another family to Glick," Rafi answered just as cautiously.

There was an overwhelming darkness before Gideon found the strength to speak. "It's Karami, isn't it?"

Rafi merely nodded.

"Quest for a Homeland took credit for the bombing," Gideon said, almost to himself.

"We know now without any doubt that it was Tamir Karami's group."

But even a name and a face didn't satisfy any particular sense of order in Gideon's head. "After so many years," he mumbled.

"He's the only one left," Rafi said softly. "After so many years, he's the only one left."

JERUSALEM, ISRAEL
1974

For a winter night in Jerusalem, it was unseasonably cold. The old woman gathered her terrycloth robe around her bulky frame as she shuffled into the kitchen. These temperatures would have been nothing for Pinsk or even for Milwaukee, but for Israel, they were cold. Putting the wooden ladle to her lips, she blew on the gravy, sucking a taste through her teeth, adding a pinch of salt, smacking her mouth, pouring in some nutmeg before sprinkling in a touch of flour to make it thicker. Cold or not cold, there was no doubt that this was Israel since when did anyone ever have brisket like this in Pinsk or even in Milwaukee? There it was usually turnips or gruel or maybe a fire if there was enough wood to burn just for the luxury of keeping warm.

Satisfied that the meat was cooking evenly, the woman sat down at the kitchen table to leaf through the pile of newspapers and magazines that had accumulated these past few days. But it was hard to concentrate tonight. Distracted by the sound of the pendulum on the wall clock, her mind wandered to the final day of teaching school in Milwaukee when she had been given that clock as a farewell gift. Restless, she stood on swollen feet and moved slowly over to the counter where she had been slicing carrots. And as she worked, she found herself once again engaged in that familiar Friday night exercise that retraced her journey from Russia to America to Palestine in 1921 when she was still a young girl.

After all these years, it never ceased to amaze her

that still she guarded the same first impressions of the land; the rustle of pine needles underfoot in the hills of the Golan, the bizarre sensation of floating on the brine and salt in the Dead Sea, the wailing of the muezzin at dawn and dusk in Jerusalem. Not that there weren't other impressions as well, memories of those early years that weren't as pleasant or as romantic. She raised her arm to pin several strands of hair back into its bun, remembering how all her old friends shared similar losses and pain in the beginning, regardless of where they came from or what their lives had been. There was a distant look in the old woman's faded eyes as she recalled how together they had battled the British, planted trees on hillsides near Haifa, settled new immigrants, irrigated orange groves near Tiberius and negotiated peace with superpowers or made hurried deals with Third World countries for a vote in the United Nations. What began as Palestine, a receptacle for trauma and tragedy, soon became Israel, a country with enough traumas and tragedies of its own to last a lifetime—several lifetimes.

Lately, she found herself dwelling in the past rather than thinking much about the future. Perhaps that was because there wasn't much of a future left for her, especially since the doctors had discovered that the cancer was back. But even if it had remained in remission, how much of a future did a seventy-five-year-old woman have anyway? Brushing some crumbs from the cloth, she glanced at the headlines of several newspapers—killing, murder, terrorist attacks, war. When would it stop? When did everything change, she wondered, so that pogroms in Russia could almost be considered as a cultural frame of reference? When did the moral issue of killing become an issue of choosing between death and disgrace? And when did the opposite of survival become negotiations? But the question that really plagued her was if she was doing enough to guarantee a basic survival. Barely moving her lips, she gave thanks for having been allowed to survive the journey from Pinsk to Milwaukee to the prime minister's office in Jerusalem. At least she knew that for her, Golda Meir, the journey would end in Israel.

Adjusting the flame under the meat, Golda tucked several of the newspapers under one arm and headed for her dimly lit study. But just as she was about to settle down, the telephone rang. Reaching over a stack of books to answer it, she found herself hoping that it wasn't a crisis. It was only her secretary, Edna, calling to confirm a speech she was scheduled to deliver tomorrow to a group of visiting American Jews. The bankers have come to collect their interest, Golda commented and not without irony, the Jews in the diaspora have arrived to judge those of us on the front lines. Yes, she would be at the Civic Center Auditorium in Tel Aviv tomorrow at six, and yes she had a decent dress—maybe the one with the white piqué collar—and without doubt, she'd give them their money's worth—didn't she always—and don't nag, Edna, she'd even put on a little lipstick. Now, if the phone didn't ring again, maybe she could get a little work done before she fell asleep sitting up. Already it was eleven o'clock and she still had two, maybe three hours before she could end the day without feeling guilty. She lit another cigarette, crumpled up the empty pack, aware that it was the second she smoked that day, and reached down into a drawer for a third. Again the telephone rang, but this time she did nothing to mask her annoyance. Yes, she snapped before lapsing into a stunned silence, eyes narrowed, mouth set in a grim line.

There would never be words to describe the chill that ran through her bones as she listened to the head of the Mossad recount the latest terrorist attack on Israeli soil. Six Palestinians infiltrated the Kibbutz Hashtul Ecov, Rafi Unger informed his prime minister, and Golda could have sworn that Rafi's voice broke. Three of them stopped at the entrance of the kibbutz just long enough to kill the two guards, while the other three fanned out to penetrate the building that housed the nursery. They opened fire, Rafi reported, on twenty-four sleeping children, murdering them all before they even had a chance to cry out. The killers had been caught, two alive and four dead, but the survivors proclaimed without exception that they did it in the name of their revolution—Al Fatah—and for the sake of their homeland—Palestine—and all under orders from their leader—Tamir Karami.

Golda managed to stand, one hand leaning on the desk for support. With the cigarette still dangling from her mouth, she assured Rafi that she would call a meeting immediately, the usual night jury would come, the kitchen cabinet, she added, and Rafi, don't forget to wear a sweater because the weather is unseasonably cold tonight.

Without bothering to put down the receiver or to remove the cigarette from between her lips, she pressed her finger down on the button, released it and with studied calm dialed the number first of her minister of defense, Amos Avneri, and then of the chief of army intelligence, Uzi Sharon. Each answered on the first ring and each assured her that he already knew and would be there within minutes. Whoever said that Hitler didn't have nine lives, Golda muttered, didn't live in Israel.

The children, she thought as she paced; the babies. And what if it had been her daughter's kibbutz or her son's children, then what? But nothing would have changed how she felt since she considered every last Israeli soldier, civilian, child and adult as one of her own flesh and blood. Sitting down at the kitchen table, she began to write, slowly at first, deliberating after each word, until the pen flew across the paper with a vengeance, until she was consumed by her own thoughts, stopping only when she realized the doorbell was ringing.

"Come sit, Rafi." Golda greeted the head of the Mossad, "The others aren't here yet."

"Go negotiate a peace treaty," he said in his raspy voice, a condition caused by nodes in his vocal cords, one that could be remedied by surgery if he ever found the time. "And for what? So they can improve their terror machine."

"We're going to put an end to this," Golda told him.

"You dream, Goldala, it won't end unless we surrender."

"There's no word in Hebrew for surrender," she snapped, "or is your Hebrew suddenly better than mine?" She turned to lead the way into the kitchen, motioning him into a chair before she began moving around with a renewed surge of energy. She filled the percolator with water, brought in more chairs, spooned coffee into the basket, plugged in the pot and was through the archway and standing in the foyer to open the door before Rafi heard the bell ring.

"Amos," Golda warned her defense minister, "don't talk to me about compromise."

"Did I say a word?" he asked as he gathered her in his arms. "I'm so sorry," he added, comforting her as if the loss was hers alone. A handsome man with fair hair and blue eyes, Avneri had been a career diplomat and an avid soldier and war hero before turning to politics. But after witnessing the carnage during the Yom Kippur War, he became a dove, claiming that he was more apt to turn over his wallet to an unarmed mugger than to one who held a knife at his throat.

"Why do I feel responsible?" Amos asked as he entered the kitchen.

"Maybe because you promised they'd settle down and accept all the terms that were rammed down their throats after Yom Kippur."

"Sit, sit," Golda said, "you'll argue when Uzi gets here." Again, she headed for the door, leaving the two men glaring at each other across the kitchen table.

"There's a message here," Uzi said, "and it's *kish mir in tocas*."

"Land for peace, that's the message," Amos said.

"And what do the dead get," Golda asked, "besides Kaddish?"

Uzi Sharon ran a hand over his bald pate, a familiar sight around Hakirya in Tel Aviv where his office was right across the road from the Defense Ministry. But it could have been on another planet, given the two men's disparate political views.

"What kind of human beings slaughter children?" Golda added.

"Who said anything about human beings?" Uzi answered calmly.

"It was Karami's group," Rafi announced. "Apparently they came in through Saham on the Jordanian side with the advance knowledge of the border guards."

"How do we know that?" Uzi asked.

"Because at last count they were alive and that was fifty minutes ago when our patrols checked in."

"What makes you so sure they knew in advance?" Amos pressed.

"They're alive, that's enough," Golda said.

Rafi spoke patiently. "How many Jordanian guards are there at the outpost at Ein al Jemal?"

"Two," Golda answered for the others.

"So, Amos, how would you explain enough food and drinks in the garbage for at least eight people?"

"Women?"

"Women don't go there to dine with Mr. Hussein's border guards."

"If that's the case, we can hold King Hussein responsible and go through official diplomatic channels to launch a complaint."

Rafi looked disgusted as he poured some milk into the coffee cup that Golda set in front of him. "And what good will that do? Or, maybe when it does no good and there's another massacre, we can go to war with Jordan and lose more Israeli lives."

"Not to mention destroy Israeli morale," Uzi added.

Rafi leaned forward. "Is that what you want, Amos, you of all people? Or is it that you enjoy groveling to the United States for money and weapons?"

"Amos wants peace," Uzi answered cynically.

"And so do they," Amos said with passion.

"Sure they do," Rafi agreed. "They want *peace* all right, a *piece* of Haifa and a *piece* of Tel Aviv."

"There're other ways to hold Hussein responsible without starting another war," Amos protested.

Rafi looked around. "Maybe we should hit the little king where it hurts most, right in his royal comforts. No more Israeli humus smuggled across the border, how's that?"

"So he'd run to the British for his imports," Uzi predicted.

"Who'd trade their mothers for the price of a good suit on Saville Row," Rafi answered.

"Or he'd go to the French," Uzi suggested.

"And you think it's any coincidence someone coined the phrase 'French whore'?" Rafi inquired.

Golda continued to bustle around the kitchen, checking the meat, tidying up the counters, pouring more coffee, offering pound cake that she sliced or fruit that she washed.

"There's only one way to handle this," Rafi finally said.

"I was waiting for that," Amos said glumly.

"What did you expect, that I'd turn the other cheek? Well, unlike you, I don't have to be a conciliator because I'm afraid Labor won't put me up as defense minister in the next election."

Amos was red-faced. "I don't give a damn about the next election," he shouted. "I care about the Jews who live in Israel and the ones who live abroad. I don't want to make them targets anymore."

"Oh, and up to now, things have been so good for them?" Rafi asked. "Maybe you'd like me to remind you?"

"Don't remind him," Uzi said wearily, "or we'll be here all night. He knows, he knows, he just doesn't want to face it."

"Well, I'm prepared to sit here until he does," Rafi announced.

"So, it's better to sit here and plan murder?" Amos asked.

"So, it is better to do nothing while our children are killed in their beds or our women are blown up in stores or our men are stabbed to death in bus stations?" Uzi exploded.

"Enough!" Golda said suddenly, looking at each of them, "Enough!"

The three men looked at their prime minister with mild surprise although not one of them said a word. "Amos is right, it's no good just to plan murder anymore. One of them is killed or two or maybe we wipe out an entire cell, but it makes no difference. They move from one place to another like cockroaches, rebuilding and surviving." She shook her head. "No, it's no good anymore, it's not enough anymore to kill the snake." She paused. "What I want this time is the head of the snake."

"What does this mean, Goldala?" Amos asked softly.

"The leaders," Uzi answered for her. "Am I right,

Golda? What you want now are the top men in each terrorist organization.''

Instead of answering, she reached into the pocket of her robe. ''I made a list,'' she announced, her eyes fixed on the piece of paper she held in her hand.

''What kind of list?'' Rafi asked.

''Hisul.''

Amos glanced around. ''What does this mean, *Hisul*?''

''No one speaks Hebrew here tonight, or maybe it's my American accent?''

''She made a hit list,'' Rafi said incredulously, standing to lean against the counter. ''I'm almost speechless, Goldala.''

''We should only be that lucky,'' Amos mumbled.

''Look, Golda,'' Uzi chose his words carefully, ''usually I agree with you, but in this case, I've got to say that you've gone too far, getting into things that should be left to Rafi and his people.'' He reached over to pat her hand. ''Leave this to the men, Goldala.''

''And where were the men tonight when the children were killed?''

''Sit down, Uzi, and listen to your prime minister,'' Rafi said and not without a glimmer of amusement in his eyes.

''What I want to know is just who is going to carry out this little mission?'' Amos asked.

Golda looked around the kitchen. ''Why, all of you.''

''So much for our image,'' Rafi mumbled.

''Let's see the list,'' Uzi coaxed, holding out his hand.

Golda turned it over without a word, her cheeks coloring as she did.

He looked it over briefly before asking, ''Should I read it or do you want to?''

She nodded.

''Their real names or by Abu?''

"Abu schmabu," she cut him off, "just read it the way I wrote it."

"Abu Yussef, Mahumad Najar, Kamal Nasser, Kamal Adwan, Hani el Hassan, Abu Hassan, Abu Marwan, Musa Abdullah, Hassan Kanafani, Mahmoud Hamshari." He paused. "Goldala, maybe you want to read the last name?"

She didn't bother to take the paper from him. She knew. She whispered the name. "Tamir Karami. And this one I want before all the others." From the cuff of her robe, she pulled out a crumpled Kleenex. "For the children of Hashtul Ecov and for Lod Airport and for the Munich Olympics and for God knows what else he's thinking up right now."

"I won't go along with this," Amos refused.

"Amos, please," Rafi said gently, "times change and we've got to adapt to those changes or we're finished."

"So this is what we've become—mindless criminals? I thought we were Zionists."

"Sixty years ago, I learned about Zionism in a little room in Pinsk and I watched that idea grow from a dream into a country. But let me tell you something"— Golda stopped to wipe away tears—"that reality won't survive another year by intellectualizing. We've got to be willing to play by their rules and that means doing what we hate them for." It took several moments before anyone spoke.

"It's not very different than what happened in '48," Rafi finally offered.

"You can't compare 1974 and 1948," Amos argued, "We're a regular country now with a regular army."

"Now you want to argue armies?" Uzi inquired, rubbing his eyes. "For sure we'll be here until next *Tisha B'Av.*"

"Let's vote," Rafi suggested. "All in favor of Golda's idea."

Three hands went up while Amos's remained clasped together under his chin.

"Please, Amos," Golda said, her own hand resting gently on his arm, "this is too important not to have a unanimous vote."

He picked up his head. "So, we've come to this," he said sadly, but his hand was already raised . . .

Golda Meir lived for another four years, finally succumbing to the cancer that had been ravaging her body for almost a decade. She died shortly after the Israeli-Egyptian peace treaty that was signed on March 26, 1979, although had she lived longer, she would have seen that any attempt at a lasting Middle East peace remained elusive. Constant border skirmishes, terrorist attacks both in Israel and abroad, strikes by the Israeli Air Force against PLO headquarters in North African countries and finally, an incursion into Beirut in 1982 caused hope to wane even more.

Ironically, Minister Amos Avneri, having retired from public office six years before, died of heart failure during a routine gall bladder operation at Hadassah Hospital in Jerusalem on June 6, 1982, the very day that Israeli troops crossed the border into Lebanon. Three years later, also in June, Uzi Sharon was killed in an automobile accident near Cambridge, Massachusetts, where he had been invited to lecture at Harvard University on the question of Palestinian statehood.

By March 1986, the men on Golda's list had been eliminated, except for the one she had ordered destroyed before the others. Tamir Karami, or Abu Fahd as he was also known, was the rising star within the ranks of the PLO, the number two man after Arafat and head of his own splinter group called Quest for a Homeland. But his strength was made even more blatant when the uprising or Intifada broke out in the Occupied Territories in December 1987, a direct result of his planning and strategy. In April of that same year, Rafi Unger, still head of the Mossad, had finally gone in for the operation to remove the nodes from his vocal cords. They were benign.

"After so many years," Gideon said sadly, "it's not my fight anymore."

Rafi shuffled some papers, consulted a few notes that he had taken from his pocket. "I need you," he said simply.

Gideon wanted to sleep, a long sleep that cancelled out all of those other destinies. "Go away, Rafi," he finally said, "leave me alone for a while."

"How long?"

He wanted to say a lifetime, except that it occurred to him that that wasn't long enough.

Chapter Three

SASHA'S REPORTS from Rome came across the television screens in America with visible emotion, doused with a certain pain that somehow translated into proper media drama. Every night, she faced the cameras and talked coherently and concisely, all the while her mind on that little boy who had died on that sidewalk. Hours were spent each day trying to learn anything she could about him or about that woman whom she suspected was with him when the bomb exploded. Anything at all about where he came from, his family, anybody who knew him that Sasha could talk to and tell that she had been there when he died. But a wall had descended right after the attack, constructed by armies of international bureaucrats and politicians who made it more difficult to get information about the victims than about the terrorists.

By the time she was almost ready to leave Rome, her obsessions had turned to rage. Every last scrap of self-control and reserve evaporated and all her anger and frustration were unleashed and directed at anyone who, in her judgment, had a part in the bombing. She recited the offenders: the Germans for creating the problem, the British for compounding it, the Israelis for prolonging it, the Arabs for using it, the Palestinians for misusing it. And her wrath wasn't limited to nations when she included those who had come in at the end of the story, the ones who were just trying to sift through the rubble of misinformation to come up with decent excuses. But unlike her, most of them hadn't actually been there when it happened.

"I don't have enough on Tamir Karami," she announced one morning. "I need more."

"Everything we've got is right here, either in the files or in the computer. Just punch him up."

She knew she was driving Bernie crazy and she didn't care. From the moment that she found out that Karami was responsible and that she was going to be interviewing him on the first segment of her new show, she drove Bernie to the brink of distraction. "This is a high school term paper," she said evenly, "I need to know reasons why he kills people."

Bernie shrugged. "Maybe he had a lousy childhood. A joke."

Her voice trembled. "Nothing about this is funny."

"Then ask him when you meet him," Bernie said, leaning across his desk. "And maybe he'll come up with a whole list of unfunny reasons for you."

She dismissed his poses and opinions and bad taste with a wave of her hand. "If I don't have a more complete file on him, I can't ask the right questions to get the right answers."

"Sasha, why don't you just tell me to fuck off?"

She didn't even flinch, not that it hadn't occurred to her about a million times since she met him. "Because I don't use that kind of language."

"Never?"

"Not when I'm standing up." She gathered several files on Karami to take with her.

"Do I have the right to know where you're going today?"

Exhaustion had set in again even though it was only ten o'clock in the morning. Already she was looking ragged around the eyes and mouth. "I've got a couple of appointments with the diplomats."

She had worked until four in the morning, to sleep for only three hours before starting all over again at seven. The conclusion that she finally reached was that while there was some sort of collective rapping on the breast of humanity in general, specifically no one wanted to take responsibility for anything. No one except Tamir Karami, who had announced to the world that Alitalia had been his handiwork. More would be said, he promised, during an exclusive interview with an American television network.

"Did anyone ever tell you that you could be a very attractive woman if you stopped trying to act like a man?"

She took a deep breath. "Don't worry about it, Bernie"—she tried a different approach—"if you can't get anything more on Karami." She even tried smiling. "But could you try to get something more on the victims, anything other than numbers. See if they'll release names and nationalities. Please, Bernie."

"Dinner?" he asked, cracking his knuckles.

She nodded. "I intended to invite the staff, everyone who's been busting their ass on this thing. Make a reservation anywhere you like, it's a good idea." She smiled again. "Dinner tonight."

Closing the door behind her, she chose to ignore what he called her under his breath. And anyway, the group deserved dinner, they deserved more than dinner. The three researchers were reduced to tears at least once on any given day when Sasha demanded endless files of police reports, forensic studies, literature written by the PLO, texts on explosives and newspaper clippings that went back to September 1970—Black September—when Tamir Karami and his Quest for a Homeland became a significant name in the movement.

But her abuse and impatience and fixation on the disaster didn't end with the people at the Bureau. When Agence France Presse had the misfortune of being the news agency to receive the call from a man speaking in ''classical Arabic,'' who took credit for the bombing, Sasha went off in another direction. Hours were spent on the phone with one of their staffers who sat at the euphemistic ''Mideast desk,'' and who tried very hard to answer all her questions. Where was that particular dialect found, who used it, who taught it, what was its genesis, why was it spoken, how many people in the world knew it and on and on until the man took his vacation time early.

But regardless of where Sasha went or whom she talked to or how superficial their involvement, she encountered evasive answers that were only platforms for rhetoric or prepared statements. Few people really wanted to discuss terrorism since it only cloaked the more fundamental problems that somehow couldn't be solved. At least that was the official word.

For the Italians, it was a deepening disgrace that it had happened once again on their soil. Hadn't that been an issue in the last election, especially after the *Achille Lauro* incident, hadn't they guaranteed that it wouldn't happen again, hadn't they made deals, even buying out the Libyan interest in Fiat for far more than market value, for God's sake? What else did these savages want? And when Sasha latched onto that particular question of economic prostitution, the suggestion was that she accompany several government officials to the city morgue to take a look for herself at the result of a lack of realpolitik. But when she agreed, a little too readily, they took back their offer and pretended not to understand English.

The American ambassador was pleasant, properly subdued, and completely useless when he quoted from an obscure *New York Times* article, circa 1950, something about William Faulkner and his obsession with perversion in Mississippi, something about rape and incest being un-American subjects. Something Sasha was sure she had read recently in an airline magazine, although she refrained from calling him on it. Just like political murders and terrorist attacks were un-American, the ambassador continued, miraculously pulling together some semblance of order for the camera, it was equally un-American to ignore the plight of all God's children suffering under oppression. What the hell did that have to do with the current death toll of twenty-four innocent people? Was he justifying the bombing perhaps and, if so, would he mind doing it for the American people? He refused. Murder can never be justified, he preached solemnly, except of course during times of war. But to the men who set those explosives on the Via Veneto the other day, the Palestinian issue was one that fell under the heading of *war*. Therefore, she continued, baiting him, the bombing could perhaps be justified, could it not? He changed the subject, waved the camera away and suggested instead that they take a tour of the embassy, have a "peek" at a Botticelli that hung in one of the ballrooms. Perhaps Sasha refused because the ambassador had dredged up that tired dispute over fifty square miles of land somewhere along the Jordan River. Standing in the driveway, he took her hand. *"Arrivederci,"* he said, "if you ever get down around these parts again, give us a call." Help, she wanted to scream.

The Palestinians that Sasha talked to called it *el nakba*, the disaster. But when she pressed them on exactly whose *nakba* it was, she found herself seated with the Palestinian representative to Italy, a pretentious little man who fancied himself a poet rather than a politician. He wrote prose not propaganda, he claimed, and then without being asked, produced a thin volume of his work, scribbled a dedication in Arabic and handed it to her. The disaster, she brought him back to the streets of Rome, could he make a statement about that.

The blood was on the hands of the Israelis since they were the ones to blame for this tragedy. His people were tired of waiting, of believing in empty promises, of trusting the United States. If the Intifada had done anything for the Palestinian people, it had united them, made the PLO strong and harmonious and solidly behind the children of the stones. But of course Quest for a Homeland was a radical splinter group, out of the mainstream of his Al Fatah, so he couldn't comment about the bombing, he knew nothing about it. And as far as Tamir Karami was concerned, the rumors that he was the leader of that group were lies, all Zionist lies.

Sasha left with her nerves in a shamble, tripping over a chair and then bumping into a man carrying a water pipe into the representative's office. But before she walked out, she asked the little poet if, by any chance, he spoke classical Arabic.

The Alitalia office issued all the correct statements of chagrin and outrage. But when Sasha pressed them on their security methods and precautionary tactics for just such a horror, suggesting that perhaps there had been a breach in security, they became defensive. Privately and off the record, they said they were in the business of making reservations and not in the business of fighting wars or securing battle lines, so would the American journalist kindly remove herself from the premises and stop the accusations. Not accusations, Sasha answered, as she told the crew to pack up, innuendos, she was making innuendos. The accusations would come later. And by the way, she inquired sweetly, one foot still in the door, how come the security guard on duty that day was seen halfway down the street guarding the office with his dick instead of his gun? Specifically, getting a blow job in a doorway and yes, she had the name of both the blowee and the blower.

If the Palestinian representative was pretentious, the Israeli ambassador was near-smug. It was no shock, he proclaimed, this kind of thing happened every day at a bus station or a school or on a kibbutz in Israel. Since when did the rest of the world think they were immune to Arab violence? It's happened before and it would happen again as long as the Americans were fooled by talk of negotiation and peace. But wasn't peace necessary, she practically pleaded, isn't that what everybody wanted? No, peace was not the ultimate Arab goal, that was a naive interpretation of the solution to a problem that would never go away. Never, that was, until Israel was pushed into the sea. It was then that Sasha glanced around the room and noticed the maps, all drawn with hostile red missiles pointed at Israel. The United States didn't understand, the ambassador continued, that the Palestinian revolution was one of corruption and imagery, money and oil, it was all contrived. But she understood, Sasha assured the ambassador, it was like the emperor's new clothes. Only the survivors and the families of the victims could see the bodies of those people killed in the Alitalia bombing.

On the morning that Sasha was leaving Rome, Bernie came into the office with a bouquet of flowers wrapped in plastic. "You've been working like a demon," he said, "and if I've been unsupportive or short, it's only because I've had my hands full with the technical end of things." But something was off, since *unsupportive* and *short* described her behavior, along with rude, uncivilized and generally unbearable. "Peace?" he asked her, extending his hand.

She studied him cautiously before answering. "Peace."

"It's a tough assignment," he began, offering her a cigarette, "especially for a woman."

She declined the cigarette. "In what way?"

"You have to know how to deal with these fuckers, that's all. Instinctively, they're all going to say no when you want a yes." He played with his cigarette before lighting it. "Like women, which is why it's a tough assignment for a woman, because you don't understand like men do."

"That makes sense," she said with a perfectly straight face. "By the way, did you get the victim list?"

"That's what I meant about dealing with those fuckers, they're out to lunch, patzo, stupido, dumb, lazy sons of bitches, typical bureaucrats."

"Is that a yes or a no, Bernie?"

He stopped playing with the cigarette. "I want to produce the Karami segment of the documentary," he said without any preamble.

What was the point of fighting. "That's a good idea, Bernie," she said without emotion, taking him by surprise as she glanced at the flowers wrapped in plastic.

"I'm glad you're not opposed to it."

"Did you talk to Maury about it?"

"I did," he said, putting his feet on the desk.

She would have opened her veins and bled to death on his office floor before she asked him Maury's response.

"He thought it was a good idea."

She nodded slowly, her eyes somewhere over his head.

"You know, Sasha, what can I say about what had happened except that life is a question of fate. You come to Rome and there's a terrorist attack, a lot of people get killed and now we're probably going to end up working together. Fate."

Another example of preferring to open up her veins and bleeding to death, except this time the choice wasn't hers.

"Keep trying about that list," she managed to say before standing. Thanking him for all his trouble, she also apologized for all of hers, taking a deep breath as she bent down to pick up her tote bag and purse. As she was about to walk out of the room she was struck by her own thoughts of fate . . . It was many things, like walking across the floor and tripping somewhere in the middle, or missing an airplane and meeting the love of your life in the airport coffee shop, or working in a laboratory and having the petri dish that grows the mold that cures cancer. But for those people who died that day, it was something else, and what she couldn't understand was who or what chose the way fate struck.

Chapter Four

THE NEXT TIME Rafi came to visit Gideon, the visit had been arranged in advance. Showered and shaved and wearing a clean sweater and jeans, Gideon led the older man into the same cluttered room. Nothing had changed in the past week, ashtrays were still piled with cigarette butts, dishes remained unwashed in the kitchen sink and stacks of cards and letters were unopened and unread on several hall tables. If anything, Gideon looked even more exhausted, as if the week just meant seven more days of sleepless nights.

"Have you eaten today?" Rafi asked when he settled down on a sofa facing Gideon.

Gideon shrugged. "I don't even know when the days end anymore," he said simply.

"I brought you something."

He held up a hand. "Please, don't feed me."

Rafi leaned over to pick up several files. "Not even food for thought," he said with a small smile, offering the manila envelopes. "What I'd like you to do is read the file we've complied on the girl and study the rest of the pictures."

"What's the point?"

"So when you meet her, you'll know everything about her as well as recognize her."

"I'll recognize her," Gideon said, a strange expression on his face as he pulled out a photograph from one of the files. It was a grainy shot of Sasha coming out of the shower, obviously taken with a telephoto lens. "Why was this necessary?"

Rafi shrugged. "Our man in Rome got a new lens, I imagine, and he was probably just anxious to try it out."

"It wasn't necessary," Gideon repeated.

"Why don't you look at the others?"

Gideon shook his head. Somehow he knew he wasn't capable of pretending that he no longer possessed those same instincts that made him set out every time as if it were the first.

"Just some publicity shots," Rafi explained, "and there's one that goes back when she first started out. It's the one that went with her job application."

"How did you get it?"

"From the FBN files, naturally."

"Rafi," Gideon began, "this isn't going to work."

"What isn't going to work?"

"I can't."

"If you can't, Gideon," Rafi said quietly, "then Karami will."

Throughout all the years and all the acts of terror by Karami's hand up to now, the incident that remained most with Gideon happened eleven years before. Miriam was in her last month of pregnancy, which also happened to be the only time an El Al aircraft had been blown up. But that wasn't why Gideon had been so affected; his feelings had nothing to do with metal or machinery or any macho embarrassment that Israeli security had finally been penetrated. In his opinion, that particular attack had been the most immoral example of sacrificing the weak and defenseless, of playing on the emotions of one woman who was naive enough to trust a man she barely knew.

One of Karami's men had seduced a young German girl, impregnated her and then promised to marry her. Arrangements were made for the girl to travel to Nablus in the Occupied Territories, via Tel Aviv, to meet the man's family. Her belly full of baby, her suitcase full of bomb, she died along with two hundred and sixty-four others when the plane exploded somewhere over Greece. It took only two weeks for Gideon to piece it all together—on the night that Miriam went into labor—and find the man who had murdered his unborn child. The time he spent waiting for the birth of his son was mostly spent thinking about that other baby who had been killed in utero.

Gideon gestured to one of the photographs as he rubbed his eyes. "Does your man in New York know about your interest in her?"

"All Glick knows is that he was politely asked to get Karami to agree to star in the first episode of his documentary."

"And what does she know?"

"Only that her first subject has been changed."

"And after what she saw in Rome, she's agreed to interview Karami?" He amazed himself that he could refer to his son's killer so dispassionately.

"She's no fool. She knows that with her or without her, it's going to be done." His eyes squinted, he added, "But she's shaken up."

Gideon said nothing.

"That's not our concern. Glick will handle her, so why don't we concentrate on who she is and where she comes from?" Shuffling some papers, he didn't wait for any sign of agreement. "She grew up in Washington Heights in New York City. Her father owned a newsstand until he gambled it away at the track, the newsstand and the house, and just about everything else they had—loved the horses. And loved the ladies. Anyway, he picked up his family and went off to live on some kind of Marxist chicken farm in rural Connecticut." Raffi smiled slightly. "Oh, he was a Marxist, a typical New York Jewish left-wing Marxist, whose last valid causes were the Rosenbergs or maybe segregation, but nothing especially relevant since the 1950s. Frankly, the reasons for running off to that chicken farm probably had more to do with escaping his creditors than anything else.''

Rafi arranged his papers again. ''Two children, Sasha and Eli, except Eli was a mess, got himself on drugs and then killed himself in a motorcycle accident.'' He shook his head. ''After a violent fight with the father, who by the way, was tough. What happened after that was predictable, father runs off with the town beautician, some girl younger than his daughter. The mother, that's another case, gets herself and Sasha back to civilization.'' Leaning over, he put the papers on the floor. ''Mother drinks, not nasty, just never quite right. Sasha helps her out financially and goes to see her once a week although the word is that she drives Sasha crazy. It seems that she reads tarot cards in some tearoom near Times Square, she's been doing that on and off all her life but since she lost her job in Bloomingdale's, she's been doing that full-time. But Beale's loyalty is clearly with the mother.

''Let's see, what else.'' Reaching down, he picked up the papers. ''She survived the lousy childhood after the chicken farm because she buried herself in books. She once wrote a paper for her high school magazine explaining how she had been raised by Joan Didion and Eric Hoffer, the same magazine where she also wrote that acting was her only love, her only dream—graduation dreams, I think it was.'' He paused. ''Anyway, it's all here.'' He tapped the folders.

''What happened with the acting dream?''

''After high school she started City College, worked odd jobs at night, waiting tables, cashier at a movie theater, anything to pay for acting lessons. Her dream was to be a stage actress, which was just asking for failure since her looks overshadowed her talent. She would have done better in the movies but she refused to consider it. Her first big break came with some walk-on part in a soap opera that was supposed to expand into a regular bit part except she got pregnant.''

''What happened to the child?''

''Funny, I would have wondered about the boy-friend.'' Rafi read from an official blue sheet of paper. ''According to the hospital records, a curettage was performed on the patient after massive bleeding prior to admission. Best guess, six weeks.'' He put down the paper. ''The boyfriend went off to California to star in a television series about a man who had a special re-lationship with his car. It's still in reruns.''

Expressionless, Gideon shifted in his chair.

''When she got out of the hospital she had to get a job, her mother was in some treatment center by then, the first of many, and Beale had to pay the rent. So she took the first job that came along, which happened to be answering phones for an answering service, which also happened to be where she met the congressman from Vermont. It's all in the file as well.'' Again, he tapped the folder. ''Briefly, she was disillusioned enough to take him up on his offer and move to Ver-mont as his assistant. About a year later, when the guy's term was up and he lost his bid for re-election, he joined the local television station as their political media ad-visor and took Beale along as his researcher.''

Rafi flipped yet another sheet. ''Rumor was that he was her lover, not that it mattered since she apparently worked her ass off, ten, twelve hours a day until some-one at the station noticed her and decided that with her looks, it wouldn't be a bad idea to put her on the air as the weather girl.'' Rafi smiled slightly. ''That was in 1980. Two years after that she was at some broadcasters convention in Washington, which was where our man, Glick, met her and brought her to New York as a re-porter, a fill-in for the local news.''

"Another lover?"

Rafi feigned a hurt look. "Now, Gideon, really, how would I know that?"

A muscle moved in Gideon's jaw although he said nothing.

"Unfortunately, I don't have the list of the ones she turned down either." Rafi moved along. "Within six months she caused a big scandal at the network by launching some investigation into tax-rebate funds concerning some big-shot builder who also happened to sit on the board of the company. As a result of her report he was indicted and asked to resign."

"She seems uncontrollable," was Gideon's only comment.

"Committed and tough and brave were the adjectives used at the time."

"Uncontrollable," Gideon repeated.

"Anyway, the calls and letters that came into the station were solidly behind her, so Glick did the only smart thing under the circumstances." Rafi paused. "He promoted her to cover crime on the local news show every night, which prompted her to do what most successful people do in television."

"Cocaine?"

"No, she hardly drinks, and when she does, by the way, it's Tattinger's or scotch." He shook his head. "No, our Miss Sasha Beale started seeing a psychiatrist, which was her first mistake, because in 1985 she married him."

"The ultimate seduction scene," Gideon remarked quietly.

"Especially for an American woman, it's either a priest or psychiatrist. Anyway, since it was more in her character to lie down to confess her sins and examine her soul, she chose the confessor who charged by the hour. It was a bad choice because he was a sonofabitch—good-looking, sophisticated, successful, Ivy League, who screwed around from the beginning. Never with his patients, that honor he saved for Beale.''

Gideon cut through the past. ''Where is she now?''

''In Rome but leaving for Paris. Glick intends to meet her there to go over format and questions and to rough out a script. They'll gather a crew from the Paris Bureau before he goes back to New York and she goes off to PLO headquarters in Tunisia.''

He could hear the sound of his own uneven breathing when he asked, ''And what exactly would I do with her?''

''You'd get as much out of her as you could, as much as she's willing to give without making her suspicious.''

''What makes you think she'd give anything?''

''I have faith in you. Besides, women love to share things with men, or so I'm told.'' He rubbed his hands together. ''But how would I know that, an old married man like me, forty-seven years next month and to the same woman.''

But Gideon was barely paying attention. ''To go back into this insanity,'' he muttered, picking up a color headshot of Sasha. Black eyes, perhaps a bit too close together, cheek bones like ski slopes, small smile playing at the corners of a full and sensuous mouth, nose a touch crooked at the tip, hair tousled, face not particularly symmetrical but there was no doubt that it all worked, somehow, to create quite a beautiful woman.

''What does it take, Gideon?'' Rafi said abruptly.

''What it *takes* is not buying failure from the beginning, which is what you're doing unless you realize there's something missing.''

''You're right, we need more.'' He took a breath. ''You'll work it out.''

Gideon shot him a look, one finger idly tracing Sasha's

eyes, nose, and mouth on the photograph that was still in his lap.

"She'll be spending every day in the Karami house and that means that she'll know schedules, household staff, bodyguards, times of meals, visitors. And what she'll also know is a daily emotional reading, whether Karami appears nervous or whether his wife plans to take the children on holiday or if she's fearful or if he's got more work on his desk than usual, whether his fax machine is spitting out reams of papers, anything that points to his mood and that tells us if he's taking extra precautions because he's worried about another attack. Because the only time he's going to be concerned is when he knows to expect retaliation on our part."

"What's the rest of it?"

"We need you to figure out who's in a position to give us background and habits and interior layout that's more technical than what Beale can give us. You can't push her like that because she's a woman who's gotten by on instinct and second chances. So, we need someone else who's familiar with alarm systems and locks and keys and windows, the usual count and method. Or we ruin our best shot, maybe our only shot."

Gideon asked, "Who would I be this time?"

Rafi breathed a sigh of relief. "Your identity card, passport and travel documents make you a French national working for Renault as a hydraulic engineer out of the Paris office. Paris, because there are twenty thousand employees and a hydraulic engineer because it's normal for you to be traveling to several North African countries scouting locations for a new Renault plant."

"Tunisia?"

"Exactly."

He was suddenly exhausted, and not only from a lack of sleep.

"She'll be staying at the George V in Paris," Rafi went on. "Do you have any questions?"

"I haven't agreed to anything."

"Well, in case you do, Gideon, she jogs. Every day, regardless of weather or where she is in the world, the lady jogs."

"How healthy of her."

"But if that doesn't work, she'll be having dinner with Glick on the night he arrives, at a little restaurant next door to our embassy."

"How do you know that?"

"Because he's in touch with one of our people."

Gideon said nothing.

"The point is, Gideon, if you can't manage to find her and interest her in a dinner with you alone, you could be sitting at the next table with a briefcase stuffed with hydraulic designs for the 1992 Renaults. And if you comb your hair and put on a nice blue shirt to match your eyes, she might notice you."

Gideon's expression was somber. "Let me think about it, give me a couple of days." But he knew better.

"We don't have a couple of days. She's scheduled to begin taping in Tunisia within the week, she'll only be in Paris for a couple of days."

For the next hour the only sound in the room was Gideon blowing out smoke or rustling papers as he read through the rest of the pages in the Beale file. Or, Rafi's shifting around in his chair or standing up and pacing back and forth or sighing deeply. Until finally the older man spoke, announcing out of the blue, "She made chicken."

Gideon glanced up. "Who?"

"My wife, she made chicken. It's in the car."

He didn't budge, although when he spoke, his tone was resigned. "To feed the rabid dog?"

"Should I get it?"

But it was clear that the question transcended chicken. "Go ahead," Gideon said, aware that the commitment had already been made.

Chapter Five

IT WAS GRAY and misty on the afternoon that Sasha arrived in Paris, drops of moisture streaking across the windows of the aircraft as it landed on the runway of Charles de Gaulle Airport. The vacation was over, at least the three hours that she had to herself in the plane where she could just sit and think without phones or people or pressure to produce.

By five-thirty, she had already cleared French passport control, collected her bags, and spotted the FBN chauffeur holding the sign with her name. Wrapped in a large, drab sweater and wearing loose-fitting trousers and sensible shoes, horn-rimmed glasses that covered most of her face, she followed the driver to the car. And as glamorous and charming as she could be, she could also be dowdy and behave with a chill that discouraged any conversation. Right then, as she settled back in the seat, she was aloof and detached, on a downward social spiral mostly from lack of sleep.

Gazing out the window as the car sped toward Paris, she thought about all the trips from all the airports throughout the years. As usual, it could have been Des Moines or Caracas or anywhere on earth since every ride from every airport into every city held the same sights and sounds for her: industry to poverty to polite commerce to a hotel in an upscale section of town. Even the literal translations of advertising had an uncanny similarity to the American slogans, even the graf-

fiti on the sides of the overpass seemed to be written in
the same handwriting all over the world. But what filled
her mind just then was something that happened long
ago, in a motel in Vermont one summer afternoon, one
of the last before moving to New York.

There had been a commotion around the pool when
a woman dove in and never came up, a woman dove
into the water and somewhere in the middle of that dive
stopped living. But what had impressed Sasha more than
the plastic bag containing the body was the plastic bag
filled with vitamins that had been removed from the
room. From one minute to the next, regardless of care,
maintenance, upkeep or age; from one minute to the
next, regardless of politics, religion, allegiance or nationality, life could end. It always came back to Rome.

She walked through the lobby of the George V, followed by the bellboy wheeling the trolley with her bags.
Approaching the reception desk, Sasha checked in and
retrieved two messages as she did—both from Maury
Glick and both confirming his arrival tomorrow as well
as dinner tomorrow night. At least she still had tonight
to herself and if she was smart, she'd rest or take herself
to dinner or just wander around. It was hard to plan
anything because she was fading fast, so fast that by
the time she entered the elevator, exited and trailed after the bellboy down the hall, she could barely keep her
eyes open.

Once in the room, she tried to unpack a few things
and jot down a few notes before the idea of taking a
shower, ordering a snack and just putting her head down
for a few minutes seemed too appealing to resist.

Ten hours later, at six-thirty in the morning, she
awoke with a start and only because of the cacophony
of horns in the street below. Sitting up, she reached for
the phone to call room service before climbing out of

bed. Thirty minutes and breakfast would arrive, the
voice with the fake British accent assured her on the
other end of the receiver. Nude, she wandered into
the marble bathroom, filled the tub, poured in an entire
bottle of hotel bubble bath and got in, getting out only
to answer the door exactly thirty minutes later. Wrapped
in a terrycloth robe, her hair dripping droplets of water
down her forehead and nose, she directed the waiter to
set the tray on the bed. She signed the check and fumbled for a five-franc tip before turning to look out the
window while the waiter fumbled with the cart and the
door.

There was something almost healing about Paris,
something that made it less brutal to be unhappy here
than anywhere else, especially New York. Not that the
images weren't still fresh in her mind of the night that
Carl packed his worn leather suitcase, carted up his
worn leather-bound first editions and trotted his per-
ennially tanned and leathery face out of their cooperative apartment on Manhattan's Upper West Side. No
notice, no warning, just a few tears and the promise
that he would always be there in an emergency, the
assurance that she would always be "family" to him.
"Family," had been her response, "the relative you put
away in a home."

For the next few weeks, the spaces on the walls where
his low-numbered lithographs once hung and the holes
in the shelves where his books once stood drove her
mad. It was as if she was living with a deranged jack-
o-lantern whose gap-toothed grin assaulted her in every
room of the apartment.

How had it all begun, it seemed so long ago when
she tried to remember that night in Carl's office. She
came to him after having had a cyst removed from her
left breast and asked him to help her off with her coat.
There was a brief discussion about personalization, mo-

tivation and transference before he acquiesced, before
his hand somehow found its way on her unwounded
breast, before there was a stunned and tense silence in
which neither moved nor spoke. Flashing through her
brain then in neon lights were choices: an affair that
could possibly end in marriage and children, a home
that she never had, other libidinous encounters with
less-desirable shrinks or similar discussions about or-
gasms, fantasies and masturbation during boring dinners with a slew of nameless and faceless men. She
opted for the affair, developed a unique relationship with
Carl's body, a special rapport with his tongue and was
ultimately rewarded with marriage.

Children were another story, since every time she
brought up the subject he talked travel—Tahiti, Bora
Bora, Machu Picchu—why have a baby when there was
a world to see. After a while, he began complaining
that her biological clock was keeping him up at night,
and what she probably should have counterclaimed was
that his geographical clock was doing the same to her.
But she didn't. Instead, she woke up one morning realizing that all those things that came up when the lights
went down just weren't enough to dull the ache or the
hurt that he didn't belong solely to her, that there were
always furtive telephone calls and excuses of late night
emergency sessions with suicidal patients. Yet, even after the separation and the divorce, he was somehow still
embedded in her life, right up until that last morning
in New York before she went away to forget, before
Rome, before the bombing, before that child somehow
substituted for all those other aches and pains.

Sasha had congratulated herself every step of the way
on the morning she was leaving for Europe, as she had
every morning since Carl left. As she poured the coffee,
showered, dressed, mostly for not having stumbled over
any signs of him. With trepidation, she opened drawers,

closets, cabinets, suitcases, even the cereal box as if a
piece of him would pop out to ruin what little progress
she was making. But when the doorbell rang, her heart
began to pound in her chest as she moved cautiously
toward the foyer—as if there were land mines under the
rug—to answer it.

Minutes later, the handyman was leaning over what
had been reported as a faulty flush mechanism. Apparently, the work sheet had just reached the basement
bulletin board, which was why he had come to do what
was no longer necessary. And despite Sasha's assur-
ances that everything was in working order, he insisted
upon not only examining the bowl and the tank but also
discussing Carl's method of repairing it.

It had been a matter of a simple manipulation of the
lever and the rubber ball, she explained, which Dr.
Feldhammer had accomplished before using the plunger
to free up the flush. What had struck her then as she
stood there, wrapped in his old seersucker robe, her
hair a mess, dark circles under her eyes, was if Carl
realized when he was fixing the toilet that he was fixing
it for her alone since their days of sharing toilets were
drawing to a close.

And what struck her now as she pulled on her sweat-
pants and T-shirt for her morning jog was how nice it
had been to see a human face that morning, to have had
someone to talk to, even if the conversation was limited
to the care and repair of a clogged-up toilet. Bending
down to tie her running shoes, she realized how much
she resented Carl, if for nothing else than for leaving
her so all alone. For that and for the fact that not only
were there still traces of his hands and mouth all over
her body, but also his fingerprints all over the flusher,
lid and plunger.

Chapter Six

THE TUILERIES were deserted at eight o'clock in the morning except for the regular fixtures. Several clumps of knapsacked bodies—nationalities and itineraries unknown—were strewn near the first set of wrought-iron gates that opened onto the Place de la Concorde. Further along and to the right was the resident mime curled up against the stone wall that served as his stage during peak crowd times. Now, he slept soundly with his bowler hat resting on his stomach, white makeup streaked across the collar of his pink shirt. To his left and already wandering the dirt paths with a container of coffee between his hands was the Tuileries photographer, there to chronicle the vacations of those tourists who would forget their cameras. But what drew Sasha's attention more than those other resident transients was the man who was playing St. Francis of Assisi at the edge of a small pond in the center of the first garden.

Jogging slowly toward him, she watched in fascination as dozens of sparrows flocked to rest on his outstretched hand and arm as he clucked and hummed and directed them with an index finger. Passing him, she picked up her pace to run the first lap around the small pond. But it wasn't until she slowed up a bit to readjust her headband that she first noticed another lone jogger in a country that hadn't yet caught the fitness bug. Except that he didn't look particularly French, perhaps

American, judging from his running shoes, and perhaps an American who found it as extraordinary as she to be jogging through these gardens, between statues of writers, gods, and kings—the Louvre on one side, the Eiffel Tower in the distance.

The man seemed in no apparent rush as he jogged down the ramp from the upper level to take the first lap around St. Francis and his congress of sparrows. Sasha kept up her pace as well, watching him from the corner of one eye, his unhurried and even strides, broad shoulders that moved only slightly forward as he did, rear-end solid and well-shaped. And for a man who was in such obviously good shape, he didn't look like one of those manic runners, the ones with skinny heads, hollow eyes and rock-hard calves, nor did he have that perpetual look of desperation on his face, like one of those typical marathon sprinters. And upon closer inspection, he didn't give the impression of being an American, more Italian or Greek or South American. Dusky, was what registered immediately, that and a certain elegance as he ran, a feeling that he did it solely for pleasure, and with great ease. She had the right to look, she told herself, she was alive and single and so had the right to look at an attractive man running in the park. Except tears came to her eyes when she thought about being alive and breathing air and running in the park, so far from Rome, so far from the others who couldn't and wouldn't ever again. Just thirty minutes, she pleaded with herself, just half an hour without thinking about it, without seeing those images before her eyes. Turning, she ran faster until she was well ahead of the stranger, feeling the trickle of sweat dripping between her breasts as she did. And anyway, what difference did it make, admiring a man in the Tuileries, a man whom she would probably never see again.

But when he disappeared suddenly somewhere between a statue of St. Augustine and Baudelaire, she wasn't prepared to have never seeing him again happen that soon. A sigh of relief when she caught sight of him as he emerged near a patch of grass bordered by naked Greek goddesses and an ersatz bust of the Winged Victory. Blowing air from her mouth, Sasha sprinted toward the shade and under a row of oak trees, changing directions at the last minute only to find herself trapped in the middle of an outdoor cafe. Weaving in and out of the chairs and tables, she exited just near enough to hear his breathing, yet found herself completely taken aback when he actually glanced over his shoulder to look at her. Looking down at the ground, she kept up, following him as he ran toward the glass pyramid in the courtyard of the Louvre, past an archeological dig on the left, a construction site on the right, before she had a sudden surge of energy to pass him. Again he glanced at her, vague interest it seemed, just long enough for her to meet his gaze. What registered was blue, clear blue eyes with tired lines around the rims, undoubtedly belonging to a wife or a mistress or a friend, depending upon where he came from and what were his priorities. She had the right to be curious, anything to fill her head while she ran, anything to relax and think vacant thoughts, anything to allow her a respite.

Deftly, she cut across the street, dodging several cars just as she reached the curb and an onslaught of tour busses. Jogging in place, she waited for the light to change to head for the square and the statue of Louis XIV on his horse. The man was right behind her, having appeared from the other side of the Sun King on his way to the right side of the pyramid. What was it Erica once wrote about a zipless and unknown encounter? No strings, no commitment, no questions, just something that might make her forget about everything else. If only she could, she went on in her head, if only she was mentally and emotionally constructed so she could operate and perform and function without guilt—which was when she tripped over a metal loop in the ground near the tale end of Louis and his horse and fell flat on her face. "Shit," she cried out as she felt herself going down.

The stranger was beside her in a flash. "Are you hurt?" he asked in accented English.

But she was too embarrassed and furious, certainly too stunned to be even civil at that point. "What makes you think I speak English?"

"I suppose because French girls would have chosen another expletive."

It didn't help that his tone was so self-assured, his expression vaguely amused, even if she had already made a mental note about the "girls."

"Are you able to stand?"

Whether she was or she wasn't didn't concern him right then, she decided, which was why she neither answered nor moved. She merely lay there feeling like a total idiot, her biggest dilemma should she just give in and curl up in a fetal position to block out the world, especially him.

"Can you stand?"

"If I wanted to, I suppose I could."

"Do you think you want to?"

"It's fifty-fifty at this point." She braced herself with her arms and turned over. She winced, not moving for another moment before sliding up to a sitting position. Her pants were torn over one cut-and-bleeding knee. "Shit," she said again.

He reached into his pocket. "Here, it's clean," and offered a white handkerchief. She could have used him in Rome. "What a dumb thing to do," she said. "Thanks."

"Why don't I wet it for you at the fountain?"

"Thanks," she said again, amazed that up close he was even better looking than from a distance.

He was back in seconds, patting her knee with the damp cloth until she took over to do it herself.

"Do you do this often?" he asked, that same glimmer of amusement in his eyes. There was no wedding ring, she noticed, but then what difference did it make and what was wrong with her anyway? "Every day," she answered with a look that dared him to make jokes. But he said nothing. "I jog every day," she went on, "and as surprising as it may sound, I've never fallen." But it was ridiculous to remain so serious and more than ridiculous, it was out of character. She smiled and was relieved when he did the same. "Do you know the trouble with keeping in such good shape," he asked, "other than the obvious hazards?"

She shook her head.

"Chances are you'll outlive your friends, so between the ages of about seventy and ninety you'll be lonely."

It struck her as odd before it struck her as amusing. "Then the trick is to stop exercising and start drinking and smoking at about sixty-five or so."

"Something like that."

"You're not French," she announced, pressing the handkerchief against her knee.

"Why do you say that?"

"Your accent is British."

He smiled slightly. "That's because over here we learn English and not American. Actually, I'm half French and half English," he said, reaching into another pocket for a pair of wraparound sunglasses.

The effect was startling and she wondered briefly if he knew it. "Well, the English half of you speaks perfect English." It occurred to her that to have said something less interesting would have taken a monumental effort. "Do you do this often?" she asked quickly, squinting into the new sun.

"Rescue fallen women?"

She grimaced. "No, I mean jog."

"Yes, when I have the time and when I'm not traveling."

"What do you do?" she blurted out before closing her eyes and leaning her head back. "I don't believe I actually asked you that."

"It's very American," he said, studying her a moment, "although usually the first thing American girls are curious about is if a man is married."

What she was most curious about was when "girls" became women to this man. "I wonder why."

An ironic smile. "For all the obvious reasons, although the question should probably be how many times a person has been married."

"What do you mean?"

"Let's see, five marriages, for instance, equals no marriages, or a hundred lovers equals no lovers since quantity can reduce everything to zero." His smile was charming this time around, more than charming, almost irresistible. "Are you married?" he asked without warning.

"No," she said, wondering what the hell . . .

"Does that mean never or five times?"

For some reason, she felt a small victory. "You're the one who created that little problem," she said, waiting for more. Of what, she wasn't quite sure.

"So I did," he said, and then went further. "Never?"

"Maybe once," she answered, watching a muscle move on one side of his jaw.

He laughed out loud and to her it was nothing less than a standing ovation. "Maybe? Don't you know?"

"Well, if quantity reduces everything to zero, then a bad experience can sometimes cause memory loss. How's that?" But the expression in her eyes closed that particular discussion. "It seems to have stopped bleeding," she announced, inspecting the handkerchief and then her knee.

He held out a hand. Another killer, she observed,

hands that were thick yet graceful and strong, she added silently as she took hold to be pulled up.

"You could have broken your nose, you know."

"At least."

He took his time, about one second, before offering, "Would you like a coffee?"

A coffee, not just *coffee* the way an American would have said it, but *a coffee*, a very specific coffee, as if it belonged to her alone. But then the wounded, neurotic side took over as she interpreted that to mean that the coffee offered was limited to one, no long-range plans for more, the boundaries already set in advance. Like the men in New York who wouldn't commit to dinner with a woman they hadn't yet met. Drinks were one thing—a viewing before the auction—which meant that *drinks* in America were perhaps the same as *a coffee* in France. Even internationally, it remained a buyer's market. "I'd love a coffee," she said, wondering where she found the nerve to allow herself to be picked up in a strange country. But at least this man was living proof that someone existed after Carl who she actually wanted to talk to. Someone who wasn't under indictment or whose president wasn't busy amassing plutonium and heavy water or someone whose life's work wasn't putting bombs in airline ticket offices. She held out a hand. "I'm Sasha Beale," she introduced herself. He took it in his. "And I'm Gideon Aitchison."

It wasn't a Truffaut film, so it made little sense to turn a cup of coffee into an unrequited love scene in Toulouse or a tearful reunion at an orphanage in Quimper or a parting at a train station in Grenoble. But since Sasha had a tendency to be literal when she should be vague, practical when she should be romantic, it was difficult to trust her own instincts. For one thing, the man currently holding her arm was a total stranger. Even if he was charming and attractive, those attributes didn't make him any more familiar. For another thing, she was the only person she knew who viewed *Last Tango in Paris* as a film concerned with that city's apartment shortage. So, the fact that this person named Gideon Aitchison was now steering her toward an unpretentious cafe on one of those side streets near the Jeu de Paume museum didn't make her any less apprehensive, even if she was smart enough to realize that this wasn't exactly champagne with Pablo Neruda before the Nobel Prize ceremonies.

There was a long bar and about half a dozen tables with various groups of people either on their way to offices or on their way into construction ditches. Coffee and bottled water, barely breakfast in New York or even at the George V for that matter, was being served to most. She could probably wangle a croissant if she were clever, although if she were very clever she would just shut up and forget about food. The smart thing to do would be to practice being a woman out with a man—something she hadn't done in years—and start off with a comment or two about the chances of an economically sound and united Europe, or about how France was faring within the international community, or which left-wing or right-wing newspaper was more thorough. Or, she could ask Mr. Gideon Aitchison something really significant, like whether he often picked up strange women in the Tuileries in the morning.

"Should we have hot milk for our coffee?" he asked, peering at her over the rim of the half glasses perched on his nose.

What was this "should we" and "our coffee" about. Even wondering something like that left her certain that she was losing her mind. After all, it wasn't exactly an invitation on his part to open a joint checking account. "Yes," she replied, watching as he consulted with the waiter, glasses off, pointing with a stem to something on the menu, glasses on, gesturing to something else on the counter, discussing the choices as if they were dining in a gourmet restaurant.

A flurry of activity followed as plates and cups were put on the table, a napkin dropped discretely on her lap, a basket of croissants and rolls set before her, a glass of pulpy orange juice, a pot of jam, a pitcher of warm milk, coffee and two hard-boiled eggs.

"If there's anything you want, just tell me," he said, taking her all in with a look that counted her pulse rate and the number of lashes on each lid.

"This is really too much," she said, wondering if an offer of breakfast signified a lifetime commitment since *a coffee* seemed to signify breakfast.

"It's important for athletes to eat well in the morning," he said solemnly.

She felt her face color as she broke a sugar cube in half, plopping the piece in her coffee, aware that she never took sugar in her life. "Are we back to my fall?" she asked, even managing a touch of humor in her tone.

Stirring and pouring, he went on. "Actually you fell quite well, which is almost as important for a woman as knowing how to cry. Don't you agree?"

Nothing was perfect in life. Obviously, she had the misfortune of finding someone who wasn't completely normal, not that she was such an expert, but the comment struck her as off the wall. Or, perhaps he was kidding or perhaps he was just as unenlightened European male, a bit too aristocratic, which made him a bit too archaic. Still, he was extremely attractive and for the moment didn't appear to be threatening her life or limb. "Are we having a language problem here," she inquired with a charming smile, "because I don't understand the question."

"A woman who cries well is seductive," he explained matter of factly, "because she evokes all those protective male instincts. It can be very sexy."

She was willing to play along. "What's the difference between crying well and not crying well?" And who knew, maybe she could learn something.

"Crying well doesn't include doing it in a group or breast-beating or screaming or scrinching up face muscles." He watched her closely. "But what I wanted to say was that you fell with considerable grace."

She broke off a piece of croissant, her mind somewhere else when she asked, "Were you here during the war?"

He seemed slightly surprised by the question. "Which war?"

Not any more surprised than she was for asking it. "The Second World War," she answered, quite aware what the whole point was, although a more subtle approach eluded her. But in her present state of emotional disarray she was capable of touching on anything from collaboration to circumcision to get where she wanted to be.

"My family was in Europe," he responded, still watching her intently.

She had a stake in knowing, since Rome. It was part of this obsession of hers that concerned genes that turned into habit that turned into hatred. If his family had gotten out of Paris in anything less than a potato sack on the back of a truck, it wasn't a good sign, unless they happened to be driving the truck carrying other potato sacks. As it was, ever since arriving in Paris and hearing that augmented-fourth sing-song siren, all she imagined were attics and ominous-looking men in belted trenchcoats dragging people out of buildings. "Were you in Paris, too?"

"You're making me older than I am," he chided gently. "And my family wasn't in Paris. They were in London during the war."

"Which wasn't as bad, I suppose."

"In many ways it was worse because of the constant bombing raids and food shortages. London was in deplorable condition for years after the war, but if you ask a Brit, he'll tell you that it was better than living under Occupation or suffering through daily deportations."

It was all so neatly avoided with polite words like "Occupation" and "daily deportations" substituting for the real horrors. Even now, there were already euphemisms for terrorist attacks that killed random civilians, little boys with red jackets who didn't even know how to spell the words. Revolutionary actions committed by "freedom fighters," she mused to herself, feeling suddenly chilled.

"Did you lose relatives during the war?" she asked.

Confusion for a moment and then embarrassment before he replied softly, "No."

Suddenly she wanted out of this conversation. She had nothing concrete to offer to explain her grief.

"Middle-aged men can be seductive," she announced, picking up on the age thing, safer ground than exposing her deeper feelings.

"Are you an expert on the subject of men?" he asked.

"A student, I guess."

"Until what age are men seductive?" He leaned forward and for an instant she thought he would take her hand.

"There's no age limit for men."

"Why is that?"

If he didn't already know, there was no point in arming him with the knowledge. There was no reason to explain that it all had to do with something subtle and even subliminal that could make men sexy and dashing for years, mainly because there was no age limit for fathering children. Just as there was no need to explain that for those same subtle and even subliminal reasons, women were redefined as their reproductive years diminished, as it became less and less feasible for them to have a child. "Probably because men shave," she chose to reply, "so their skin is tougher, which means they don't wrinkle as much."

He watched her carefully, to see if she were even mildly serious. "Or perhaps wrinkles on men make them appear more dependable."

She watched him just as carefully. "And on women?"

"More experienced."

What the word "experienced" conjured up were sexual images of benefit to men, while "dependable" made her think only of plumbers and accountants, also of benefit to men. Men could have it all, an impeccable tax return, a working toilet and a great piece of ass. But how could she tell him that, this man who rated women's tears in the arena of seduction. "Of course, men can behave in ways that call attention to their age."

"How's that?"

"When they take out only women who are young enough to be their daughters." And in case he judged her to be younger than she was or in case he was slightly older than he admitted, she decided to qualify and not take such a hard line. "But sixty to forty or fifty to thirty-five isn't as bad as forty to twenty or thirty to late teens."

"A sure sign of decay," he said gravely, and then surprised her. "But what would I say to a girl that young?"

"How young?"

"Certainly younger than you." He seemed to calculate. "Say, twenty."

She played with the pattern of crumbs on the table, not even bothering to look up when she answered, "Oh, I don't know, maybe you could tell her about that duel."

He seemed taken aback. "What duel?"

She had him or at least that battered grin of his belonged to her for the moment. "The one where you got that scar under your right eye." She looked up.

"You don't miss very much, do you?"

"Not when I'm concentrating."

"I won, you know."

"I didn't doubt it."

He dropped it without warning. "Did you win as well in your marriage?"

There was an edge to her tone when she replied, "I'm divorced."

"Surely, there was a winner there," he said affably.

She felt trapped. "Let's see," she began, "the party was a total disaster," the buzz going off in her head before she could control it, "mainly because the caterer forgot the caviar and the champagne wasn't properly chilled and a hundred other details just got lost in the confusion." Her words slowed to a halt and she looked about fifty or sixty. "It was your typical American love story," she said quietly, "we met, fell in love, got married, got divorced and then survived because we're both driven people with high-powered careers." But the sarcasm was evident.

"Am I allowed to ask what makes you so driven?"

"My work."

"Obviously. But what is it?"

"I'm a television reporter," she said, relieved to be on the professional side of her existence.

"Sounds exciting."

"Sometimes, and sometimes it's horrible." She was feeling a bit shaky. "And you? Is it still too American for me to ask what you do?" She tried a smile but it felt all wrong. But then she noticed there was something not unlike tenderness around his eyes and mouth when he answered. "No, it's not too American at all, especially since you were wounded in action." He gestured somewhere to the side and down. "How's that knee?"

"Fine," she said, "I can hardly feel it."

"You're very brave," he said with mock seriousness, and then added as if a bargain was a bargain. "I work for Renault."

"The car company?" she asked, hoping the disappointment was not too evident. "What do you do for them?" A test driver, she sort of hoped.

"I'm a hydraulic engineer. Do you know what that is?"

"Not exactly." A pause. "Actually, not at all." Slouching in her chair, she folded her arms across her chest and waited.

"It would take about four months to explain just the basics and you'd be bored to death." He said it as if he had been saying the same thing for years, to countless others who asked.

"No, please," she insisted, "I'm interested, tell me."

"Well, hydraulics has to do with the conveyance of liquids through pipes. Clear?"

"Clear."

"And that has to do with mysteries of motive power. Clear?"

"Not clear."

"I don't wonder," he said, patting her hand, leaving the flesh burning when he stopped, although she was the one who pulled her hand away. "But what I do for Renault, without getting into specifics, is travel around North Africa. In fact, the day after tomorrow I'm leaving to scout out locations for a new plant in Tunisia."

She almost knocked over the coffee. "Tunisia? But so am I, leaving for Tunisia, I mean, on assignment."

"Really," he said, his level of interest not exactly spinning off the charts, piqued but far from carried away. But she wasn't about to let his under-reaction put a damper on this happy coincidence. What she had to remember was that in Europe, London was to Paris what Philadelphia was to New York. Or, taking it toward the sun spots, Tunis was to Paris what Miami was to New York. And who in his right mind would fall off his seat when learning that someone he had just met was also going to Miami. But the other thing about him was that he was partly British, which explained that restraint, partly French, which accounted for that reserve, nothing that she was used to—American spontaneity, television exuberance. This man had looks and brains. What he seemed to lack was a touch of suffering, a pinch of soul, a dab of history.

"Have you ever been there before?" he asked graciously.

"No, never," she replied, taking it down a decibel level or two.

"How long will you be there?"

"For about two weeks."

"Where?"

"In Sidi Bou Said," she replied.

"Yes, I know it very well. It isn't very far from where I'll be."

She tried not to, for about thirty seconds, she really tried. And failed. "Where's that?"

"In Tunis."

Suddenly she wanted to know everything: who owned him, who packed his suitcase, who waited for him to come home, who missed him while he was gone, who loved him, who didn't. "We'll be staying at the Abou Nawas Hotel," she offered, hoping he'd wonder about her companion or companions. "Have you ever heard of it?"

"Yes, it's one of the best and right on the sea. I hope you like fish."

"To eat or swim with?"

He laughed. "Both."

"I love fish, especially to eat," she replied before informing him of what she imagined was a little-known fact. "The hotel is named after a poet who was born in the eighth century and died in the ninth." She smiled. Not exactly hydraulics but something that could help someone win at Trivial Pursuit. Where that came from was a mystery since she never played the game in her life nor any other game where her every move was confined to a board.

"You've certainly done your research."

"That's probably because that's what I do for a living," she said, waiting still for him to ask all the obvious questions. And when none was forthcoming, she decided to help it along. "Would you like to know why I'm going there?"

"Of course," he said more politely than eagerly, "I was hoping you'd tell me."

"We're taping a segment for a documentary we're doing for American television."

"On what?" he asked casually, busy with pouring another cup of coffee for both of them.

It was her seduction scene, something that she knew by heart and she played it to the hilt. "Have you ever heard of Tamir Karami?"

He hesitated. "The Palestinian?"

"A terrorist or the freedom fighter, depending on where the show is being aired, I suppose." She paused, gathering her thoughts to present her credentials as an expert on the subject. "He's number two in the PLO and also the head of his own group called Quest for a Homeland. You've heard of them."

"There's certainly been enough in the papers lately."

"What we're doing is going to Tunisia to do a special on Karami and his family. We're going to be interviewing him and his wife and children right in their house."

"Isn't that dangerous?"

"No. He needs the press too much to jeopardize all the publicity he'll be getting."

"Then why do it if it gives him publicity?"

Her mouth twisted slightly. "Because that's what television is all about."

"Aside from the publicity, what other advantages are there in his giving an interview?"

"His revolution is a media revolution."

"I see, and do you approve of helping that along?"

A thousand images again were racing through her head. "The audience will know who he is the minute he begins talking about his cause, so I can't see where anybody would have any sympathy for him, even if his reasons might be valid—"

"Are they valid?"

"My opinion doesn't matter."

"Do you have an opinion?"

She felt the lump in her throat. "It's pretty hard not to." A barrier had been raised between them, one that she had created. "A week ago I might have said that the Palestinian position was understandable." She looked up. "But it's hard to feel that way after what just happened. It clouds the issues."

"It must be fascinating," Gideon said, obviously having little interest in politics, "meeting people like Karami. But what really fascinates me is all that behind-the-scenes arranging that's done before the program actually goes on the air, all the details the public never sees. For instance, how was the decision made to choose Karami and not someone else?"

She was suddenly weary. "If you've read any papers and been watching television, you'd know why."

"Yes, of course," he said, shaking his head, "Rome. It was dreadful . . . Did you make the decision then?"

"No, my boss did. In fact, he's arriving from New York today."

"I see," he concluded. Nothing more. Which was when she noticed the two deep creases on either side of his mouth. "You must do a fair amount of traveling," he added pleasantly.

"Not all that much up until now since I've been either chasing fires or drug busts or welfare scams right in New York City."

Again, he changed lanes. "Will you accuse Karami of that attack?"

She frowned. "Accusation isn't exactly necessary since he already took credit for it."

"But think how dramatic it would be if he said it himself, if he explained how he organized his people, how he made the bomb, how he smuggled it into Rome, how he planted it there. Step by step by step." He grinned. "You see how boring I am? That's the hydraulic engineer talking now."

But she took her job very seriously and so began to educate him about the world of television and terrorists. "People care less about the how than they do about seeing the aftermath, the blood-and-gore part of it. Unfortunately, that's television and the more shocking the images, the higher the ratings."

"And that's what you give them?"

"And that's what I give them." But her voice was sad.

"So, I'm having breakfast with a famous person."

"Famous within the boundaries and suburbs of New York, New Jersey and Connecticut." She smiled modestly. "My show is local, which means that not only am I not famous in Paris, France, but I'm also not famous in Paris, Texas." She frowned again. "Except for lately."

"Lately?"

She took a deep breath. "I was in Rome when it happened."

He appeared stunned. "For your network?"

"That's how it ended up, but I was there by accident, right across the street, in fact."

"Were you hurt?"

The performance ended abruptly. Subdued, she began to explain. "Barely, at least not physically." Her voice faltered. "It's something I'll never forget as long as I live. It's beyond description, it's something I'll never get over." He didn't make a move to comfort her, nor did he offer any comment, merely stared as if he had suddenly removed himself to another level of understanding. "There were bodies everywhere," she went on, "some of them dead, some so badly injured that it was hard to tell who was who, and some who were in shock from having survived." She fiddled with an ashtray.

"The worst part is that the victims are forgotten quicker than anything else," she went on. "They serve a purpose as props, at least for television they do, and then they turn into statistics, which is when they stop existing as far as the media is concerned. They're only dragged out again if a recap of the year's horrors is broadcast."

He said nothing.

"What we should be doing is a documentary on who those people were before they walked into an Alitalia office alive and were carried out dead or injured." Her eyes were narrowed in concentration. "But nobody would be interested in those people's lives before they were killed. All the audience wants is bloody images. After it's over, they can go on with their lives and forget. That way they can't get emotionally involved. It's hard to get emotionally involved with a corpse." She bit her lip. "I'm rambling," she said, "but it's something I can't stop thinking about. The unbelievable thing is that the people who did it won't get caught, they'll get away with it because it's a political issue that has to do with money and oil and power."

Still he said nothing.

She had gone too far to stop. "I can't forget a little boy," she said quietly. "One of the victims." She took a breath. "When I first saw him lying there, he was alive, barely alive but alive, and then he died, he called for his mother and he died.'' She shook her head, tears filling her eyes. ''He looked so *small*, with his red jacket all torn, a piece of it in the hand of a woman lying nearby.''

He went pale on her.

''Are you all right?''

''Yes, yes, fine,'' he said hurriedly, ''but your descriptions are rather vivid.'' He signaled for the check. ''It's late and I've got to get to work.''

''I'm sorry for going on like that.''

''No, please, don't apologize. Something like that is naturally shocking.''

''What I can't understand is how anyone can survive such a thing, I mean, a parent for instance, how can anyone survive such a loss?''

He reached into his pocket for those wraparound glasses and put them on. Leaning over, he touched her nose gently with one finger. ''Did anyone ever tell you that you cry well?''

She shook her head. ''Did I cry?''

''Barely,'' he said, ''but well.'' He counted out some change to leave on the table before picking up his reading glasses. ''Shall we?'' he said as he stood. She stood as well, feeling awkward and clumsy and ridiculous.

''Where are you staying in Paris?'' he asked, his manner almost distant.

''At the George V,'' she answered, feeling like a balloon with a puncture.

They walked in silence for half a block before reaching the corner, where they waited for the light to change. He looked at her very intently then, so intently that it made her self-conscious. But when he spoke, his tone was unexpectedly casual. ''And of course, there's no chance I'll forget which hotel in Tunisia because of that poet.''

"Eighth- and ninth-century poet," she added, feeling like a plank of wood.

The light changed and again they walked in silence until they reached the other side of the street. "I'll be in touch, Sasha Beale," he said without warning, a finger briefly on the tip of her nose. And then he was gone, vanished down the steps of the métro.

She had to stop recounting her experience in Rome. Telling Maury was one thing but telling a perfect stranger she had just met was not very smart, especially since she still wasn't able to control her emotions when she talked about it. At least she'd better learn to control herself before she actually met the monster who ordered Rome, the man who was, in her mind, nothing less than quintessential evil.

But as far as breakfast was concerned, it was too late to change anything. Either he'd call or he wouldn't. Over and over, the choices played in her head as she walked, as if she were picking petals from an imaginary daisy. And if he didn't, she'd survive, and if he did, she'd be surprised, although there were other good-looking men in the world who were less distant and more effusive. What bothered her about this one was that apparent emptiness behind those spectacular eyes of his, which could very well mean a lack of depth. But then, he was a hydraulic engineer, whatever that was, so his frame of reference was certainly different than hers. And anyway, what did she expect him to do—break down and tell her his entire life story? One thing was certain, she was glad that Maury would be here for a couple of days, she needed an infusion of good old Jewish neurotic, she craved the company of a man who had suffered in life, she decided as she entered the lobby some twenty minutes later.

There were two messages at the reception desk. Maury had arrived while she was out making a fool of herself and intended to sleep until noon, when he hoped to see her in his suite for coffee. She was about to ask for her key when the concierge approached her. "Mademoiselle Beale?"

"Yes?

"There's a telephone call for you. Please, you can take it over here next to the flowers."

Undoubtedly Maury. "From the hotel?"

"No, from the outside."

There was no doubt. She knew. But she just didn't "take" the phone as the concierge suggested, she grabbed it, almost knocking over three Japanese businessmen in the process. They were still bowing, she noticed, long after she apologized and shortly after she shoved the receiver under her chin and over her ear. "Yes," she said breathlessly.

"Sasha Beale," he said in that intimate tone of his, almost obscene for nine-thirty in the morning, "how is that knee?"

"Fine," she answered barely above a whisper.

"How about dinner tonight?"

"Fine," she said again, aware that he somehow had reduced her to an inarticulate muddled mound of mush.

"I'll pick you up at your hotel at about eight."

"Fine," she said once more, wondering if she would be able to say anything else ever again.

"See you then," he said before clicking off.

So maybe it *was* a Truffaut film.

Chapter Seven

THE ISRAELI EMBASSY in Paris was a dull yet imposing structure on a street named after a writer whose prose was considered by many to be equally dull though no less imposing. On the rue Rabelais, next to the embassy, between the metal barricades, electrified gates, armed guards and a permanent contingent of gendarmes who spent most of the time inside a bus playing cards, was the Dreyfus Bank. It was this particular bit of information that the ambassador delighted in telling his guests when he dragged them to a musty window. "After all this time we find ourselves not only vindicated but also sharing the same view, trash bins, and guards," as if he had a hand in either the real estate transaction or the outcome of the *Affair* itself. The latter connection had been made rather blatant after the Alitalia bombing, when the ambassador lifted Emile Zola's words in an open letter to one of the right-wing newspapers entitled *"J'Accuse."*

Down the street from the embassy on one side was the Time-Life Building, while on the other was a pretentious but decent restaurant that catered to the lunch crowd in the neighborhood. Which was to say, it catered to those who didn't take exception when asked to produce identity cards or passports before they were allowed entry onto that heavily guarded stretch of pavement. But regardless of who came and who went, the ambassador had his usual table in the corner every day, where he drank a half bottle of Vichy and ate a grilled piece of sole drenched in mustard sauce. It was a routine that drove his guards wild but one they couldn't do much about given the diplomat's opinion of himself as a man of impeccable taste and judgment, a mystic no less, inexplicably protected from an assassin's bullets. Not that anybody agreed with him, least of all his PLO counterpart, who was surely the culprit behind those rumors of homosexuality. But in all fairness, the reason that nasty scuttlebutt had taken hold in polite French society was undoubtedly due to the man's Syrian origins. Which of *them*, his illustrious colleagues asked each other in insouciant tones, with that kind of background, wouldn't be just slightly *pédé*?

But despite the innuendos, the foreign ministry in Jerusalem had unanimously nominated the man for a second tour of duty as ambassador to France. And it wasn't that the boys back home were so cavalier about the sexual practices of their representatives serving abroad. God knew, they had their rules about sending out strapping or not-so-strapping single men for fear they would be grabbed up by local women and not return home to till Israeli soil or guard Israeli borders. In the case of the ambassador, however, it was a question of pragmatism or good old Jewish *sechel* that made his superiors more than tolerant. After all, the man had cultivated strong ties with the Elysée and the Quai D'Orsay as well as maintained a consistently hard-line policy against any Western conciliation with the PLO. But what the ambassador mostly had in his favor was the special relationship he shared (as well as that daily meal at that corner table in the local bistro) with the French bureaucrat responsible for all permits and custom forms relating to every civilian aircraft landing on French soil.

It was, therefore, no coincidence that barely any notice was taken of the unmarked white Boeing 707 that flew into Charles de Gaulle from Israel in the dawn hours that morning. Nor was it a matter of dereliction that no entry was made in any official log book or any papers checked as to nationality or purpose and length of visit of the male passenger who was carried on a stretcher from the plane. While the craft stood on an abandoned portion of the field, the drugged and tightly bound man was placed in the back of a private station wagon to be driven off to that dull yet imposing building on the rue Rabelais. After that, it took only thirty-seven minutes to refuel the craft, enough time for the pilot, the copilot and navigator to stretch their legs before they and it took off into French skies.

In a room that was far removed from the Chagall stained-glass windows and hand-carved winding mahogany staircase, Yacov Agam geometric wall designs and showy Bucellati silver tea service that were all part of the cultural and historical decor of the Israeli Embassy, Rafi Unger presided over a meeting.

The main advantage of that top floor section of the embassy was that it was the only area in the entire building where visiting dignitaries could speak in normal tones or make uninhibited gestures without fear of any fancy French audio or video devices recording words or movements. Or, as Rafi was fond of putting it, ''The only place in Paris where a man could confess a marital infidelity and scratch his balls at the same time.'' And all because each day a team of Sabras equipped with earphones and machines resembling Geiger counters swept the large conference room, two adjoining briefing rooms, bathroom, kitchen and bedroom, checking for unusual frequencies, hidden eyes or microwaves.

In the case of the Alitalia bombing, it had taken less than twenty-four hours to make the decision for an assassination and to gather the four-man team that had been scattered throughout the world. The group of men who now sat around the battered oak table in the embassy had been handpicked by Rafi from an elite commando unit attached to the Mossad called the Sayaret Malkal. A decision such as this was not always reached that fast; sometimes it took days or even weeks for the people who pushed paper back at the office to make up their minds, discussing the dissecting when a terrorist was a terrorist. But despite the time involved, the guidelines remained the same: when innocent people were killed in the name of a political cause. Alitalia had all the markings of just such an attack.

Unfortunately, most of those being killed were Jews, which meant that most of those taking retaliatory action were Israelis, which didn't exactly translate into their being welcomed with open arms into European clubs, hotels and spas. "As if we were ever welcome," was Rafi's constant retort. Or, as the defense minister put it in a speech delivered before the group on the day of their arrival in Israel, "Is it our fate to be both vanquished and victor without benefit of either tears or applause?"

Gideon did not attend that first meeting, and it was just as well that he did not or he would have heard the minister's speech in its entirety. Jerusalem expected results not only for Rome, but especially for the Intifada. Rome was unspeakable, savage, but Rome was Rome, while Gaza was only one-hundred and fifty kilometers from Haifa, Jericho only thirty minutes from Jerusalem. What nobody mentioned was that Tamir Karami was not only responsible for the bombing and the riots, but was also the only man left on Golda's list.

After Gideon agreed to lead the mission, the most minute facts and details on Karami began accumulating rapidly. Flight numbers, airports, train schedules and rental cars were all recorded in an effort to find some sort of pattern before everything was checked and re-checked and entered into the computer. Not only was Karami's every move being tracked by then but every move of every person he came into contact with as well. Which included the travel agent who booked all his trips, as Gideon had managed to tap into the unsus-pecting woman's computer. Before long, word came down that the Palestinian was getting suspicious, changing names and passports more frequently, nation-alities and identities more easily as he chose circuitous routes to take him from one Arab country to another. Yet none of that worried Gideon as much as coming up with that someone else besides the girl to guarantee the success of the mission. There was still something miss-ing, a key ingredient that had not yet been covered but one that he knew would make all the difference. It wasn't until seventy-two hours before Gideon was due to leave for Paris that he was sufficiently confident of what it was to give voice to it. And when he did, Rafi not only agreed but insisted that the information be lim-ited to only the people involved in the mission. Gideon would explain everything to the four-man team when they were all together in Paris.

"Ya'Acov, Ya'Acov and the birds," Rafi said, glanc-ing around the table. "How they always come to you, no matter where you are is something I'll never under-stand." He smiled at the diminutive man who sat to his left.

"It's the crumbs and the whistle," the man replied modestly.

"So tell us, Ya'Acov, did she notice the bird act?"

"When she wasn't looking at Gideon."

Rafi smiled again. "So everything worked out. But you know, Ya'Acov, I'd swear you were a Catholic the way birds and animals love you, or do you just have special talents?'' But Ya'Acov's special talents went far beyond amassing strange birds in foreign parks. An expert underwater diver, formerly a member of the frog-man contingent of the Israeli Navy, he gained most of his experience sabotaging Egyptian ships in the Suez Canal during the Yom Kippur War. Recently, he had led the squad that permanently disabled the Palestinian ship, *Al Awad (The Return)*, patterned after the *Exodus*, as it prepared to set sail from Limassol, Cyprus, to the Israeli port of Haifa. Most recently, he had been living in Rhode Island and learning new underwater weaponry techniques to bring back home.

''So, Yoram, did you take beautiful pictures?'' Rafi spoke to the man seated on his right.

A thin man with a mop of black curls, Yoram smiled slightly. ''All you like, two rolls of film.''

''So you could have taken a few of the tourists and made a couple of dollars,'' Rafi carried on.

''Too early for tourists,'' Yoram answered in a small voice. Yoram and his dark-haired partner Ben were in charge of the video portion of the mission. They always worked together, most recently at an internationally renowned resort in Morocco that was a playground for former monarchs, rock stars and other dubiously employed millionaires. Yoram served drinks around the pool while Ben maintained the fifty or so air-conditioning units. In their off-duty hours, the pair had participated in no less than twenty missions throughout the Arab world. Their presence in otherwise hostile countries and their work with certain splinter terrorist groups were not at all suspect, given their physical traits, command of Arabic, and lifelong false identities as two brothers from a Palestinian family scattered in the diaspora. Lately, it hadn't hurt their reputations that their origins were Iraqi, distant cousins, it was rumored, of the current Arab lunatic, Saddam Hussein, whose troops had goose-stepped into Kuwait as if it were a neighborhood 7-Eleven in Skokie, Illinois. Between them, Yoram and Ben had eliminated some seven or eight Arab luminaries and were still fresh and functional and ready to eliminate another.

"Did you get a final shot of her?" Rafi asked as an afterthought.

"When she fell for Gideon," Yoram said, a grin spreading across his emaciated face.

"So, Ronnie," Rafi continued in a pleasant tone, "how's the new baby?" He watched as the blond man's face lit up.

"Wonderful and fat and happy, they tell me," he said.

"No pictures?"

"Not here."

"Is he as beautiful as his mother?"

Ronnie Elan nodded emphatically.

"Do you miss being there?"

"Of course, but it's only until this tour is over." It had been decided that Ronnie's wife would remain on the family kibbutz during the emergency, which coincided with his current one-year tour of duty as political attaché at the Israeli Embassy in Berlin. Officially, it was Ronnie's job to deal with the press in all matters that concerned the Middle East. Unofficially, he kept careful account of every terrorist safe house and the movements of every occupant or visitor throughout what was once considered the Eastern Bloc. It was an assignment that suited him, fluent as he was in four languages.

But specialized qualifications were not the reasons Rafi chose the team for the mission. Devotion to Gideon was his primary concern, friendship that went back to the beginning when each started out, whether Gideon was young with them or whether he was already a leader. It was Rafi's instinct this time around that more than anything else, Gideon needed a support team that understood all the conflict and pain.

"Who wants to pull down the screen so when Gideon gets here we can start the slide show?" Rafi asked around the room.

Yoram stood. "I can still hear the shower running," he said as he adjusted the tripod.

"That's because he's probably still under it," Rafi replied. "That job must have been too much for his tired old bones."

"She didn't seem to mind them," Ya'Acov said.

"How many miles this morning?"

"About two," Ya'Acov informed the group, "and she kept right up with him."

"Or maybe it was Gideon keeping up with her," Rafi said. "But we can review the film later and see who's in better shape. In the meantime, Yoram, will you take charge of the projector?"

"Are all the slides in?" Yoram asked Ben.

"Almost," he answered, taking a few minutes to arrange the slides in their proper sequence. "I'll put the girl first to cheer up Gideon."

"Too late now," Yoram said, "Karami is our star today."

"One of his final performances, no doubt," Rafi said, but stopped abruptly. Everything stopped abruptly, in fact, all conversation and banter, when the door opened and the man they had been waiting for stepped inside.

From the moment that Gideon entered the room, it was hard to escape all their loving assaults. Yoram and Ben embraced him, greeting him as "Gidi," a name that went back to their university days together. Ronnie hugged him as well, kissing him on each cheek.

"Tell me about the baby," Gideon said warmly and when Ronnie hesitated, Gideon squeezed his shoulder. "Go on, Ronnie, tell me, I want to hear." The sentiments were genuine, but it was nothing less than a test of his own strength as he listened to his friend's words.

"Four kilos small," Ronnie said.

"And Anat?" Gideon asked.

"Still about ten kilos too big."

He nodded and hugged him once again, but the gap had already been sealed. "Ya'Acov," Gideon greeted the bird man, "how are you? I noticed you looked a little tired this morning."

"Jet lagged," Ya'Acov replied, "only I'm working such long hours that I'm jet-lagged even when I don't fly."

It was generally expected that Gideon would still be in shock and functioning under enormous strain. It was also expected that he would never allow his personal grief to interfere with his work. Both expectations were correct. Eyes crinkled in concentration, he listened politely as each imparted his own word of wisdom on how best to handle those waves of anguish, as if any of them had experienced those same waves for those same reasons. Still, he behaved with his usual grace and dignity, assuring everyone that he was managing as well as could be expected under the circumstances. Only, he practically choked on the words. Still, he held tough, kept up a calm controlled front until Ya'Acov made the mistake of mentioning the last time he had seen the boy riding his bicycle around the neighborhood in Herziliah. Like a man who had been shot, Gideon visibly crumbled, one hand on the back of the chair for support until he was able to gather enough composure to continue. And while Ya'Acov kept apologizing, while the others just stood and stared, dumbstruck and at a loss, Gideon was the one to comfort the man and put the others at ease. Judging that the moment had passed and that any further reaction would be self-indulgent, he changed subjects.

"What has Rafi told you?" he addressed the group.

"Nothing," Rafi responded for all. "I wanted you to start from the beginning. We have slides to show as you speak or after you speak, as you wish."

Wet hair plastered back from his face, his shirt opened at the neck and tucked into a pair of jeans, loafers worn without socks, Gideon tried to sound as casual as he appeared. "Let's show the slides later because there's too much ground to cover in a very short time and I don't want any distractions. We'll put faces on all the players soon enough." He glanced at each man and to his dismay saw his own sorrow reflected in their eyes. His mourning had apparently become a communal matter. Not that it surprised him. In those circles bad news traveled fast, especially news that had more to do with emotional trauma than the usual trauma dealt with on a daily basis. Everyone knew every detail of everyone else's life even under normal circumstances, including the state of his marriage. What nobody bargained for, least of all Gideon, was that the professional and personal trauma would become one and the same, which was what made it so difficult not to justify and explain. The temptation to begin the briefing with the announcement that Rome was supposed to be a new start for his family, that the problems with his marriage were supposed to have been forgiven and forgotten forever, was almost impossible to resist. Except that *forever* turned out to be very different from what had been planned.

"It could have happened anywhere," Ben offered.

"It was meant to be," Yoram added.

"It was fate," Ya'Acov put in.

Gideon turned, his regard glacial as he forced himself to remain on the outside, to swallow every bitter retort . . . To those of you who consider what happened to be fate, he answered Ben silently, let me make it clear that fate had nothing to do with it, goddamnit. He pretended to study some notes before him, waiting for the tightness in his throat to disappear. Fate played a part in death, he continued silently, only in those cases when a road was chosen where a drunken driver was heading in the opposite direction or when a vacation city was selected where there would be an earthquake or when a can of food infested with botulism was picked from a supermarket shelf. Fate was absent on the day that my wife and son happened to stroll down the Via Veneto in search of a street map. That just wasn't up for debate, the words blasted away inside his head, since it was all within my ability to prevent such a disaster, since it was all because of my misjudgment, miscalculation, misinformation. Hands lying flat on the table, his expression was placid, his tone calm when he finally spoke. "When Rafi asked me to come up with someone who could tell us everything we need to know about Karami, from the contents of his agenda to his childhood diseases, to every last nail, screw, lock and door in his house, I thought it was impossible. Unless, of course, we could convince Karami himself to help us out." He wondered how many more times he could say Karami's name and remain sane. "But when I thought about it some more, I realized there was only one person who was in a position to give us that kind of information." He devoted his attention to a pencil. "The coffee man," he said before glancing up. "The one loyal member of Karami's household staff whose brother happens to live in the village of Bet Forik." He paused. "In the Occupied Territories."

"Which means he needs an Israeli identity card and work permit and tax papers to exist," Rafi added.

The others nodded, their eyes filled with what appeared to be admiration although it was hard to read. Admiration for what, Gideon wondered, a well-tuned machine, a well-nurtured robot?

"For those of you who forgot, Bet Forik is a charming little village near Nablus with an overabundance of olive trees and stones and a shortage of indoor plumbing.'' Turning to Gideon, Rafi said, ''Go on, tell them about the coffee man, and my apologies to Yoram and Ben, who know it all by heart already.''

Every Arab of means employed one, Gideon began, since serving coffee in that part of the world was a sign of peace and conciliation, even if everyone knew there were no guarantees after the last drop was drained from the cup.

''Be precise,'' Rafi prodded.

''The coffee man is the one person who knows who comes and who goes and how long they stay. He's the one man aware of how the Palestinian takes his coffee and what brand of liquor he prefers, what cigarettes he smokes and whether he has breakfast in the dining room with his advisors or alone with his wife in bed.'' Gideon hit his stride. ''This is the one employee who knows where Karami keeps his gun because he's the one who loads it and cleans it. He's the one who also knows if Karami prays to Mecca three times a day and whether he faces Allah with or without this weapon.'' He paused to run his tongue over his top lip when he was hit with the notion that his son would never again come through the front door after school. ''How many keys, how many doors,'' he went on, ''how many windows and most important of all, the telephone number and whether or not it's regularly changed.'' What was it she said about that red jacket, that it was scattered everywhere, a piece of it clutched in Miriam's hand. ''Which means we can place a small box on the wires that lead from the house to the main telephone station.'' He glanced around. ''So we can hear every conversation he has with the wife he loves so dearly.'' He moved papers around, remembering his son as a baby before imagining him as a grown man, either image something that would never be again. ''You see, Karami calls her several times a day when he's traveling and tells her everything. He apparently values her opinion. Everything comes right back to the coffee man, the one person on the inside who can make this operation work.'' He felt sick.

''Then why bring the girl into it?'' Ya'Acov asked.

Given that he had already lived and died, still it felt odd to exist without any thought of risk. ''The girl is already in it,'' he answered, determined not to let any spark of the human element enter into things.

''With or without us, she's there to do a television interview,'' Rafi explained, ''which means she'll be with the family almost every day for about a week. She's the only person on the inside who is an outsider, who has no personal interest in lying or misleading Gideon. She's our corroborator, our second opinion, our insurance policy just in case the coffee man thinks that giving us wrong information is more amusing than giving us right information.'' He smiled slightly. ''Two Israelis, three opinions,'' he continued. ''If you prefer, consider Sasha Beale the doctor you go to when the first doctor tells you it's terminal.'' He nodded to Gideon.

''She's an innocent,'' Gideon said without even glancing up. ''And innocent observations can be more valuable than if we sent someone in who knew exactly what to look for. This is her first time in international waters, her first contact with a political criminal, her first exposure to a terrorist attack.''

''A virgin,'' Rafi muttered.

But Gideon went on, hustling the group with a smattering of his own convictions. ''There's an in-bred level of paranoia among Palestinian leaders that begins with American reporters. They think they've got an inside track to the CIA, which has a direct line to the Mossad. So, it's not unlikely that any interview Karami gives is meant as a message for top officials in Washington or Jerusalem.'' He looked directly at Rafi. ''If they had a legitimate platform, perhaps they wouldn't look for alternative routes to be heard.''

"Getting back to the doctor," Rafi quickly changed subjects, "what would you do if he said you had two weeks to live?"

"Is that the time frame here?" Yoram asked.

"We do what we can," Rafi answered.

"How do you intend to get the coffee man?"

"Where is he now?"

"Do we pick him up in Tunisia?"

"What about the brother? Do we get him in Bet Forik?"

"What makes you think one brother will hand over the other?"

"Suppose he agrees and then changes his mind?"

"What do we have on him?"

One by one the questions were posed, Gideon remaining silent until each of them had finished talking. And when he finally responded, his comment was evasive. "It's odd, isn't it," he said, "how everyone wants to be part of that mythical solution called peace in the Middle East."

"It's a sad state of affairs," Rafi shook his head. "But why don't you tell them the whole story, Gideon."

He inclined his head over the file before him on the table.

"Go on. Gideon, tell them," he repeated.

Gideon reached for a cigarette. "Saba Khalil, the coffee man's brother, was picked up two nights ago."

"Where?" Ronnie asked.

"It seems the American Colony Hotel put out a call for extra laborers. All the windows on the ground floor level were blown out, one of the more minor casualties of the Intifada."

"What happened?" Ben asked.

Gideon began the story. "It went something like this . . ."

JERICHO—OCCUPIED TERRITORIES

The car was parked on the side of the road that ran between Jericho and Jerusalem, the route that cut through an Arab village rather than the Israeli settlement of Maale Adumim. Gideon sat next to Rafi in the backseat, his eyes fixed on the road for any sign of approaching headlights. Within minutes, an army jeep appeared in the distance, weaving its way toward them, and within seconds after that, a Mercedes taxi approached from the opposite direction.

"Here we go," Rafi said, tapping his driver on the shoulder. "Stay behind the Mercedes until it makes a full stop and then pull up alongside."

Gideon watched as the two men in the army jeep, both dressed as Israeli soldiers, began the routine. The driver cut the wheel sharply, swinging the vehicle around to create a barrier in the middle of the road while the other "soldier" jumped out to wave the Mercedes over to the side. "When they bring our man over here," Rafi said, "I'm going to move to the front seat so he sits next to you in the back."

Gideon said nothing, intent on watching everything that was going on, a ritual that was played out at least ten times a day all over the country.

The car that was stopped was an Arab taxi carrying four Palestinian workers on their way to the American Colony Hotel in East Jerusalem, where there had been a call for extra laborers. Rafi's instructions to his men posing as soldiers were that they not deviate from the Army's regular procedures when it came to random road checks. They were to look at identity papers and work permits as well as to inspect underneath the Mercedes and in the trunk for any hidden weapons and explosives. Then they were to get their target out of the car, detaining him under the false pretense of having an expired identity card.

Fortunately there were no complications or discoveries of hidden weapons so that within fifteen minutes, the cab driver and three of the passengers were checked, cleared and hustled back into the Mercedes for the trip to the American Colony Hotel. The fourth passenger was escorted over to Rafi and Gideon with the explanation of an expired identity card. The plastic-encased document was handed to Gideon, who examined it before leaning over to open the car door. "Get in," he ordered the terrified Palestinian.

The man was chunky, Gideon noted, and fair-skinned, with enormous black eyes and light brown hair. His shirt was worn at the elbows and his trousers were soiled and faded although the medal he wore on a chain around his neck was gold—five fingers, the hand of Fatima, a *hamsa*, good luck to the wearer. "Are you Saba Khalil?" Gideon asked, studying the photograph on the card.

"My card isn't expired," the man protested in Arabic, responding to Gideon's use of the language.

"Do you know what happens to Palestinians who collaborate with Israelis?" Rafi asked from the front seat.

"But I'm not a collaborator," the man protested even more strongly.

"They're chopped up with hatchets or hung from telephone poles," Rafi continued as if no one had spoken. "Tell him."

But Gideon said nothing until the confusion was evident on the man's face, until he was satisfied that Saba Khalil had no idea which side of the struggle was present in that car. And when he finally spoke, it was in a pleasant tone. "You are Saba Khalil?"

"Yes," the man answered warily.

Gideon offered him a cigarette. "You have a very sick baby," he stated in the same innocuous tone.

The man appeared stunned. "Yes, but how—"

"He needs an operation or he'll die," Gideon went on.

The man held the cigarette between trembling fingers. "Yes."

"But you don't have the money."

"No."

Gideon lit his own cigarette before leaning over to offer a light. "And your family doesn't have the money either," he said. "So, tell me, Saba, what are you going to do?" He waited, watching the man carefully, trying not to disbelieve himself even more, reminding himself why this was necessary, who the target was. "What are you going to do, Saba?" Gideon repeated.

"I don't know."

"Perhaps you could ask your brother for help," Gideon said casually.

A look of understanding appeared in the man's eyes.

"Perhaps he could go to his boss for the money." Gideon paused. "What do you think, Saba, could your brother go to Tamir Karami for the money?"

"I don't know," Saba replied, looking down.

Gideon smiled warmly. "But that could get complicated, I understand, that could put your brother in a difficult position."

"He wouldn't want to ask Abu Fahd," the man mumbled.

"Who?" Gideon leaned over, "I couldn't understand the name."

"Abu Fahd," the man repeated. "He wouldn't like to ask him for the money."

"Of course he wouldn't," Gideon agreed, remembering that Abu Fahd was Karami's *nom de guerre*. "If everyone asked that poor man for help, there would be lines of sick children and starving old people in front of his villa.'' Gideon shook his head. "No, that wouldn't do at all, would it?''

The man shook his head.

Gideon took a breath before making the announcement with as much flourish in his voice as if the man had just won the Palestinian National Lottery. "Here's the good news. We've decided to help you.'' He waited barely long enough for the man's head to snap around. "Your wife and baby and two other children are safely in Jerusalem, Saba, waiting for you at a hospital, so as soon as you get there, your baby can have that operation.''

Tears streamed down the man's face. "Who are you, what do you want from me?''

"Nothing that will harm you or your family,'' Rafi told him, turning around.

"What we're offering you is help, Saba,'' Gideon added, "providing you help us.''

"But what can I do?''

Gideon had already made the decision not to appeal to the patriot in the man, one zealot in the family was enough. And anyway, the baby born with the hole in the right ventricle of his heart had long since rendered Saba Khalil passive and apolitical. Not that he hadn't uttered the word "Palestine" in the past, his voice even rising an octave or two during a demonstration, challenging the authorities to arrest him for saying the name of a country that didn't exist, but that was long before he was a man who gave life to a dying child. "What you can do,'' Gideon said quietly, "is help us prevent Karami's murder.''

"But I know nothing of him—''

"Your brother is very close to Karami.''

"Are you Shin Bet?'' the man dared, referring to the Israeli internal security force.

"No, I'm not Shin Bet,'' Gideon answered honestly.

"It's my brother you want, isn't it?" the man suddenly asked.

"You love him, don't you?"

"Of course, he's my brother."

"And he loves you?"

"Of course."

Gideon seemed to consider the relationship for several moments, counting on what he had read in the file,
that Saba Khalil was not stupid.

"You want my brother because of Abu Fahd," Saba
realized.

"Why do you insist on calling him by his *nom de
guerre*?" Rafi asked. "Is he *your* leader?"

"There are no leaders," the man replied with surprising cynicism, "only victims."

They drove on a few more yards until Rafi ordered
the driver to stop the car at the base of a small hill,
where several rusted wagons stood, a memorial to some
who had died during the 1948 War of Independence.
Gideon wondered briefly about the older man's sense of
drama. "Unfortunately, as long as people use those
names," Rafi commented wearily, "there will never be
a chance for a real peace."

"My brother belongs to the PLO," Saba said. "I
don't."

Gideon shook his head. "But that's the whole problem."

"You see, Saba, there is a radical faction of the PLO
that is planning to kill Karami," Rafi lied.

Gideon continued it. "They believe he's willing to
negotiate with the Israelis."

"But my baby," the man moaned softly, "why my
family?"

"Because you're so close, all of you," Gideon said.
"If one of you is in trouble, everyone helps." He smiled
briefly. "And because if anything happens to Karami,

your brother would be held partially responsible because he's there to watch over him.''

''But if he does something to save Karami's life,'' Rafi put in, ''then everybody is happy.'' He smiled briefly as well. ''And grateful.''

''But you're not Palestinians, why do you care if something happens to Karami?''

Gideon ignored that small discrepancy. To try to explain would only complicate matters. Leave the man confused. ''Unfortunately, your brother can only save Karami's life if he cooperates with us. Only if he tells us certain facts we need to know.'' By using the ''we'' he had somehow united all entities, whatever they might have been in Saba's mind. ''The most important thing, of course, is that your brother must never mention anything to Karami, either that there are people trying to kill him or people trying to save him. Because if he does, Karami will get suspicious and change his routine.''

''And if he does that,'' Rafi interrupted, ''the killers will get nervous and hit when we least expect them to.''

''When we're not prepared and not there to stop them.''

''But what can my brother *do*?'' Saba begged, although the question clearly concerned his wife and children.

''Right now, it's you that we need,'' Gideon said. ''Your brother will know what to do once he understands the problem.'' He rubbed his eyes before putting on his half glasses. ''We want you to tell your brother that there is someone who needs to talk to him.'' His shoulders shifted slightly. ''Tell him it's a matter of life and death.''

''*Whose* life?''

Gideon took another deep breath, hating this. ''Your son's.''

''*Allah akba,* why my child, why my child? My child

was born after the Catastrophe, after the Intifada, why my child?''

''Your child was dead when you stepped in this car,'' Rafi said coldly. ''What we're offering now is a chance for *life*.''

''Just tell your brother the truth,'' Gideon said, thinking that at least some semblance of truth had been created within the confines of the car. ''Explain that someone came to you for help because they had information about a plot against Karami. Tell your brother that he's the only person in a position to save him. But the rest of it must be said in person, no telephones, no fax machines, no messages, no third parties. In person.''

''There isn't much time,'' Rafi added evenly.

''It's up to you, Saba,'' Gideon said, pausing then to change subjects in case the man had forgotten the beginning of the story. ''We're going to drop you off at the Russian Compound so that if anyone notices they'll see that you've been taken to the detention center because of your expired identity card.'' Gideon cracked open the window to flick his cigarette. ''You'll be kept in solitary tonight and then tomorrow, before you're released, you're to call your brother in Sidi Bou Said at Karami's house.'' If the man seemed hesitant, Gideon pretended not to notice. Instead, he settled back against the seat and glanced out the window while Rafi continued. ''You'll tell your brother that you've got to talk to him, that it's an emergency and that he's to meet you at your parents' house in Jordan as soon as possible.''

''You'll go there the way you usually go''—Gideon turned to the man—''across the Allenby Bridge from Jericho and then bus sixteen to Jebbel Hussein.''

''You know, Saba,'' Rafi said quietly, ''your brother is really quite fortunate.'' The man appeared bewildered. ''When this is over he's going to be one of the heroes of the revolution.''

Saba looked to Gideon, as if for verification. Gideon looked away. "Why do you care if Karami is killed?" Saba repeated the question that Gideon now judged he had to answer.

"There are important meetings going on, secret meetings between the Americans and Arab leaders, Israelis and the PLO. If Karami is killed, it will set things back at least six months until there's someone else who thinks like he does to replace him. That means that every Palestinian living on the Riviera and driving a big car will go on living like that while the Palestinians living under Occupation in the camps will stay like that as well." A little fact, a little fiction.

"After you've visited with your family and explained things to your brother"—Rafi got back to the subject under discussion—"you'll both leave Amman together. Only for obvious reasons, you won't come back over the bridge into Israeli territory." There was no need to explain to Saba that from the moment his brother joined the PLO, he was forever banned from reentering Israel and the territories. "Instead, you'll cross the Jordan River through the wadi where it narrows into the Yarmuch."

"We'll be waiting for you at the abandoned power station," Gideon continued, "and as soon as your brother is safely inside it, you'll be driven to the hospital to join your wife and children." Gideon watched as the man nodded his understanding and acceptance. For Gideon it wasn't unusual that the man didn't resist when instructed to walk back over that heavily patrolled border. Given the same circumstances, he would have done the same and more; he would have crawled on his belly to Beirut or to Tripoli to save his child. "Tell me," Gideon asked the man, "do you really care whether or not there is a Palestine?" Not that he expected a rational response, since there was a limit to how much a man could sacrifice for his people or for a cause or for a political mistake that was made before he was born.

"I'm tired of all the fighting," Saba said, "but not for myself. I'm afraid for the children."

It was a mutual malady, fatigue and fear for the children, although for Gideon, half that equation was over.

The car pulled out onto the highway, heading once again toward Jerusalem. No one spoke for the next ten minutes or so until they had driven past the Knesset and were already on Nablus Road nearing the Compound. It was then that Saba gestured to Rafi to ask the inevitable question. "He speaks Arabic with an Israeli accent. Is he a Jew?"

But for Gideon, that willingness to talk was a sign that the man suddenly realized his worth, enough to afford himself the luxury of asking questions. "Does that make a difference?"

Saba shrugged.

"Either way, your child needs that operation."

"But what if we get caught crossing the wadi?" Reality had replaced the dream. "What if the Bedouins see us and the Israelis start shooting, what if the Jordanians start shooting?" The adrenalin was on the decline. "What if I refuse?"

"It's too late now," Rafi said quickly.

"You let us worry about the Bedouins and the Israelis and the Jordanians," Gideon told him. "You just worry about convincing your brother to come back with you." Reaching into his pocket, he produced an identity card. "Take a good look at it," he instructed Saba, "so you remember the exact date it expired and the date it was renewed."

"But this isn't the same card," he protested before a look of understanding crossed his face. "For my brother," he whispered knowingly, "so he'll see that I was arrested."

But Gideon chose to ignore the man's transition from victim to accomplice. Instead, he firmly clutched his shoulder. "Good luck, Saba," he said as the car drove through the gates of the prison compound. "And remember, you've got the best doctors to operate on your child."

As if there were degrees of hopelessness, the man nodded. "Israeli doctors," he said softly. "Jews," he added before his wrists were snapped into a pair of handcuffs.

"What if there hadn't been a child who needed an operation?" Ya'Acov asked.

"Then there would have been a father who needed a kidney or a mother who needed a sack of rice or a sister who needed chemotherapy or an uncle who needed to know that his house would still be standing when he came back from work or someone who needed something, even if it was just an identity card or a work permit not to starve."

"Where's the coffee man now?" Ronnie asked.

"Sound asleep in the room next door," Rafi replied, "and recovering from a slight injury."

"What happened?" someone asked.

Gideon tried to sound unconcerned. "He was shot in the leg."

"Why?" Ronnie appeared confused.

"Did you want him talking to us or talking to Allah?" Rafi inquired. "He was shot in the leg because it was better than being shot through the heart."

"But why was he shot at all?" Ronnie pressed.

"A Jordanian border guard spotted them as they were crossing the wadi, fired, and missed. The coffee man could have been killed, so one of our men thought fast enough to injure him, aiming for the leg so he went down and out of range."

"What's Karami going to think?" Ya'Acov posed the question to everyone in the room.

"The same thing his coffee man thinks," Rafi replied.

"What's that?" Ben broke in.

"That one of their own *meshuggeneh* factions took a shot as a warning," Rafi explained. "With the Arabs, it's easy, in the leg is a reminder to pay attention, in the other leg is a warning, through the heart and the discussion is over."

"But why bring him here?"

It was a question of technique rather than logistics, although Gideon decided to answer literally. "The girl is here," he said, "we're here." He glanced around the table. "You're here." He closed the file folders. "And now, he's here."

"When he wakes up, Gideon will have a talk with him," Rafi said, ending the discussion. "Now, Yoram, please shut the lights so we can see some of those slides."

"Is that it?" Ronnie said.

"That's it," Gideon answered, his eyes already focused on the screen.

Chapter Eight

THEY HAD SOME TIME alone, Sasha and Maury, while Bernie was on the phone in the next room and while someone named Bendex was downstairs buying shampoo and toothpaste.

"Who's Bendex?" Sasha asked.

If she didn't know him so well, she might not have noticed that he stumbled. "She's here to help with a few things."

Curled up in one corner of the couch in Maury's suite, Sasha had no intention of making it easier for him. She smiled. "What kind of things?"

"Oh, you know, things, odd jobs."

Odd jobs, blow jobs, hand jobs. "What kind of jobs?"

"Why do you have to know everything?"

"Because you always tell me everything."

He made a face. "All right, she's your basic twenty-five-year-old blond with big tits."

"So, she's here for the regular *S* and *S* routine."

"What's that?"

"Shopping and sex."

"Don't get critical, you know I hate to be alone."

"What am I—a figment of your imagination?"

"You," he said, sitting down and lifting her legs onto his lap, "are my best friend."

"Which means I don't qualify as company, no drinks

and dinner and little conversation, is that it? A new variation on the madonna whore syndrome—friends are limited to telephone talks and brief encounters between planes.'' She nudged him in the groin with one toe. ''Why do I love you, Maury?''

''Because I'm blatantly insecure, needy, deeply neurotic and completely devoted to you.''

''Do you think one thing has anything to do with another?''

''Just don't get chummy with her,'' he changed subjects.

''With whom?'' She gave him a blank look.

''With Bendex.''

''Why would I do that? Unless she runs to me for comfort.''

''Why would she do that?''

''The same reason they all do that, at least the ones you drag along on assignment with me. At least they do it when they realize all they've ended up with are a couple of designer dresses and a ticket home.''

''You're jumping to conclusions,'' he protested. ''I told you she's here to help out.''

''Why don't I believe you?'' she accused him with affection.

''Why don't you?'' he answered, but it was hard not to smile.

''I suppose it's because of that neon sign that keeps flashing the data: twenty-five, blond and let's face it, with a name like Bendex, just Bendex, she's not exactly the nice Jewish girl your mother dreams about for her son, which makes her exactly your type.'' She nudged him again. ''You forget, Maury, I know you, I know about that ardent Zionist, that perennial Yeshiva boy who makes it a point to *shtup* only *shiksas*.''

His face crumpled. ''And what were you?''

She flinched. ''A Jewish girl who knew how to twirl a baton.''

"That was out of line and I apologize because I never just *shtupped* you in my life." He shook his head. "Why do I say things like that?"

The admonishment was gentle. "Because you're blatantly insecure, needy, deeply neurotic and completely devoted to me." But it was suddenly bordering too close to the real for comfort. "I shouldn't have brought up your mother."

He tried to sound casual. "Why not, she's a nice lady."

"Then I shouldn't have reminded you about my not being a *shiksa.*" She smiled, but it was short-lived.

"You were perfect and my mother loved you."

"The kiss of death," she answered, and then nodded that Diane Keaton nod she once saw in the movies when the character Keaton was playing looked like she wanted to be anywhere but in that particular scene.

"By the way, Carl called me last week," Maury announced.

Her face hardened. "What did he want?"

"He just wanted to make sure you were all right."

"I was on the air for four straight nights after it happened. He must have noticed that I was in one piece."

"It was your emotional state he was concerned about."

"I doubt that."

"Be fair."

"If Carl taught me anything, he taught me that being fair doesn't count."

"He must have had some good qualities. You were married to him for six years."

"Being married to Carl was a non-event, sort of like having an affair with Hugh Hefner." She nodded that Diane Keaton nod again.

"Try to talk about his good qualities, you'll feel better."

"Why?"

"Because it's healthy."

"All right. When we first met he used to listen to all my problems but maybe that was because I was paying him to listen. Then, after we got married, he used to listen to me when we were in bed and I said all those little things he taught me to say so he could keep it up all night."

"Now, there's a good quality."

She shrugged. "But the best of all was after he left, when his instructions to me were to call his service if I ever got upset. So I can't help but be amazed that it took a terrorist attack for him to pay attention to my emotional state."

Maury winced. "He's going to call me again. Should I tell him how you feel?"

"No, why don't you tell him that I've got this really terrific idea for a self-help book on how to recover from a divorce." She snapped her fingers. "Works every time."

"I'm sorry, Sasha, so sorry that you landed in the middle of that thing. I'm so sorry that it happened to you."

Again, that facade. "Nothing happened to me, nothing can ever happen to me again after seeing that," and the damn tears gathered in her eyes, a reflexive response each time she thought about it.

Maury moved closer to take her in his arms. "Sasha," he began. But she was out of his embrace in the time it took to twist around for a Kleenex. "Talk about something else, like your trip to Israel," she said, escaping into the safety of the Middle East.

He followed her lead. "The same as always, seeing the same people, listening to the same complaints, eating the same food and too much of it." He patted his stomach. "Every time I come back from one of these junkets—"

"Fact-finding missions."

"I forgot, taxpayers pay for junkets, sponsors pay for fact-finding missions. Anyway, every time I come back I look like a blood sausage stuffed into one of my thousand-dollar English suits." Which was only a slight exaggeration, Sasha thought, and which didn't make Maury any less attractive as far as she was concerned. For despite the added weight, thick glasses and short stature, Maury was sexy because Maury was smart, because his energy was contagious, because there was something reassuring and familiar about his intellect, because Maury genuinely loved women. Even if he could somehow never quite manage to give them that happy ending. "Well, at least you look rested." She touched his cheek.

"I wish I could say the same about you. You look pale and drawn and too thin and unless you rest up these next few days you're not going to make it through the schedule we've set up."

"We? Now we're a 'we'?"

He settled back. "Bernie's a pro, he's been around and he's aggressive. Nobody's going to intimidate him, so he'll take a lot of the flack for you." He smiled. "It's not so bad, is it, working with him?"

"Whenever you've asked me that in the past, it's turned out to be a disaster. But no, it's not so bad."

"Do me a favor, then, and make him feel welcome." There was a touch of apprehension in his tone. "For some reason he thinks you don't like him."

Eyes wide when she answered, "Me? Whatever gave him that idea?"

"Incredible, isn't it? Anyway, he's going to be coming in a few minutes to discuss format and tell you about an interview he'd like you to do."

"Who?"

Placing her legs to one side so he could get up, he walked over to a small refrigerator in the corner of the room. "Let him tell you, it'll make him feel good."

He reached inside to take out a split of champagne. "Want some?" She shook her head, remembering when she and Eli were children and how she was always told to give in to her brother so he wouldn't feel bad or so he would feel good, how careful her parents were of his psyche because he was a boy. Or later, because of his penis. As if she didn't merit care and repair because she didn't have one.

Holding the bottle and the glass in each hand, Maury headed for a chair that faced her and sat down. "Sasha, as horrible as this is for you, there's one thing that's come out of it that's positive." He paused. "At least I've got you where I've wanted you for a long time now."

"Where's that?" she asked carefully.

"On the international scene." He twisted the cork until it popped. "Right in the middle of the on-going Middle East story that's the core of every damn issue that happens in the world." He caught the bubbling liquid in the glass and took a sip. "And I don't care where or who or how or what else is happening, it's right up there in the forefront."

"You've always had this fascination with the Middle East, haven't you?"

"It's my profound love of uniforms," he replied before taking another long sip.

"Come on, be serious, what's this thing you've got about covering a bunch of maniacs?"

"Which side are we talking about?"

"Both sides. One side kills and the other side kills back and so on and so on until one day there'll be nothing left except a pile of flags and banners and old newspapers. I don't get it."

"That's because you've never had an Arab or an Israeli lover."

She was a long way from understanding his logic. "What's that got to do with anything?"

"Don't you know the best way to learn a foreign language is to get close to a native? If you were close to someone from that part of the world, you'd begin to understand the mentality, the justifications and reasons—''

"Thanks, but I'd rather relive those last few months with Carl then get involved with someone armed."

"They're not all armed." He laughed. "At least not like that."

"At the risk of sounding limited, I try not to get involved with men whose countries owe enormous debts to the Chase Manhattan Bank." She leaned over to untie one running shoe. "And don't change subjects," she added, looking up, "tell me about this Mideast thing of yours." Untying the other one, she took them both off and dropped them on the floor.

"Uniforms," he repeated, "but you don't believe me. Someone once told me that uniforms turn women on. So, from the time I was a kid and got interested in the opposite sex, I wanted to be a fireman, and then when I was a teenager I wanted to be a cop, and then when I got to college I thought seriously about making the army my career, until I realized what it was all about."

She took off her headband to run a hand through her hair. "What's that got to do with the Middle East?"

"I realized that uniforms turned women on all right, but mostly on the guys who opened doors at Maxim's or the Côte Basque or the '21' Club." He kneaded one pock-marked cheek with the knuckles of his right hand.

"Are you saying that every doorman at every expensive restaurant is either an Arab or an Israeli?" It was meant to be funny but somehow she already understood Maury's grief.

"Don't be ridiculous, what I'm trying to say is that women cost money, especially for someone like me, and that's why I went into television, maneuvered a big expense account and lived happily every after."

"Did you?" Her expression was serious.

"What?" He leaned his head back, gazing at the ceiling.

"Live happily every after?"

He looked at her a moment, and when he spoke it was with forced energy. "Television gives me a feeling of accomplishment, and doing the news gives me a feeling of power, and without the war and the terror and that whole Middle East lunacy, there wouldn't be much hard news. And if that happened, I'd run out of product and probably lose my job or at least lose my importance around here as the resident expert on anything that happens over there and—"

"And without that, you wouldn't get laid, is that it? It all boils down to that, no blood and gore, no Bendex?"

"That's pretty rough, Beale."

"Maybe, but ask her or any of the others if they'd sleep with you without twenty-four people getting killed just because they happened to walk into an airline ticket office." It was choking her again, the memories, the images, the child. "Oh God," she said, taking a breath, "it's going to start again." Hand over her mouth, she willed back her tears.

Maury looked helpless. "What can I do?"

"Help me find out about that little boy who died in that bombing," she said.

"Sasha, let it go."

But she wasn't going to. "I can't," she said simply. "Please, Maury, if I keep coming up with nothing, help me."

"What good will it do?"

"This isn't about good, it's about evil," she said softly, "and I can't explain why I feel this way about that child except I do." She studied her hands. "He was so fragile and so still . . . How can I explain why from that whole horror, he was the one thing that stayed with me to make me remember.'' She looked up. ''I can't explain it,'' she repeated.

''Whatever you want,'' he said quietly, ''you know I'll help you.''

Her tone was stronger then, her face more relaxed.

''And something else,'' she said, her tone not as severe as her words, ''someday you're going to explain everything to me and you're going to stop bringing it all down to one meaningless and ridiculous sexual level. And one more thing, you're going to stop this self-denigrating ugly Jewish guy routine because, frankly, it's insulting.''

''To whom?''

But she knew he knew. ''To me.''

''When you get back from Tunisia,'' he answered, ignoring the rest of it, ''I promise, we'll have a long talk about it.''

''I'm going to make you keep that promise.''

As if the thought just occurred to him, he said, ''Give Carl a call. He sounded really concerned.''

Thinking about something as unpleasant as her ex-husband was a welcome change. ''Concern might give Carl some character.''

He didn't push. ''We're all having dinner tonight, by the way, you, me, and Bernie.''

''Not me, I've got an appointment.''

''What kind of an appointment?''

''An appointment appointment.''

''Who with?''

''Someone.''

''One thing about you, Beale, when you don't want to report it you sure don't report it.''

''Take Bendex.''

''It's business.''

''Try something different,'' she said, ''try treating her like a real person, let her into your world.''

He ignored her. "How'd you tear your pants and cut your knee?"

"Without these pants getting torn and my knee getting cut I wouldn't be busy for dinner tonight."

"Bruised knees are supposed to happen after dinner."

"You're beginning to sound like Bernie."

"How's that?"

"Not funny."

"Is that how he is?"

"Why don't you get him in here so we can start the meeting and you can see for yourself."

He glanced at his watch. "You're right, it's getting late and we've got a busy day." He paused before picking up the phone. "You've got an even busier two weeks, Sasha, so take it easy. This isn't the time to start up with new . . ." he seemed to search for the word. "Friends," he finally said.

It was a relief to be busy after all the drifting. It was therapeutic to have finally found a straight line, even if it was for all the wrong reasons.

The way Bernie would have told it was that he had been drafted for the job as producer of the Karami segment because Maury gave him sole credit for the Rome scoop. But then, Bernie would have taken sole credit for the bombing if it had guaranteed his ending up in the same place. At least that's how Sasha judged it as she watched him flatter and fawn his way through coffee, croissants and champagne in Maury's suite. But if she was at all worried that he wouldn't swing into his typical overbearing mode, she needn't have bothered. For as soon as the discussion centered on the interview, he became the Bernie she knew from the last encounter. Put another way, if life was a poker game with Bernie holding the big winning hand, he would have raked in the pot with too much gusto.

"What about Sasha's Jewish background for this one?"

"Karami won't care. To him, she's just his ticket to Middle America."

"What about the fact that she's a woman?" Bernie went on. "You know how these guys treat women."

She remained calm. "How do you treat women?" she asked innocently.

Bernie shifted in his chair and spoke directly to Maury. "The problem is really not about women, I suppose, it's about the way Sasha gets human with her subjects. It's that Jewish-mother technique she uses where she goes right for the gut via the heart. The natural viewer response is to see this guy as likeable, human."

"I don't see that as a flaw," Sasha said, wondering if she could pull off that little technique at dinner tonight.

"Let's get back to the Jewish issue," Maury suggested.

"These guys don't hate Jews, just Zionists. At least that's the party line."

"It's not so much a religious issue," Bernie said, "as it is that she doesn't have that cool Wasp approach."

"Look, Sasha's had the same background and approach for as long as she's been in this business and she's come up against some pretty crazy people like the Klan in the South or Louis Farrakhan in New York last year. As I understand it," he said lightly, "she doesn't make them fast on Yom Kippur and they don't make her observe Ramadan or burn crosses. It works out fine, trust me."

"She gets motherly."

"I only sew buttons on overcoats and only in winter."

Bernie persisted. "You know how Arabs think of women."

She was adorable. "No worse than some American television folk."

Maury seemed to be looking for a corner to turn. "Let's get back to Karami," he said quickly.

Bernie didn't protest. "What still concerns me is that he'll come across as a nice guy, normal, rational, even justified in his cause."

Sasha didn't push it. Instead, she listened and took a few notes.

"What we seem to have here is the beginning of a debate on professional integrity," Maury said. "Do we represent Karami as a good father and husband or a murderer?"

"I'm a bad one to ask," Sasha answered grimly, "since I've only seen the end result of one of those sides."

Maury looked from one to the other. "In my opinion we should show him as both and let the audience judge."

"I'm not sure I agree," Bernie said.

"Let me remind you that this show is called 'Family,' " Maury said, "which means it's supposed to be about people talking about the people they love and not about their jobs."

Bernie laughed. "You call bombing an airline office a *job*?"

"Look, you both know how I feel about this, but I don't want to lose the . . . intimacy of the show. We're going into this man's house so the audience can see him doing the everyday mundane things. The fact that he also happens to blow up planes and people is what makes it so provocative. They wouldn't want to watch you or me brushing our teeth or talking about our kids. And if we do it right, without any overt challenge to him, we'll get a much more dramatic result."

"He'll hang himself," Sasha nodded.

"He's charming," Bernie warned.

"So was Ted Bundy," Maury said.

"Nobody's charming enough to make mass murder popular," Sasha said.

"Forget the morality for a minute. People tend to block things out the minute we stop giving them visuals. The thing that sticks with them is that this guy or anyone else with the same agenda cuts into their freedom. All of a sudden, thousands of tourists have to stop to think whether or not they want to take a plane or go to a certain city or walk on the street." His eyes squinted in concentration. "And nobody, especially Americans, likes anybody who cuts into their freedom."

"Maybe," Bernie conceded, "but if you watch his tapes, he's articulate and—"

"That's just the way we want him," Maury shot back, "and while he's projecting all that sweetness and light, we flash images across the screen of Rome or one of his other little numbers."

"Maybe," Bernie said slowly, "and while we're at it, why don't we show some shots of how the Palestinians live in those refugee camps as a contrast to how he lives in his villa overlooking the sea?"

"It's a good idea, but it's not relevant to the interview."

"It's relevant to the people living in those camps to see how their leader is living," Sasha said.

"Not too many of those people are going to be watching the show, I don't think there are too many refugee camps in your ten major markets."

"One way or another, that part of it won't disappear," Bernie argued.

"We can discuss this all day, so let's not."

"Why don't we go through my file instead?" Sasha suggested.

"Good, and then Bernie can tell you about the interview."

Sasha picked up the file marked Karami, opened it and put on her horn-rimmed glasses.

"Are those supposed to make you look intellectual or intimidating?"

She looked through him. "Karami is educated, and highly intelligent," she began.

"How old?" Maury asked.

"About forty-five."

"English?"

"Fluent."

"And the wife?"

"Fluent as well," she replied, aware that the conversation was between the two of them, Bernie excluded.

"Where did they meet?"

"At the Sorbonne during the May '68 riots."

"Do we go in-depth so our viewers understand the significance of May '68?"

"I've already requested file footage from the Paris Bureau. What we're going to show, briefly, is how the students joined the workers to paralyze the city. But we'll focus mainly on Karami's role as head of the Palestinian Students Union, which was when he became 'someone' in the whole movement."

"What was his big claim to fame?"

"One of the more spectacular actions during that period was when Karami took over a hotel on the rue de l'Ancienne Comédie and held a group of German tourists hostage." She rearranged some papers. "It wouldn't have attracted that much attention except they were handicapped."

"Nice guy," Maury muttered.

"Karami's wife was one of four students who carried food and water and messages back and forth between the police on the outside and the militants on the inside."

"How long did it last?"

''Sixteen days before the hostages were released, and the two of them were in love.''

Maury shook his head, the dark circles under his eyes looking darker than usual. ''Touching, really touching.''

''Karami spent only a couple of weeks in jail,'' Sasha went on, ''because nobody was hurt, and the French used that as an excuse to calm the Arab population. Anyway, there were more important issues at stake.''

''Like getting Paris running again,'' Bernie commented.

''But while he was in jail, his wife did the usual, visited him, brought him cigarettes, took care of his mail, mimeographed his pamphlets.''

''I've got to tell you,'' Maury interrupted, ''that in the order of topics that grab media attention or has any kind of sexy international appeal, Arab women rank just about last—right after scalp problems among the Sikhs.''

''She's French,'' Bernie announced, as if he had a hand in it.

''And she's attractive and charming, so our male viewers will watch her,'' Sasha continued, ''but not too attractive to turn off our female viewers. She's also a devoted wife and mother, which should get the seal of approval from everyone and give the women something to identify with.''

''Except how many women pack a grenade in their husband's lunch box?''

''Or what about this? How many married couples do you know who are still crazy about each other after twenty-three years? And here's the best part, after all those years and two teenage children, they just had another baby last year. So, something's still going on in that house.'' She closed the file. ''Karami carries that baby around on his hip and takes him into meetings and doesn't care if the kid drools all over his maps and papers. That I got from the PLO representative in Rome.''

"I love it," Maury said, "cuddles his own baby while he plots the murder of other babies.''

"Mrs. Karami's mother still lives in the same apartment where she grew up," Bernie began. "My idea was to have you go over there and talk to her, get some background stuff, find out from the mother how thrilled she was when her daughter ran off with a terrorist.''

"Do you have her number? I'll call her right away.''

"All here," Bernie said, patting the leather Filofax on his lap. "I'll give you everything." He reached over to pick up an envelope. "I forgot, Rome gave me this for you. You must have requested some information on the victims.''

A look of alarm appeared on Maury's face. But she was already across the room, the envelope in her hand and ripped open. Seated, she read a surfeit of information that pulled her away from them and brought her back to the sidewalk in front of the Alitalia building.

"What does it say?" Maury asked.

She glanced up but it was clear that she was too upset to reply for a few moments. "It's unbelievable," she finally answered, "but they don't give any specifics about the victims, not even names. All they list is sex, age and nationality." She read on. "That little boy was only ten years old, an Israeli, it says. One other Israeli," she mumbled, "a woman." She glanced up again. "The woman with the piece of his red jacket," she said softly, "I knew she was with him." She shook her head. "I bet the Israeli Embassy here in Paris would have their names and probably the names of their survivors in Israel." She dropped her arm, the paper fluttering. "Thanks, Bernie," she said, her face drained of all color. A breath then, a nervous gesture to her hair, another breath. "It was really short notice for them to come up with this for me." She tried to make sense of things or change the subject because she wanted to stop what was about to happen. "So, if you talk to them in Rome, will you tell them I'm very grateful." It was the same thing every day, every time she thought about it, it was this same overwhelming sadness, and tears. "Maybe I'll go over to the embassy and check it out," she said sensibly. But there was a note of hysteria in her tone. She bit her lip, her eyes filled.

"Why go over there?" Maury moved toward her.

She held him off with an explanation or at least she tried to even if she could hear herself babbling. "I just feel that I want to know who he was," she began, "and who the woman was." She stopped a moment. "Maybe I want to talk to the father, the husband, tell him how . . ." It made her sick to go on. If only she could remember how it felt not to grieve for people she didn't even know. "Why are the murderers the only ones to get air time?" she blurted out, as if that was the issue.

Bernie looked pale. "Because television is mostly about the bad guys. Not the victims."

"Sasha," Maury said, kneeling next to her, "it's over now."

Face streaked with tears, she shook her head. "No, it's not over, not if we're doing Karami."

"Let it go," Maury urged gently, "you've got no stake in it anymore." He pushed some hair from her face.

But she did have a stake in it and more than that, she couldn't let it go.

"We've gone beyond Rome," Maury said, "you've covered that part of it, now we're onto something else."

There was no doubt that progress had been made, although somehow it didn't quite include anything that had to do with her own healing.

Sasha sat crosslegged on the floor, her back leaning against the couch, and dialed the number. Maury sat at the desk in the corner organizing papers and credit cards. Bernie was in the next room again, on another telephone.

The phone rang six times before it was answered. In broken French Sasha asked, "May I speak to Madame Villeneuve, please." And in perfect English the voice replied, "This is she, who is this?"

Sasha took a breath. "My name is Sasha Beale and I'm with the Federated Broadcast Network in New York—"

"I'm sorry, but I don't know anything about it," the woman cut her off.

"Please, don't hang up, we're doing a television interview of your daughter and her family in Sidi Bou Said."

"Really," the woman said slowly.

"Yes, but in the meantime I've got this very difficult assignment." She waited.

"What is that?"

The hook found its mark. "You."

"But what do you want with me?"

"I thought we could talk for a few minutes about your daughter when she was growing up in Paris. Anything that would give me some background information for the interview."

A brief pause before she asked cautiously, "Then this isn't about . . . what just happened?"

Closing her eyes, Sasha went deeper into the role. "I don't know what you mean."

"Well, I assumed you were calling me about what happened in Rome, and I really don't know anything about it. I'm only the grandmother."

"Only the Grandmother," a title perhaps for another program. "Oh, you mean the bombing," Sasha managed, wondering if she could have actually pulled that one off had she been sitting with the woman in her living room. Not that it was any less stupefying to be mentioning it and referring to it as if it were a minor traffic accident or a *faux pas* at a garden party. *The Bombing*. Not that the whole conversation wasn't unreal—an elderly woman living in Paris inextricably linked to a fanatic Arab revolutionary living in Tunisia.

"My producer is going to have my head if I don't get to talk to you. Do you think we could get together today?"

"I don't think so." The woman hesitated, "I was just in the middle of making a veal roast."

At least the excuses were improving. Sasha's mind was moving at a fast pace as she reviewed the file she had just perused—one dead husband and an only daughter who lived in another world, limited contact with grandchildren on Christmas and birthdays. "That sounds good," Sasha said with a smile in her voice.

"What does?"

"The veal roast."

"So many journalists," the woman said vaguely, "so many newspaper reporters have written so many lies that I just don't know anymore."

"First of all, I would never do that and secondly, I don't work for a newspaper or magazine so I wouldn't be writing anything. All I need is a little background," she repeated, "and I'd be coming alone, no cameras, no crew, just me."

"How did you get my number? It's unlisted."

Truthful when she could be truthful, she replied, "My producer got it from your daughter."

"I see," the woman said.

"What I'd love to do," Sasha went on, "is to look at pictures of your daughter when she was young, if you have any."

"Her father loved to take pictures," she said distantly before suddenly asking, "Have you spoken to my daughter recently?"

"No, I haven't." Sasha tensed. "Was there something you wanted me to tell her when I see her?"

Defensive, she rushed to reply. "No, nothing."

Sasha rushed to ask, "If you did agree to see me, what time would be convenient?" And in response to Maury's sudden interest and questioning look from the other side of the room, she rocked her hand back and forth in the air—a fifty-fifty chance at that point.

"It's not a matter of time," Madame Villeneuve said tightly.

The perspiration was dripping down Sasha's right wrist from her grip on the receiver. "Please, I've only got two days before I'm due in Sidi Bou Said."

"Well, if I did agree . . ."

"I already know the rules," Sasha preempted.

"Nothing about what happened in Rome."

A thumbs-up sign for Maury when she answered, "Nothing, I promise."

"All right, if you're absolutely certain that it's going to be only about Josette." Said as if it were all beyond her control, as if she were dependent upon the whims of others.

"I swear."

"Do you have my address?"

"Why don't you give it to me just to be sure."

Address, directions, floor, building-entry code, Sasha wrote everything down. "When would be convenient for you?"

"Tomorrow at four o'clock."

"Perfect," Sasha said, "and thank you very much."

After she put down the receiver, she turned to Maury. "Tomorrow at four o'clock and nothing about Rome."

"You'll get around to it, I'm sure." Leaning back in the chair with his hands behind his head, he seemed suddenly disturbed. "I'd take you to lunch today, but I promised Bendex we'd go shopping."

"That's nice," Sasha mumbled, concentrating on finding a number in the Paris telephone book.

"I'll take you to lunch tomorrow."

"Great," she mumbled again, still buried in the phone book.

"By the way, do you know the difference between a mortician and a television reporter?"

"Uh huh," she said, dialing.

"A mortician waits until you're dead to bury you."

But by then she was barely listening, asking instead to be connected to the press attaché at the Israeli Embassy.

Chapter Nine

THE SLIDE SHOW at the embassy was momentarily interrupted when the door opened and one of the staff padded quietly over to Rafi to whisper in his ear. Cocking his head, he listened before his gaze swept around the table. The group was silent, the projector still, an image of Karami frozen on the screen. "It seems we have a visitor, gentlemen," he announced as he stood.

Gideon glanced up although he had neither to wonder nor to ask, his instincts were on high this morning.

"Miss Beale is downstairs with our press attaché and this might be a good opportunity for me to meet her."

Gideon didn't understand the proprietary feelings that overwhelmed him, this urge to protect her from people he knew were shrewder. It made no good sense.

"Obviously, Gideon, you'll stay upstairs."

"Obviously," he replied, giving no sign of ever having considered the alternative, nor of being even the slightest bit interested.

Legs crossed, skirt hiked up above the knees, notepad balanced on one thigh, Sasha sat on a hard-back chair upholstered in torn green naugahyde. Facing her from behind a Formica desk was a small, dark-haired man who resembled an owl, and whose round tortoiseshell glasses made him look even more wise and solemn. "Actually, there are two reasons I wanted to talk to you," she said, answering his opening question and pushing her own glasses on top of her head.

"Before you begin, would you like a cup of coffee?"

She thought a moment, mostly about poison and truth serum, mostly truth serum. The last thing she needed was to explain how her father had denounced Judaism in favor of a Marxist chicken farm in rural Connecticut before denouncing the chickens in favor of a beautician thirty years his junior. But that was another story. "Yes, thank you." She decided to risk it since this religion depended on the mother, and her mother wasn't sober enough to know what she was anyway.

The man spoke in Hebrew to an intercom on his desk, a contraption that looked as if it had been salvaged from a Judy Holliday movie, circa 1950. Obviously, money wasn't wasted around here on anything that couldn't fly or shoot. In fact, investment in the area of general office decor was less than minimal, a nightmare, in fact, of plastic flowers and furniture that looked like it was picked up at auction from a defunct hotel. "By the way," the owl said, "I hope you don't mind, but my assistant would like to meet you. He's seen you on television."

Instinctively, it occurred to her that while one official Israeli in a room constituted perhaps a meeting, two could be considered an interrogation. "How nice," she replied.

Frankly, she would have suspected someone other than an "assistant" when the door opened behind her and the press attaché leapt to his feet to welcome the older man with the glittering black eyes and white hair. But perhaps it was a cultural phenomenon to be deferential to underlings who were senior in age. "How do you do," she said, withdrawing a hand whose fingers were throbbing from the man's grip.

"Welcome," he replied, smiling warmly, "I'm Rafi

Unger. And I've enjoyed all your reports on television.'' For some reason she found herself nonplussed, as if that was the first time someone enjoyed watching her on television and told her so. Which was probably why she went on the attack. "Did you live in the States?"

"Yes, I was attached to the embassy in Washington."

"And you saw me on television?"

"All the time."

Her eyes never left his. "Your receiver at the embassy in Washington must have been incredibly strong, because I've done only local news out of New York." She smiled.

If he was embarrassed, he didn't show it. "I traveled to New York quite often," he said smoothly.

The smile was frozen on her face as she sat down again after he made a sweeping gesture toward her chair.

"I've asked for some coffee," the press attaché informed his "assistant."

"Good, fine," Rafi responded, rubbing his hands together.

Sasha put on her glasses to consult some notes, although it could have been her grocery list written on the pad for all she cared. "I started to say that I came here for two reasons. As you probably know, I covered the Rome attack." She glanced at the man who claimed to be her biggest fan. Nothing, not a flicker of a reaction. "Now, we're about to go to Sidi Bou Said to interview Tamir Karami and his family for a special we're doing called 'Family.' " Nobody stood up to cheer or do cartwheels near the dusty bookcase with the cracked glass front. "Anyway, I thought you might be able to give me some additional information on Karami and his group Quest for a Homeland." Apparently, gaining access to a terrorist's den wasn't enough to impress anybody around here.

"If you want information on Karami," the older man

finally said, "why come to us? Why not go to the PLO?"

Her smile this time was wintry. "If I wanted a pep talk I'd go to the PLO. What I need is propaganda, which is why I came to you."

Rafi laughed. "Do you always break ethnic groups into such categories?"

"Lately, I suppose that I do."

"Please, I'd love to hear more," he encouraged her just as a woman entered the room carrying a tray with cups of coffee and a plate of cookies.

The tray was set down on one corner of the desk before the press attaché spoke to the woman in Hebrew. "I've just asked that all our file material on Karami be brought in," he told Sasha.

"Go on," Rafi said, "please."

Any hesitation on her part to play ethnic-classification games might end with her out on her ass with nothing, she decided.

"For example, what would you get from the French?"

"Rationalization, I suppose."

He smiled. "And the Americans?"

"Morality."

"And you came to us for propaganda. Milk, Miss Beale?"

"No, thank you."

He put three cubes of sugar in his coffee and stirred. "And the second reason you came to see us?" he asked.

"The second reason," she said, the cup and saucer in one hand, the coffee as yet untouched, "was that I wanted to know about the two Israelis who were killed in the attack." What she thought she noticed then was a distinct if still silent reaction. But she wasn't sure. "What I'd be interested in trying to do is a piece on the family who survived back in Israel." She was on overdrive. "It falls back under the heading of our documentary."

"Why the Israelis?"

"For all the obvious reasons, but also because the little boy was the only child killed. And I have a feeling that the woman killed was his mother. Is that true?" She looked from one to the other.

The owl said nothing. The "assistant" shrugged. "We can certainly check that out for you," he finally said.

"You mean you don't know?"

"Please understand, Miss Beale, that while the Rome terrorist attack was a major media event, for us it was just another atrocity." Rafi spoke quietly. "We have them nearly every day in our country. To keep track without checking official records which victims are related to which victims in which attacks is difficult. But of course I can fax Jerusalem and try to get those answers for you."

She didn't buy it, not one word of it. But before she could argue, the door opened again and the same woman who had brought the cookies and coffee now carried a manila envelope. She handed it to the press attaché, who handed it to Sasha. "I think you'll find this helpful."

"Thank you," she said before turning once again to Rafi. "Can you at least tell me the names of the victims so I can have our Tel Aviv bureau check it out from that end?"

Rafi smiled. "I find it fascinating," he said.

Slightly taken aback, she asked, "What's that?"

"That you're even more attractive in person than you are on television," he replied. Which was when Sasha realized that the meeting was over.

Chapter Ten

SASHA CHANGED TWICE. The first outfit made her look like a Sicilian streetwalker, or at least Hollywood's version of one. Black cotton leggings, a mauve bodysuit, black spike heels, all set off by her hair fluffed around her face and shoulders, eyes rimmed in black, lips pale, the whole impression not unlike Anna Magnani in *A Streetcar Named Desire*. The second outfit made her look like an escapee from the A-list at the Waukegan Country Club, notwithstanding those lace-up thigh-high stockings that kept wrinkling at the knee. To get the full effect, she stood on a small stool in the bathroom; short Armani red skirt, long Armani red jacket, yards of rainbow-colored chiffon scarf, set off by her face now scrubbed and her hair pulled back in two barrettes. Or, if not an escapee from Waukegan, then perhaps Giuletta Masina in *La Strada*, had the carnival passed through Illinois and had Masina dressed for the occasion. It was raining lightly in Paris and rain always made her think of Italian actresses in hopelessly tragic movies. Rain made her think of Rome. But then, everything made her think of Rome.

When there were only fifteen minutes left to pull herself together and get downstairs to meet the man she had just met in the Tuileries this morning, she reached into the closet and grabbed. The result wasn't bad at all, since most of her appeal was in her imperfection, which translated into a kind of sexy dishevelment. She ended up wearing a short black silk skirt, typical that the Band-Aids showed, a V-neck white silk shirt, no bra, a black-and-white cashmere shawl that kept slipping off one shoulder ad sling-back pumps that never quite stayed on her heels. Hair refluffed, eyes rerimmed in black, lips painted peach, she felt suddenly nauseous, a dab of blush, she felt the beginning of an anxiety attack, a string of pearls and some Arpege between her breasts, she thought she would keel over, gold watch clasped on her wrist even though it was still on New York time. The stockings were useless, she decided as she sat down to take them off, they looked sloppy. They would never stay up, they would end up somewhere around her ankles when she got out of the car or the cab or just up from the table after dinner. Pantyhose were the only sensible answer; good old unsexy all-American pantyhose that Carl always said created a subconscious barrier. Although he was a fine one to talk about subconscious barriers, since any attempt at pre- or post-coital conversation with him was like talking to a priest through the grill of a confessional. What it all boiled down to was that she felt like an idiot dressing for a date since she was a woman who rarely dated. Usually she mingled in a group after work, combined business with pleasure and often fell into love affairs at first glance or after years of benign friendship.

That wasn't to say that perfectly normal and intelligent people didn't date. They did. Out-of-town girls dated married advertising executives, middle-age divorcees dated old widowers, prom queens dated football players, serial killers dated, Gloria Steinem dated. But to Sasha, dating was nothing more than a contrived mating dance, a boring prelude to sex or marriage, publicity or murder.

Standing in front of the mirror, she began filling her purse. Makeup was strewn all over the top of the dress-

ing table along with loose change from three countries,
a comb, a stack of credit cards, passport, that envelope
from Rome plus another envelope containing stills taken
by a free-lance photographer, pictures of the sidewall
outside the Alitalia office before all that was left was a
froth of soap and water. Maury didn't even know that
she had them, neither did Bernie, and she wasn't going
to tell them that she intended to show them to Karam
for comment at some point during the interview.

Hands holding her hair away from her face, she
looked well beyond her reflection. A carefree house was
a house where cares entered freely, a handicapped toilet
was a toilet that didn't work. Granted, she didn't always
interpret things the way they were meant to be interpreted, but that didn't excuse the gods for so misinter-
preting her desire to forget Carl that they included a
terrorist attack on her itinerary. Turning away from the
mirror, she hated herself for personalizing, for viewing
the tragedy as it affected *her*, for being so helpless, but
most of all, she was ashamed for having survived it
when those others didn't.

When she thought back on why she had chosen Rome,
she could easily blame her mother. Caroline Beale had
suggested Rome, claiming that the Via Condotti was
the retailer's version of Lourdes, the cure-all for most
emotional maladies, the street where the object of every
desire could be found and charged, where every memory and hurt could be discarded. Instead, it turned out
to be a place for Sasha to witness how some came to a
city to shop and tour while others came to suffer and
die.

She walked right past him in the lobby, not because
she wanted him to notice her but because without her
glasses she was blind. After several blurry moments she
gave in and put them on. And there he was.

He had gotten a haircut, which made him look a

least five years younger, or maybe it was just that he had taken a nap. But suddenly she needed time to regroup, to collect herself before switching into a charming and social mode, which was when she concentrated on his shoes. Her mother had taught her after their first crossing that shoes told everything about a man; her mother had taught her as well to refer to their trip abroad as a crossing even though they had flown on an Apex ticket out of Newark. Shoes, she was suddenly back on the shoes. Gideon's were black, which with brown were the only acceptable colors. Not gray or blue or tan or, God forbid, white, and why Caroline's rules regarding shoe color to be worn after Labor Day and before Memorial Day were uppermost in her mind was a mystery.

He was next to her then, his hand briefly holding hers. "Hello," he said, his eyes traveling the length of her body and back, "I've missed you."

"Hello," she answered, her eyes taking him in as well, the dark blue suit whose fabric stretched across his muscular back each time he moved, the light blue silk handkerchief stuffed into the breast pocket, not folded or halved or pointed, just crammed right in there any old way, his eyes, blue as well, unchanged from this morning. He gripped her around the waist as he steered her toward the exit, where the doorman actually touched the tip of his cap in greeting. An expensive black Renault was parked in the driveway, the passenger door held open by another doorman while she slid inside, settled back, crossed her legs and waited while he slid in next to her. She felt him staring. "You have beautiful breasts," he announced. Turning her head, she considered that thanking him would be ridiculous while expressing shock or anger would be hypocritical. After all, nobody forced her to wear that white silk shirt without a bra. But when she didn't answer, he seemed concerned. "Have I offended you?" Sixty seconds with this man and already her body was under scrutiny and

up for discussion. Again, there were choices. A nega‐
tive response and she was a silly tourist, a positive re‐
sponse and she was a silly woman. She opted for the
Talmud. "And if you had?"

"Then I would have asked you to forgive me," he
replied, again pressing her hand before a cacophony of
horns sounded. Releasing her hand, he pulled out of the
driveway onto the Avenue George V. For lack of any‐
thing else, she asked for a cigarette and watched as he
pushed a button under the dashboard. The glove com‐
partment snapped open and as he braked for a light, he
reached over her legs for the pack of Marlboros. "I
didn't know you smoked."

"I don't," she replied, taking one.

He seemed amused. "I thought about driving to Nor‐
mandy for dinner," he announced, heading toward the
bridge that would take them over the Seine to the Left
Bank.

"Why Normandy?"

"Because it's beautiful. Have you ever been there?"

"Yes, on my honeymoon."

"What a pity."

"Why?"

"To let bad memories spoil Normandy."

She smiled. "But I don't have bad memories, at least
not of Normandy," she said before realizing that ar‐
guing in favor of Normandy was surely arguing in favor
of another breakfast.

"Perhaps," he said, "it's not such a good idea after
all. It's crowded this time of year. Mostly with visiting
Arab royalty."

"You say that as if it's an affliction."

"I was just reporting on the occupancy quota. Or are
you the only one in this group who can report things?"
He smiled.

She liked that, they were a group, although she said
nothing, merely fiddled with the lighter.

"Do you really want to smoke that?" he asked as he guided the car to a stop at another light, this time in front of the Assemblée National on the Left Bank side of the Seine. She took the cigarette out of her mouth and ran her tongue over the filter. "No, not really."

He must have pushed another button just then because she heard the doors click shut. "Or, I could take you dancing in the métro," he continued, his hand holding her hand, which just happened to be available on the seat between them.

"Dancing in the métro," she repeated in a voice that sounded not even remotely familiar.

He squeezed her fingers. "I'd be willing to wager that you've never done that before."

"And if I had, would it spoil it for us?" she asked with what she hoped was an airy lightness.

"Never." His glance was penetrating. "Because we'd do it better than the others." He let the words linger a moment before going on. "I happen to know they're playing Cole Porter downstairs at the Place de la Concorde."

Delighted, she laughed. "Now, how do you know that?"

" 'Cheek to Cheek,' in fact. At least, that's what they were playing this morning when you left me there."

As if she had driven him to a suburban train station for the trip into his city office.

"Usually they play baroque at the Hôtel de Ville stop." He shrugged. "But that's Paris, isn't it?"

"That's Paris," she repeated, wondering when she'd catch on to the rhythm around here and think up something original and witty. But for some reason her timing was off.

"So, Normandy is out," he said after several moments of silence.

"Normandy is out," she agreed, the possibility occurring to her that she would never exit from this parrot mode of conversation.

He had her hand again, just a pat this time, nothing lingering except the sensations that remained after he withdrew. "I'm glad I jogged this morning," he announced, his eyes on the road, a muscle twitching in his jaw.

She was bad at this, making banter or worse, making sweeping pronouncements that had no future. "I'm glad you jogged too," she replied, coming up with what sounded like an appropriate compromise.

Nothing seemed lost on him. "I wasn't asking for a lifetime commitment, you know."

"And that's the bad news?" was her instant retort.

He steered slightly to the right to merge onto the Boulevard Saint Michel from the Boulevard Saint Germain. "So, dancing in the métro is still a possibility after dinner."

"What time does the métro close?" Not brilliant but at least she was able to formulate a sentence that, except for the word métro, didn't repeat any of his words.

"Long before dawn."

"Before it's time to jog," she added, feeling a bit more relaxed.

He gestured to Notre Dame. "We have quite a past here, don't we?"

"Yes," she said before asking, "What about your past?" With a touch of humor then, "No wives or children and that doesn't count your zero-to-one-hundred theory."

He seemed only mildly surprised although he answered as though he was delivering a prepared statement that had been around for years. "Wives long gone and children probably the main issue although if they hadn't been, perhaps the wives would still be with me or at least one wife would be."

"What happened to them or to her?"

"One left me and the other I left, or it was the other way around, I left the first one for the second who left me because of children." He smiled briefly. "There's a lesson to be learned, I suppose, that there's a price for everything in life."

"Did you want children?"

"She wanted them right away and I wanted to wait and make sure that things worked out between us. She didn't give me a chance so I guess she would say that I didn't want them, which was why she left."

For some reason, she liked him more on the Left Bank than on the Right, more this evening than this morning, although what touched off those feelings was an abstract hypothesis concerning unborn children with a now nonexistent wife. He ran a light then, his hand extended as a shield across her waist. "There's a place I know that's not far from here, a little different, almost like a split-level cave. But it's usually difficult to get a table."

"Then why bother?"

"They know me. What do you think?"

What should she think except that he took all his women there, that when she stepped inside, the maitre d' would give him one of those and who-do-we-have-tonight looks hidden beneath a proper "Bon soir, Monsieur Aitchison." Not that she expected to be the first in his life or even the best or, perish the thought, the last (how had he put it—that he wasn't asking for a lifetime commitment). What she didn't want to be was Friday's breakfast that had turned into Friday's dinner as if the Tuileries were nothing more than his personal singles bar. But getting back to his original position about dinner in that split-level bistro that he knew so well, she smiled, demurred and wondered what exactly provoked the brush of his lips against her cheek before he got out of the car.

* * *

He had retreated behind that chilly European manner of his, as if restaurants brought out the worst in him. She noticed it at breakfast and now here it was again at dinner. "Can you believe it," she was saying, "that the Israeli Embassy doesn't even know the names of the Israeli victims killed in that Rome attack."

It wasn't that he wasn't attentive, it was more an air of boredom that surfaced when he replied. "Odd, but bureaucracies are not exactly known for their efficiency."

"Doesn't that go beyond a question of efficiency?"

"You know," he began, leaving the pâté unattended, "I'm a bad one to ask about governments on any level because I'm something of a libertarian, or maybe I'm basically an anarchist. What I'd be much more interested in hearing about is you." A command performance. "Tell me about your family, start from there," he said, his gaze boring a hole somewhere near her top lip. "What does your father do?"

"He's in the news business," she heard herself saying, "or at least he was." Remarkable how Harry Beale had somehow found his way to her dinner table in Paris, France. Harry, the secretary-treasurer of an almost defunct chicken farm in a small anti-Semitic town in Connecticut. It was almost funny; the man who couldn't manage his own finances was put in charge of running a commune or running it into the ground would be more like it. Another funny thing, most of the people living on that chicken farm were far away politically from the Republican redneck community that tried for years to close them down and finally did. Which was when Harry went to work in the local beauty parlor with his wife—when he wasn't at the track. Harry, the man who told his only son right before that last motorcycle ride that the better part of him ran down his mother's leg; the person who claimed to know exactly what his children were up to—so how come he didn't know that poor

Eli was constantly stoned and Sasha was constantly miserable.

"What does he do now?" Gideon asked.

Where was it written that she had to tell all just because this man was paying for her dinner, reason enough to hate dating. "He's, uh, he has an interest in race horses."

Gideon nodded. "And your mother?"

"They're divorced," she replied as if that was an occupation, which to Caroline Beale it was. "She was in the millinery business until she got interested in parapsychology." Caroline, who worked in the hat department in Bloomingdale's until she showed up drunk one too many times and was fired. Caroline, the most popular tarot-card reader in Madame Rose's Tea Room, which was right above a temporary employment agency in Times Square that gave Caroline ten percent of the fee for all referrals.

"What kind of parapsychology?"

She shook her head. "It's beyond me." She laughed a nervous laugh.

"Are you an only child?"

"Now, I am."

"Sasha," he began, a look of concern.

"My brother died in a motorcycle accident when I was fifteen," she said quickly.

"I'm very sorry," he said, drawing her close, "poor Sasha."

"No, not poor Sasha, poor Eli." Poor Eli, funny how she could hardly ever say her brother's name, even when he was alive, without adding *poor* as a prefix. "My brother was on drugs," she explained, "and he had already overdosed twice before the accident." She was quite rational, she had learned to sound that way, almost objective and dispassionate when she talked about it. "There was a horrible fight with my father that night and Eli jumped on his bike." She could still remember begging him not to go. ''Whether it was really an accident is debatable.'' She could still remember the anger at feeling cheated and abandoned when he never came back. ''The outcome is the same in either case,'' she said quietly.

For Gideon's part, he was like a moth drawn to a flame as he leaned closer to her, an abruptly serious, pained expression on his face. ''Whatever happened or however it happened, it's a tragedy.''

''Not as tragic as that child who was killed in Rome,'' she said, retreating behind her most recent anguish. ''Eli made decisions, he was twenty years old. That little boy didn't.''

He seemed suddenly shaken. ''You seem obsessed with that child. Why?''

''I'm not sure. For some reason it's terribly painful.''

''Perhaps it's the shock of seeing something so horrible and surviving it.'' He studied her. ''What do you think?''

''Maybe. Or maybe it makes it easier not to think about those other things. Who knows?''

''Maybe,'' he said softly.

''Maybe,'' she repeated.

Neither moved, their eyes on each other, until he finally broke the silence by changing the subject, surprising her. ''Is your mother as beautiful as you?''

Sepia was the word that came to mind. A sepia-colored photograph of a woman dressed in a tight sweater and ankle-length flared skirt, flat shoes, hair in a page boy, lips painted red, one hand on her hip. The image wasn't exactly original, since there seemed to be a squad of mothers, circa 1950, who posed like that, dressed in similar outfits and all backdropped by what appeared to be the same white porch. What happened, she always wondered, so that some of those plump and pretty girls ended up rail-thin and bitter and hardly ever sober. ''Once she was beautiful,'' she said quietly.

"And now?"

"When she's sober she can still look nice."

His eyes were soft. "Are you close?"

She wanted to leave, to throw down her napkin and run out of the restaurant. Instead, she answered, "Yes. We're close because she needs me, and because I guess I feel responsible for her." She closed her eyes a moment. "Actually, what I feel mostly is sorry for her."

"And your father?"

It was the point during dinner when there were more bones on her plate than salmon, when there was almost no wine left in the bottle, when her defenses weren't on high. "My father was abusive," she said without emotion, "so it was hard to be close to someone who could sometimes wake up smiling and other times swinging." She took a breath before demanding something in return. "And your family, are you close?"

"They're dead," he answered, not only shutting the door but turning the key as well. *Why was he like that?*

Like a duel, she found herself once again defending. "My ex-husband," she began carefully, "who happens to be an analyst, always claimed it was because of his traumatic childhood."

"Was he abused?"

"He was an orphan."

"So he took it out on you?"

"My ex-husband says he never worked out his own anger at his parents for abandoning him."

"He should have made it up to you."

"My ex-husband felt he needed someone to blame."

"Your ex-husband certainly has all the answers," Gideon observed with a smile.

"Unfortunately, what he never had were the questions."

"And then?" he asked her. And then, and more, until she found herself going through so much of her past . . .

The painful childhood was the reason that she fled, at least that was her justification for running off to Vermont with that ex-FBI agent turned congressman turned political media advisor, the married man twice her age whom she elected caretaker of her body and soul. Vermont, she called him, never by his given name, Vermont was supposed to protect her and shield her from all things painful except that it would have taken more than an ex-FBI agent, it would have taken a lobotomy to protect her and shield her and make her forget. But she stayed, overlooking that he was right-wing from another era—no, Hoover was not a vacuum cleaner—limited intellectually—no, Vladimir Nabokov did not write the words and music to *Evita*—and had this little drawback about having a wife. Twenty years with the same woman even though he swore on his next election that he hadn't laid hands or anything else on her in about ten of those years. And when he lost the next election, nothing changed, Mrs. ex-FBI agent remained the guardian of his Marine Corps sons, antique gun collection and scrapbook filled with reports of his astounding arrests.

Everything happened quickly after that, she told Gideon. She worked at the television station as Vermont's research assistant before being noticed by several executives and sponsors who thought with her bones and teeth she'd make a spectacular weather girl. Four years at the American Academy of Dramatic Arts and she found herself talking high pressures and low pressures as if she had been born with a barometer in her mouth. But looking back, she considered herself lucky because from there she met Maury Glick, the man who not only offered her New York but who also became her best friend.

"Is he the one who's here now?"

Cautiously, she replied. "Yes."

His eyes fixed on hers. "Was he a lover?"

She felt somewhat defensive. "He was my lover and now he's my friend." Not that she could quite figure out why she had folded so fast.

Gideon appeared unfazed. "And when he was your lover, was he an enemy?"

She smiled. "We all say that, don't we? I mean, if someone asks, we either classify people as lovers or friends, as if we only make love to our enemies." Her face felt hot.

"Was he an important lover?"

She considered it. "The whole affair went from oh-my-God-how-could-I-have-done-that to I-can't-wait-to-do-it-again."

"You were in love with him." He stated rather than asked it.

"Probably."

"And that spoiled the friendship part of it." Again, he said it as fact. But this time she felt a fair amount of irritation, mostly at herself, for responding to every last question he posed, and even to the ones he didn't. "No, it didn't spoil it, it made us closer in a way."

"But it's over, or at least I assume it is."

This time she didn't make it easy. She made him rephrase it to get a response. "What is it now, the relationship, I mean?"

It was still her turn. "What would you like it to be?" she asked him, her gaze steady.

"Over," he replied, taking her hand.

"Then, it is."

He inclined his head toward hers, and for a moment she thought he would do something . . . She was wrong. "Does one first have to be your friend to become your enemy before he can be your lover? Which category have you put me in?"

For a moment she almost told him that he had already qualified as all three, having outdone himself in the enemy part of the equation with that early interrogatory style of his. "None yet," she answered.

"Then may I choose?"

"Choose," suddenly feeling weak in the knees.

It went from a chaste kiss on the cheek to a polite peck on the lips to one where he devoured her mouth and her tongue, where he held her face in his hands and looked directly into her eyes, as if for approval, before he began all over again. The impression she had was of being kissed by a man who hadn't touched food or water in years, of a man who needed to fill a void of sadness that showed only in his eyes.

When he took her hand and gently pulled her to her feet, she didn't hold back. "Where?" she managed, still spinning from the kiss. He didn't answer, merely led her to the exit and down a flight of narrow stairs.

The room at the bottom of that split-level cave was dimly lit, filled with smoke and couples swaying on a small dance floor to a Patricia Kass song. Without a word, he took her in his arms and held her so close that she could scarcely breathe. Linking her hands around his neck, she moved against him, but only as he moved, which somehow had nothing to do with the tempo of the music. "Gideon," she whispered. "Tell me," he whispered back, his hand clasped at the nape of her neck. But there was nothing to tell. "Let's get out of here," he finally said, as if suddenly he had noticed what was happening.

They were back at the table, not that she cared how they got there, not that she was the least bit embarrassed about the kisses he gave her on the way up the steps or how he caressed her breasts when they reached the landing. She watched him call for the check, sign it, tip the maitre d' before he leaned over to kiss her on the tip of her nose.

Taking his hand, she followed him outside. But once there, she stopped to test something that she needed to know. Again, she linked her hands around his neck and pressed against him, aware of who was the aggressor this time, aware as well of his instant response. She kissed him and then withdrew her lips ever so slightly so they barely touched his, kissed him again, withdrew, kissed him, withdrew, relieved that if she had lost the debate, there was still some victory forthcoming. "You're driving me crazy," he murmured, reaching for her just as she slipped out of his embrace. Walking slowly, several steps ahead, she stopped only when she reached the car. Turning, she received him in her arms, as if he had been away for months, her head tilted back to allow him to run his mouth along her neck. One arm through hers to steady her, he bent down to unlock the car door.

She never took her eyes from his face while he fumbled with the key, started the ignition, shifted into first and then put the whole mechanical operation on hold to take her in his arms again. He nibbled her mouth, working his way down to her breasts, his breathing audible, his kisses more passionate, his embrace tighter until, without any warning, he pulled back, as if somehow he needed to stop in order to survive. "I'd like to take you home, Sasha," he said with a regretful sadness. If she was surprised, she was mustering every bit of composure from resources she never knew she possessed. Smiling her most sincere and kind smile, her very best, she never for an instant handed over all the confusion. "That's very nice, Gideon," she said primly, "but I think I'd better get back to my hotel."

A moment of hesitation. "But that's what I meant."

As though she didn't know. "Oh," was all she said before she turned her head.

This wasn't about her, she told herself as the car sped along the quai of the Seine, past the houseboats and the glaring lights from the *paniches*. This little performance was about him, she consoled herself as they passed a miniature Statue of Liberty and modern sky-scrapers owned by the Japanese. She wasn't a tease, he was. She didn't enjoy playing power games, he did. Not that she was without her own problem; responding as she did to withholding and punitive men. Which meant, if she judged Gideon correctly, that he was her perfect mate. What he seemed to be was a contradiction, a mystery, a man who doled out his affections as prudently as the French gave direction or the Swiss gave credit. Except that none of it mattered right then because she still wanted him so badly that she ached.

They said nothing as they crossed the bridge at the Rond Point of the Champs Élysées, drove up that wide boulevard until they arrived onto the Avenue George V. Pulling into the small roadway that ran parallel to the street, she felt the car coast to a stop before she felt him reaching for her. She was having none of it. "Thank you, it was really lovely," she said with a smile. Call me when you decide who you are, she didn't say. Call me when you decide who you want me to be, she also didn't say. Rather, he was the one who spoke, not that what he said made it any easier. "We're going to have a love affair, Sasha Beale." There was no appropriate response except to touch his face and get out of the car. Without glancing back even once, she walked toward the hotel and into the lobby, aware that he hadn't moved, aware that he was watching her, aware that she didn't even have this man's telephone number.

Sleep was out of the question. Instead, she went through the routine of taking off her clothes, hanging up her clothes, washing off her makeup, brushing her hair, brushing her teeth, creaming her face. Knees tucked under her chin, she sat on the radiator cover and gazed across those Paris rooftops, wishing that she had that cigarette.

Not that she would have made love to him. After all,

she barely knew him, but it should have been her decision, goddamnit, not his. Everything tonight seemed to come from his lead, questions about her life, judgments about her desires, decisions about her body, as if she had nothing to do with any of it. And what baffled her was that she allowed it. It certainly wasn't a matter of inexperience. At some time or another in her life she had functioned as wife, lover, friend, mother, sister, nurse to a variety of men who could or could not do a variety of things.

There were the closet cases at the network, the men with boyish haircuts and social wives, season tickets to the ballet and lovers who lifted weights in Upper East Side health clubs. There were the tax accountants and lawyers who had downed one too many martinis and could no longer get it up and who gave gifts to satisfy other desires. Or, there were the older and richer men who had it all and after a coronary or two wanted only to watch. Or, the nice men who began the seduction by dragging out photographs of wives and children and who, at the moment of compliance, fled in regretful but desperate haste for the 9:07 to Scarsdale.

Gideon Aitchison fell into none of those categories. In his case, the equipment was surely in working condition, the experience evident in his eyes, the desire apparent in the way that he kissed her and moved. Still, by three o'clock in the morning she was no closer to figuring out his game or, had she been more charitable, to understanding his problems. She crawled into bed.

It came to her suddenly, several hours later, when the dawn light filtered through the shades, the moment that fell somewhere between dreams and fantasies. With this one, she would have to take him all in, body and soul, because with this one, it was a package deal. That was, if she ever heard from him again.

Chapter Eleven

GIDEON SHOULD HAVE BEEN concentrating on Ali Khalil, who had just come around in the next room. Instead, he sat at a desk piled high with papers and files and thought about Sasha.

Considering that they had dealt mostly in abstinence and good manners, his feelings were irrational. Not so bad, he argued with himself, if one considered that so many words had passed between them, so many ideas in so short a period of time. Business aside, he sought another label for what consumed him now but could come up only with something not unlike a postponement, a minor delay of sorts until negotiation turned to intimacy.

Somewhere along the way he had broken the rules by going too far in the game. In the car, when he announced his intention to take her home (whose home, she hadn't asked), he kept it vague enough to leave himself a way back in. And then held strong—wasn't he the clever one to end up as guardian of his own frustrations? It surprised him when she came back with that quick response that was meant to turn everything around. Still, the truth had been evident in her eyes, the extent that he hurt her. Her confidence seemed to erode visibly even if she knew enough to say *no*, even if she said it after he had already refused. But then, he knew how to say no and decline better than most, having done it many times before in his life, regardless of what his wife thought. Of all the women he *had* known, none had particularly distinguished herself for reticence. Yet this one had aroused him both sexually and intellectually from the beginning, and not only because he had aroused her. Not this time.

He found her incredibly attractive—encouraging, wasn't it, that at forty-five with all the cynicism and experience and pain he wasn't immune to good looks. At least he wasn't immune to her brand of good looks. From that first moment, he wanted to kiss her, when he found her on the ground in the gardens, cut and bleeding, dazed and embarrassed. And then, when he left her in front of the hotel and watched her in the rearview mirror, he was only seconds away from leaving his car in the driveway and going after her into the lobby. He wanted her even now, even after the distance of a night. He felt the desire so acutely that he ached. Like a novice, he sat and thought about her breasts, soft skin, the way her hair had brushed against his face when they danced, about her smile and that habit she had of biting down on her lip when she needed time to consider. At the time his excuse had been that she fit into him, from breast to knee, from mouth to thigh, her body had blended into his. Now, he had no excuse.

How long ago that he had counted backward or thought of soccer scores or climbed imaginary steps on a ladder, one at a time, anything to control unwanted responses. He shrugged, painfully aware that he had no right to these thoughts. Walking over to the sink, he splashed some water on his face, patted it dry before slipping into a fresh shirt. More and more he reminded himself of his late father, eighty when he died and right up to the end he needed a woman to live for or to die for, as it turned out. That was how it happened—at eighty with a woman.

For Gideon, however, most similarities between himself and his father had ended when the natural order of

life and death had been reversed. There were no longer
any suitable excuses to permit himself the luxury of
diluting the pain and the loss, and for that he was
ashamed. Karami was another story, along with Ali
Khalil. Not as exciting perhaps or as unpredictable, but
one that was easier to control and certainly one that he
had a right to ponder. Not that he had a choice in the
matter; not that he had a choice about what he felt for
her.

Rafi was waiting for him in the corridor. "How was
dinner?"

"Overrated."

"Did the maitre d' make a fuss?"

"He was properly fawning."

"You can thank the ambassador for that."

"You can thank him for me."

"Was she impressed?"

"You really don't have any idea about her, do you?"

Rafi shrugged. "I don't have to," he replied. "You
do."

"I'll do my best."

"Our guest is waiting."

Let everyone wait, let the whole world wait, he had
other things on his mind. "Good," he said, glancing
down at the sheaf of papers he held in his hand. For a
variety of reasons, this part was easy.

The room smelled vaguely of sweat and stale tobacco. Fortunately, the coffee man had suffered no ill
effects from the drugs other than a disorientation which
worked in his captor's favor. The gunshot wound
seemed to be healing nicely, no visible infection, but
why not take the antibiotics just as a precaution, Rafi
suggested amiably.

The man was lanky and slim, Gideon noted, with
wild hair and eyes, flat cheeks and thin lips; not as

placid or round as his brother, nor as clever or emotional. But that wasn't surprising since in his line of work, the qualities most needed after blind faith and servility were a working knowledge of the rhetoric and a good memory to parrot—on demand—rhyme and reason for the cause.

Leaning against a row of blacked-out windows, Gideon crossed his arms over his chest and watched Khalil. Occasionally he'd move to sit at the desk in a pretense of studying some papers before resuming his pose against those windows.

In the beginning, Khalil was generally cooperative. He didn't protest when given several versions of the fiction that had been created for him, not that his options were overwhelming. It started with his arrival at the airport in Amman, proceeded to his reunion with his brother Saba at their parents' house in Jebbel Hussein, and ended with the hike to that abandoned power station where he experienced his last moment of consciousness. The resistance and the hostility surfaced when Rafi launched into a brief discussion about ideals and justifications and dogma, nothing too deep, just enough to set the boundaries of agreement before any future allegiance could be explored. That's when Gideon realized a mistake had been made, an error that would be deadly if not caught in time. It wasn't what the coffee man said but rather his expression, inflection, a glance, nothing particularly concrete, just a series of nuances that signified a bad choice.

It was in Beirut that the latest chapter in the narrative of the Palestinian grievance had been written, Rafi suggested, or at least that was its most recent genesis. But of course not, the man shot back, there was no recent genesis, the beginning was the beginning and the end was the end. And the beginning came from the children of the stones, from the land that is occupied by the Zionists, the territory illegally settled by the invaders from Eastern Europe—Jews—and they wear the reasons from their exodus like a badge of honor. A little past, a little present, Rafi mused, but no, the Intifada is too current, although that forced exodus is too past— invaders who still wear their numbers carved into their skin like a badge of honor. More to the point, the older man continued, why is so much said about the Israeli occupation of the West Bank and so little about the Palestinian occupation of southern Lebanon or the Syrian occupation of the entire country? Are they merely two chunks of land that make people blind in Beirut but not in Gaza? Or could we assume that had Lebanon possessed oil, there would have been the same concern as there was for Kuwait?

Ali shifted his weight so that his injured leg was stretched out on the floor. Leaders were forcibly scattered in the diaspora, they settled where they could to direct and to guide, some in Tunisia, others in Libya, still others in Iraq. It was an occupational hazard, Rafi interrupted, a question of weapons and resources and friendly countries harboring different groups, which of course created the problem of unity. Rafi shook his head. Again, the Palestinians are manipulated for the gains of others, again, they are used as the front-line force when all else fails. The man merely glared.

That lack of response was not out of stupidity but fear, Gideon thought. Perhaps Khalil needed to be reassured that the blacked-out windows were for his safety, that the guards who spoke Arabic with vague Iraqi accents—Yoram and Ben, for example—were brothers-in-arms. It made no difference how the leaders got where they were, since the road was twisted and confused for all of them. And more, the man asked Gideon with his eyes, where were they now and how did it happen that he had been shot?

Sweet cakes and coffee were offered from a tray that had been brought in at least thirty minutes before. Yes, he was still in Jordan, in Amman to be precise, a guest of the plucky little King, oh, not officially, of course, but then nothing in this war was official, not even the declaration of war itself. It seemed, however, that the question of Palestine was no longer merely a question of land, it was more, much more, considering that everybody suddenly had a stake in Tamir Karami's life. And death. True, every last one of them is either on the same side of the struggle or in different factions on the side of the struggle and has his own agenda for wanting the Palestinian question to be buried underneath all that talk of Jihad and Arab unity. The man turned his head to spit on the floor when Rafi paused.

Let's review reasons, Rafi went on, paying no attention; let's review excuses ranging from exports through the Gulf of Aqaba to the oil fields in Saudi Arabia to the Soviet's interest in destabilizing the Middle East— once again—as it was clearly a new vision of what had been the Eastern Bloc. A slight shift in geography, that's all, Rafi concluded sorrowfully before brightening up, but you, Ali Khalil, are going to help put an end to the Palestinians being used and murdered. Finally, justice will be done.

The man sighed before downing the coffee and asked for some water, which Rafi seemed in no particular hurry to provide. We all have our roots, Rafi continued, the same places, the same problems, the same conflicts, and who exactly are the chosen people anyway and where exactly were they chosen to exist or to survive? He gestured to Gideon sitting at the desk. "He's going to explain everything, how you got here, who took that shot, a little background." He leaned closer and in a conspiratorial tone, added, "He's English, so perhaps it's his way of making amends." He shrugged. "Who knows?"

"Why should an Englishman care?" the man asked bitterly.

"Where is it written that only someone who has made the pilgrimage to Mecca can care?" Rafi gestured with his chin. "Certainly not you, since you're a Communist."

"A Marxist," the man corrected.

"Of course, a Marxist who studied the doctrine in a Zionist jail from books supplied by the Red Cross." He shook his head. "What a world!"

Gideon stood to hand Ali a glass of water before he pulled his chair around to face him. "Did you actually carry the bomb into the Alitalia office or did you drive the car?"

The man blanched. "But, but I—I wasn't there."

Ignoring the denial, Gideon continued, consulting several sheets of paper. "Let's see, two Palestinians carrying Libyan passports, one also carrying that pigskin briefcase." He glanced up to study the frightened man. "Two hundred and twenty kilos of dynamite crossed wires buried in three-fourths of an ounce of semtex, cheap wrist watch and *boom*!"

The fear was more evident. "But I know nothing about it, I swear."

As if his reference to the bombing had been a mistake, Gideon went on. "First of all, I want to thank you for agreeing to talk to me. Did your brother mention why I wanted to see you?" His heart was beating faster than usual.

The expression on Ali's face was now more suspicious than relieved. "Abu Fahd," he said slowly before adding, "and the child, my brother's son."

Gideon nodded, having no intention this time around of correcting any use of the *nom de guerre*. "You're aware that his life is in jeopardy?"

The man took his cue nicely. "Which one?"

"Both."

Ali nodded, his hands wrapped around the glass, although he made no effort to drink.

"If you don't mind, Mr. Khalil, let's concentrate on Abu Fahd, since the child's future seems brighter." Reaching back to the desk, Gideon picked up a pencil to make a brief note on one of the pages. "Mr. Khalil, I'm going to go very slowly and in the order that things happened." He smiled briefly. "Did the pair meet Abu Fahd in Sidi Bou Said or in Europe?"

Confused, Khalil asked, "Which pair?"

"Rome, Mr. Khalil, the pair that so brilliantly pulled it off. Did they meet at the villa or abroad?"

"I don't know," he muttered, "so many people visit."

"But some are more important than others." He flipped a page. "That's your job, isn't it, Mr. Khalil, to know who is who so they can be treated with the proper respect?" He leaned forward. "Tell me, are the soldiers treated as well as the commanders?"

"As well."

"Where did they meet?" Gideon reverted, "in Tunisia or abroad?"

"Death is welcome." The man was suddenly defiant.

GIdeon took it up. "For you, Mr. Khalil? That I believe. You're a brave man." He stood. "But I'm afraid I can't help you," he said with regret, "I'm afraid you're going to have to find someone else to save Abu Fahd's life."

"No, please," Ali said, "please, I'll tell you."

There was nothing to say.

"It was hard for me to think," he begged, "please, I'm ready now, I remember things."

"We're not accusing you of holding anything back," Rafi assured him.

"They met in Baghdad. Abu Fahd traveled there to meet with them," the man rushed on, spittle glistening at the corner of his mouth. "One of them went to Bonn where he stayed at the apartment of a friend's sister, the other one came back to Sidi Bou Said with Abu

Fahd and stayed for two weeks until it was time to leave for Rome . . .''

It sickened him, all of it. "Was Abu Fahd pleased with the result?"

"Yes, yes, everyone was pleased, everyone was very happy except they said it wasn't enough."

"What wasn't enough?" Rafi interrupted.

"There were only two Israelis in the bombing and many other people." The man glanced at Gideon. "We have nothing against the others."

"You should have bombed El Al," Rafi suggested pleasantly. "Why did you bomb Alitalia?"

He shrugged. "Accessible."

Gideon flipped a page. "Let's start with your injuries. Shall we?"

He seemed to take the dismissal with relief. "Yes," he whispered, the uncertainty still evident, wondering perhaps if he had given enough information for the moment.

The world was insane. He was insane. "You'll probably have questions of your own, so feel free to stop me," Gideon said.

The man didn't speak, although he made eye contact.

"Let me caution you of one thing, Mr. Khalil. You must be accurate. Above all, you must be precise. If you can't answer a question or don't wish to answer, don't. It doesn't matter, we understand. But if you do answer, make very sure that the answer is correct or it can cost lives and do irreparable damage." Gideon looked away. What difference did it make anymore, except if one more fact could be learned? "Shall we begin?" Unstable, weak, loyal to the last person who threatened him, it was all there, the writing on the death warrant.

"The power station," Rafi suggested, "why don't you start from there since that's where our friend was shot?"

Gideon could see it in Rafi's eyes, too, that it was over, that a mistake had been made. And caught. In time. "Are you interested, Mr. Khalil?"

The man nodded.

"A little history never hurt anyone," Rafi winked at the coffee man before turning back to Gideon. "And you English are so good at history."

"Are you familiar with the Israeli-Jordanian border?" Gideon asked.

The man shook his head, the water glass still clutched in his hands. "Was that where I was shot?"

"The *where* seems to interest you more than the *who*," Gideon observed genially.

"Who shot me?" the man tried to catch up.

"Perhaps we should begin with the where," Gideon agreed.

The abandoned power station stood on the banks of the Jordan River at its narrowest point, where it was called the Yarmuch and where it created a natural boundary of about sixty miles between Israel and Jordan. The building itself was technically divided down the middle with one side considered Israel and the other Jordan.

From 1948 until 1967, years that included three wars, it was in neither side's interest to destroy the building that served as the main supplier of electricity for both countries even during times of conflict. Later, after it slid into obsolescence as more efficient means of power were pulled from other sources, a "hands-off" policy was still in effect that kept the station intact. Conflicting explanations were heard from each side of the river and each end of the political spectrum.

Dovish members of the Knesset along with idealistic members of the Jordanian Parliament cited the power plant as a symbol of peaceful coexistence, what had once been and what could be again. Predictably those references were almost always followed by calls for an independent Palestinian state; and depending on which side happened to be delivering the speech, those calls would be carefully phrased so that neither Jordan's shaky Hashemite kingdom nor the controversial Israeli settlements would be sacrificed.

There were other opinions as well. Some claimed that the plant had been preserved only because no one was prepared to assume that it wouldn't be needed again, while others maintained that any connection between the abandoned structure and the peace process was nothing more than a slick public-relations ploy. Yet all agreed that in that volatile part of the world, power was essential, the most coveted commodity after water. Whether the power was real or symbolic was rarely the issue.

The building had found its way back into the news during the more than three years of the Uprising, the Intifada, in the Territories. Articles appeared regularly that alluded to brotherhood and blood ties while editorials trotted out that "love they neighbor" routine for the whole world to read. The bus trips resumed, tours of the country that included a stop at that dreary stone structure where journalists and tourists were escorted by strapping Israeli soldiers. There, distances would be judiciously measured to show where both Syria and Jordan touched Israeli soil. Visitors were encouraged to wave to King Hussein's border guards or to count Hafez al Assad's tanks in the near distance. But what made the area most notorious were the infiltrations that occurred regularly, which was why Rafi chose the power station as the place to meet the Khalil brothers.

Better to meet for the first time on Israeli soil, Rafi reasoned, even thinly disguised Israeli soil, than on Tunisian. Still, it was his hope that nothing would go wrong, his fervent hope that if something did go wrong it would go wrong on the Israeli side of the Yarmuch.

After all, nobody shot so fast on his side, mostly they captured and interrogated, which in some cases wasn't much better. Unfortunately, things didn't work out exactly as planned, although everyone agreed that they could have been worse.

At precisely 2:13 in the morning Saba Khalil crossed and was greeted at the northeast entrance to the power station by two of Rafi's men dressed as Jordanian soldiers. He was immediately hustled into a waiting car. Seconds later Ali Khalil crossed and was also greeted by two of Rafi's men dressed as Jordanian soldiers. Having just seen the fate of his brother, he made a dash back over the wadi. It was then that a legitimate Jordanian border guard fired a shot at the Palestinian. And missed. One of Rafi's men calculated that the next shot might not miss and decided to shoot him in the leg to incapacitate him. Those were the facts, including the drugs that had knocked him out, the car ride to Magido, the air base in the north and the plane trip to Paris. The fiction that Gideon related to the man that morning in the embassy was a little different.

Terrorists from Black June, Abu Nidal's group, had followed Khalil from Sidi Bou Said, said Gideon. Imagine how close they had come to penetrating Karami's villa. The renegade Abu Nidal suspected that Karami was not opposed to holding secret talks with low-level American diplomats or high-ranking Israeli military, or worse, with less militant factions of the PLO. They had followed Khalil from Amman to Jebbel Hussein, across the wadi and into Israeli territory where they took a shot. Nothing fatal. A hit like that went in stages with the next round the final round. After that it would be Karami himself, except with him there would be no warning bullets in the leg.

"But what about Rome?" Ali pleaded. "That proves Abu Fahd is not a moderate."

Rome proved nothing, Gideon said with disdain. One

bomb more or less didn't alter the overall picture, anybody could arrange one attack, it didn't necessarily change fundamental philosophies . . .

"Then I can tell Abu Fahd the truth?" the coffee man asked hopefully.

Unfortunately, said Gideon, he couldn't tell Karami the truth. The Palestinian, learning about the plot to assassinate him, would rush to change his routine or worse, go into hiding, which would make it impossible to protect him. No, it was just too complicated at this stage.

"Does Abu Fahd know what happened to me?"

"News travels fast in this part of the world," Gideon answered.

The man said nothing.

"Karami already knows what you tried to do and what happened for your efforts."

The blood drained from the man's face. "But what did I try to do?" he cried.

It was stupid, Gideon scolded the man gently, imprudent and extremely risky—and here he rose to put a comforting hand on the man's shoulder—but emotions had obviously gotten the better of good judgment when he made the decision to steal across the Yarmuch River. Totally unrealistic, Gideon continued, to plan on crossing with Saba, hiding out during the daylight hours until reaching East Jerusalem, where arrangements had been made to stay with sympathetic friends and where papers had been prepared that would allow Ali to venture outside and to the hospital to see the baby. Touching, Gideon judged, to watch the child through a glass partition as he lay fighting for his life. And why? All because the Jews had forever banned him from entering Israel or the Territory again, making it impossible to come in legally and satisfy his brother's request at his hour of need. And for what reasons were the Zionists so harsh? Simply because Ali had been vocal in his hatred for the

authorities, because he had served time in various jails
for reasons of security infractions or at worst, demon-
strations at Bet Zir University in Nablus. Gideon read
the charges dispassionately. "A knife attack on two
Swedish tourists at Dung Gate in the Old City, another
knife attack on a group of visiting Greek Orthodox pil-
grims, hanging a PLO flag from the town municipality
in Gaza, PLO membership, escaping after killing a political official in Nablus, running off to fight in Sabra
Camp." He looked up. "Taking a job as one of Karami's bodyguards until being promoted to coffee man."
Gideon put down the papers. "Impressive," he complimented him, "very impressive."

"You were needed elsewhere," Rafi judged, "your
place was not with the women and the children. That's
what Karami would say, your place was with the fighters."

Still, that was the exact version he was to tell Karami,
in just those words and sequence—no deviation or elab-
oration except for the admission that he had been stupid
for taking such an enormous risk. Shot in the leg by
one of Abu Nidal's men, carried on his brother's back
over the wadi and to the temporary safety of a Jordanian
outpost before being moved to a small clinic near Amman.

When Rafi finished, the look on the man's face said
he realized he had committed the gravest error of his
life. If only he could recapture the days, if only he could
go back to the beginning, he said miserably, he would
have refused to meet his brother.

It was then that Rafi told him to get dressed in the
same clothes he had worn when he woke up. He was
going home. Gideon cleaned his wound and changed
his bandage, gave the man his shoes, an act in itself
which increased his optimism.

"You look spiffy," Rafi said as he settled back in his

chair. "Just a few questions," he added. "You don't mind."

"When can I return home?"

"Soon, very soon," Rafi assured him.

"A few questions?" Gideon smiled.

The man was taking no chances. He responded only with a barely audible word and a cautious movement of his head. Gideon eased himself back into the chair near the desk. "Sabra Camp," he began innocuously, "was Karami there with his family or was he alone?"

"He never goes anywhere without her."

"Her?"

"His wife, he never goes anywhere without her."

"Josette." Gideon said the name, hoping to fill the gap between them. "Never?"

"Except on business."

"Rome?"

Ali looked away.

"There aren't too many Western women who would sacrifice so much for their husband or their husband's people."

"She is very brave," the man said with pride, as if she was his own creation.

"He works very hard as well, I suppose."

"Late into the night."

Faster now. "So, he sleeps late in the morning."

"He's up every morning at six-thirty."

"Out of bed after his prayers?"

"He says no prayers."

"Do you bring him coffee in bed?"

"He walks along the beach before his coffee."

"Alone?"

"Two of us follow."

"At night, does he always work in his office at home?"

"Yes, unless he is out of town."

"Near her?"

"His office is right next to the bedroom with a door connecting the two rooms."

"He must disturb her each time that he goes in or out."

"No, there is another door leading out to the landing."

Gideon smiled. "You have a nice life, Mr. Khalil, and a good job. Do you have a lot of spare time?"

"Never, I'm always outside his door, waiting, in case he needs me."

"And if not you," Rafi asked casually, "then who?"

The man's shoulders sagged, as if it were no surprise, as if on some level he had been expecting it all along, shoes or no shoes.

"Guns, Mr. Khalil," Gideon said cheerfully, "if they were to come into the house." He stopped. "No, that wouldn't be possible." He studied the man a moment before beginning again. "There must be too many guards outside for them to break in." He smiled. "And you, Mr Khalil, a gun or a rifle? Or both?"

"A gun."

"Only?"

"Except in the car."

"And then?"

"A Kalishnikov."

"Too many guards," Gideon mumbled, gazing off into space.

"What do you mean, too many?" Ali appeared offended.

Gideon turned. "What I mean is, the guards on the outside are the ones who protect Abu Fahd from any harm. Once people are inside the house, you . . ." He waved his hand. "You're helpless."

"No," he protested, "that's not so. There's Talil, the kitchen man."

Gideon laughed. "But if Talil cooks, how can he guard? Unless he guards with a leg of lamb."

"He always keeps a gun in the kitchen."

"Outside the house," Gideon calculated, ignoring him, "there must be two, no three guards, and then you and Talil inside."

He shook his head. "Outside there are *five* guards, including the driver who stays in the car."

There was silence then while Gideon gauged the possibility of going a bit further without the man facing what he suspected and making a last attempt to sabotage. "We've talked about guns and guards," Gideon said slowly, "guards outside the house and inside the house, Talil, the cook and the driver who sits in the car." He rubbed his eyes with the heels of his hands. "But there's something that's bothering me." He waited. "Abu Fahd is too clever not to have some kind of an internal electronic security system. Or is he that arrogant?"

Provoked to defend, he answered quickly, "Video camera in the children's room, in the study, outside in the courtyard, even in their bedroom."

Gideon was brusque, his manner changed without warning. "Where's the television screen?"

There were tears visible then. "In the basement in a small room near the washing machine. There's a bathroom on the other side and a kitchen for coffee and water and even a place to heat up a meal." He was rushing, scrambling now for his life. He knew it now. "Two men watch the screen all day and then at night," he stopped to swallow, choking on his own saliva. "That's when they turn it off sometimes, the camera in their bedroom. But always it stays on in the children's rooms and outside. When she's alone, when he's away, it stays on in the bedroom as well. Please," he said softly to no one in particular.

"The gun, Mr. Khalil," Gideon cut him off sharply, "does she keep a gun in the room?"

The man shut his eyes, snapping them open only

when he was prodded by Rafi. "The gun," the older man repeated, "does she keep a gun?"

"Yes, the gun, under her pillow, always there," he said wildly, "a German gun. Please, please . . ."

We are all mad, Gideon judged silently before glancing at Rafi. "Where is the entrance to the basement?"

"Inside the courtyard and to the right of the front door near the swings for the children—"

"In the house, where is the entrance to the basement?"

"In the kitchen down a flight of stairs at the back of the pantry. There's a long hallway where she keeps earth for the plants and fertilizer for the flowers—"

"Draw it," Gideon ordered, motioning to Rafi to hand the man paper and pen.

He labored with pen and paper, scratching out lines, crumpling several sheets, beginning again, the tears threatening to spill from his eyes, his hands shaking as he concentrated on whatever it took to satisfy them. Gideon saw it and understood the panic and the desperation for a chance to save a life. His life. One chance. And it was Gideon who judged when the picture was finished, not Ali, even though the man tried twice to hand him a sketch of the courtyard and the house and the basement. "Please," the man said, "please help me save Abu Fahd." But both men knew that the plea was really for himself.

Gideon walked over to the window then, to open the wooden shutter just enough so there was daylight, not enough so Khalil could see outside.

"When will this be over?" the Palestinian asked with a newfound calm.

"You know, it's interesting," Gideon responded, staring out the window, "sometimes these things take weeks and sometimes they even take months and sometimes they're over when we least expect them to be." He turned and snapped his fingers. "Just like that and it's finished.'' He saw it clearly in the man's eyes, something resembling resignation, as if he had already departed, as if he had given all that he would ever give for the fight. ''Perhaps you should rest now,'' Gideon suggested, following Rafi toward the door. He saw the tears then, for the loss perhaps, for what he couldn't do, for what he would never see again. Without another word, Gideon walked out of the room.

Rafi was waiting for him in the corridor between the two rooms. ''What do you think?''

Gideon postponed the inevitable. ''I think someone will come out of this better than when he started.''

''Who's that?''

''The child.''

Rafi presented the ending. ''I hope you got enough information because that's it.''

Gideon knew enough not to ask about Ali Khalil's future, because he suspected he already knew what would happen. The brother was another story, one that he allowed Rafi to recount. When the child was fully recovered from surgery the family would be thrown back into the garbage heap otherwise known as the Occupied Territories.

''At least you can feel good about the child,'' Rafi added.

But Gideon was too weary to explain that most of the time the only emotion he could feel was *dead*. Even if his impression of *dead* included all the same sorrow and remorse he carried around when he once thought he was alive. But now there was a fantasy added to his purgatory.

''Sasha Beale is all you've got now,'' Rafi warned him.

As if that was news to him.

Chapter Twelve

LUNCH HAD BEEN Maury's idea, the restaurant was Sasha's, a Left Bank bistro on the rue de l'Ancienne Comédie, near the Odéon, a place called Procupe, which dated back to 1686 and which happened to be right next door to that hotel where Tamir Karami staged his first hostage drama. Which meant that Maury could deduct it as a business expense. Which made Maury happy. Sasha was another story. For some reason she needed reassurance on the most basic level of her own insecurity. "Maury, am I attractive?"

He was startled. "Why would you ask such a dumb question?"

Easier to separate church and state than to separate the professional from the personal. "Just answer, am I?"

"Of course you're attractive."

She forced herself to go further, to confront the most absurd possibilities that she should have passed long ago. "Would you take me out, forget that you once *did*, would you do it again?"

"Does this by any chance mean that I haven't lost you to that dashing European?" He took her hand. "What's he like?"

"Dashing," she said morosely.

"We're planning to leave the day after tomorrow," Maury changed the subject, "providing there aren't any complications."

She followed. "How long do you think we'll be there?"

"About a week, again if there aren't any complications."

She thought about not telling Maury. "He's going to be there, you know," she said without warning.

"Who?" The tone was casual but the expression was intent.

"Last night's dinner."

Clearly, he wasn't pleased. "How did that happen?"

"He always travels to North Africa on business."

"Does that mean I'll have your divided attention?"

Something was off. "Do we have yours when you bring a Bendex along?"

"A Bendex is busy in the shops. Somehow I have the feeling your visitor to Tunis will be with you."

"He works."

"By the way, so is Bendex, working, I mean. She's manning phones back at the hotel."

"Not my phone."

"Your phone too."

"Maury, why?"

"Because I don't trust the hotel operators here to refer calls. It could be something important." He paused. "Come on, Sasha, get your mind on the documentary."

"It's on the documentary," she said evenly.

"I need you, Sasha," he said gently.

"You'll have me to absolute maximum," she assured him. "I love this assignment, I'm really looking forward to this."

"Let's be specific—to what?"

"Maury, cut it out. I'm looking forward to the interview."

"I can believe *that*," he said, settling back, "because you seem to have found your field. Amazing, but you really seem comfortable handling this terrorist thing.''

''I am.''

''How do you explain that?''

''I've worked for *you* all these years, haven't I?''

''I just hope you don't do anything stupid, that's all.''

''It's not only up to me, you know.''

''That's not very encouraging.''

''I wouldn't worry about it. I'm not exactly getting inundated with flowers and phone calls here.'' She tried a smile.

''Why are you so insecure when you have so much?''

The lighter, the better, although it was harder and harder to be flip. ''Probably because no one ever told me I was a nice kid.''

''You're a nice kid.''

Why were they back to that again?

The maitre d' came up to the table and spoke to Maury. ''Is there a Mademoiselle Beale with you?'' As if she didn't exist, as if she would only materialize if Maury responded in the affirmative to give her substance and form. What she wanted to say was, ''What do I look like, chopped liver?'' But that was Carnegie Deli talk and even adapting it for Paris by saying, ''What do I look like, fish choucroute?'' didn't quite make it either. ''I'm Miss Beale,'' she said, refusing to acknowledge or repeat the one French word that he had thrown into that perfectly phrased and accented English sentence, as if they took a course in tray-carrying and pronunciation. ''Telephone,'' he said with a bow.

She paled.

''Relax,'' Maury said, ''it doesn't have to be him.''

''You're right, it could be good news, like the show's been cancelled.''

Five minutes later she was back at the table, slightly flushed as she collapsed against the back of the banquette.

''So, is the show cancelled?''

''No.'' Her eyes were shining. ''He's meeting me here. He wants to see me before I've got to run off for that interview with the mother-in-law.''

''Good, you can introduce us.''

''No, Maury, please.'' She looked startled, as if the possibility never occurred to her. But he was good-natured about it, offering little resistance when he said, ''I know, you don't want him to feel threatened by me.'' He grinned. She kissed him on the cheek. ''Let's order since it seems we're on a time limit now,'' he said with good humor. And, after all, it was his Bendex who had directed that phone call to this restaurant. ''I'll have a scotch on the rocks,'' she said.

''Like always. That doesn't surprise me,'' Maury said, signaling for a waiter.

''What doesn't surprise you?''

''The smarter the girl, the less complicated the drink. Don't ever disappoint me and order a sloe gin fizz with two green cherries. Promise?'' His eyes no longer held amusement or humor but rather an intensity that startled her.

''Promise,'' she said.

''So, don't lose it with this guy.''

''And to eat,'' she ignored him, ''I'll have oysters.''

''Is he really that good?''

''That isn't fair, is it?''

''Was I that good?''

''You were different, Maury.''

''And what's Mr. Dashing European?''

Again, the reality hit her. ''How should I know? He's a total stranger.''

They passed each other at the door, Maury and Gideon. The whole transaction took no longer than thirty seconds. The passageway was not quite wide enough for two broad-shouldered men to pass abreast. Sasha watched, aware that Gideon was at a disadvantage in this round. After all, Maury had an idea who Gideon was when he walked through those creaky, ancient doors. Gideon didn't know Maury. Maury stepped aside, Gideon did as well, so that part of those thirty seconds were spent signaling right of way in the most polite manner. After you, no, after you, no please, I insist, after you, until Gideon gave in with a quick nod while Maury stood there and waited until he was seated at the table.

Instantly, he reached across the white cloth and took her hands. "Sasha Beale," he said in that throaty voice and then stopped. As if the wonder of seeing her and saying her name was just too much for him. At least that was her take on what he was trying to convey. She didn't withdraw from him, nor did she offer anything more, not a single word of encouragement or a look of appreciation at his wonderment. "You look beautiful," he went on, "I haven't stopped thinking about you or wanting you since last night."

This was the moment to do it, to come back with the rules on foreplay or to get sucked into a conversation where nothing was being said at all. And there was a way to do it without sounding like Roseanne Barr or Marilyn French, but until she heard her own words and tone of voice, she just couldn't make any assessments or give any guarantees. "Gideon, do you think there're fifty thousand women in Paris?" she asked innocently. If he was surprised by the question, he gave no clue. He didn't drop her hands the way some men might have, but pressed them to his lips while he seemed to consider. "Of course not," he replied with a twinkle in his eyes, "There are millions of women in Paris."

"Could we just keep the figure at fifty thousand for my purposes?" she asked, a smile in her eyes as well.

"Of course, please, go on."

"Well, I bet that forty-nine thousand nine hundred

and ninety-nine of them would love to hear what you just told me.''

''Except?''

''Except that I wouldn't or at least I wouldn't want to hear it from a man I know nothing about.'' She took back her hands and smiled a dazzling smile.

He smiled back, an amused smile, his gaze never faltering. ''Would you like a glass of champagne?''

''What are we celebrating?''

''Your wit,'' he replied.

In control, poised, calm; in control not to laugh, poised enough not to blush, calm enough not to get angry. ''I'd love one,'' she said.

He caught the waiter's attention and ordered before he sat back, once again prepared to listen to anything she had to say. He put her on center stage and never gave her the option of retreating. She noticed that his expression had changed to one of tenderness and patience, as if he were about to deal with a child's compliments or forgotten promises of coveted toys. It fueled her, not unlike Bogart having a tantrum about leeches in a swamp while Hepburn just hung around him waiting for him to finish. Role reversal perhaps although the focus again seemed to be on the delivery and not the leeches. ''No phone number,'' she heard herself beginning, ''no address. I admit it's my fault since I picked you up in the park or allowed you to pick me up, which is something I wouldn't recommend and something I've never done before.'' She waited, not so much for a reaction as she did for emphasis, to give her audience a needed pause. ''You knew where to call me to invite me for dinner, you even know where I'll be in Sidi Bou Said, but I don't know anything about you.'' She waited another moment, just long enough to moisten her lips with the tip of her tongue and consider the imbalance of it all. He wanted into her body, she wanted into his past. ''You could be anyone,'' she said quietly, "and there's something not quite fair about this, uneven, do you know what I mean?" It was over then, the monologue with the almost-rhetorical question at the end. "You must be a terrific reporter," he said. If she could possibly manage not to offer another word, not a single sound to fill the silence that was enveloping them, she might just make her point. "Was I that stupid?" he finally asked her. Still, she didn't move, not a flicker of an eyelid. "I was that stupid," he announced, shaking his head.

"It's not a question of stupidity," she said.

"No, it's not," he agreed. "Not giving you my number was complete thoughtlessness." He took back her hands. "I was stupid about other things."

"What things?" she asked. But she knew it was a mistake the moment the words left her tongue.

"I should have kept you with me all night and made love to you."

A barrier at this point was irrelevant. "Gideon," she began, noticing that his grip on her fingers was tighter. "You're assuming a great deal."

"I could feel you all night."

"You're very spoiled," she said lightly.

"Will you give me another chance?"

"Could we talk about something else?"

"Anything you like."

"Could we talk about you not talking like this?"

He folded her fingers back into her palms and placed them neatly on the table. "Does it make you uncomfortable that you made this"—he searched for the word—"impression on me?" Deadly serious then, no small-boy lilt this time, no expression in his eyes that undressed her, just a straightforward matter-of-fact announcement. "I apologize if I've offended you." Tenderness was back, not as much as before but enough to make her feel vaguely guilty. "I'm not used to these feelings, especially so quickly, and I suppose I'm not used to a woman like you.'' He took a sip of champagne. ''In the back of my mind I keep seeing the end because it's an unrealistic scenario, three days here or there. That's the stupid part of this, that I'm going way beyond the reality in my head.'' He grinned. ''But I find it extraordinary that we'll both be in Tunis at the same time, don't you?'' He didn't wait for a reply. ''So will you give me another chance?''

Too late for decorum. ''Yes,'' she said, although somewhere it struck her that despite the tumbling and tousling and jousting, she was exactly where she had been at the beginning of this conversation.

''Why don't we take a long drive in the country this afternoon and then have dinner tonight?''

Her foot touched the briefcase that was under her chair, the Helene Villeneuve file inside, the detail that brought her back to earth. ''I can't take a drive this afternoon,'' she said, ''because I've got to interview the terrorist's mother-in-law.''

''When will you be free?'' Said calmly, casually, to cover his surprise at this unexpected opportunity.

''I'm not sure. Sometime after seven.''

''And after that?''

''I'm yours.''

He reached for her. ''You're mine now.''

Back and forth, on and off, she threw him out, she took him in, possible, not possible. ''Gideon, why don't you give me your phone number''—the tone was teasing—''so I can call you when I'm about to finish?''

''My nemesis, the telephone. Of course I'll give you the number, except I won't be home. I'm going to be running around some this afternoon.''

She was patient. ''Why don't you give me your office number then?''

''It wouldn't do any good, I'm afraid, because my secretary is out sick.''

She said it in a whisper, ''So, tell me, how would I

reach you, say tonight, if I suddenly had this big desire for you?''

''But why would you have to call me, Sasha Beale, when you'll be right next to me?''

''Not if you don't know where or when to pick me up after the interview. Look, why don't you call me at the mother-in-law's house at five-thirty? I'll give you the number and then if I'm not finished, at least I'll have a better idea when I will be.'' She reached down and picked up the leather briefcase, took out the Villeneuve file and waited while he produced a pen and a slim leather notebook.

She read him the woman's name, spelled it, gave him the phone number, address, floor, access code for entry into the building—just in case. ''I've got to run,'' she said softly, glancing at her watch, ''or I'll be late.''

He called for the check, paid for the two flutes of champagne, took her arm and walked her in the direction of the exit. ''Could you give me a minute?'' he asked. ''I've just got to check in with one of my people at the office.''

She nodded. It didn't take long, just long enough for her to pop into the ladies room to fix her makeup and comb her hair. He was waiting for her.

They were outside then, standing in front of the restaurant, when he pulled her toward him, taking her in his arms. ''Do you remember what I told you last night?'' he asked, his lips brushing against her hair. She shook her head. ''That we were going to have a love affair.'' She nodded. ''Well, in case you haven't noticed, we're having one,'' he told her before tilting her chin to kiss her on the mouth.

She decided to walk. She needed time to think about the interview, something she hadn't even planned out since making the appointment. It was a question of finding the best way to get the woman to talk about her daughter, and not about her childhood—Sasha couldn't have cared less—but about her life now, in the Arab world, with him. That was what she had to draw out of her.

The street map indicated that off the Étoile was the Avenue Wagram, which, if followed to the very end, became the Place Wagram, where, off to the right, was a small street that was called an avenue, Avenue des Chasseurs, where, in the building marked 6 *bis*, lived Helene Villeneuve.

It was getting late and cloudy. Sasha hadn't realized how far it was, all the way to the other side of Paris, which was why she decided to call the woman to explain that she might be a little late. There was no problem, at least about the time, it was the weather that concerned Madame Villeneuve, it looked threatening, there could be a downpour at any moment, typical Paris climate, changing constantly.

By the time that Sasha had crossed the Seine and was halfway up the Champs Élysées, the sky had grown overcast and a fine mist was dampening the streets. And by the time that she reached the lively and commercial Place des Ternes with its row of flower stands, not far from Madame Villeneuve's street, Yoram and Ben were already in the basement of 6 *bis* Avenue des Chasseurs installing a tap on the wires leading to the woman's telephone.

Chapter Thirteen

THE APARTMENT SMELLED of stale Campbell's vegetable soup, metal walkers, musty slipcovers and soiled litter boxes. Helene Villeneuve was a wiry woman with faded green eyes, a distant smile and an out-of-date gray chignon pinned at the nape of her neck. She moved in nervous spurts as she searched the wall for the light switch, clasped her hands together as she made excuses for the disarray, blaming it on the maid who was ill, smoothed down the skirt of her shabby silk dress, waved Sasha into the living room.

"I didn't expect someone quite so young," she greeted Sasha.

"Neither did I," Sasha returned the compliment with a warm smile.

The woman blushed, her bony fingers flying to her hair. "I hope you understand why I was reluctant to see you."

Sasha smiled again before she glanced discreetly at several ancestral paintings that hung on one wall. "Of course, it must be very difficult for you."

"I've been alone throughout most of this ordeal. My husband died eight years ago."

Right then, Sasha knew that if there was any veal roast left over from yesterday, she would be having it for dinner. Gideon would have to wait.

"At least he didn't linger," the woman continued.

"He was a gambler, collapsed after losing a game of bridge at the Racing Club."

"I'm sorry," she said, Olivier Villeneuve's obituary flashing through her mind. And even before the words were out of her mouth, she knew how she would play it. "Unfortunately, my father isn't so lucky."

"Isn't or wasn't?"

"Isn't. He has a lingering illness." Poor Eli would have loved it. Acute malice, terminal for anyone within hearing distance or even more dangerous, acute gambling disorder, terminal to anyone who happened to be dependent on him for food, education and housing.

"It must be very hard on your mother. Are you an only child?"

If she hated anything that she had become over the years, it was being an only child. "My brother was killed in a motorcycle accident when I was fifteen."

The woman was properly horrified. "Oh, my dear," she exclaimed, a variation on what everybody said when they heard. "At least your mother has you. A daughter is so important. Unfortunately, Josette was in Beirut when her father died, and with the war and the children, it was impossible for her to get back for the funeral."

War and children. Words that had found their way into this threadbare, baroque living room in the 17th Arrondissement, the good section of the 17th Arrondissement, the one that bordered on the 8th. Paris, the city of lights, nuance and inches.

"I can assure you," Madame Villeneuve added, "it means a lot to your mother, having you around to talk to." That established, she moved on. "Will you have a chocolate?" she offered, producing a box from a drawer in a barrel-shaped commode. Coated with white film, the candies looked as if they were contemporaneous of the people who had posed for the ancestral portraits. Sasha took one and bit into it. "Do you talk to your daughter often?"

"As often as possible, although it's difficult because she's so busy with her work and with the baby."

"Isn't that wonderful, having another child after so many years?"

"Yes, it is," Helene answered carefully, "and from what I understand, the birth wasn't at all difficult. Surprising, isn't it, for a woman in her forties?"

It wasn't hard to figure out what the woman wanted Sasha to know. "Weren't you there?"

"No, I wasn't."

She reviewed the file in her head, a widow alone with a limited pension, few friends who were still alive and lucid, a daughter who lived in another world and grandchildren who appeared once every year or less. "Tell me a little about Josette when she was growing up." Sasha went back to more pleasant times.

"Well, let's see, she was extremely bright but very shy and timid, not like the other children. Josette preferred to be alone and read."

"Did she have friends?"

"There were a few little girls whom we encouraged her to see, children who came from similar backgrounds."

"You mean, whose fathers were also in the military?"

"Not necessarily in the military, just families with similar political leanings and religious values." She smiled. "Families who felt the same social obligations as we did and who wanted the same things for their children."

"What was that?" Sasha asked pleasantly, "What kind of political leanings?"

"We believed in France for the French, the way General de Gaulle believed in France, the way Monsieur Le Pen believes now." She laughed softly. "What you people would call right-wing or even fascist." She patted Sasha's hand. "Not necessarily you but all the journalists. They condemn without understanding any of the background. You see, my husband fought in Algeria so he knew the mentality of those people and how their attitudes and desires were contrary to our Catholic morality. We wanted that for our daughter, a good solid French life where church was important and France was important.'' She paused. ''For the French.''

Sasha let the woman talk a bit more, about her husband's career that seemed to begin and end in Algeria, their politics, which seemed to be unchanged from that same era, everything that led up to the social explosion in 1968, the year that changed her daughter's life. ''Did Josette have plans for a career or a job when she was studying at the Sorbonne?''

The woman looked baffled. ''A job? Why no, she was studying art history with the intention of getting married and having children, at least that was what we assumed.'' Her voice grew distant. ''Josette did like to paint. She would spend the afternoons at the museums after classes sketching and drawing.'' She looked at Sasha. ''But the ultimate plan was marriage and a family.''

''Things changed after May '68, I suppose.''

She frowned. ''Life changed after May '68. At least for us it did.'' She bit her lip.

''Is that when she became political?''

''I don't know about political but that was when she stopped bathing and combing her hair and dressing properly.'' The woman became engrossed suddenly in several stains on the arm of her chair, licking a thumb, rubbing the fabric, licking, rubbing until Sasha asked, ''Have you ever been to Sidi Bou Said? I understand it's very beautiful.''

The woman glanced up. ''I visited them in their last house, the one the Israelis destroyed when they bombed . . .'' she hesitated.

"PLO headquarters," Sasha finished the sentence, aware that the dreaded words had finally been spoken.

"Yes, that's right. My daughter lost all her good china."

"Then you haven't seen the new baby?"

"Josette brought him here for a visit last fall, shortly after he was born. In fact, the whole family came because my son-in-law had meetings with the President of the Republic, Monsieur Mitterand, on the Gulf crisis."

Now that he was out in the open, Sasha pursued the subject, even if that meant the end of the visit. "He must be a very unusual man."

"Monsieur Mitterand?"

"No, your son-in-law."

She seemed to waver for only a moment. "You promised me."

"I haven't mentioned Rome, that was our agreement."

"Please, we agreed."

"And that agreement stands."

She sighed once. "Unusual isn't the right word." A brief smile. "Another chocolate?" Removing the embossed gold lid from the box, she held it toward Sasha, who chose one that was wrapped in foil this time. "No, he isn't what you might imagine at all. He is very quiet and thoughtful and loves to play backgammon."

Sasha nodded. Tamir Karami, the quiet one. His toys made the noise.

"The children adore him," the woman chattered on, "and he adores them, even though he can be strict when it comes to their progress in school." She smiled again but for some reason the smile did not quite reach her eyes. "My oldest grandson, Fahd, goes to school in England and only comes home in June for the summer vacation and for Christmas and Easter . . ."

Sasha wondered if this woman had ever imagined that

she would have a grandson called anything but Yves or
Pierre or Jean-Michel.

"My granddaughter Camilla lives at home and goes
to a French school near Carthage, but you should see
the baby, Tarek. He is adorable with big black eyes and
black hair. Tarek," she repeated, "the baby's name is
Tarek."

"Your daughter must be very happy."

"Oh, I think she is, yes, I would say that she's very
happy. She loves her children and the garden and her
work at the hospital and the weather is warm but not
too humid except of course in August." She brushed a
strand of hair from her face. "Nothing is perfect, you
know," she confided.

"What do you mean?"

"Well, things could be easier, but given his work,
some things can't be changed."

"Could you give me an example?"

"Well, all those security guards, young toughs roaming around the house." She shivered. "They're wild-
looking boys, badly dressed, shoes never polished and
always carrying those big guns. They eat in the kitchen.
Josette insists that they take all their meals in shifts in
her kitchen."

Sasha smiled and touched the woman's arm lightly.
"You know, you're really very lucky." She paused.
"My mother would love it if I were happily married
with children. That's every mother's dream." She
turned things around to give the woman a break from
the questions.

"Are you married?"

"No, I'm not, but I wish I were," Sasha replied
sweetly.

"Why aren't you then?"

"It's not easy to find the right man. Your daughter
was lucky to have fallen in love with someone who
loved her back." She nearly choked on the words.

Madame Villeneuve twisted around in her chair to pick up a crystal decanter and two shot glasses from a tray behind her. Sasha expected that would happen from the moment that she walked into the house. She recognized the setting and the symptoms. It wouldn't have come as any surprise if Helene Villeneuve believed what Sasha's mother believed, that if it was kept in a crystal bottle and poured by shot glass it didn't really count as drinking. "Would you like a whiskey?" she asked primly.

"I'd love one," Sasha replied.

The woman poured steadily until each glass was filled to its worn gold rim, handed one to Sasha before taking a long sip from hers. "You are such an attractive girl that I'm sure you'll find the right man some day." Taking another swig, she emptied the glass and turned to pour herself another. Sasha waited until she had taken a sip from that one before asking, "Did you try to stop her?"

"Stop who from what?"

It was a risk, but then, she was practically an expert on the subject of afternoon drinking as it affected certain women. "Did you try to stop your daughter from marrying him?"

Another gulp produced another empty tumbler. "My dear," she began, the words slurring slightly, "not only did I try to stop her, I forbade her from even talking to him." Turning around, she refilled her glass, unaware that Sasha's hadn't yet been touched. "And her father was even more severe. He threatened to order her out of the house when he found out." She shrugged. "But by then it was too late."

What amazed Sasha was not the reaction of these parents but her own reaction to this woman's drinking problem. For the first time she was able to think of her mother without feeling all the anger and disgust and sadness. "Why were you so opposed to him?"

"Because he was an animal." She spoke the words very distinctly. "My husband knew *them*. I told you that. He fought in Algeria, that was his life. He knew about how they stuck a knife in your back when you weren't looking. Only this one, he was worse than any of them."

"Why?" She pushed a little more.

"Because he was a political vagrant without a future or a job. Could he take care of our daughter?"

She pushed even more. "But he had a political future within the system of the PLO."

The woman looked at her as if she were demented. "Do you really think that was something we valued for our child?" She laughed. "Do you really think that was the kind of future we planned for her, living with a bunch of savages?"

It seemed to have been more a matter of social disappointment than prejudice, Sasha thought, and waited for more.

"Not that we side with the Jews on the Mideast issue. We believed then and I believe now . . . those of us who are still around and realistic enough to follow Monsieur Le Pen . . . is that most of the trouble in the world comes from the Middle East as a result of all the fighting between Arab and Jew."

Sasha was silent, as if she were thinking about it, as if that particular thesis actually had some merit, as if it was a relief that the woman practiced such evenhandedness in her dislikes. "Do you think your daughter knows some of the things her husband is involved in?" Curiously, instead of the reaction that Sasha expected— an angry referral to that agreement between them—the woman seemed to diminish and wilt. Defenseless, she sank down into that large French provincial chair with its ragged maroon velvet upholstery and chipped gilt-trimmed arms. "We don't discuss it."

"You're probably right not to," Sasha chatted away,

"since it's doubtful that your daughter knows anything anyway." Had she not taken that position, it would have been rude; had she judged, it would have been pointless; had she accused, it would have been over. Now, the transition belonged to Helene Villeneuve. "Don't be ridiculous," she snapped, "she reads the newspapers like everyone else, doesn't she? Even if he told her nothing, she is not a total idiot!"

Sasha pretended surprise. "And yet you don't discuss it?"

She rallied. "What do you say to a woman who is blind, who is so irrationally in love that she was willing to destroy her own father?"

There was no need of an answer.

"My husband died of a broken heart," she continued, "but how would you have him feel when his only child, a daughter, betrayed him as she did?"

Sasha was exactly where she had planned to be, but for some reason she wanted out. "You must be very strong," Sasha said gently, "because you survived it."

A hand shook slightly as it arranged a piece of hair that had fallen from the chignon. "Sometimes I wish I hadn't." She looked at Sasha. "But perhaps I had more time to adjust since my daughter confided in me from the beginning of the affair."

There was nothing left to say about the marriage. "Do you have any photographs?" Sasha asked.

Placing her empty glass on the commode behind her, the woman turned back to position the leather album in the center of the table. She sat back while Sasha leaned forward to look.

Each page was filled with snapshots held down at their corners by yellowed tape, mostly pictures of a child with haunted eyes that stared dully into the camera, something wan and fragile and terribly sad about her. Then the child as an adolescent, that same tragic regard, the bony brow covered with thin wispy blond hair.

More photographs of the adolescent young woman as she passed through the stages of teenager, sloppy revolutionary, bride, stylish matron, militant wife. A newspaper photo of Josette standing between her husband and Yasir Arafat on a boat with a caption explaining that she had come to Lebanon to fight and die at her husband's side. Sasha glanced at Helene after reading it and saw tears in the woman's eyes. Turning back to the album, Sasha paused again over a picture of Josette leaning against a palm tree, a flowered dress pulled over a pregnant belly. "Why does she look so unhappy?"

The woman glanced over and then away. "That was taken in Egypt when she was pregnant," she evaded.

"With her first child?"

"No," she said softly, "that was taken after the tragedy."

"What tragedy?"

The woman looked suddenly haggard. "After the accident." A breath. "After Tarek, the first Tarek, fell off their balcony in Damascus and was killed."

How had she missed that in all the biographical material? "What a horrible *accident*."

A shrug of her thin shoulders. "In their world they call it an accident."

"Wasn't it?"

"The only accident that took place was that the men who burst into their house that night did not realize that my son-in-law was in prison and not there." She twisted her fingers. "The child was thrown off the balcony, probably out of spite." She paused, as if she was gathering the strength to bring up the memories. "Apparently there was a disagreement." The sarcasm was evident. "And apparently, that's how they settled disagreements."

"I'm very sorry," Sasha said, and then wondered if

that was reason enough to obliterate the rest of humanity.

"Before that happened," the woman went on, "we thought maybe, just maybe, they had outgrown those revolutionary ideas. We would have accepted him had he taken a job with an American company in Cairo, for example, and made a normal life for them. We were prepared to accept him," she repeated, "under those circumstances, but unfortunately we were wrong to hope."

Sasha knew enough not to interrupt or question this explanation for decisions made so long ago.

"The tragedy happened in December 1969," she continued, "and three months later, in March, they dropped everything and moved to Jordan. In September of 1970," she added disdainfully, "the king decided to expel all the Palestinians from his country, an event called Black September." She paused. "Which was when my son-in-law became someone in the movement and when my daughter became an inspiration to all Arab women. Can you imagine such a thing?" She shook her head. "The worst was only beginning. The attacks began and then Tamir's name was in the newspaper taking credit for the attacks and then pictures of my daughter and the children and then the excuses and the reasons and the politics and suddenly he was known as a man who killed for his country. Except he didn't have a country. But then, that was the whole problem, wasn't it? It's almost a blessing that my husband died. At least he didn't have to suffer through what happened these past few years."

For Sasha, it was the beginning of the story, something she could never understand regardless of how many people she asked and how many explanations she heard. Still, she had to pose the question. "As a mother, how do you think Josette feels when she reads that an innocent child was killed in—"

"In a bomb blast caused by her husband?" Helene finished the sentence. "I don't have the slightest idea." "Slightest" was the operative word in that response, Sasha judged, since the woman had already passed tipsy to emerge as, simply, quietly drunk. "Here we are talking about the one thing I swore we wouldn't discuss." Her eyes filled with an inordinate sadness.

"We said we wouldn't discuss Rome and we're not. What I'm interested in understanding are your daughter's feelings about violence."

"I can't speak for my daughter."

"Of course you can't."

"But if you happen to ask her and she happens to answer you, I'd be curious to know too."

Sasha decided she had nothing to lose. "How do you feel about all that violence?"

"How should I feel? You would like me to say that I feel ashamed and shocked and angry, isn't that right? Well, I once did feel all those things until I just stopped feeling anything. I started numbing myself."

"Do you think she shares his opinions?"

"She shares his bed, doesn't she, and his children and his life. How does a woman share all of that and not the rest of it? Of course she shares his opinions. My daughter never had an original bone in her entire body."

"It took some originality for her to marry him and not someone more conventional." She was pushing again.

"That's not originality. My cats go into heat too, you know."

Sasha flinched inwardly. "Yet your daughter and her husband seem to lead a relatively normal life, considering . . ." She watched closely.

The woman leaned forward. "Do you think it's *normal* to have television cameras all around the house? Little hidden eyes in the bedrooms and the kitchen and outside on the veranda? Do you think it's normal to have men sitting in front of a television screen in the basement watching everything they do? Do you think it's normal for my daughter to keep a gun under her pillow or for those disgusting men to wander around the house with submachine guns and walkie-talkies?''

She pushed harder, but only because she sensed that it was almost over. "But most of the PLO leaders move from house to house every night, and he doesn't. There's a sense of permanence about him—"

"He's insane to live like that. In the end it's going to kill him. He can't have it both ways." Her expression was grim. "He just renewed the lease on the villa because of the children. He wants them to be able to enjoy the sea and keep the same friends, as if they were like other children. Stupid. He refuses to let the Tunisian police guard the house at night because, he says, he doesn't want to make the neighbors uneasy, and he refuses to have an alarm in the house in case one of the children sets it off by accident and his bodyguards start shooting. And then there's the key he leaves under one of those potted palms near the front door in case someone gets locked out or there's an emergency. More stupidity." Her eyes glistened with anger. "Don't think that I care what happens to him, or to Josette . . ." That last said with lowered voice. "It's the *children* I worry about. They're the innocents. There's no blood on their hands. Not yet . . ."

"You sound angry."

"Not anymore," the woman said.

"I hear anger."

"What you hear is my loneliness. I lost a child."

"But so did your daughter, *madame*. Couldn't that be a common point of compassion between you?"

"She has other children. She has her husband. I have no one."

"Have you ever told her how you feel?"

"They should never have gone to Jordan."

Somehow Sasha had lost her. "Did you tell her that, that she shouldn't go?"

The woman was far away. "I sat next to her mother at the Collections last spring."

"Whose mother?"

"The Queen of Jordan's mother. I sat next to her at the Saint Laurent show. She only wears Saint Laurent, you know."

"Really," was all Sasha could manage. "Small world."

The woman nodded. "Smaller than you think. My housekeeper's sister works for the woman who alters all her clothes."

"Amazing," Sasha said, unable to come up with anything more substantial as she watched the woman fade.

"I get hate mail," she announced without warning, "sometimes I even get death threats. Me, can you imagine, death threats, Me, a target for assassination." She laughed but there were tears in her eyes. Reaching out, Sasha touched her hand.

"Isn't your number unlisted?" Sasha asked.

"It is now, but before it was changed I used to get obscene phone calls." She blew her nose.

"What did my daughter say when you talked to her?"

"I don't know, I didn't talk to her. But I could ask."

"No"— she waved her hand weakly—"it doesn't matter." She gazed off somewhere in the distance. "Nobody calls me anyway."

"Don't you have friends?"

"My husband was my friend."

"And now?"

"My neighbors barely speak to me. Oh, it's not a racial or political thing, they're just afraid, and frankly, I don't blame them. I'm afraid too."

"Can't your daughter be your friend?"

The woman stared at her hands, her bottom lip trembling slightly. "My daughter belongs to them."

If Sasha had entered this dialogue concerned about making an emotional connection for the sake of the documentary, her problem now was how to extricate herself gracefully—even if that meant missing Gideon's phone call, even if that meant relying on Gideon's having sense enough to reach her back at the hotel. She made the first gesture. "I should really be going," she said, glancing at her watch.

Helene Villeneuve appeared shattered. "But I made a veal roast yesterday," she murmured before saying in a stronger voice, "it's a shame to waste it. Won't you stay? Please?"

"Of course I'll stay," Sasha replied with hardly any hesitation. Seconds later, the telephone rang. It was exactly 5:30.

Chapter Fourteen

DRIVING GLOVES. Gideon was giving out clues. Chances were that he went home to get them, which meant that he had a home and a telephone, which meant that Sasha had a good shot at getting the address and number, if she would only remember to insist. Or maybe he didn't go home at all, maybe he kept the gloves in the car and didn't have a home, maybe he was—what was it that Helene Villeneuve said about her son-in-law—a "political vagrant." Maybe Gideon was a political vagrant, which was why he hadn't given out much information about himself, nothing concrete, just a lot of short sentences about dead family, departed wives and never-born children. But getting back to those driving gloves. Clearly, he was giving out clues. A distance drive? Normandy perhaps, or a spin along the Seine, or maybe he intended to strangle her.

Sasha came striding out of the courtyard of No. 6 *bis* Avenue des Chasseurs high on her interview, high on the expectation of seeing Gideon, and there he was, sitting in a black Porsche that was parked in front of the building. A black Porsche, she registered the color and make, what happened to the black Renault and what was this thing with black anyway? Ridiculous, she dismissed the thought instantly, as if there was something significant about black, or as if there were rules about a Renault employee driving another make of automobile. She walked over to the passenger side and peered in the window. His eyes were shut, a condition that didn't make his profile any less fetching. Opening the door, she recognized the music as Albinoni. "Hi," she said softly, which was when she noticed them. Driving gloves.

"Sasha!" He straightened up, eyes bright and alert as he fumbled with the door, stepped out, long legs touching the pavement. He was next to her then. A kiss on the cheek and a clutch, that was the only word that came to mind as he pulled her close to him, nothing tentative about the way that he grabbed her—nothing less than a clutch. She saw the approval in his eyes, more than approval, what she saw was lust. "You're beautiful," he said, holding her. His body felt hard—everything felt hard—and taut and she found herself missing him the instant he released her. "Get in, I've got a surprise for you."

Glancing toward the Porsche, she asked, "This?"

As if he hadn't noticed. "The car?" He turned slightly. "No, something better. Get in." Holding open the door, he waited until she tucked in her legs before he placed her canvas tote bag at her feet. Once inside and seated next to her, he didn't waste any time. Taking off his gloves, he reached for her and kissed her, exploring and tasting with his tongue, nibbling and devouring her lips, his hand finding its way under her sweater, under her bra, on her breasts. It went too far somehow and she didn't know how—oh my God, she thought, the way she shifted around to meet him, she was exhibiting more than a passing familiarity with the front seats of sports cars. "Gideon," she sort of protested, feeling his hands on her buttocks.

His breathing was audible. But, then, so was hers. "Not here."

"Isn't this where nice American girls learned to fuck?" His tongue was running along her neck.

She shook her head slowly, hair tumbling in her eyes, hands on his chest. "I thought you only drove with your gloves on." The look he gave her was a combination of surprise and admiration. She felt like a whore without a hallway.

The pause lasted only long enough for his mouth to find its way back to her breasts. "Not here," she whispered. He seemed to give the matter serious consideration. "Take me home," she added softly.

"My pleasure."

Bastard, as if the whole thing were her idea in the first place.

Makeshift. That was her first impression of the apartment. Thrown together with the barest of necessities, it was spartan, without thought to color or texture or design. A haven after an emotional rupture, a divorce, a foreclosure or a flight from political oppression, something done in haste to provide only the essential. Sasha wandered through the rooms while Gideon did something in the kitchen.

A wine rack with bottles of Châteauneuf du Pape, Lafitte 1982, not bad, a decent Burgundy, compact disc, again Albinoni, books piled on the bare floor, mostly French writers, a copy of *Constanza and Other Stories for Virgins*, by Fuentes, preference or passion, she wondered, some English standards like Byron and Chaucer and Shakespeare, nothing particularly original on that score except for *Tristram Shandy* and a book on mourning by C. S. Lewis. The couch, the seduction pit, she decided, suede and soft and taking up most of the living room, with its floor-to-ceiling windows, faux balconies and dusty brown velvet drapes. A low glass table on which were several pieces of Steuben, a thick candle and an enormous marble ashtray filled with cigarette butts. Next came the bed, located in the only other room in the apartment, neatly made in crisp military fashion, corners tucked in tightly, quilt spread on top, beige and brown, masculine colors, of course, pillow shams to match; a dresser, no photographs, no past life, no memories, only a silver brush and comb and a flask—she unscrewed the top and sniffed—filled with brandy. Bathroom adequate enough, fixtures old, nothing there to suggest anyone else had visited recently or ever for that matter, no remnants of women who had left behind shampoo, cream, makeup, Tampax or douche. Just a razor, toothbrush—one only—soap, cologne—a splash on her hand to know that it was his, the scent she had grown to recognize. Touching a damp towel slung over the rack, she took a deep breath before heading into the kitchen to join him.

The room was unremarkable except that he was in it, arranging things for what she supposed was dinner, before or after, she posed the question silently, and what if she didn't feel like eating, what if she didn't feel like staying. A coffeemaker, blender and orange squeezer were lined up on a butcher block table; knives, plates and cups were drying in a dish rack near the sink, an intricate fish poacher sat on the stove. On a large wooden tray, he was busy piling an assortment of food; pâté and cheese and biscuits and fruit and a bottle of wine chilling in a silver bucket. Surprising to see engraved initials from another era, his mother's perhaps, or one of the two wives, the only item in the house even remotely personal, left over from an English childhood, she mused, leaning against the refrigerator, who ever accused him of ever having been a child.

"Hungry?" he asked as he scooped out some tarama from a small glass jar, adding it to the collection on the tray.

She was aware of tarama on his index finger. He moved in then, offering first a taste of the fish spread.

Without thinking, she took his finger in her mouth, running her tongue up and down and around, taking more than a taste before holding his hand in hers to press the palm against her lips. He was nuzzling her neck. "Gideon," she heard herself. Warning him? Inviting him? Whichever, it was too late. He had her pinned against the cool refrigerator, his tongue in her ear. Oh God, they were going to do it for the first time right here, banging up against the Hotpoint. But then without warning he stopped and held her off, both hands on her shoulders, a quick kiss on the lips. "Do you think you can wait until I take the tray inside?" Her body stiffened, her face felt hot although whatever his game, she had had enough experience to be confident of the effect she had on him.

He turned back to the preparation of the main course. Assuming, no doubt, that she was dessert. How long since someone had so shaken her poise? She decided that she would rather win at playing the whore than the idiot. "So, what's the surprise?" she asked, striking that same pose, arms crossed over breasts.

"Something you'll enjoy, I promise."

How many times she had heard that one—the have-I-got-a-surprise-for-you coming in all different packages. "How long have you lived here?" she asked, needing time to regroup.

"Not long."

On more familiar ground, she moved to an attack. "It's a little barren, isn't it?"

"For the moment it's adequate. The problem is always time, something I never seem to have enough of."

"Did she get everything?"

"She?"

"Your ex-wife."

"Ah, that she. She took almost nothing. The man she went off with owns a large château in the country." He paused. "Filled with antiques."

That still didn't explain the lack of possessions. "Were you very hurt?"

He moved closer. "What would hurt would be if I didn't excite you, or even bored you."

Nothing fit; not his casual sexuality with that tenderness around the mouth. Not that teasing lilt to his voice with the warmth in his eyes. She had assumed, arrogantly, that she had it all under control when the truth was that she had already fallen at least a little in love with him. Unfortunately there were problems like geography and time and the fact that she was from earth and he was from where? The moon.

"Why don't you help me? Carry the wine glasses and the bottle inside," he said, apparently expecting her to do what she was told. He turned to pick up the heavier tray. "Come with me," he added, clearly assuming she would automatically follow. He was right on both counts.

She took it quite well as he took that last bit of control from her, after he got her out of her boots and jeans and sweater and bra, leaving her on his bed in only a pair of lacy bikinis. On his knees, he took her in, for interminable seconds watched before releasing her, then reached for her to draw against him. A reward, perhaps, for being so willing to please. She actually saw it that way.

He told her she was beautiful, that he loved her body, that he wanted her more than he had ever wanted anyone. He told her he couldn't wait, not then, not the first time, later would be better, and there would be a later, all night. Stripped, in more ways than one, of her illusions, Sasha didn't resist.

Lips pursed, head thrown back, she gave him his fill of her. Eyes closed, she heard his throaty voice as he entered her, told her she felt wonderful and coaxed her along. And when it didn't happen, he withdrew and tried with his hand, and then with his mouth, until it did. Everything in insistent slow motion until she thought she would scream.

With his fingers he explored the small of her back, her spine, her shoulders, her neck until he took her in his arms, lying to the side of her to cradle her face in his hands when he kissed her. Bending her right knee, he slid his hand between her legs, along her thigh, her abdomen. Her eyes were fixed on his, watching his every expression. Limbs entwined, she felt his every response, the sudden races and skips of heart as she ran one fingernail down his skin, down the creases of his leg, skimming the full length of his erection. Licking her palm and fingers slowly before she touched all of him, she waited.

He teased with small pecks at the corners of her mouth, her eyes before he kissed her again deeply, before he moved down to her breasts, his tongue making small circles around her nipples, before he parted her legs to keep his promise. He had an idea, he told her, that surprise he had mentioned, and she followed because his touch already enveloped her, because she was already an addict.

Eyes closed, she let it happen, allowing him to bring her along with his tongue, only for her, she was the center of attention, the sounds were hers alone.

When he entered her again—finally—a momentary stab of surprise before she relaxed enough to slip her arms around his back to draw him into her. She had him now, all of him, she knew it, her imprint would last for days, she heard it in his breathing and then felt it in the rush—warm and smooth—as it spilled inside of her. And still, he wanted more. And yes, so did she.

The rain was coming down harder now, pelting the windows of the living room, flashes of lightning across the suede sofa where she lay against him, naked, in his arms. They were sharing the last of the wine. Sometimes he would hold the glass to her lips, sometimes he would hold his lips to her lips, feeding the wine into her mouth.

"She broke my heart," Sasha said softly, "it was so sad."

It wasn't the bottle of wine, she wasn't the least bit high, just satisfied and lazy and full of him. She leaned against his chest, drifting, feeling him over and over, a residual effect of what had been, like a pebble making endless circles on a pond. She turned her face for a kiss on her cheek, settled back once again, her hand on his hand on her breast. And talked.

The woman was so sad and so lonely, all by herself and virtually cut off from her own daughter and her grandchildren.

"Were they ever close?" he wondered.

She had the impression that they were close when Josette was in college and naive and confiding in her. Just after she met Tamir and had already fallen in love with him and was afraid of her feelings and her father. What was even sadder was the tragedy with the baby, the first child, who had been thrown off the terrace in Damascus.

He looked at her. "When was that?"

Everything terrible happened at the same time it seemed, in 1969 and 1970, the tragedy with the child and the events in Jordan when Karami became a rising star in the PLO. But maybe if that first tragedy hadn't happened, the rest of it wouldn't have escalated into such violence. After all, who wouldn't want revenge after a child was murdered.

His voice was distant when he finally spoke. "Who killed the child, did she say?"

No, she didn't actually say although the inference was clear. A political disagreement in that part of the world usually erupted between Arab and Jew and usually ended in death. Maybe the Mossad, or maybe some intramural fight in the PLO?

"Maybe," he said, ". . . so many enemies, so much violence."

It frightened her, Sasha said, all this violence. And it wasn't limited to that part of the world, anybody was a target, anywhere was a battleground, any street, any country, any damn reason. Look at Rome, she said, an innocent child who had no connection to any of it . . . And that wasn't the end of it, it would happen again and again if something didn't change. If something wasn't done about it.

He kissed the top of her head. "I think you're a Mossad agent."

She would probably make a very bad one, she told him, because she was too emotional, she did care about people, and those kind of people, the kind who went into that kind of work, didn't. Still, after being caught in the middle of Rome, of witnessing death and destruction, she wasn't too sure about anything anymore. Including herself.

"Don't talk about it," he said, his voice abruptly intense.

They lived an abnormal life, she went on, having cameras focused in the bedrooms and on the veranda with strangers watching everything on a screen in the basement. What kind of life was that, guards watching every move, every kiss, every cross word—it was a nightmare.

"Is that how they live?"

That was part of it, she said, although the other part was even more bizarre—Karami refused to install an alarm system or have Tunisian police patrol along with his regular PLO guards. For the sake of the children he tried to maintain a normal facade, not like the other PLO leaders who never slept more than one night in the same bed. And most incredible was that he actually kept a spare key under a plotted plant near the front door in case someone was locked out. It would do him in, at least that was what Helene Villeneuve predicted, all that play at maintaining a normal life.

"Why do you suppose she told you so much?"

And who exactly would she tell, someone out to use that kind of information. The woman was lonely, sad and not entirely sober, she needed to talk to someone.

"Maybe there'll be a solution before anything else."

A solution, she responded innocently, was impossible when people were so committed to a cause, so webbed to the problem so that any solution became lost in all the hatred. And if she hadn't understood or realized it before, she did now, after Rome, after pouring over all the files and tapes and documents. Imagine, sleeping with a loaded gun under her pillow, which was what Josette Karami did.

He pulled her closer.

There was something perverted about the whole screwed-up situation, she said against his chest. A baby sleeping in the same room with his mother and father, a gun under a pillow, guards roaming around with machine guns, television cameras in bedrooms. She pulled back, looked at him. What kind of a life was that? "They become prisoners of their own damn revolution," she said.

"Are we going to talk about this all night?"

"No, and anyway, there's nothing left to say except that the veal roast was tough."

"Which is why you ate up all my tarama."

"I loved your tarama."

He turned her around. "What else?"

She kissed him lightly. "The cheese and the biscuits."

"What else?"

She read his eyes then but somehow it wasn't the

moment, she needed time to breathe. "When's your flight?"

"When's yours? The next thing you'll want is my phone number." He reached behind him. "Here's my surprise, the real one." He offered a piece of paper. "Name, address, phone number, what else would you like?"

She took it, not showing her delight. "My flight is at five tomorrow from Orly," she announced.

"And mine is the day after at five from Orly. I'll call you at your hotel when I arrive."

"What if I want to call you?"

"Then you will." He smiled that all-purpose smile of his.

"Where, for instance?" But it didn't matter anymore.

He studied her. "More, you always want more." He had her then, in his arms, his lips on hers. And it seemed debatable which of them wanted more.

But what if he vanished, she wondered along the way, what if he continued being different people until he disappeared forever, one man in the park, another at breakfast, still another at dinner and another in the car, in the kitchen until finally he couldn't hide behind what was happening between them? Interesting, she thought, how she had never been made love to like that. Certainly not by a man who wasn't even completely there.

Chapter Fifteen

FLIES BUZZED AROUND Sasha's head as she stood on line waiting to pass through the metal detector at the airport in Tunis. Where else, she wondered, was there a metal detector *after* disembarkment, where people were checked for weapons and bombs and anti-government pamphlets. At least that was the explanation written in four languages that hung above the entrance to the terminal.

Guards in too-tight jeans swaggered up and down the line, ready to pounce on any infringement or infraction, to confiscate contraband that ranged from liquor to salami to radios to explosives, revolvers on their hips, machine guns cradled in their arms.

The pungent odor from black tobacco cigarettes surrounded her as she stood there. Music poured in through a crackling sound system, melodic Oriental strains, bongos and strings and high-pitched wailing that somehow brought to mind undulating belly dancers in nightclubs in Astoria, Queens. The heat in the airless terminal was oppressive, the stale odor of nerves from hours on a cramped airplane was stifling as she moved slowly past the security and toward the baggage area.

Men in soiled white floor-length robes stood around the carrousel in front of Sasha and behind her and off to the side, waiting for their possessions. Kaffiehs were draped around their heads and shoulders as they nodded and watched and muttered, *Inchallah*, God Willing, when questioned about their plans, *Hamduallah*, Fine thank God, when questioned about their health. Or they merely stared passively when one of their oversized cardboard suitcases tied with dirty rope was dragged up onto the table for inspection.

Older men dressed in shiny Italian suits milled around as well, too much gold on cuffs and fingers and wrists, hair slicked back, shirts white on white, the collars too long, ties covered with initials by mass-marketed designers, briefcases highly polished and all with combination locks, pointy-toed shoes tapping impatiently on the scuffed linoleum floor.

Women held sleeping children in their arms while toddlers clung to their long gowns, the hoods of which draped half their faces so all that was visible were hopeless eyes staring into nowhere. The little girls were mostly skinny while the little boys were mostly round with fleshy breasts that protruded through thin cotton shirts.

The older, more polite youth, eyes glittering and intense, stepped aside for Sasha, the Western woman with sunglasses that hid her face. Were these the cockpit killers, she wondered, the ones who hijacked airplanes and carried weapons, the same breed who drove cars along the Via Veneto to place suitcase bombs among crowds of innocent people, the boys who kissed the guns and caressed the grenades. Her heart pounded in her chest as she pointed to one of her suitcases, the ragged porter hoisting it up to place it on the floor. Her prejudice was astonishing even to her, her automatic stereotyping of an entire race of people.

The more brazen of the youths whistled and stared and clucked and brushed against her as she bent down to move her possessions over to the side. Were those the unreliable ones who were sacrificed because they turned, even for an instant, to admire the pretty girls and so were left for dead by their cohorts? Were those the foot-soldiers who were fed drugs before being strapped into explosive-charged trucks that would ram hotels and military installations; the wild-looking boys with gold teeth and too many religious medals hanging from their necks, the pinky fingernail longer than the rest, tattered shoes and expressions of vacant hostility.

They waited on yet another line, this time for a taxi or rather three taxis. One for Sasha and the suitcases, another for Bernie and the cameras, yet another for the two-man FBN crew and the lights and sound boxes. A woman in the line in front of them, old and bent almost in half, was laughing with indifference before she turned her wrinkled face to fight the wind that had just kicked up. A young man stood next to her, her son perhaps or grandson, a submissive-looking youth with bad skin.

It was seven o'clock, dusk in Tunis, the setting sun hung over Carthage Airport, a musty smoke-filled taxi waited for her, a driver who spoke only a bit of English. Journalist, reporter, he repeated her response, here to talk to our father, Bourguiba, no longer our president but always our father, living peacefully in his region. Sasha held onto the strap over the door, hardly daring to answer or smile or react as the cab rattled along the two-lane badly paved road on the way to the sea and Sidi Bou Said. Now there was President Ben Ali, the new leader, it was all explained with a note of pride as the driver pointed to the picture of the man plastered on the windshield. He was handsome, smiling, yes he was *beau*, that was well-known, too many women, a national pastime here; a coffee perhaps, he asked Sasha, turning around, he would show her the sooks and the mosques for a good price. Watch the road, was her reply. She could feel her features harden. But the driver was oblivious. He could tell, he said, she was a very sensual woman because he was a very sensual man. She wasn't into men, she snapped, so just watch the road and get a move on because she was late. Yes, too many women he sighed, reason enough to love Ben Ali, for that and for socialized medicine and public housing and no more secret police.

But she was already far away, concentrated on the interview, focused on her first encounter with Tamir Karami. Could Miss Journalist please justify the reason for Israel as only a Jewish state, she put the words in the Palestinian's mouth. Better to have given the Jews Berlin after the war, Carl once said at a dinner party. It would have perhaps saved the trouble of building walls only to tear them down; avoided incidents where Carmelite nuns barricade themselves where Auschwitz once stood. Race, she would argue with Karami, reason then to justify Israel. Racist, he would argue back. Still not a good enough reason to commit mass murder, would be her parting retort.

By the time the cab drove up the circular driveway of the Abou Nawas Hotel she had already exhausted every last argument and was still left with the dilemma. By the time she took the camellia from the basket offered by the young boy she had already become a prisoner of her own ambiguity. There must have been easier ways to make a living.

Chapter Sixteen

SHE BELONGED TO THEM. Wasn't that what Helene Ville-neuve said about her daughter—that she belonged to *them*? Standing in the driveway of the villa in Sidi Bou Said, Sasha observed Josette Karami: the black-and-white checkered kaffieh that was tied loosely around her neck, her ease as she conversed in Arabic with her husband's guards, the gestures that she made with her hands and head as she talked. Yet the woman's resemblance to her mother was uncanny, her resemblance to the photographs of that child in that album was remarkable. She seemed unchanged, still delicate and slim and pale and blond, graceful and vulnerable and charming as she walked over to greet her. "Hello," she said, extending her hand, "you must be Sasha."

Sasha's voice shook, she heard it herself. "Hello Mrs. Karami, I'm here alone, you know." An expla-nation, as if she had been asked. "Your driver brought me." Another, as if there had been a doubt. "The crew and my producer won't be coming until later on this afternoon."

Josette merely smiled, the pale eyes crinkling into a hundred fine lines, that same weariness as her mother's evident around her mouth. "I'm delighted we'll have some time alone," she said in a soft French accent. "Unfortunately, my husband is very busy with meet-ings so he won't be able to welcome you until later." She gestured vaguely toward the house. "But he made time for you this afternoon. I think he said that he put aside an hour so you could get acquainted before the cameras began.'' Another diffident smile.

''I was hoping we'd have some time alone as well,'' Sasha responded, her heart racing, her head pounding. Silence. Glancing around the enclosed courtyard, her eyes focused on a low white stucco fence bordering the clay tiles. ''Your flowers are beautiful,'' she said, ''I've never seen such brilliant colors.''

Josette inclined her head toward the garden. ''They are one of my passions,'' she said slowly, one hand shading her eyes from the glaring sun.

It was an invitation to inquire. ''What are the others?''

But Josette was evasive. Walking to the border of the flower beds, she bent to pick a fuchsia jasmine. ''For your hair.''

Sasha took it, unsure whether to stick it behind her ear—silly—or twirl it—also silly. ''Thank you,'' she said, holding it like a candle in the dark.

''I love to watch them grow, like children, to feel as if I'm a little responsible for that growth.''

Sasha felt the despair of having to suppress a hundred questions about children and flowers, of wondering if this woman was forgiving of her husband for causing a child to fall among magnolia leaves on a Rome sidewalk one afternoon.

''Come,'' the woman said, her arm through Sasha's, ''why don't we go inside so I can show you the house? Afterwards we can have coffee on the veranda. It looks over the sea.''

''Where are the children?'' Sasha suddenly remembered.

She smiled. ''So many of my children are living under Occupation. You see, I have many more children than you think, and I carry them with me always. But you mean my flesh and blood, don't you?''

Through that gentle and calm facade, that demeanor of infinite patience and nurturing femininity, Sasha clearly recognized a steel band of militancy.

"I did," Sasha replied carefully, "but if you want to talk about the others, we can." She waited.

The woman took her arm again to head toward the house. "Our son Fahd is in boarding school near Manchester, England, and our daughter Camilla is very French." She smiled. "She goes to a French school near here, not far from Carthage. She'll be home in a little while. And the baby, Tarek, is with his father. But then, he's always with his father." Another slight smile. "And you, do you have children?"

"No, not yet."

They reached the door, walked into the house and stopped in the foyer.

Sasha stood still, registering white walls, blue-and-white tiles on the floors, two caned chairs on either side of a low table inlaid with mosaic, a leafy green plant against one side of the room, several rugs and paintings on the opposite side. A circular staircase was straight ahead leading up to a New Orleans-style balcony that surrounded the entire second level. Josette turned. "My husband's study is upstairs, our room, a dressing room, bathroom and Camilla's room. Our son sleeps downstairs when he's at home, away from the other children because he's the oldest and the man in the family." She shook her head, "Time flies," and seemed lost in thought. "Tarek sleeps with us."

"Your surprise child," Sasha said softly.

"We'll go up later when the others have gone," Josette said, ignoring her. "There are so many problems. As usual." She continued toward the set of double French doors and stopped. "Please." She motioned to Sasha to follow. Opening them, she stepped aside. "This is the dining room. We try to eat in here all together every night whether it's only us or whether we have guests.'' A long rectangular table with fourteen chairs stood in the middle of the bright and airy room, a colored Venetian glass chandelier hung from a high sculptured ceiling, a sideboard covered by a heavy brocade cloth held a silver tea service, a samovar and several miniature paintings on tiny easels. Sasha found her voice. ''Do you entertain a great deal?''

She shook her head. ''Not formally, but our house is open for anyone who is in the general vicinity. My husband has two sisters who have families and of course there are dozens of cousins who visit.'' She took a breath. ''Sometimes we have visitors from Gaza or Ramla, my other children, who come here to recover from being tear-gassed or beaten.''

Argue, the voice urged inside her head, accuse, talk about cause and effect and which came first, the stone or the club, the bomb or the tear-gas canister. ''Not that I'm against recovering from an injury,'' Sasha began, looking around the table at all those imaginary guests, at all those imaginary victims.

''My children are all ages, from newborn to very old.'' She waited for a reaction and when there was none, she added, ''Without any thought to age, they are tear-gassed and beaten.''

''At least they recover,'' Sasha said, echoing Josette's sentiments.

''We have those who don't.''

''There are some forms of violence that eliminate any possibility of recovery.''

Josette ran her hand across the top of a large mahogany arm chair, upholstered in pale green silk. ''We have children who have been in that situation too.'' Her gaze never wavered. ''I assume you're talking about bombs.'' Her eyes remained fixed on Sasha. ''Guns can have the same effect.''

There it was, victim for victim, bomb for bomb, reprisal, retribution, revenge—the three *R*'s of basic Middle Eastern studies. And the refugee camps, another *R*, what about them and the people who lived there—Josette Karami's children of all ages—who slept on thin mattresses on dirt floors, sat on chicken crates to eat rice and beans, used outdoor plumbing—one Chippendale chair might feed several tents of Palestinians.

"We rent the house furnished," Josette said carefully, as if mind-reading was another of her hobbies.

"Isn't it unusual for someone like your husband to make a commitment like that?"

"Like what?"

"A lease."

"Many people come here to talk and try to find a solution."

"Then your husband isn't a revolutionary. Would you call him a politician?"

Josette appeared annoyed. "People come here to talk to the head of a government in exile. This is our White House, my husband is Abu Ammar's second-in-command, like your vice-president." A tight smile crossed her face that did nothing to hide the determination.

"Then he is functioning as a politician within your movement," Sasha pressed.

"We can't define positions the way you can in America, that's a luxury of a government that is established."

"Was your husband a politician when he planned and executed the Rome attack?" She felt her heart beating faster, her hands getting clammy.

"Why don't you ask my husband?" Josette replied calmly. "Come, I'll show you the kitchen."

In time, she cautioned herself, she would debate the issue in time. Playing different parts in this household was a common practice it seemed. Now, between women, there was the question of flowers and gardens and children. And the kitchen.

The man named Talil squatted on the floor in one

corner of the immense tiled room, a large wicker basket before him filled with green beans, a bin next to him, a ceramic bowl on the other side. Snapping the ends of the vegetables, he tossed the stems in the bin and the beans in the bowl.

"Talil," Josette spoke very precisely, "we have a guest." She turned to Sasha. "He speaks very little English." She turned back to Talil and continued in Arabic and when she finished the man stood. *"Marhaba,"* he greeted Sasha.

"Marhaba," Sasha repeated, glancing at Josette.

The woman smiled. "You don't know any Arabic, do you?"

"No, none."

"Well, now you know how to say hello." She took Sasha's arm then, guiding her around the kitchen, pointing out the earthen cylindrical ovens where the flat bread baked pressed against the sides, the molds for the fish, the main food caught daily, the china, the pans, the cupboards filled with the children's snacks, the closets for the grownup's treats—caviar and olives and chocolates. "All gifts from visitors," Josette rushed to explain, "guests who come here from Greece or from France or from Iran."

To discuss a solution, Sasha didn't say, to negotiate a peace with everyone in the world except the other side. A dog barked, a deep ferocious bark that hovered somewhere around a Pavarotti *A*. "That bark sounds like it belongs to a very big dog," Sasha said.

"It does. That's Shwai-shwai, which means slowly in Arabic."

"An unusual name."

"My husband named him that because when he was training him, he kept telling the dog, *'Shwai-shwai'* until the poor animal only responded to that name." She shrugged. "It just stuck."

"What was your husband training him to do?"

"To kill," she responded matter of factly. "During the day he stays downstairs with the men who watch the closed circuit television screen. There's an enclosed pen for him to exercise in or he's walked on the beach on a leash. At night he roams around inside the gates of the house." She smoothed her hair. "He's trained to attack anyone who comes in and who doesn't know his name—Shwai-shwai. Those are the only words that stop him."

"I'm glad you told him," Sasha said.

"Don't be afraid. Whenever you're expected, the dog will be downstairs. It's the people who aren't expected that have reason to be afraid." Josette turned her attention to several clean plates and saucers on the counter.

"Your dishes look French," Sasha observed, although her mind was still on the dog.

"Yes, my mother gave them to me." She closed the cabinet. "All my things were destroyed when the Israelis bombed PLO headquarters."

"Your mother told me."

"My mother," she said quietly before talking once more to Talil in Arabic. "I've asked that he bring out some coffee and cakes. Come, let's sit on the veranda and talk."

Sasha nodded, eyes fixed on the long stainless-steel counter. Cutting boards and tins of sugar and flour and coffee were lined up next to boxes of cereal and a knife rack, copper pots, wooden ladles, a bottle of oil, a basket of oil, a basket of dried peppers, a metal mesh basket filled with sterilized baby bottles and a machine gun.

They sat on the veranda on top of a cliff that overlooked the pleasure-port of Sidi Bou Said. When they first sat down and Sasha admired the deep blue water and masts of dozens of white sailboats docked in the harbor below, Josette explained that the port was no longer used for commercial trade. A rich man's paradise, she confessed with a touch of irony, Arabs and Greeks and European tourists came to sail and to sun. Originally, the cliff-top had been built as a *ribat*, a monastic fortress during the early years of Arab rule, part of an intricate chain that ran through the neighboring towns of Sousee and Monastir and all the way to Tripoli. Eventually this particular village grew around the tomb of a holy man named Sidi Bou Said who was still worshipped in the central mosque.

"In the summer when my husband and I sit out here in the evenings we can hear the *malouf* music coming from the cafes below."

"It's a beautiful place."

"We are strangers." She gazed out toward the sea. "I feel like a stranger in my own house sometimes, certainly in a strange country, and I probably will until I can live in our own land."

"Israel?"

"Palestine."

"But you have a country and a passport if you choose to—France."

"Not any longer."

"By your choice."

"There were reasons that went deeper than simply being born in a country where there is a government and a system that apparently work."

"That's what fascinates me about you," Sasha began, "this commitment to your husband's cause . . ."

"My cause."

"When did it become your cause, before you fell in love with him or after?"

"My husband is my life. How can I explain? His blood is inside of me, his pain and his joy. Without him I would not exist, I would have no life."

"Then you took up his cause after you fell in love with him."

"Nothing in this world happens without a reason and I believe I was guided to this struggle, sent to my husband not only as his wife and mother of his children but to help liberate his people from oppression."

"You've taken it on, his history, his people, his fight as if it's your own."

"It is not my own, it is ours, my children's and therefore mine, my husband's and therefore mine."

In any other place with any other woman discussing any other man, this communal thinking might have been about something else, like stocks or bonds or real estate. Here, it was about pain. "You sound as if you had no interests or identity before you met your husband."

"What did I have? What have I given up? An obsession with the perfect sauce or my father's hatred over the outcome of the Algerian war or my mother's materialistic view of the world? Would that have interested you?"

"I think I might have found something in my own country to interest me, challenge me."

"I found my husband."

"Is he more important than your children?"

"Without him there would be no children." She considered. "Yes, perhaps he is, and perhaps that makes me a bad mother, I don't know."

"Do the Palestinian people mistrust you because you're not an Arab?"

"Some still do, less now than in the beginning. They used to say it was impossible to understand without having lived through the humiliation and the violence. But what is going on now is as bad, what is happening at the hands of the Zionists is perhaps even worse."

"I was in Rome," Sasha announced in an even voice.

"Yes, I knew that," Josette replied in a subdued but not apologetic tone.

"There were dozens of dead and injured lying all over the street including a small child who was killed instantly, a little boy who had nothing to do with your revolution.'' Still, her voice was flat. "That can't possibly make you feel vindicated or proud. You can't believe that his death will help other people.'' The climb had begun, a steep and winding road that inevitably ended in a fork where one way was a dead end while the other was mined. Anything would have been easier at that point, anything instead of five thousand years of hatred.

"In 1948,'' Josette countered, "the Zionists murdered two hundred and fifty men, women, and children in the village of Deir Yassen near Jerusalem.''

Sasha felt a sudden and overwhelming fury for having been elected to the defense. "And what about Hama?'' Hama, she reviewed quickly in her mind, the Syrian city where President Assad's troops put down a rebellion and in the process murdered twenty thousand of their own people.

"That was a family feud.''

"What wasn't?'' Sasha shot back. "Families have been splitting and branching off and wandering over other people's borders for centuries.'' Six million murdered in Europe, she didn't say, and there was still guilt for not resisting. "There's no excuse in the world for killing innocent people who aren't responsible for your . . . situation.''

"The world is as much responsible for our oppression as it was for the Holocaust.''

"We didn't—'' she began and then stopped when she realized she had taken it on. It was official now, for some reason she had made herself a part of it after all these years of ignoring her involvement.

"Are you a Zionist?''

"No.''

"But you are a Jew?''

Being a "Jew,'' especially as Josette Karami said it, sounded much worse than being "Jewish.'' "Yes.''

"Really a Jew, or the way I am a Palestinian?" Josette said.

"Really a Jew, but also a Jew the way you are a Palestinian."

"I understand."

"What I was going to say was that the Jews didn't kill innocent people during the Holocaust to call attention to what was happening to them."

"Perhaps we learned from them and perhaps they would have if they had the chance and perhaps that's the reason for all the aggression now, to make up for that passivity."

"There's resistance and then there's mindless violence like Rome."

"We struggled peacefully until we were pushed to this point." But the words seemed to jump off a poster, slogans that were spoken over and over again. What struck Sasha was that the more this woman spoke of violence and war, the more serene and calm and sure she became.

"Violence is a cry from the heart of our people. The world never listens to anything else. It's only because of violence that anybody ever stopped to consider what was happening to our land, only then was the possibility of an injustice considered." She glanced around. "More coffee?" A brief look of distress before she clapped her hands once. "Our coffee man isn't here. Unfortunately, there was an attempt on his life," she said without further explanation. Talil appeared then, carrying a tray with two more small glass cups filled with thick coffee. *"Shukran,"* Josette said before turning her attention back to Sasha.

"Where is he now?" Sasha asked.

"Recovering from a gunshot wound near his family's house in Jordan."

"Who tried to kill him?"

"You're getting an instant lesson in our revolution,"

Josette said quietly. "We were told it was Abu Nidal's group but then, every time there is an attempt on a Palestinian's life we're told it is Abu Nidal's group." She took a breath. "You see, the Jews use Abu Nidal to kill our people, or even to kill their own people as a pretense to begin a war."

Sasha's mind rebelled against further argument with such a closed mind. "The program we're going to do is called 'Family,' " she said, abruptly changing the subject, "so maybe we should talk more about your relationship with your husband."

There was barely a pause. "My husband is a fatalist," Josette began, "which means that he knows his life can end at any time. He needs us near."

"Doesn't that make you afraid? Haven't you tried to modify his priorities?"

Josette sounded subdued. "Our whole existence is devoted to the struggle. It's not possible to separate emotion or to modify priorities."

"But there must be something else that binds you, something else that you talk about, something else that concerns you."

"To ignore something doesn't make it go away. And then there is the question of our mission. We can't let the world forget."

She needed to find common ground here or the whole interview would turn into nothing more than a bitter debate—Josette Karami for her adopted cause, Sasha Beale for hers. "As a woman, don't you feel revolted by the violence?" But even before she heard the response, she knew it wouldn't work. She was cuing her for the predictable.

"When you ask that question you're referring to the violence on our side, aren't you?"

"Probably," Sasha said. "Yes."

"Maybe we should talk about my relationship with him," Josette said, "your viewers will understand that.'' She paused a moment. ''My husband is better at explaining the other part of it.''

There was no resistance, in fact, there was only relief. Both of them, Sasha reasoned, were in unfamiliar territory. ''How do you love someone that much,'' Sasha asked, ''to the exclusion of everything else?'' The first genuine question since the conversation began. Help me, she thought, explain it so I can recognize the symptoms and know how it starts, that passion and obsession that eventually turns into commitment and sacrifice and forgetting about who the hell you really are. What was it Josette's mother said in Paris—''My cats go into heat too, you know.''

''I loved him from the first moment I saw him.''

''It must have been an incredible physical attraction.''

''It was much more than that.''

''What can be more than that—especially in the beginning?''

''It was as if I had known him all my life, in another life, as if there had never been anyone else before him, as if I had been waiting only for him.''

''Didn't that frighten you, that intensity?''

Josette smiled a wintry smile. ''Life is frightening, isn't it?''

''Some lives are more frightening than others.''

''Emotional risk can be as frightening as physical.''

''More,'' Sasha agreed. ''And as your love grew, it became more and more wrapped up in your husband's cause?''

''Our cause.''

''Did you ever wonder how different your lives might have been if the situation were different?''

''Wondering is a luxury.''

''Sometimes sacrifice is a luxury,'' Sasha said, and saw a look of annoyance cross Josette's face.

"Tell me," Josette said, "have you ever made a total commitment to another human being?"

"I chose a career," Sasha said tersely, not prepared to hand over a piece of herself. "Or maybe it chose me. Sometimes I seem to be a prisoner of my job."

"Everyone is a prisoner of something," said the true-believer.

She was due back at the hotel for lunch with Bernie. Past the white stucco houses with flat roofs, down the winding cobblestone streets toward the sea, along the outdoor sooks and the stands with rows of fresh fruit, the same thought kept running through her mind. Had she finally joined that not-so-exclusive club of women who found themselves obsessed and passionate about a man? Impossible, she argued inside her head, at least it wasn't that kind of obsession and passion Josette Karami had about her husband. With Gideon, it wasn't a question of giving up her politics, friends and family. With Gideon, the big danger was just another disappointment and she was becoming an expert at handling something like that.

Chapter Seventeen

AGAIN THIS MORNING Gideon was awakened by the same dream. He sat up in bed and reached for a cigarette, that same image so clear before his eyes.

A little boy, his curly hair falling over his brow, his mouth set in determination, his pudgy legs bare below the knees, was peddling his tricycle as fast as he could across a suburban street. The car in the distance was an American model, an electric blue trimmed in chrome, tailfins near the rear bumpers. Gideon was certain about the tailfins.

Everything happened so quickly, it seemed. The car turned the corner to accelerate just as the child reached the middle of the street. But for some reason the driver was momentarily distracted either by a companion in the passenger seat or by a road map or by the sun glaring through the windshield.

Helpless and unable to move, Gideon watched from a distance, his feet encased in some kind of cement, his voice lost somewhere in the wind when he tried to call out to warn the boy, to signal the driver to swerve or to brake. Move, pedal faster, he mouthed the words silently in his dream, his jaw sore from twisting the muscles; hurry, move, his silent screams echoed in his head. And then the crash that he couldn't avoid watching. He was unable to turn his head or to avert his eyes, he was forced to witness the impact, to see the broken body of the child after it landed yards away, to view the twisted pieces of metal all over the road, the mangled grill of that American electric blue automobile on somebody's front lawn. And finally, to notice pieces of the boy's red jacket caught on the tip of those tailfins. Gideon was certain about the tailfins.

Just a dream, he told himself when he woke up this morning, just a dream. It hadn't happened like that and anyway, he hadn't been there to see it. Just a dream, because the reality was even worse. Nothing was fading, he knew that only too well, nothing was getting easier except that somehow he always managed to end every unbearable dream with the image of Sasha's face. He only managed to calm himself by summoning her into his consciousness. Until the next time.

Rafi ordered the last of the slides shown this morning before everyone went off in different directions.

Yoram brought down the screen while Ben adjusted the projector, both men stepped aside when Rafi got up to take control of the remote. Ronnie was seated at the far end of the table looking fresh and well-rested, dressed in a button-down shirt, striped tie and conservative gray suit. Next to him was Ya'Acov, also cleanshaven and dressed for an office, a leather attaché case lying on the table before him. Gideon sat alone, silent, deep circles under his eyes, badly in need of a shave, his collar open, a sweater wrapped around his shoulders. He was drawing attached rectangular boxes on a yellow pad, half of the lined page was already covered with neat and precise little rectangular boxes.

"The plane leaves at noon," Rafi announced, looking over at Ronnie, "which means you should be at the airport no later than eleven-thirty. The cargo will be in the back of the ambassador's station wagon for the trip to the airport. I'm glad that you'll have a few days in Israel, Ronnie."

Ronnie nodded.

"It gives you a chance to see the baby," Rafi added before looking at Yoram, who asked, "Who takes the cargo from Israel?"

"With no complications, Ya'Acov will accompany the body as far as the power station."

Gideon lit a cigarette and sat back in the chair. "What kind of complications?"

"Who knows?" Rafi shrugged. "We could have another bunch of suicidal heroes waiting for us at the border."

"Is that the final stop?" Gideon asked.

"As far as we're concerned it is," Rafi answered. "The body will be held under guard at the power station until you're finished with business at Sidi Bou Said. Then Saba Khalil will be notified of his brother's death. We'll arrange for the body to be transported over the border into Jordan." He looked around the table. "Where he's buried is their business, although I suspect it won't be in the Territories." Pulling the long cord over to the table, he sat down. "Let's get this over with so we can keep some semblance of a schedule." He consulted his watch. "I understand the ambassador has visitors this afternoon to discuss the Gulf crisis so he'd like the embassy cleared out before then." He smiled. "Tell me, how much time is needed before a crisis gets reduced to a political state of affairs?"

As Rafi clicked on the first slide he told Gideon, "There's a room upstairs for you to work, your flight to Tunis doesn't leave until five."

"I've changed it. I'm on the two o'clock out of Orly."

Karami was the first image to appear on the screen. Gideon's Quest, Rafi called him. He was dressed in a suit, walking surrounded by his bodyguards on what looked like a Paris street. In the next frame he was wearing robes and a kiffieh, in the next he was in jeans and a T-shirt and in a bathing suit at the beach in the last one. Whatever he was wearing, the man was easy to recognize. He was unchanged except for the weight gain, the same as at the beginning of his career, his expression somber, his gestures and movements calm and precise. Sixteen years of tracking and waiting and missing, Rafi thought, mostly waiting, but then patience was something rewarded with results.

The next series of slides of Karami was taken at the Palestinian National Council meeting in Algeria the year before. "Before he got the gut," Rafi commented.

"The good life," Ben added.

"Before he rediscovered pistachio nuts," Yoram said, "thanks to his new Iranian friends."

Gideon glanced up. "No pistachio nuts in Iraq?"

Another slide of Karami walking with two other PLO luminaries through the streets of Larnaca. Two days later his two friends were blown up in a late model BMW. Someone said it was a pity since the car had been fitted with a brand-new emission system and handled beautifully on the winding Cyprus roads.

Next, Karami was shown in a meeting with King Fahd of Saudi Arabia in the good old days when Saudi petrol dollars still flowed into Palestinian coffers, before Abu Ammar put his money on the wrong horse.

"Long before King Fahd discovered which side of the desert his friends were on," Ronnie said.

"Long before the King refused to take his Palestinian brothers' phone calls," someone else put in.

"Even the ones that weren't collect," Rafi ordered.

The last slide was of Karami on a boat as he prepared to sail out of the port of Tripoli in Lebanon after the 1982 war. Flanking him were his wife and several senior Fatah officers, all of them grinning into the camera.

"Look at them, all smiling and making the V for victory sign," Rafi said. "Yet they had just been thrown out of Lebanon, which meant they had lost their base of operations.''

"Tossed out without any warning by the Syrians," Yoram added.

"They lost their home," Ronnie said.

"Not to be confused with their homeland," from Rafi.

Accompanied by her children, Josette Karami was next, wandering in a sook not far from the villa in Sidi Bou Said. Fahd, the oldest boy, looked exactly like her except for his dark coloring, and Camilla, the daughter, also looked like her except she too had dark hair and olive skin. But it was the baby, Tarek, whose looks were the most startling, or rather, whose resemblance to his father was the most noticeable. It was uncanny how much the child looked like Tamir, especially in profile.

Not a hair on their heads, Rafi now warned, the wife and children were not to be touched, avoid contact at all costs. If there was contact and if there was no other alternative, then the carotid artery was to be pressed for not more than thirty seconds to induce only unconsciousness. But what if Sasha Beale's information was correct, someone asked—and they had no reason to believe that it wasn't—and Josette Karami did keep a gun under her pillow? Shoot in the leg or in the hand or in the foot, were Rafi's instructions. Then pump every last round into Karami's head. Regardless of what appeared to be his condition, never mind if indications were that all life had already seeped from his body, the rest of the bullets into his head. Ideally, of course, the gun under the pillow should be removed and disposed of in advance. He turned to Gideon. "If you could somehow arrange that, without arousing suspicion, that would be helpful.''

"Three of you," Rafi gestured to Yoram, Ben and Ya'Acov—"keep a remaining nine bullets among you. Ronnie, make sure you've got an extra clip for your twenty-two.'' And of course Gideon would be the last one out, so it was his job to make sure that there was no one left alive, no one—except the wife and the children and if, by any chance, they were injured, then an ambulance was to be called and the front door left unlocked and open. ''Crazy Israelis,'' Rafi muttered, shaking his head before clicking the remote to the next slide, Sasha Beale.

They had her from the beginning, shots from her broadcasts in Rome after it happened, looking haggard and unsteady. And vulnerable, Gideon thought to himself. They had her in Paris before Gideon, in Paris after Gideon, that jog through the Tuileries and then walking out of the FBN Bureau somewhere near the Trocadero, looking professional and chic and energetic. And beautiful, Gideon observed silently. At the airport with Bernie Hernandez, boarding the plane for Tunisia, arriving in Tunisia, checking into the hotel accompanied by her two-man French crew, looking apprehensive and nervous and weary. And tough, Gideon noted. Sasha in evening clothes getting into Gideon's car and then getting out of Gideon's car, all action limited to the driveway in front of the George V Hotel. ''Gideon's assignment,'' Rafi explained as if any of them needed reminding. ''She's our only remaining access inside the house now since we discovered our error concerning the coffee man.'' He jotted something down on a piece of paper. ''Which means that we'll be at a disadvantage about precise distances around the interior from room to room or about head counts when it comes to guards.'' He looked at Gideon. ''Unless you can manage to get that information without arousing her suspicions. Remember, if you do and if she calls you on it, we'll have no choice but to postpone.'' He coughed. ''Questions, anyone?''

There was some shuffling of paper, but no questions.

It was all Gideon could do not to jump up and rip down the screen. He felt a searing pain in his gut and a shortness of breath. He ground out his cigarette as Rafi enlarged and froze the last frame of her face on the screen. She filled up the room—every line, pore, blemish—with that quizzical expression of hers, hair that looked as if it needed a good brushing, eyes bright and clear as they focused into the unseen telephoto lens. Nothing surprised him about her. After all, he was already familiar with every detail of every inch of her face and body.

Rafi stood to walk over to a credenza where a tray holding six crystal glasses and a matching decanter filled with brandy had been placed earlier. He poured slowly, filling each one before turning to invite everyone over to lift a glass. They all came except Gideon. "A toast," Rafi told him, "come and make a toast." Gideon stood. "To what?" he asked, walking slowly toward the door, pausing with his hand on the knob. "To health and a safe return," Ronnie began. "To Israel," Yoram and Ben said in unison. Gideon waited. "To Golda," Ya'Acov said reverently. "To life," Rafi added. "I was afraid of that," Gideon said softly as he turned to walk out of the room.

Chapter Eighteen

EVIL HAD A POT BELLY. Sasha didn't expect that. Nor did she expect the receding hair line, average height and slumped posture. Neither did she expect the plaid flannel shirt, sleeves rolled up to the elbow, baggy pants and crumpled blue handkerchief protruding from the back pocket. Nor did she expect the way he kissed his baby on the forehead before handing him to his wife, touching his wife's cheek as he did. It didn't fit the way he shifted his shoulder holster and repositioned his gun before walking slowly toward where Sasha stood with Bernie in the driveway of the villa.

Hand outstretched, Tamir Karami focused first on Sasha. "Hello, Sasha Beale, welcome."

"How do you do, Mr. Kamari." She told herself she couldn't show fear or intimidation or this whole exercise in television drama would be ruined from the start.

"If you don't mind," he said, "please call me Abu Fahd or Tamir. The Jews used to call my father Mr. Karami in a tone that was pseudorespectful." He turned to Bernie. "And you must be the producer, Mr. Hernandez."

"Call me Bernie. The cops used to call my father Mr. Hernandez every time they came to collect their protection money." Tough-guy Hernandez, Sasha observed, certainly didn't sound frightened even though he looked pale and his bottom lip trembled

236

slightly. "You've got a spectacular view here," Bernie added.

"Unfortunately it's a borrowed view. We would prefer looking out over our olive groves in Ramla." His expression was so serious. Sasha expected different. But did she think fire would stream from his mouth, that he would have small black crosses for eyes and three sixes carved over his brow?

"What are the chances of you getting that view in the next few years?

"There is no time frame at this point, but if we let up in our struggle the chances diminish." His eyes never wavered, his face never changed its expression. Countless times throughout her career when she interviewed criminals in New York, she had seen that blank cold stare that warned her that they were of a different species, not necessarily human. They appeared to her without remorse or reason, unable to offer rational explanations or regret for murdering or mutilating. Tamir Karami, she had to acknowledge, was different—educated and clever, a politician, like other politicians, skilled in logic or at least rhetoric . . .

Bernie seemed ill at ease. "Well, uh, good luck on those olive trees," he said.

"Let us pray that your next visit to us will be in Palestine."

"Would there still be room for an Israel?"

"As far as we are concerned there is room for everyone." There it is again, that political glibness, that ability to say the right thing, to rationalize every act he had ever committed in the name of the cause.

"I guess I'd better get going to scout out locations for the show," Bernie announced. Sasha might have pressed that other point, about there being room for everyone. In fact, she did press the point. "What about the PLO charter, the covenant that calls for the step-by-step elimination of Israel?"

"Sasha," Bernie jumped in, "come on."

Tamir smiled. "No, it's all right." He turned to Sasha. "We will discuss everything. I'm sure we'll be seeing a great deal of each other. Do you play backgammon?" he asked Bernie.

"One of my favorite games."

Karami turned to Sasha. "Do you?"

"I'm afraid I don't," she said.

"Perhaps we'll have a chance to play a few games," he said to Bernie before turning back to Sasha. "We'll go upstairs to my office to talk."

Two bodyguards with submachine guns slung across their chests and revolvers stuck in the waistbands of their pants materialized. Several words of Arabic were exchanged before Karami spoke to Sasha. "I've asked that we not be interrupted for about an hour. Is that enough time?"

"More than enough," she said, and glanced at Bernie, who dissolved into the car to be driven off to explore the area for good outdoor sites.

The office was uncluttered. A desk, a chair; two chairs for visitors, a small sofa, a rug, four file cabinets and a fax machine. On the walls were photographs of men, martyrs, he explained, Palestinian leaders who had been "gunned down by the Israelis" or who had died during battles and wars "to liberate their land." Eleven of them had been on the old woman's original list back in the 70s—Golda's hit list. And they had all been eliminated, one by one over the years. He was the last one who remained and for how long was anybody's guess. He started to say something about his coffee man and then stopped. "I don't want my wife to be upset, but we have reason to believe he is not coming back. I've had reports that he has been murdered by the Jews." He shrugged. "So you see what I mean, it's only a question of time before I'm next." The subject was apparently closed. "Coffee or green tea?" he asked.

"Green tea," she replied, prepared to take it all in, from tea to terrorism, the Stanislavsky method of reporting, except she hoped she wasn't around when *it* happened. One disaster a year was sufficient. But how could anyone be so philosophical about his death, unless it was all an act, a ploy to make her favorably disposed toward a man who admitted he had killed. "How can you be sure that the Israelis killed your coffee man?" she asked.

His eyes smiled. "Should I trust the press enough to tell you my sources of information?"

"No, of course not," she answered quickly, "but it's a strong accusation, or assumption on your part."

"It is neither an accusation nor an assumption. It is the truth."

"And you deal only in truth?" She was challenging him too soon. Save it for the camera.

"No, not only," he said patiently. "After all, we're human beings, just like you Americans." He smiled. "Does your government always tell the truth?"

He was Yul Brynner playing the King, Zero Mostel playing Tevya. he was too good at it, too practiced. "Why do the Palestinian people always seem to sabotage themselves politically?" she asked casually.

He appeared more interested. "Perhaps because we have too many leaders or we have one leader trying to please too many people."

"I was being more specific than that."

"Are you referring to our taking the side of Iraq?"

"Before Iraq walked into Kuwait, when the PLO and the Americans had a dialogue going in Tunisia. That dialogue was broken off because of an attempted terrorist attack on an Israeli beach."

"The Americans broke it off because Chairman

Arafat refused to condemn Abbul Abbas for that attack.''

''Wouldn't it have been better for the PLO if Arafat had condemned it?''

''Why should we have taken sides with the Americans and the Israelis and risked our own position of leadership within the PLO?''

''At this point, it doesn't matter, it's done. But when there was an opportunity to get back into the good graces of the Americans, you didn't. When Iraq took over Kuwait, there was an opportunity to side with the other Arab nations who were supporting you all these years. Instead you sided with Iraq.''

''Those other Arab nations were only giving us money. Iraq offered us the chance for dignity and a homeland.''

''Without the money you can't have survived.''

''The object of our revolution is land.''

''And if you got that land, would you live there?''

He took a sip of coffee. ''What happened to the Jews when they settled on our land was interesting. They were once poets and musicians and political strategists and thinkers. Did you know that after the Second World War, after the 1948 War of Independence, the Israelis had the greatest symphony orchestra in the world? Those who survived were the first violinists and first cellists from all the orchestras all over Europe. And then came prosperity when their homeland changed into suburban communities with wall-to-wall carpeting, Sweet and Low, the good life, except for those thirty days a year when the men played soldier. Only a handful remembered what it was like to sacrifice for a belief, and that handful is dying out now.'' He leaned closer. ''That will be the downfall of the Jews, not nuclear weapons coming from Iraq or rushes across the border from Jordan or even attacks by us. Their downfall will be their own Americanized comforts.'' He smiled. ''You've created a monster, you see, you've created the worst of what you are.''

''How do you explain the fact that the Arabs keep losing wars to that complacent little country?''

''Because we have the misfortune of constantly underestimating the enemy.'' He paused to remove his shoulder holster and gun, to place the gun in the top desk drawer and the shoulder holster on top of the desk.

''How would you describe yourself?'' she asked, her eyes on his props.

''I'm the military commander of the Palestinian Liberation Organization.''

''Then why do you live like this,'' she went on, ''with all this suburban comfort and luxury?'' She gestured around the room. ''What are you doing here when your people are living in camps?''

''You think I should be with them? I was.''

''Why did you leave?''

''Because it became more useful to live here to receive world leaders who could help us take back what is ours. Palestine.''

''So you're looking for a political solution.''

The lights dimmed in his eyes. ''Of course we're trying to arrange a political solution, we're trying anything we can.''

''A political solution and a military one and I'm not even using the word—''

''What word?''

''Terrorism,'' she said, having to say it. Killing, murdering, she didn't say it although they were all part of the same thing.

''Use it if you like.'' He shrugged. ''It's been used before.''

''What happened in Rome wasn't exactly an example of a political solution,'' she began slowly, her eyes never leaving his face.

He ignored it. "We know you were there, we didn't know you were an expert on the Middle East."

"I'm not, but something like Rome cuts away the abstract to the real. It's a crash course in your politics." She smiled.

"It's too bad we don't have you on our side. If nothing else you'd confuse the issues sufficiently." He shook his head. "You could probably present any argument and have people walking away not quite sure what you really said or meant or how they lost . . . Tell me, how long have you been a Zionist?"

"Your own wife decided I wasn't a Zionist, only a Jew and maybe a Jew the way she's a Palestinian." Actually, she wasn't quite sure what a Zionist was anymore. Tilling the soil, planting trees, those were the activities Golda wrote about when she first arrived here. Now it had something to do with surface-to-air missiles and nuclear warheads. Now most of the trenches dug were for missile launchers, most of the trees planted were to camouflage airstrips. Toss it back to him. "What is your definition of Zionism?"

He was all prepared, as he had been many times before: "Zionism is the existence of one state at the expense of another. Zionism is citizenship in Israel that applies only to Jews. Zionism is racism."

The old U.N. General Assembly Arab-driven resolution. She felt her face grow hot. "And I suppose they allow Jews to become citizens in Jordan or Kuwait or Saudi Arabia?"

"No, they don't."

"Then what's the difference?"

"Those countries are not in territorial dispute."

"You're mixing up issues. And several of them are— in territorial dispute."

"I will give you a little background. We should start at the beginning, about my family and why I am less careful about my life than most of our other leaders."

He gazed at the men who had been on that list. "You see, the men in those photographs were very careful. Now they're dead. In the end it's all a question of fate."

"I want you to know, Abu Fahd," she began, using his *nom de guerre* as though she accepted his profession, "the name of this program is 'Family.' You can talk about the personal side of your life if that's what you prefer. You're under no obligation to discuss anything else."

"Did you explain that to my wife?"

"We talked about it briefly."

"And what did she say?"

"Probably the same thing you're going to say."

He extended his hands, palms up. "At least on that issue we're harmonious."

"I got the feeling that you were harmonious on all issues."

It was his turn to smile briefly. "There are always disputes and disagreements in a marriage, and my wife is a determined woman."

"Can you give me an example?" It struck her then that this little get-together, this little getting-to-know-the-family session could be viewed as either a day in Hitler's bunker with the original tenants or a bizarre version of "The Newlywed Game." But Maury had created this documentary and chose to star people who were different from most people in most families.

"Any convert to a religion or to a cause is usually stricter than those of us who have been born to it. My wife feels that I'm too lenient, for example, and forgiving because I would be willing, under certain conditions, to negotiate with the Israelis. Not just with any Israeli, and certainly not with an Israeli from the Labor party. I've always said that I'd be willing to sit down with Ariel Sharon, the worst of them all, because if he made an agreement I'd know that it would be honored by all the other Israelis. No one could accuse him of selling his people or sacrificing his beliefs.''

''Then any treaty made with the PLO should be made with someone as fanatic, like Ahmed Jebril, for instance, the man who blew up the Pan Am plane, and not with Yasir Arafat.''

''If we all agreed with such a scenario, as you call it, Chairman Arafat would be long gone. One suspects the reason he's still alive, the reason the Israelis haven't killed him is that they're afraid of who would follow.''

''How else do you and your wife disagree?''

He settled back in his chair. ''She thinks I'm too lenient with the children, but then that's because I never really had a childhood and she did. She thinks I keep too much inside, that I suffer silently instead of talking things out more with her or with my colleagues.'' He touched his holster, brushing off some dust from one of the straps. ''She thinks I work too hard and take on too many problems that could be delegated to others.''

A terrorist henpecked husband?

''She thinks I eat too much of the wrong foods.'' He patted his stomach. ''That I am beginning to look like a grocer from Nablus.''

Butcher. That was the word that came to mind, and she wondered if it showed on her face. ''It would be good if you talked about your marriage and your feelings about each other on camera.''

''Will that make your audience think of us as human beings?'' There was a touch of demeaning sarcasm, more than a touch. ''Isn't that the idea? The man behind the gun?''

She had no intention of getting involved in what was obviously a test of wills that could only end up diminishing everything she had come here to do. But then again, she had no intention of wasting time, either hers or his or the audience's. "I think it will help viewers to relate more to you, although I can't predict reactions."

"Are you interested in reasons?"

"What kind?"

"Why we do what we do."

"Your wife mentioned getting the world's attention for your cause. Isn't it a steep price when innocent people are killed?"

"Innocent people are killed every day in Hebron and Gaza."

"By your choice those places have become battle-grounds."

"Are you saying morality is a question of geography?"

"Aren't you?" she came back, as if the entire issue hinged on whether or not she could win this debate, a debate with a man whose life's work was staged disaster.

"Let me begin at the beginning."

And the beginning sounded as if it came straight out of a propaganda brochure, PLO material that was passed out to visitors who came to PLO headquarters from all over the world . . .

"When I was a small boy the Jews came to take over our town of Ramla. What I saw then remains with me as clearly as the day it happened, Jewish soldiers shooting women and children, breaking down the doors of houses and dragging old people into the streets, beating them to death in front of their families and friends. We hid in mosques and it was only because a holy man walked out into the middle of the road with a white flag that the soldiers didn't storm the mosque. They came inside quietly and separated us, women and children and old people in one group, men and boys in another." He took a sip of tea. "They were taken away to detention camps."

"Were you among them?"

"No, I was under twelve so I remained with my mother and little sisters and brothers. Our house was destroyed so we went to a neighbor's. Every night the soldiers would push their way inside to rummage through everything under the pretext of looking for weapons. It was their way of intimidating us so that we would give up and run away from our house and our land." He took a breath. "One night the Zionists announced over the town loudspeaker that we were to come to the town square. They told us that busses would take us to Nablus but they couldn't tell us when. We were told that we had to live on the side of the road. We slept there and waited there for five days and nights until on the fifth night, soldiers ordered the old men to begin walking toward Nablus.

"Where were you?"

"Still with my mother, my grandmother, my aunt and my three little sisters and brothers." He seemed far away then. "The next night the busses finally arrived and we were told that we could take only one suitcase with us, everything we owned had to fit into one bag or it would be taken away." His eyes focused on her once again. "We expected that we would be driven all the way to Nablus but the busses stopped about twenty miles away and we were ordered off."

He glanced at a map of the Middle East that hung on the wall. The portion that was Israel was blacked out and on it was written "Zionist Entity." "We were told that we would have to walk the rest of the way to Nablus. Some of the women were sick and old, others were pregnant or carrying two and three small infants and children. The Jews wanted us to arrive in Nablus exhausted and frightened. They counted on us telling the others about the horrors we had suffered on the road. It made it easier for them to capture the country city by city. As the word spread, there would be less resistance.''

''But you had a chance in 1947 to have a state of your own. It was offered to you by the United Nations. Why did the Palestinians refuse it?''

''Why doesn't matter. It was a mistake.''

''Then why didn't the Arabs try and remedy that mistake by giving you a country when they controlled the Territories between 1948 and 1967?'' She leaned forward. ''Why did the world wait until Israel controlled the Territories after 1967 to make a claim on that land?''

''Because the Arabs wanted us for other reasons.''

''What reasons?''

''Homeless, we would fight the Jews for them, we had an incentive, an interest in it. After all, they had been humiliated in 1967, then again in 1973. They believed we would be complacent and comfortable settled in a homeland, not interested in rushing into a war.''

''Under those circumstances you should hold the Arabs at least partly responsible for the outcome.''

''Don't think that I have ever accused the Arabs of doing what was best for my people.'' He sighed. ''But that's another story and one that would do no good now to talk about. We need them. They are our only allies regardless of what any other well-intentioned country claims.''

''Go on with your story.''

He seemed pleased to oblige her. ''We walked or at least we tried to walk, but the Jews kept shelling us with artillery and mortar bombs. We dove behind rocks for cover, except for some of the women who ran out in panic with their children . . .''

She waited.

''They were killed. But the ones who were able to continue actually believed that once they reached Nablus they would be safe. Some of the women were so exhausted they had to abandon their children on the road so they could go on for help. Even my grand-mother advised my mother to leave three behind, she was so sure my mother would be killed trying to run with four little ones in her arms or clinging to her skirts.''

''Why didn't they leave some of the women with the children to watch them while the others went for help?''

''Do you want me to say it's because we're primitive?''

''I want you to say whatever you believe,'' she replied calmly.

''We were under siege and it was impossible to reason. Did the *Jews* reason when they walked into the ovens?''

She could hardly accept the comparison, but she said nothing.

''Most of the other families didn't have an older child to help carry the younger ones. Many infants and little ones were left behind because there was no one to carry them. Others were left behind because their mothers had been killed by the shells and mortars.'' He carefully studied his hands. ''That is something I can never forget.''

''How old were you?''

''Four years old.''

''Four? A remarkable memory for details. And that was the beginning?''

''That was the beginning for me.''

''Shouldn't it have made you hate violence instead of using it as a means to an end?''

He had a ready answer. ''We were silent for years. Violence brought our cause to the world, the media brought it to the world's attention. Actually I have you to thank for the recognition.''

Afraid that her rage would show, she almost whis-

pered her response. "Your cause hasn't advanced because of that violence."

"Dialogues have begun because of it."

"And ended."

"And will begin again."

"Out of fear."

"The reasons are immaterial."

She turned her head. "That map next to the map of
the Middle East, what are all those red pins for?"

"Military actions that we have organized in the last
six months."

There was no suitable response. Changing the subject, she asked with an icy calm, "What surprises me,
Abu Fahd, is that the death of your first child seems to
play a less important part in your justification of violence. At least you haven't mentioned it." She paused.
"Your wife hasn't mentioned it either."

"My wife has difficulty talking about it even though
she tries very hard to be brave." He glanced away. "She
was there when it happened. I was not."

"Do you know who did it?" If he said it was the
Jews who had murdered his child at least she could
bring herself better to understand the reasons for his
life's work. That bus ride to Nablus wasn't enough.

"The Israelis did not kill my son," he said. "It was
the Syrians."

She was relieved. "Do you want to talk about it?"

"Not now, perhaps later."

"But wasn't that worse than what happened to you
when you were four?"

"For me and for my wife, it was worse. But we don't
consider ourselves individuals with the luxury of thinking about a personal loss. Our people are losing children every day."

The door opened then to admit Josette carrying the
baby in her arms. Tarek Two. "I'm sorry to interrupt
but I've got to go to the market." The child leaned over

toward his father, hands outstretched. Josette looked at Sasha. "Will I see you tomorrow?"

"Could we come here in the morning? I know my colleague would like to begin taping when the sun isn't too strong."

"Fine," she said, "and perhaps our coffee man will be back tomorrow, or at least we will have some news. It would make things easier . . ." She spoke a few words in Arabic to her husband as she smoothed down his hair. "Until tomorrow then," she reverted to English. A casual adjustment to her black-and-white kaffieh and she was gone.

"When will you tell her what you think happened to your coffee man?" Sasha asked.

"As soon as the extra guards are in place. I've requested five extra policemen from the Tunisian government. They will be on duty every night for a while."

There was nothing left to say as she gathered her notebook and pencil, preparing to leave. She had not written anything down nor had she taped a single sentence, but somehow she knew that she wouldn't forget what was said and not said during this meeting. "Are you available tomorrow morning?"

"Yes."

"What will you do with your baby today?"

"He'll stay with me while I meet with my military advisors."

She glanced at that map with those red pins. "Are you planning another . . . military action?"

"We are always planning military actions as well as political meetings. We are open to everything. We are at war, you know."

She stood, watching the child pulling at his father's nose. Plotting the murder of other babies while he held his own baby on his lap. She felt sick. Nothing physical, more something that resembled impotence and heartbreak that she didn't know quite what to do with, feelings that were almost choking her.

She took one last look at that map, counting fourteen red pins, wondering if another would appear before the week was up. And what she could not explain just then were new feelings that were suddenly enveloping her, a dread of some kind of impending doom.

Chapter Nineteen

GIDEON'S SUITCASE was leather, covered with straps and buckles and giving the general impression of belonging to a gentleman who wore cashmere jackets, smoked pipes and drank calvados. His passport was French with all the expected stamps and visas, entrances and exits into Tunisia, Morocco and Algeria, several trips to London, several more to Italy.

Dressed in a dark gray suit, white shirt and striped tie, he looked more like a man who had boarded the flight on his way to a dinner party. Walking from the tarmac to the terminal to stand on line or pass through the electronic surveillance, he thought about Sasha. And he thought about the ways of the world . . .

The Americans would have taken a month and sent in twenty-five thousand men, making it an international news event and a general prelude to war and missing their target in the end anyway. The French would have sent in three thousand men and taken a week to get here, denying that they were even involved in any conflict and negotiating a deal while their target was allowed to escape.

The Jews worked differently. Five men would take no longer than one night to accomplish the job. Or, as Rafi put it before everybody left, eighty minutes from start to finish with a minimum of conversation and cost; one hundred and fifteen minutes if the human element somehow got in the way.

* * *

Gideon checked into the Hotel Africa in downtown Tunis and unpacked his valise. It was six o'clock in the evening, an earlier arrival than he had expected since he had taken the earlier flight out of Paris. What was the point of hanging around Paris when she was already here?

Picking up the phone, he arranged for a rental car to be delivered at eight before he asked to be connected to the Abou Nawas Hotel. There was no answer in her room, but then, he hadn't really expected one. He left a message that he would be there at nine, that he would ring her from the lobby to take her to dinner. Another call to his hotel operator with instructions to wake him in one hour. And as he drifted off to sleep, he could feel the battle begin, all his efforts and energies up-front to fight off another nightmare. This time he won. The dream was of Palestine, the land where there were no sunsets. Not for any of them.

She was cool, distant. In her mind it was self-protection because she had come to care so much so fast, because he had this power over her that made her die a little each time he left, long for him while she waited for the next time, wondering always if there would ever be a next time.

When he called her from the lobby she told him to come up, not exactly up, she corrected, since the suite was on the first level of the two-level hotel, at the end of a series of very long corridors and past a clump of indoor shrubbery and a chatty parrot in a white cage. There were doors that opened onto a rose garden with a view overlooking the sea. They could have a drink on her veranda, so much nicer that sitting among strangers in a noisy bar. Hurry, I've missed you, she didn't say because she was still acting remote . . .

Dressed in beige silk pants and a beige silk shirt, she

shoved her glasses on top of her head and grabbed a notebook and pen. She wanted to look preoccupied, as if he was nothing but an afterthought to a busy day, as if she had been immersed with work until the very last moment, with things that had nothing to do with him— as if she could have concentrated on anything in the past two hours while she waited for him to appear.

A knock on the door and there he was. He surveyed the situation, taking it all in—the room, the decor, the windows, the view, checking her temperature and her pulse and her emotional level. Carefully, he kept his distance. Subtly. There was a kiss on the cheek. She offered the other cheek for a second kiss, less a tribute to his French mother or time spent in Paris than an excuse for being close, for brushing against his skin and smelling his cologne.

Dark blue suit, dark blue shirt, black and blue Nina Ricci small-patterned tie, everything chosen to make his eyes a smoldering blue tonight, or perhaps it was just the dim lighting and stream of golden sunset that filled the room that did it. A package was tucked under one arm as he came slowly through the door, no rush, without words, his eyes never leaving her face, gauging the decreasing chill, she was certain.

"Is that for me?" she asked, her nerves a shamble, her heart thumping in her chest.

"For you," he said, offering a package, a manila envelope containing books, a biography of Arafat by a pro-PLO Brit, he explained, with sections on whatshis-name as well, which he thought might help or at least be interesting. And Proust's *Remembrance of Things Past*, a new translation. More than his taking over her body and soul, he now seemed to be heading for her mind and her work.

They decided not to sit outside after all, too many bugs. Instead, they sat across from one another, he on one loveseat near the glass doors that opened onto that rose garden, she on the other. She had put down her notebook and pen—her props—and also the package of books—his gift—and now held only a glass of champagne between her hands, pressing the tulip against her cheek, a cheek that hadn't stopped burning since he entered her suite, since he entered her life, for that matter.

On closer inspection when she put on her glasses—another ploy at not appearing so interested or seductive—he didn't look as rested or robust as the last time. Still, that didn't stop her from telling him what was on her mind.

To begin with, what happened between them happened too quickly, it was the exception, not the norm, something she didn't make a habit of doing and, yes, in case he wondered, she did feel slightly uncomfortable about it.

"What happened to make you feel uncomfortable?"

She wasn't going to fall for that one, saying the words, hearing him say them too until they became a string of urgent whisperings that described what they were doing when they were doing it, what they had done, what they would do again. She was an automatic loser if the conversation went that way. If he was under the impression that she was just another American trollop, well, he was wrong. Wasn't that what Englishmen called American women who did what she did so soon?

"Nobody ever did what you did," he said softly. "Never, at least not to me."

Canvassing the Tuileries had never been that good, come on, be honest, admit it, he had really hit pay dirt with her. Imagine finding a woman who was at her most vulnerable, still recovering from a divorce, shaken from witnessing a terrorist attack. The odds on that happening were one in a million at least.

His expression was tender, his tone genuine. "I was lucky, very lucky. I found you."

God, he was beautiful. God, how she wanted to shut up and unwind and melt. But she was the one who had stepped on this ride—uninvited—and she was the one who would have to get herself off, if possible without falling flat on her face.

Proust. She changed topics for the moment, a respite from this barrage of defensive self-doubt. Her mother reminded her of Madame Verdurin, and how well Proust captured that type of woman, unhappy and superficial, but in her mother's case there were reasons. She ran her hand over the other book, the thick nonfiction one, *Arafat*, with sections on whatshisname, how thoughtful to have brought it, but actually, she was getting enough background firsthand. It was difficult, the most draining and emotional experience of her career. Interestingly, it wasn't that Karami appeared excitable or irrational, quite the contrary. He seemed completely accepting about the fate of his coffee man.

"What do you mean, completely accepting? He must be upset?" He took a sip of champagne.

"He would be more upset, I think, if his wife found out. And anyway, it's as if it's no surprise, the man was killed by the Israelis. It's as if he just waits for things to happen."

"Why does he assume the Israelis did it?"

She leaned back. "He wouldn't say."

"Well, if that's what happened you'll soon be covering a major news event."

"What do you mean?"

"Won't he retaliate? Another Rome?"

"He didn't exactly confide his plans to me," she said. "The only thing I know he's doing at this point is getting more guards for his house. He's asked for extra policemen from the Tunisians. And then there's the dog."

He looked at her a moment. "You're very involved with your work, aren't you?"

"I've never been involved with something as dramatic."

"You're passionate about everything," he said softly.

"Everything?" she asked, and felt a rush of desire.

"Tell me about the dog, if you like, but then nothing more tonight. Promise?"

"Promise," she replied. "That dog has a bark as big as his bite." He smiled. "It's a guard dog trained to kill anybody who comes around the house uninvited."

Keeping her word, she changed the subject. "What I started to tell you before," she began, "I suppose you're something I just didn't expect in my life right now."

"The last thing I want is to make you unhappy, or complicate your life."

Fight for me, damn it. Don't skulk off without a fight, for God's sake. But he was cool, too cool to plead his case right then, at least not with words. And he wasn't willing to address the ridiculous subject of her morality either, and not particularly interested in discussing Proust or whatshisname. He was more concerned, it seemed, about the damn dog.

"Suppose that beast gets loose when you and your crew are there? Do I lose you to a dog?"

She shook her head. "I was assured that the dog would never wander around when we're there. And anyway, he has a name that stops him from attacking."

"I hope you know it."

"Mrs. Karami told it to me."

"Don't forget it," Gideon warned.

"I've already forgotten it." She laughed. "At least I've forgotten the Arabic. In English it means *slowly*."

He changed the subject, getting back to them. He was willing, he said, to back off and disappear, let her function without strain. It was up to her, he would do whatever she wanted. "But I'll miss you badly," he didn't forget to mention.

"What are we really talking about?" she said. "I'm going back to the States in two weeks."

"Haven't people worked out ways to overcome geographic separations?"

He was someone who could reduce the rest of her life to a series of incidental events. She should never have come to Europe. Heartbreak in Rome, potential heartbreak in Paris. She could only imagine what would happen now in Sidi Bou Said. But she said none of this to him. She had already exhausted herself voicing insecurities and vulnerabilities. What she did say was that she found herself in a situation that was not exactly ideal. He shook his head, saying she was the most extraordinary woman he had ever met.

"Would you like some more champagne?" she said, covering her embarrassment.

He shrugged as he stood to take off his jacket, hanging it over the back of a chair. Clearly he didn't need it.

Would she? What she needed was a hypodermic filled with a drug that would allow her to do it all without reflection or fear about anything that might happen later.

She made the first move, to the other side next to him on his loveseat. He took her in his arms and kissed her and his hands were quickly under her blouse and on her breasts. And it wasn't a gesture of familiarity on his part, as if he had been there before, knew his way around and considered he had the right of way before motoring straight into the driveway. What he did then was to stand, taking her with him, unbuttoning her blouse, removing her bra, unbuttoning his shirt, removing his tie and holding her against him.

Ten steps to the bed, she counted them as she followed him there. He was out of his clothes in the time it took her to discard the bra and the blouse that had found their way around her waist and to lie down.

He was making love to her still in her silk pants, anties and shoes. Over and over he kissed her, his and under her panties but making no effort to remove em—as if that was her job. Up to her. Kicking off one hoe and then the other, she hoped the noise would aspire him to undress her. But he was suddenly lying ack on the bed, his head on the pillow, his hands beind his head, watching her as she debated how best to o it. Standing to remove her panties and pants was orse, lying down to remove them at least had its moents; legs in the air, legs bent as she slipped them ff. What was it that Carl always said? Women looked exier with a little bit on than all of it off.

He took her in his arms—this man knew when to stop laying games. First he made love with his mouth. She idn't even try to hold herself back. Hadn't she already hade her point the last time? And lost? Then with his and and back and forth, except when his mouth was n her mouth and his hand was busy on her breast or olding her face or stroking her until he began to make hore serious love to her. The impression once again as f he hadn't touched her or anyone else in years. In a oggy way it was like the first time ever or the next time ver.

He did the unforgivable then, or rather he said the npardonable. I love you, he said, not once but again nd again as if by repeating the words he were trying o bury something unseen within her, as if they had nother meaning not related to her. He said it again, I ove you, and somehow, in spite of all her presumed marts, she made the transition from being fucked to eing made love to which, after all, made everything o much easier to accept. To believe in. Strange, reardless of the circumstances, it always came back to hat. Men set the pace, she made the adjustment. But hen he did something else, a variation on the theme: "Tell me you love me," he said. "No," she answered

a little too quickly, half on the edge, his body in hers
other parts of him in other parts of her. "Of course
don't love you," she repeated. It was debatable for
whose benefit she spoke so strongly.

He flinched slightly and for an awful moment she
thought he would lose it and withdraw. Maybe some
day, she wanted to say, but right now I hardly know
you. It didn't seem appropriate to play it so tough. "It's
a little soon," she hedged politely. "I love you," he
said again. At least he didn't say "need," and he didn't
say it in the throes of orgasm, and for that she was
grateful.

A few seconds passed and he said it yet again. "I
love you, Sasha, you're part of me." Her name, he said
her name this time, which led her to believe that maybe,
just maybe, it was a specific encounter with specific
feelings. Until it was over she thought that, until she
had had her fill of three or four or five times, but who
was counting, until he held her so close that she imagined he would break her in two, until his breathing was
so intense that she thought he would break in two. And
when the heat and the dampness from his body covered
hers, he said it again, when he held her as she tried to
catch her breath and her sanity, he said it another time.
I love you. The End. Like a Taviani film. FIN. White
letters on a black screen flashed before her eyes. Somehow it was the end of something she couldn't quite define. Thirty-six hours in Tunisia and already she had
been with a terrorist in the afternoon and her lover at
night. It was her day for killers.

Of course they could talk about Proust and Madame
Verdurin who reminded her of her mother and, yes,
they could even talk about whatshisname if she needed
to after her difficult day. He was a bit of a chauvinist,
he admitted it, he wasn't very good at this because he
had never met anyone quite like her before, a woman

who was involved in literally earth-shattering world events. True, no argument, he hadn't been terribly interested in her work in the beginning because it didn't have anything to do with *them*, he said. And that was selfish, but he would try to remember that she was an American woman with a career, successful and independent and intelligent, who also happened to have the most beautiful cunt in the whole world. So tell me, darling, what happened today and why are you so drained and so nervous. Talk to me. Come here. Tell me everything.

Chapter Twenty

THEY HAD GONE through the same type of practice drill in Petah Tikvah, where they had constructed a replica of the airport at Entebbe. Nothing had changed much for the team of commandos who specialized in that kind of raid, neither tactics nor precautions nor technique nor time spent rehearsing since that fourth of July day in 1976 when an Israeli C-130 transport plane carrying eighty-six paratroopers touched down at Entebbe Airport in Uganda and in three minutes burst into the terminal building, gunned down four terrorists and rescued ninety-five passengers. Rafi expected the same kind of success in Tunisia. Nothing less.

For this particular mission, however, there was no need to construct a replica of the Karami villa in Sidi Bou Said. Gideon's house in Herziliah would serve well. Situated near the sea and surrounded by a high wall, it too was built on two levels with a wraparound New Orleans-style balcony. A room on that second level had been transformed into Karami's "study."

The entire setting was eerily similar to the target house, including the outdoor steps leading down to the basement and the flower garden that bordered the walkway and the courtyard—similar except for the interior, where scenes of the Holocaust still hung everywhere. Rafi and the others considered Miriam's graphics and paintings as nothing less than heartbreaking, a poignant reminder of the past that had somehow become a harbinger of the future within those walls. They certainly did not hurt motive or incentive. Neither did the fact that two of Karami's victims in his latest atrocity had once lived in the same rooms where the Palestinian would metaphorically fall. Not that anybody needed extra inspiration. Gideon was with them even if he wasn't physically there for the rehearsal. He was with them in spirit and in pain.

The craft, manned by two officers of the Israeli Navy, would leave the port of Haifa at midnight. Aboard would be eleven commandos, who would position themselves around Karami's house. Also aboard would be Yoram, Ben and Ya'Acov, who would penetrate the house. Ronnie would already be waiting on shore. Rafi would stay on the ship, maintaining contact with Israeli Defense Force headquarters in Tel Aviv and the commandos on the ground in Herziliah as well as with the Boeing 707 that would circle overhead, jamming all telephone lines and shortwave frequencies in the area.

On the ship that would sail down the Israeli coast, past Tirat, Karmel, Zikh Uaacov, Hadera and Netanya, would be four rubber dinghies and their accompanying collapsible oars, that would be lowered into the water when the boat docked off the coast of Ra'Ananna. Two Volkswagen vans and a Peugeot 305 sedan were already parked and waiting on the beach. The team of eleven men who would position themselves around the house plus the four who would actually penetrate it would drag the dinghies from the water, fold them and place them with the oars in the back of one of the Volkswagen vans. Then they would pile into the vehicles for the twenty-mile ride to Herziliah.

The rest was routine, providing, of course, nothing went wrong. A bullet in the head of each of the guards including the five Tunisian policemen, a bullet in the head of the men who sat before the closed-circuit screen in the basement, a bullet in the dog, Shwai-shwai, a bullet in the head of anybody else who happened to be there that night. And then the target, more than one bullet, but that was Gideon's job and Gideon's gun and Gideon's judgment. Not a scratch on the family, Rafi repeated as he stood in the bow of the ship before the team prepared to step into the dinghies to paddle to shore. Not a hair on their heads. Eighty minutes from start to finish, Rafi ordered, one hundred and fifteen at the outside.

It took one hundred and thirty-seven minutes the first time, one hundred and seventeen the second, until after the ninth attempt, Rafi had to contain his pleasure. One hundred and seven minutes from start to finish, and this was only the first day of practice, using Gideon's house as a stand-in for Karami's. By dawn it took ninety-six minutes under the worst of circumstances, the team by now hungry, exhausted and ready to punch out the boss. Once more and out of sheer fury, it took eighty-two minutes, which was when Rafi announced that it was time for breakfast.

There were no illusions that the raid would end with the same glory and global approval as evoked by Entebbe. There was no one to rescue. The Israelis could not even promise that after the hit something like Rome would not repeat itself in another city. There would be no *Plus Jamais* written on the walls of the villa in Sidi Bou Said. There would be no guarantee. Except of course for Tamir Karami. For him, the guarantee that in three days he would be dead.

Chapter Twenty-one

WHAT STRUCK SASHA this morning when she arrived at the villa with Bernie and the crew was the absence of those Tunisian policemen Tamir had talked about. There were the usual five Palestinians smoking foul-smelling cigarettes and wearing the usual threadbare clothes and scuffed shoes. All five of them carried Kalishnikov assault rifles and all five cradled them as if they were precious children. Four stood around the villa, two at the front gate, two more at the front door, the fifth behind the wheel of a Mercedes parked in the circular driveway.

The crew shook hands with Tamir and with Josette before moving over to the trunk of the car to unload equipment that they would set up on the veranda overlooking the sea. Bernie was carefully polite and softspoken. Sasha was subdued.

"We'll talk for about an hour this morning," Bernie explained, "then we'll break for lunch. We'd like to shoot inside the house after that with you and the children."

Josette looked pale and nervous this morning, Sasha noticed, her hands shaking as she drew on her cigarette. "That's fine," she said, "our daughter will be home from school at about three-thirty."

Tamir took hold of his wife's arm. "How much time until you're all set up and ready to begin?"

"About half an hour," Bernie answered.

Tamir said something in Arabic to Josette before talking directly to Bernie. "If you don't mind, I'm going to go up to my office to finish some work until you're ready for me."

He released his wife's arm and said something else in Arabic before heading into the house, pausing to smile briefly at Sasha. "Sasha," Josette turned, "will you join me for a coffee?"

"Do you need me, Bernie?" she asked.

"Not now, go ahead. We know where you are."

Perhaps it was only the anticipation of being on a television program that would reach millions of American viewers that made Josette Karami so anxious. At least that was Sasha's initial judgment until they sat down at the far end of the veranda and sipped their coffee.

"You look a little tired this morning," Sasha said.

"I am," Josette said. "So do you."

Sasha admitted she was, remembering how many times she had made love with him to wake in his arms and begin all over again. "Didn't you sleep?"

"No, not very well," Josette said, "the phone rang all night."

"When telephones ring at night, it's never good news."

A worried look crossed Josette's face. "No, it wasn't good news at all." She paused. "My husband is more upset for me and for the children. He really didn't want me to know." She lit another cigarette. "Our coffee man is dead."

"I'm sorry," Sasha said, but could not help thinking of Rome.

"We're at war," as though that explained—and justified—everything.

"It's a terrible way to live," Sasha said.

"Living without hope is worse."

"Why don't you accept a compromise so this can end?"

"What we've been offered are rigged elections in the Territories, which would only dilute my husband's leadership. The Israelis want to put their own puppet Palestinian leaders in power."

Obviously she was reflecting Tamir's view of it. Hardened, as even her husband had said, by a convert's fervor, compromise was not in the lexicon, so leave it alone, Sasha told herself, and get on with business.

The cables and sound boxes and cameras were all in place. Bernie called for Karami, then went over to the two women. Karami followed and bent down to kiss his wife's cheek before taking a seat next to her. "Do you want us sitting together with the sea behind us?"

"Looks like a perfect shot," Bernie said before turning to his cameraman. "What do you think?"

"Perfect. Let's get Sasha facing them with the house in the background from that side."

They positioned Sasha's chair so it faced Josette and Tamir, who sat close to each other, his hand on her leg, the harbor in the distance, masts from the ships visible in the camera's lens. They were ready. The crew was ready. Bernie was ready. Sasha was ready and scared, but she pushed ahead, her mind erasing her emotions. "You said before when we talked," she began, "that the price is high to achieve your goal. Tell me, was it worth losing your own child?"

Josette flinched, took the question as a direct hit while her husband merely appeared distracted, as if he had other things on his mind, allowing his wife to answer for them both. "Nothing was more horrible or more painful," was the woman's steely reply, "but giving up the struggle won't bring back my baby."

She couldn't have done it with anyone else except these people, and only because they had dubious and conflicting qualifications as victims. "Could you talk about it now, tell us how it happened?'' Sasha prodded. They would edit later. They would change the order and undoubtedly insert voice-overs that would bring the piece together for the sake of continuity. Right now, it was a matter of the conversation's substance.

"My husband was in prison at the time, in Damascus, where we were living. It was a very difficult period for us because the Syrians were trying to gain control of the PLO. Many of our leaders had been assassinated or injured in assassination attempts. I suppose it was naive of me, but in a way I was almost relieved that my husband was in prison—at least I knew he was alive and safe.'' She held her husband's hand as she talked. "Many people were coming in and out of our apartment in those days, discussing ways to free my husband or trying to convince me to carry messages to him about ways to resist the Syrians. One night, the first night since my husband was in jail that I was alone with our baby, it happened. He was eighteen months old and barely walking, mostly he crawled but at such a fast speed that it took most of my energy to chase after him. I was exhausted that night.'' Tears filled her eyes and her voice broke. Her husband was passive, allowed her to continue. "I try not to talk about it because the temptation to feel sorry for myself is so great and because it is no worse than all the horrors that happen every day in the Territories. I try to be strong for my people.'' Her people, the convert's people. She glanced at her husband, who nodded for her to continue. "It happened so fast. The door burst open and four men ran inside. They were waving pistols and shouting out my husband's name. Where was he, they would kill me if I didn't tell them . . .'' She took a breath. "It was strange, even then it made no sense to me. If those men were really Syrians, then why didn't they know that my husband was in jail? After all, they were the ones who put him there.''

Sasha said nothing, it wasn't the moment. One of the cameras was recording her expression as she listened to the rest of the story.

"They threw me against the wall and ran into the bedroom," Josette went on, "and when I tried to run after them, one of them pushed me to the floor and kicked me in the stomach. All I heard was my baby screaming and then I heard a door slam and then I heard nothing until they all rushed past me and out of the apartment." She shook her head slowly, her voice barely audible. "I ran into the bedroom and my baby wasn't in his crib so I ran to the balcony and . . ." she took another breath. "It's been so long since . . ." Another breath until her voice was stronger. "He was lying on the ground, his arms and legs all bent, his head covered with blood, and even from there I knew he was dead. Even before I went downstairs to him, I knew."

Even if she wasn't on camera, what could Sasha say? That she was sorry, that violence resulted in violence, that as a woman, as a mother, she should have considered the dangers for her children, that nothing was worth the life of a child. It was then that the direction of the interview came together in her mind: Josette was a victim of her own emotions. Tamir Karami was to blame, she decided then, making herself judge and jury, he was the devil in this union, not Josette, the convert. Converted by whom? By *him*. But Tamir surprised her.

"You know," he interrupted, "Israel's poet laureate, Chaim Nachman Bialik, said something once that moved me." A pause. Purposeful? "Ironic, isn't it, that I end up quoting an Israeli?" Also a smart move? He smiled slightly while he patted his wife's hand. "He said that not even the devil can invent vengeance for the blood of a small child."

Definitely a smart move. She had to follow up. She looked at Josette before settling on him. "How can you commit an attack like Rome where another small child was murdered? How could you order an attack on a kibbutz in Israel as you did in 1974 in which an entire nursery filled with small children were killed while they slept?'' As she listed the atrocities she knew that photographs would be flashed across the screen.

''All unfortunate,'' he replied, ''but every single day small children as well as old people are maimed and killed under Occupation.''

And now Josette's tone was suddenly hard, her expression stern. ''My baby's death was only one family's loss, our personal tragedy. It was no different for us, no greater a loss than what other Palestinian families suffer. How can we sacrifice our people and our cause and our ideals for one child who happened to die in Rome, especially when we did not give up when our own child was killed?''

Sasha wanted to shake her, she wanted to hit her, she wanted to scream and to plead and to cry until it was as clear to her as it was to the rest of the world that these kinds of things just weren't done in the name of honor and commitment. But who was she kidding anyway, since most of the rest of the world didn't understand this ancient war whose adversaries never ran out of self-justifications. Not even the people who were so busy killing one another understood it, not even when they made their pious statements of regret.

''Could you explain it a little better, Abu Fahd?'' Flatter him with the name he liked. Sasha spoke only to him now. ''Are you saying that the people who are dying from your bombs and grenades are justifiable sacrifices?''

''In every war there are innocent victims. Look at Vietnam.''

''We've acknowledged our mistake and punished people who killed innocent victims, at least the ones we learned about.''

"You entered a region that offered neither historical nor emotional gain for your people."

She owed it to her audience, to herself, to reply. "The people who die in airplane hijackings or terrorist bombings also have nothing to do with your fight."

"That child in Rome was no more important than any other child, any Palestinian child."

"Is killing any of them, on either side, bringing anyone any closer to a solution?"

"Someday it will," Josette interjected.

"You're a woman," Sasha said quietly, "isn't it different for you? Don't you see things differently?"

"There is equality among the Palestinian people," Josette replied evenly. "Look at the statistics and you will be amazed at how many men and children are beaten in equal numbers, shot in equal numbers, mourn their land in equal numbers and die in equal numbers."

"Could we be specific for another moment and go back to that child who died in Rome?"

"Why is the media more interested in our attacks than in the attacks the Israelis commit daily in the Territories?"

"That is not the case. If you want to fault the media, say we tend to be more interested in the spectacular. You provided that kind of drama. Now the other side seems to have caught up. Since the Intifada, the Israelis are on the front page and at the top of the television stories more than the PLO." But she wasn't there to defend, and dropped it to turn her attention back to Josette. "Can't you acknowledge a terrible injustice when a child is killed in the name of *any* political cause?"

Again, Josette's eyes filled with tears. "Do you think that child's parents weep for my child, that child in Rome?" She caught herself. "Do you think they weep for any of our children?"

"I can't answer that," Sasha said quietly, "but I

doubt that they are planning any kind of violent retaliation against your children." It had now gone far beyond that small victim in Rome. "As a mother, only as a mother, can't you feel any grief for that child?" If she could achieve only that, it would be enough for today. She knew they would cut and edit back in New York. Still, they would leave in the tears and the drama. And the remorse, if she could elicit it. Even if it was only a matter of ratings. Even if it was all but impossible to separate performance from genuine feelings.

Josette's voice trembled slightly when she answered, "Yes, I can weep for that child." Looking at her husband as if for approval, she added, "I cry for all the children. We all do."

There was silence for a moment or two before Bernie called out, "Cut!" And still there was silence.

Chapter Twenty-two

GIDEON LOOKED LIKE any other tourist who had just stepped off the train that ran from Tunis to the northern suburb of La Marsa. Parking his car near the railway station, he followed the crowd toward the main shopping area in the center of town. Dressed casually in a cotton sweater and jeans and with a copy of *Le Monde* under one arm, he wandered along the southernmost tip of the palm-lined beach until he reached the sook. Only ten minutes remained until Sasha was due to meet him at the Café Saf Saf for a quick lunch before her afternoon taping session.

What had begun as calculating had ended as real. Or, what began as an irresponsible admission of love during an even more irresponsible emission of lust had ended as real. He had, he told himself, fallen in love with her. And if there was conflict about it—which there surely was—it was only because his loving her could not change anything that happened. Neither for his wife nor for his son nor for himself would anything change, except that now he was able to *feel* totally disparate feelings. Love her, and grieve for them.

When he said the words, told her he loved her, he knew it could go either way. Under the circumstances the instinct on her part was to disbelieve, which gave him the automatic advantage. Either he could convince her it was so or allow her to think it was something that had been said in a moment when reason was absent.

273

And need uppermost. Even so, he knew what her immediate response would be. He could read it in her eyes, half-closed before they opened wide to study him. Say it standing, when breathing is even, as a preamble of something else, but don't just say it as a euphemism for what feels good. How hard she tried to act the way she thought a man would act when she told him that she loved him for the moment, here, now, in bed. Except a man probably wouldn't have dared. And anyway, she was wrong, Gideon thought as he lingered in the midst of a group of French tourists. He had said it as another kind of euphemism, something to do with I love you and goodbye.

He headed now toward the flight of stone steps leading to the veranda of the Café Saf Saf. Taking them slowly, one at a time, he stepped onto a large shaded patio and headed over to an empty table at the far end under a palm tree. Within minutes, even before he had a chance to summon the waiter to order coffee, he saw her coming up the stairs, a scarf tied around her neck and flowing down her back, her hair off her face, her skirt above her knees. Without a word or gesture he watched her looking around the patio until she spotted him. Pausing briefly, she removed her sunglasses and walked slowly over to his table. He stood. Taking her in his arms, he kissed her on either cheek, inhaling the scent of her perfume, feeling that same twinge whenever he touched her.

"Hi," she said softly after he released her.

He pulled out a chair, his eyes never leaving her face; still not saying a word. She sat down. "I'm fine, thank you," she said, as if he had asked, "and the taping went well this morning, a few rough spots but nothing that won't straighten out in the final cut—"

"I love you," he interrupted, pressing his hand to her lips, silencing her in mid-sentence.

"Gideon," was her only response, but her cheeks were flushed.

He reached for the menu that a waiter had dropped on the table.

"Fruit and cheese," she said suddenly, avoiding his gaze.

"What am I going to do about you?" he said, his hand covering hers. What was he going to do about himself?

"We seem to have the same problem."

The waiter appeared. Speaking in Arabic, Gideon ordered quickly. When the waiter left, he turned back to her. "We can't solve any of this over lunch, you know." She waited, she wasn't making this easy.

"The way things are going, we probably can't solve it over dinner or breakfast or even while we're here."

"We'll work something out by the time you have to leave." He took her hand. "Trust me?"

God, how she wanted to.

He needed even more now. He couldn't let go. "Tell me what happened today," he began on a different note, "and *please*, at least credit me for remembering to be interested in your work." He smiled. "Am I less archaic?"

She smiled back. "You're almost perfect."

"What would make perfect?"

"Practice," she replied with a straight face, "lots of practice."

"Have you put me on a time limit?"

"Please, let's not do this now."

The fruit and cheese arrived and the bottled water and knives and forks, napkins and plates. When everything was arranged on the table and Gideon had filled their glasses, he told her, "After you tell me about your day's work there's something I would like to discuss with you."

Cutting the apple in half carefully she glanced up. "No, you first."

"But what I have to say depends on what you say."

She shrugged, a brief expression of bewilderment before she began. "Well, it was interesting, and tough. The one good thing about them is they're devoted to each other. But they're obsessed with their cause." She peeled one half and took out the core. "I tried not to focus on Rome, but I guess I wasn't completely successful." She stared at her hands. "Half of me wanted to talk about that child to get a reaction and the other half wanted to do it because it's somewhere in here." She touched her heart.

He watched her, searching her face for more of what he knew he couldn't bear to hear. "Are you having a problem pulling in more electrical lines for your lights and cameras?"

"Not that I know of," she answered. "Why?"

"The power system in Tunisia is bad. That's one of the problems I'm running into with this new plant we're trying to build."

She seemed to relax some. "We haven't had any problems yet, but maybe that's because there are no major appliances in their house that I can see."

"It's better for you that they don't have an alarm system. That would pull a lot of power."

She noted with some vague surprise that he remembered about the alarm. "Our crew knows all about the technical end of things," she said.

He concentrated on peeling his orange, aware that he had annoyed her. Back down, he told himself. "So, how do you find it, working in an Arab country where things don't always happen when they're supposed to happen?"

She took a sip of water. "So far all promises have been kept. Not that many have been made."

"Typical Arab bureaucracy," he said. "*Bukara In-*

challah, the national credo, means Tomorrow God Willing, which is the usual response to any request or question. The trouble is when someone says that, whatever it is will never happen.''

She laughed. ''I'll remember that, in God's hands and it's all over.''

He offered her a wedge of orange, which she refused. ''Should I continue to worry about you being there?''

''Where?'' she asked even though she knew.

''In his house.''

''He just learned that his coffee man was murdered,'' she said slowly, as if that would reassure him.

''What a relief,'' he said, ''and I thought my concerns were only imaginary.''

''Karami wasn't threatened—''

''You have no idea about the Arab sense of vengeance.''

''Do you?''

''Of course. I've worked here long enough. The coffee man is the closest person to him, it's a warning that he could be next.''

''That's what he said.''

''Then I'm not wrong. Sasha . . .''

''Nothing is going to happen to me.''

''Anything can happen. This sort of man lives on borrowed time.''

''He's managed to survive this long, the odds on anything happening to him just when I'm there are pretty remote.''

''Something else,'' he said, ''I was thinking about guns. If someone got hold of a gun and if the gun went off accidentally . . .'' He touched her chin, turned her face toward him. ''I'm worried about you.'' Was he pressing too hard? If he aroused suspicions his whole operation could be compromised. But he *was* concerned for her . . .

Whatever he was doing, she didn't like it. It made

her edgy. He seemed to be picking up on things she'd told him. He was a hydraulic engineer, why all this about guns, Tamir as a target . . . ?

"There's nothing I can do about it," she said.

"Would you mind if I made a suggestion?"

"Probably," she replied, and forced a smile.

"Would you rather I keep my distance?"

"I hate that word."

He had her again back on track. "What word?"

"Distance."

A thousand thoughts filled his head, a thousand excuses to disappear, to take her and run away, anywhere but where there were traces of this commitment. "Unless the cost is too high, unless someone ends up badly hurt, my instinct is to always be honest." God, he sounded sanctimonious even to himself.

The edge was back when she asked, "What's your suggestion?"

"That you tell them you're uneasy around guns and for the time that you're in the house they might consider putting them away." He watched her. "What do you think?"

"You know, Gideon," she said quietly, "sometimes you're very odd." She considered a moment. And what she'd been formulating but hadn't pulled together suddenly came out. "Who are you, Gideon?"

He didn't answer, waited to see how serious she was and how far she would go. He kept back any show of relief when she finally said, "Because if I do ask them that and if anything did happen to him, I'd have to wonder if you had anything to do with it." She kissed him on the cheek. "It's only for another day and a half and then it's over."

"Whatever makes you comfortable," he said quickly, worried he had gone too far despite her light tone when she said she'd have to suspect him.

She continued peeling the apple, so meticulously and

neatly that only one piece of skin hung from one corner. "It's getting late," she said, almost abruptly.

"Should I get the check?"

"Yes, and then you can take me for a quick drive before I'm due back." She really did hate to let go of him, whoever he was.

The gun under Josette Karami's pillow remained an unsolved dilemma for him, but at least Sasha seemed back to normal. Bad judgment, he chastised himself silently. Still, he had little choice.

They walked hand in hand down the steps, around the crowded stalls in the sook and toward the railway station until they reached the car. He pulled her close then, before unlocking the door. "This is all new to me," he said softly, "and I'm sorry if I interfered. I guess I'm out of my element."

She nodded, not resisting when he tilted her chin to kiss her on the lips.

In silence, head on his shoulder, they drove past Gammarth, the next installment of Tunisian suburbs, past a series of beaches known as Monkey Bay, past the cemetery for the Free French who were killed during the Second World War. She commented only when the road became wedged between a salt flat and a broad expanse of empty sand called Raouad Beach and seemed interested only when he explained that it was a popular site for campers, mostly Germans and mostly nude. Coasting to a stop, he parked the car away from several tour busses and oversized campers. He was aware that she had moved away from him to lean against her door, an expanse of front seat between them. "Should I tell you something?" he asked.

"Will I hate it?"

"Probably."

"Then you had better tell me before I keep thinking you're perfect."

"I'd never allow you to sunbathe in the nude."

"Allow me? Since when?"

He reached for her. "It's a variation on the story of Androcles and the Lion." He held her around the waist, her back pressed against his chest. "After all, I saved you in the Tuileries."

"From what?"

"Who knows what kind of unsavory dangerous character could have come along and picked you up?"

"I suppose I could have done worse," she said, wondering if she could have. She fitted herself against him. "Or maybe I couldn't have," she added with a small smile.

He held her tighter, his lips against her ear. "I told you, Sasha," he said softly, "you'll just have to trust me." He kissed her ear. "About everything." Turning her around, his mouth found hers. And as he felt her respond, he began regretting it all again until he forced himself to pull away. He saw it in her eyes then, a look that told him he had opened a corner of doubt somewhere, not specific, but nonetheless something that hadn't been there before.

"I'll take you back to the villa."

"I've got to stop at the hotel first to pick up some papers," she said, her voice still weak from the kiss. "Gideon," she started, then stopped. But he had already shifted into reverse, one foot on the clutch, the other on the brake.

"Tell me."

"Let's try to figure out something realistic about us."

"Soon," he promised as he maneuvered the car onto the road, back onto the route where the scenery looked as if it belonged on the moon.

"And then all this pushing and pulling and testing will be over," she said.

"And then it will be over," he agreed.

Chapter Twenty-three

THE KARAMI FAMILY, except for the oldest son Fahd, was gathered in the living room of the villa to tape the second and final segment of the interview.

If the opening segment featured Josette, this one was clearly Tamir's show. Wearing a Palestinian combat jacket, he held his infant son on his lap, a replacement baby, he explained to the camera, for the child who had been killed years before in the beginning of the struggle.

Next to Tamir sat Josette, her hand resting lightly on his thigh, dressed all in black this afternoon as "a symbol," she said, "of mourning for the victims of the Intifada." And next to her was Camilla, the teenage daughter, who resembled her mother but had an even more uncanny resemblance to her maternal grandmother.

"Can the world expect more of the same?" Sasha opened. "More terrorist attacks in which innocent people are killed?"

Tamir acknowledged that terror was cinema, but he was not disturbed by those who condemned his methods. Whoever heard about the plight of the Palestinian people before there was a military organization behind them? And remember, those who judged weren't the ones who had suffered years of humiliation.

"You don't seem too humiliated. You seem like a man who has everything. A family who loves you, a nice place to live." She paused. "A job." There was dead silence in the room while Karami went about ignoring her observation. It would go on, he continued, until there was a solution, maybe not in his lifetime but surely in his children's. They had already faced that inevitability.

Don't push with that child who died in Rome, Sasha cautioned herself silently, the audience got it in the last segment. Just shut up, she told herself, just shut up and let him talk.

Josette came alive then, leaning forward to offer a private moment. "My husband had a dream last night. It's a recurring dream where soldiers are chasing him through the streets of Ramla . . ."

"I was running," Tamir took the cue nicely, "searching for my wife and children. In my dream I knew that only if I could find them would I be safe."

There was a vaguely ironic edge to Sasha's voice when she asked, "And did you find them?"

Tamir held tightly to his wife's hand. "No," he said. "But they say it isn't possible to die in a dream of your own creation without actually dying."

She had learned—a quick study, she was—to ignore abstractions and metaphors in this business. "If your husband was killed," she addressed Josette, "would you continue with his work?"

Josette took a breath, reached over to reposition the baby on her lap, to smooth some hair from her daughter's face. Props. For some reason the whole scene reminded Sasha of those gypsies sprawled on Parisian sidewalks who left their infants and children on tattered blankets, shoeless, filthy, small feet touching the money cup. "If my husband were killed, there would be nothing left except the struggle and, of course, our children."

Sasha felt her features soften and her tone relax when she spoke to the daughter. "How do you feel when you hear your parents talking about their commitment to the cause, when they know it could even cost their lives?''

''The same way as my older brother feels,'' Camilla Karami answered without hesitation.

''How is that?''

''Proud,'' the girl answered.

''Where is your older brother?'' Sasha asked innocently.

''In school in England.''

''Why is he there?''

''To get a good education.''

She glanced at her mother, who took over. ''Our son's dream is one day to go to a university in the Territories. But of course—''

''He is not allowed,'' Tamir finished the sentence.

''Because of you?'' Sasha led him.

''Yes, because he is my son and I am working to liberate our land. The Israelis have banned us.''

Israelis, not Jews. It sounded less harsh, and she suspected Karami knew it, was using it as a nicety for television.

''Someday if not our children then our children's children will be able to live there and go to school there,'' Josette added.

Sasha had not promised that she wouldn't mention it, there were no pre-conditions to this interview and certainly they hadn't discussed this particular point: ''When you and I talked before''—she looked at Tamir—''you said that if you ever succeeded in liberating your land you wouldn't necessarily live there. Can you explain why?''

A flicker of annoyance in his eyes before he buried it. ''What I meant was that we the Palestinian people are benefiting from the different cultures that we are exposed to, just as our Jewish cousins benefited when they lived in the diaspora. I meant I was needed here now to set the foundation for our government. Someday when we have achieved our goal, of course, I would live there. It is, after all, our dream.''

She wondered how ''our Jewish cousins'' would go down with the audience. Well, she would let him have the last word. Enough people out there could read behind the rhetoric.

''How old were you when you met your husband?'' she moved along to Josette.

''Twenty.''

''Were you already involved with the Palestinian cause then?''

Josette looked uncomfortable. ''No.''

''Did you learn about it from him?''

She made the choice right then that it was all or nothing and she chose all. ''I learned about life from him.'' She looked at her husband. ''I would have taken on anything that was part of him.''

Touching, Sasha thought. ''And you''—she turned to Tamir—''did you feel that way about your wife?''

''From the first there was a connection that went very deep.''

She asked when that deep connection first was realized.

''I knew we would spend our lives together,'' Josette took over.

Sasha led her as she described her exhilaration at being involved in a biblical struggle, as she put it, a romantic revolution that was so far removed from her bourgeois life in the Seventeenth Arrondissement.

''My wife is my helpmate. I trust her more than anyone else.''

''We breathe through each other's skin. We see things through each other's eyes. We share a single heartbeat,'' Josette said.

''And heartbreak,'' Tamir added as if on cue.

''Are you ever frightened?'' Sasha asked them.

The greeting card responses vanished. ''We don't

choose our fate," Josette the soldier replied. We can only control the degree to which we use our own strength to carry out that destiny."

The girl was next, Sasha decided, a child living among self-styled warriors. Didn't Camilla ever imagine living in a house where there were no signs of war or weapons, where the telephone number didn't change every few weeks along with the locks on the door and the guards? Didn't she ever consider how different life might be if her father's image wasn't flashed across television screens or on the front pages of newspapers after one or another of those sensational attacks?

"But how can I answer that," the girl said, "when this is the only family I know?"

"Do you know how to use a gun?"

The girl hesitated only briefly. "Yes."

"Who taught you?"

"My mother."

Said the way another daughter might credit her mother with teaching her petit point. "Do you carry a gun?"

"No, but I know where my mother keeps one, in case."

"In case?"

"In case something happens," she replied matter of factly.

"My daughter is no different," Tamir interrupted as the camera came in for a tight shot, "than those other children who were born after 1967 and know nothing except living under the Occupation. They learned about weapons from the time they were children as a matter of self-defense."

"When you talk about the Occupation you're referring to the 1967 Israeli occupation of the West Bank. The parents of these children also knew an occupation when they lived under the Jordanian occupation of the West Bank." Sasha smiled.

"If my father was killed," Camilla said as if feeling the need to explain, "he would be martyred."

"Our love is greater than our enemies' hatred," Josette intoned.

Enough of that, get back to the script. "Getting back to my original question," Sasha said, changing lanes, "can we expect more attacks such as the one in Rome in the future?" In case the world thought the main message around here was love, in case they forgot about the hatred.

"The world can expect retaliation for every Palestinian man, woman and child who is killed at the hands of the Israelis." He shifted slightly. "And the world can hold the Zionists responsible each time one of theirs is killed just as we hold them, and those who support them, responsible each time one of ours is killed."

She pressed it, what the hell, she had already gone beyond the guidelines of so-called proper television interviewing. "Can you give us an idea, Abu Fahd," she began, forcing him to make the transition from father to fighter, "where these retaliatory actions will take place?"

"They will take place everywhere, anywhere that makes the world pay attention to the systematic slaughter of my people." A chill went through her, as it would her viewers.

What she was asking for was a bloody list, and how she was managing to do that with a straight face was beyond her comprehension. She felt her hands tremble, her palms go sweaty. "Can we assume that means in stores and in airports, in Western cities where there are tourists?" Pull it together for the title "Family," she cautioned herself, now, at least, bring it back to the fold.

"I cannot give you dates and places." He almost smiled.

Now. Bring it back. "How do you feel about that?" she asked Camilla.

The girl was pale. "Palestinians are murdered every day by Israeli soldiers," she recited.

"That is fact," Tamir said quietly. "That is truth."

"True or not, this doesn't solve the problem." A pause. "Does it?"

"Sacrifice," Tamir began.

"Commitment," Josette added.

"Tragedy?" Sasha replied.

"Call it what you want," Tamir began again.

"As long as the world is aware," from Josette.

"As long as there is hope, there is struggle," from Tamir.

"So it continues," Sasha said, voice low. "And how many more innocent people will have to pay the ultimate price?"

The curtain fell. "Freeze frame," she heard Bernie say. "Cut." She could imagine the closing shot as it would appear on the television screen, the four of them sitting together on a couch in the living room of a rented villa in a borrowed country. Tamir stood to shake hands. "Thank you, Sasha," he said, "and I am even more convinced of it."

"Of what?"

He smiled slightly. "That we need you on our side."

Josette walked over. "You are very good at your job."

"So are you," Sasha replied, wondering if she understood and certain that Tamir did.

Camilla was next. Shyly, she shook hands.

Bernie walked over to them now, shook hands and thanked them all. The crew followed, shaking hands and thanking everybody for their patience and cooperation. "We'll be here tomorrow in case we need some last-minute background shots or to ask you a few questions. And thanks again."

* * *

Sasha stood off to one side, wondering what everybody was thanking everybody about. Thank you for making it possible. If appreciation was in order, then perhaps a special thank-you was also due the victims of the Alitalia bombing. After all, without their unwilling participation there wouldn't have been much interest in this particular family for the opening segment of this series. Maury would have stuck with that snap-bean farmer in Appalachia. And while she was at it, an advance thank-you might not be a bad idea for those future victims who would undoubtedly breathe life back into what the press occasionally considered a weary revolution. Consider this a joint-effort, then, a co-production of sorts, and a big thank-you to all of you out there, she signed off in her head, for tuning in before tuning out.

"We've been invited to play backgammon at the house tonight," Bernie announced.

"You know I don't play backgammon," she answered sullenly.

"If you're very nice and stop treating me as if I've got a contagious disease, I'll tell you what I found out."

She stopped gathering up her files and papers to stuff back into her briefcase. "What did you find out?" she asked in a bored tone.

"Are you going to play backgammon?"

"No, I'm not going to play backgammon," she snapped, turning back to her briefcase.

"You know that child and that woman who were killed in the bombing?" He had an annoying grin on his face. "The only two Israelis?"

She turned. "What about them?"

"Well, it seems the husband works for the foreign ministry in Jerusalem."

"What does that mean?"

"Working for the foreign ministry covers a multitude of sins, or virtues, depending on your point-of-view. He could either be a driver for some big shot or he could be with the Mossad."

"How do you know this?"

"Because the Tel Aviv bureau faxed the scoop to Paris and Paris sent it by Federal Express to the hotel."

"For whom?"

"Well, for you."

"And you opened it?"

"I honestly thought it had to do with the broadcast."

"Fuck you, Bernie," she said quietly.

"Fine!" He glared. "Okay, okay, I'm sorry, I shouldn't have opened it."

She was exhausted. She was angry. She was fed up. Oh, was she fed up. But for the sake of what she needed to know and for the limited time that remained, her instinct was to accept his apology and keep it civil. "Do you have a name yet?"

"Not yet but they're working on it." He touched her arm. "What are you going to do once you get a name?"

"Talk to him, see if he'll talk to me on camera, try to convince Maury to do a piece on the families. Not just his because he's Israeli, but families of some of the other victims."

"So far they're not releasing any names."

"They will eventually."

"Not his, they won't. Not if he's with some sensitive government organization." His smile turned charming. "Will you please change your mind and play backgammon tonight?"

"No thanks, Bernie, I'm *really* tired."

He was less insistent. "We did a terrific job," he said, "we really made it all come together. I predict the ratings will probably go off the charts."

We. The expression on her face would have made someone in a coma feel uncomfortable. Not Bernie.

"Are you going to stay cool forever?" he asked.

She barely looked at him as she gathered up the last of her things. "Do me a favor," she said wearily.

"What's that?"

"Let's not talk now. I'm kind of drained."

He tried to shift gears but not give up. "You know, Sasha, you've changed. I mean since that first day you walked into my office. You were a very different lady—"

"A lot's happened since then. I'd hardly be alive if I hadn't changed"

"You can't change the world."

"No shit. How about 'only the good die young'?"

He stepped back, eyed her. "I know what you need."

She stood still, her briefcase in one hand, her hair in her face, her eyes unblinking. "And what's that, Bernie? What do I need?"

He hesitated, but it was too late not to finish what he had started. "*You* need a good cause to keep your mind off your own problems."

She had to give him credit. It was pretty fast thinking. Taking a breath, she started to walk away. Right, Bernie, she thought, a good cause, and a man to give it to me. Just like Josette Karami.

Chapter Twenty-four

SHE HAD THE IMPRESSION of moving like a ghost through what had once been the second city of the Roman Empire. He had her around the waist, her hand clasped on her wrist, as they went up the hills and down the hills that overlooked the ruins of what had been ancient Carthage. Vaguely disappointing, was her comment, especially with all the overflowing trash bins and orange peels that were strewn around the grounds, not maintained the way she would have expected. Plodding along through the archeological sites, she was amused at the persistence of the tour guides, who approached to read the epitaphs or to recount the history. No thank you was the constant response, they didn't need any help since Gideon seemed to know it all by heart in three languages.

Sasha twisted out of his grasp to walk ahead to the edge of the park and an antiquarium where a few stunted columns and statues still stood. Excavation was certainly a major pastime around here, she remarked just as she caught her heel in a wooden plank set down to protect a future dig. "That's how it happened," Gideon said, "with you tripping." He turned her around, his hands on her shoulders as he kissed her. She actually felt dizzy. Swoon, the word popped into her head, this man actually made her swoon. June, moon, swoon . . . Shading her eyes with one hand, she followed his finger until she focused on the Punic ports in the distance.

Unfortunate that all that was left of them were two non-descript and rather dilapidated lagoons. But she was barely paying attention, still involved in that kiss, still tasting his mouth on hers. "It's almost over, you know," she said suddenly, not even looking at him, her eyes somewhere out over the sea.

"What's almost over?"

"Except for some last questions, the Karami shoot is finished."

"The stars of today are the has-beens of tomorrow in your business."

"Tomorrow is the last day," she said.

He was cheerful when he made the announcement. "You'll be finished just when I'm back."

She turned. "Back from where?"

"Algeria."

"I didn't know you were going."

"Tonight."

"Oh," she said, hoping it sounded casual. Life was too short, time with him was too short not to tell him how she felt. But if the intention was really there, the timing was hopelessly off. He took her hand to lead her to the Oceanographic Museum. Closed, they discovered when Gideon translated the sign written in French and Arabic that hung on the door. By then, the moment for telling him how she felt had passed. "Are you coming back here?" she asked instead.

"Of course, tomorrow or at the latest, late tomorrow night."

"Oh," she said again, every organ in her body in disarray. It was almost over, all of it. Unless other arrangements and rules could be created, it was ending.

The regular museum was open. He kissed her again before they headed toward the wraparound veranda on the old building. Once inside, they wandered around several glass display-cases filled with ancient jewelry and hair ornaments, goblets and cooking utensils.

Walking through a series of light and airy rooms, they found themselves in a large white marble enclosure that held a pair of stone sarcophagi, a man and a woman carved lifesize on the lids. The fact that they were dug up here in Carthage might suggest that they spent their lives here, Gideon explained, but that wasn't necessarily so.

It took all she had not to tell him to shut up, that the last thing she cared about right now was history. What she wanted to hear was the future, their future, and even if it only included what would happen tomorrow or the day after, if he returned. And if he didn't, what would happen then?

His lips brushed against hers. Judging from the characteristics of the carvings themselves, he went on, the couple, in all probability, were Greek—or did she intend to make love the same way without trying anything new for the rest of their lives?

Stunned by the implication of time rather than position or aperture, she stared before making the decision right there in front of that carved man and woman who had been joined for all eternity on the lid of that white marble box. "I want you to know," she began carefully and then stopped. "I love . . ." and stopped again before forging ahead to finish the sentence, any sentence. "I love it here," she proclaimed, disgusted that she was completely incapable of including the word in a sentence that expressed how she felt about him. A nod of his dark head. He knew. "Sasha," he said quietly, "it's complicated."

"What's complicated?"

"You wanted to discuss it."

"Discuss what?"

"I live in Paris."

"Aren't you the lucky one?"

"In some ways, yes." He lifted her chin. "Since I met you I'm not sure it's a question of luck anymore."

"Then what?"

"It's not that I'm unwilling to change my life," he said.

It was imprecise enough to be meaningless. But it didn't surprise her, since she had learned that technique from Vermont. He loved her but he couldn't leave his wife. He was terrified of losing her but he couldn't hurt his wife. Pussy-whipped on one hand, cunt-struck on the other. At the time she considered it to be ironic that either expression had him floundering about in a sea of female genitalia. "One of us has to change his or her life," she said simply.

"I don't expect you to do that," he said carefully. "I couldn't ask you to give everything up and stay with me."

She said nothing. What was it that Carl once gave as an explanation for her mother's alcoholism, that women who were rejected usually turned to booze, drugs or a string of inferior lovers. Which fabulous legacy was in store for her? She left Gideon standing there and headed toward the door.

Once outside, she paused for a moment to get her bearings before walking over to a patch of untended grass cluttered with an assortment of artifacts, pillars and arms, a plaster elephant. Without glancing back to see if he was following, she continued until she reached a hill overlooking an amphitheater. It barely resembled the drawings that were staked in the ground, yet it was clearly described as the site of countless Christian martyrdoms. Gideon was there, right behind her, sunglasses in the breast pocket of his jacket, arms wrapped tightly around her. "You'll forget about me anyway," he said softly, testing.

She shook her head, her eyes filling with tears.

"You'll be so busy when you get back to New York that you won't even take my calls."

"Why does it have to be that way?" she whispered.

"You're not even giving me the chance to make my own choices."

"Tell me how you'd like it to be."

"How would I like it to be?" she repeated the question. "Not like this," she stated.

"Not any of it?"

"Not this part of it."

She reached into her purse then. Turning, she handed him a key. "Here, take it, humor me. It's to my hotel room." She tried a smile. "At least you'll have it so when you come back tomorrow night, even if it's late, you can let yourself in."

He took it and put it in his pocket, making no mention of the transaction that had just passed between them. Turning her around so she was leaning against him and facing the arena, he continued the tour.

Felicitas and Agrippe were the most notorious of the martyrs, one a female saint, the other a male hero, who were victims in 210 A.D. He took a breath then before going on with the story about how the pair were stripped naked and placed in nets in the arena so even the Romans, barbarians that they were, were shocked to see that the girl was pregnant and that he had been beaten and tortured almost to death by the time he had been dragged there. He buried his face in her hair. "You're really such a strange girl," he said lovingly.

She didn't give a damn anymore about that "girl" business as long as she was his girl. He could have called her his broad or his old lady for all she cared as long as she belonged to him, as long as they were both clear on that.

They were taken out of the net, Felicitas and Agrippe, and carried back inside where they were dressed in white gowns before they were taken back outside again, this time to die a more dignified death, murdered by the sword of a gladiator. What did she think, he asked her, could this have been the beginnings of what was considered Roman civilization? And when she didn't reply, he simply posed the next question. "Are you going to be happy today?"

It was sunset. "Yes," she lied.

Sad eyes that looked into hers. "Things happen if they're meant to happen."

"You sound as fatalistic as the Karamis."

"Don't you believe in fate?"

"Frankly, I think it's a lazy way out."

He smiled. "Oh, you do, do you?"

"Yes, I do." The tone was adamant even though the feelings behind it were nothing less than an acute, overwhelming despair. "People can make things happen if they want them to happen, or at least they can try to protect themselves so things don't happen—"

"And how was I supposed to protect myself from you when there you were, lying on the ground so helpless?"

"You could have kept on running," she said, and almost wished he had.

He shook his head slowly. "No, I had to stop."

"Why?" she asked, suddenly angry at what she could only guess, at him, at herself, at distances, at responsibilities. At this fate business everybody seemed hung up on.

"Because like your Palestinian friends, I am a fatalist. I believe we were meant to happen. You were meant to fall and I was meant to pick you up."

"I suppose it could be worse, since my Palestinian friends, as you call them, are fatalistic about getting killed."

Gideon shrugged. "We don't all fall in love, but we do all get killed one day."

It struck her as strange. "No. You mean we all die one day, we don't all get killed."

"Dead is dead."

"It is if you happen to look at those pictures on the

Palestinian's walls. Massacres and shootings and murders, both sides the victims, then dead is dead.'' And for some reason that earlier feeling of despair turned to an overwhelming feeling of hopelessness so profound that she actually shivered. ''Gideon,'' she whispered, leaning against him. But she had nothing to say except the need to say his name.

He stroked her cheek. ''You're tired, darling, you're just tired.''

''Why do you have to leave now when we don't have much time left?''

''You talk as if we're a fatal illness,'' he said, and then his tone became more serious. ''I'm only going to Algeria to scout out some sites for the factory and it's only for a little more than a day and a night.'' His tone went light again. ''And I happen to be going with one of the most boring men in the company. So, if anyone has a right to be morbid today, it's me.''

''What if something happens and you get detained?''

''What could happen?''

''I don't know.''

''Then I'll call you.''

''What if you don't?'' she asked because pride was no longer an issue among these ruins.

Patting his pocket, he answered. ''How can I not call or come back?'' He smiled and kissed her. ''I've got your key.''

''You could always mail it back to the hotel.''

''And what about making love to you? Can I mail that back too?''

It worked, for the moment, at least, she was assured. They wandered past the cisterns and the American Cemetery and something called Antoine's Baths, which he said made her think of Bette Midler. They stopped before a framed explanation of ancient Carthage, a compendium of the entire civilization in three paragraphs in three different languages encased in all-weather plastic. Dutifully she read it although the words didn't distract her from that little problem they seemed to be having. If he had been asked to describe it, he would have said it was nothing more than a case of logistics. If she had been asked to describe it she would have said it was nothing less than what to do with the rest of her life. *Layers of ancient myths and cruelty and deception and passion and power buried within the decadence of Roman Carthage.* As if she needed something else to depress her even more, as if she needed him to inquire: "Do you know the story of Queen Dido and Aeneas?"

"How does it end?" she rushed.

"He abandons her in Carthage." And what exactly did he propose she do with *that* information, take it as a sign that the same was about to happen to her and run like hell before it did? Run where? Across the border and into Libya; back to New York and nothing; over to the Karamis for a massive dose of love and terror? As if Mr. Gideon Aitchison needed Virgil and his *Aeneid* as an inspiration to dump her in Carthage. Or anywhere else. "This has been the worst and the best time in my life," she said without warning, although somewhere she was aware that it was completely honest.

"What was my contribution to such extremes?" he wanted to know.

"The best until now."

"And now?"

"The worst."

"Why?"

"Because all vacations end."

He shook his head. "No, Sasha, this wasn't a vacation."

"What the hell do you want?" she blurted out.

"The best for you, always."

"It wasn't enough, was it?" she said, a knowing look

in her eyes. Right now she felt at least a hundred and twenty.

She left him standing there and started down the incline and toward the entrance and the parking lot, turning once to see where he was. She saw him following her at a steady pace, and the sight of him nearly knocked the breath out of her. She was mad, clearly mad, how could she feel so much for a man she barely knew, who lived halfway across the world, out of her world, who had no direct relationship to her reality? What had happened to all those self-protective instincts she had accreted? What he was, if she could be objective for a moment, was someone who had filled a void in her life, a potential replacement for a man she should never have married. And more, he was a dose of ecstasy to counteract that dose of tragedy in Rome. So, what did she expect, a lifetime commitment?

Who said that? He said that, that's who, and yes, that's exactly what she expected or rather wanted him to want. Didn't Renault have bloody offices in America? Somewhere in the midwest? Well, it wouldn't matter a bit to her to anchor the news in some small, obscure market somewhere.

He caught up with her, his blue linen jacket flapping behind him as he ran. But her eyes held him off, she didn't want to be taken lightly or even touched lightly, not this evening, not tonight. What she needed right now was a repeat of those words that he said the other night, lie a little, pretend. Why didn't he know when those half-truths would be most appreciated? He had her by the wrist. "Be careful or you'll fall," he cautioned. Too late. She had already fallen.

He walked her quickly down the rocks and over twigs, around stumps and branches, excavation pits, and dust kicking up over her shoes, the wind blowing through her hair. She followed as best she could without falling, tripping and catching herself. What the hell was the goddamn rush all of a sudden? Frustrated, confused, she struggled to keep up, calling his name once or twice to slow down, bending her knees, taking small steps until they finally reached the bottom of the hill and the pavement, several more yards until they reached the car. Out of breath, her hair caught in the corners of her mouth and sticking to her face, damp and sweaty, mascara burning her eyes and streaked down her cheeks, she asked in a voice that was unsteady, "What was that all about?"

He didn't answer. He seemed to be studying her, standing very still before he took both her wrists, holding them in the air to pull her close. She didn't have a chance even if she had wanted one.

"If you want to tell me you love me," he said with his lips almost on hers, "then say it." Closer. "Say it."

She said nothing. It was just like him to be so blinded by his own needs, his own ego.

"Sasha, I love you," he told her, and gathering her in his arms, he said it again.

And so she had won. Or had she?

Holding her wrists even tighter, he followed the pulse in her neck with his tongue until, mouth open and moist, he enveloped hers. It was her last chance to reciprocate. She saw him frown as he proceeded to make a calculated study of her face before a small smile appeared at the corners of his mouth. His instincts and timing fascinated her. Was she hungry? Starving, as a matter of fact. He was too smart to press issues right now, and she was too unsure to make proclamations. They settled on dinner.

Chapter Twenty-five

THE SHIP HOVERED eighteen miles off the coast of Tunisia in the general area of Sidi Bou Said and La Marsa. Had a direct line been charted, the vessel could have steamed right down the middle of the swimming pool of a beach club where both Jews and Muslims belonged.

The mood aboard was sober as the fourteen men gathered in the forward cabin, where Rafi sat with the deputy chief of staff of the Israeli Army. Eleven of the men who stood in that cramped room would remain outside the villa to do whatever was necessary to insure the safety of the others. Yoram, Ben and Ya'Acov would penetrate the villa to carry out the rest of it. At least that was what had been written on the section of the classified file that defined purpose of mission. Ronnie was already waiting on shore.

It was the idea of Moti, the army general who wore the knitted yamulka, to say the *Birkat Haderich*, although Rafi would have probably suggested it. It was something that certainly couldn't hurt and might even help, who knew? Anyway, who could be against covering all the bases at a time like this? Something Golda would have done. Golda. Please God, the men recited to each other and to themselves, keep us safe on the ground, on the sea, on the road, in the house; keep us safe from harm, Lord, so we can carry out this mission and return to our families and our country, please God, safe there, safe back, safe, safe. In the air, Moti added, keep them safe in that Boeing 707 that was circling overhead. The same plane that had jammed all the telephone lines in the area, Rafi reminded them, the one that would link all communications between the ship and headquarters in Tel Aviv and on the ground at the villa. Clutching each of them by the shoulder, Rafi moved around to say a final private word of encouragement before he took a deep breath and watched as they filed out to do a night's work.

Without any lights or radar, two rubber dinghies were lowered soundlessly into the black water with six men climbing into one and eight into the other. Attaching the collapsible oars to the slots on the sides of the crafts, two men in each raft rowed steadily toward shore, a beach covered with fallen needles from surrounding pine trees.

Two Volkswagen vans and a Peugeot 305 sedan, their engines idling, were parked at the far end of the sand near a wooden fence that marked the perimeter of the beach club property. Gideon sat at the wheel of the Peugeot, a cigarette illuminating the otherwise pitch-dark scene. Next to him was Ronnie with the cherubic face, sunny smile and newborn baby back home in Israel; Ronnie, who tonight was dressed up in black toreador pants, black tunic top, flat-soled rubber shoes, black gloves, full face of makeup and a shoulder-length blond wig. The Uzis and Barettas were on the floor in the backseat.

The rubber dinghies were dragged from the water, deflated and folded, the four sets of oars fitted neatly into a side compartment of one, both placed in the back of one of the vans and covered with a beige tarpaulin. Moving in graceful harmony, six of the men piled into one van, two seated in the front while four crouched down in the back next to a pile of weapons; eight in the other van, four seated in the front, three in the back while one crouched down in the rear next to the boxes of extra ammunition.

Without a word, Gideon shifted into reverse and backed the Peugeot until its tail-bumper lightly touched the wooden fence. Swinging around, he drove slowly over the sand until he reached the parking lot, then through the chain-link fence that had been cut and spread wide enough for the car and vans to pass through. Entering the narrow two-lane highway, he accelerated before turning up the car radio full blast to an all-Arab music station. His attention alternating between the radio in front of him and the rearview mirror to make sure the two vans were following, he slung an arm around Ronnie's shoulder, in plain view of anyone who happened to pass them on the road.

It took forty minutes to drive the twenty miles to Sidi Bou Said, where the Palestinian lived with his family.

Unable to sleep, Josette had spent the last hour restlessly leafing through a pile of magazines and newspapers that had just arrived that morning from Paris. Every month without fail Helene Villeneuve sent her daughter a package of reading material that covered everything from fashion to gossip to real estate, to help her keep up with what her mother considered the civilized world.

The baby slept soundly in his crib near the window, four feet from where Josette sat up in bed.

Tamir had just finished playing backgammon with Bernie, having beaten him soundly four out of six games. Summoning one of his guards to accompany the man to his car parked near the front gate, Karami walked with him as far as the door. Several last words were exchanged before he bid the man good night. From there he headed up to his study adjoining the bedroom.

There were fax messages to read and a letter to answer from an English film star interested in making a movie about the PLO.

Camilla was asleep in her room at the other end of the corridor.

It was 1:07 in the morning.

The commandos parked the two vans and the Peugeot at the end of the street. One man remained at the wheel of each van; the Peugeot was left empty. Dividing into three groups, seven of them fanned out to surround the villa, two continuing over the gate to penetrate the courtyard.

Bernie had just taken his keys from his pocket and was about to get into the car, the guard holding open the door, when Ben came up from behind and put a bullet in the guard's head. At the same moment Yoram fired one shot into Bernie's temple.

Leaving the bodies on the ground, they continued to the right of the front door, stopping only while Ben leaned into the window of the Mercedes to put another bullet into the head of Karami's driver. Running down the flight of stairs leading to the basement, they headed for the room containing the closed-circuit television monitor. The dog was nowhere to be seen.

Ya'Acov and Ronnie circled around to the back of the villa and came upon a guard who was about to talk into a walkie-talkie. Two bullets into him, two more into another guard who was relieving himself on one of Josette Karami's azalea bushes.

Gideon stood near the door, counting silently to twenty, waiting for Ben and Yoram to reappear from the basement, when he saw the dog. The animal had just turned the corner from the other side of the house and was bounding toward him. Gideon issued the command in Arabic when he saw Ben raise his gun to aim it at the animal. Too late. In mid-leap the dog was struck by two bullets, landing with a thud at Ben's feet. They had already lost seventeen seconds. Nodding to the others, Gideon walked over to the potted plant on the left side of the door and reached down for the key.

Karami heard the noise at exactly 1:11, the clicking of the front door downstairs. Pushing back his chair from his desk, he reached for his gun at the bottom of the third drawer. Somewhere in his mind he realized what was about to happen although as he moved around his study it was less fear than rage rising in his throat. Another sound downstairs confirmed what for an instant he tried to convince himself was not about to happen.

The group was downstairs and inside the house; Ben, Ya'Acov and Yoram were surrounding Gideon on either side while Ronnie stood slightly off to the front and left. For the first time in one minute and fourteen seconds no one moved.

But not for long. Within seconds Tamir Karami appeared at the door of his study. Josette appeared at the door of her bedroom, clutching the baby to her. Later she would say that it was a choice between grabbing the gun under her pillow or Tarek. Seconds more and Camilla also appeared, running the length of the hallway toward her father.

With a gesture that would later be considered imprudent at best, arrogant at worst, or as someone suggested, done by a man in a state of shock, Karami fired one shot in the direction of the downstairs entrance foyer. He never fired another. The first bullet from Gideon's gun blasted the weapon out of his hand. Four more bullets in rapid succession nearly severed the hand from his arm. As his wife and daughter and baby watched, Karami stumbled forward and down several steps, his other arm looped around the bannister. Gideon was immediately upon him. Holding his gun in both hands—trained in Israel, three wars, a revered member of the Sayaret Malkal, Mossad operative, bereaved father and husband—he fired two shots point-blank range into Karami's head. A barrage of bullets followed from other guns while someone . . . perhaps Josette . . . screamed "enough."

But it was not enough. Not yet, as another fusillade poured into Karami from five different weapons.

Josette raced down the stairs, covered her husband's body with her own, still holding the baby. Camilla followed, hanging back as she made unintelligible sounds.

Later, mother and daughter would remember different first impressions . . . Camilla would recall the blond woman who stood to one side with what looked like a video camera in her hands, as if she was taping the murder. And Josette would describe the man who knelt beside her husband's body to check the pulse in the side of his neck. Not because he appeared to be the leader nor because he was the one who fired the first shot but because she had never seen eyes that were so blue before . . .

After Gideon was certain that Karami was dead, he stood and took the girl's arm to lead her away from the body, which was when Josette did something that stunned the half dozen men who were still in evidence throughout the downstairs of the house. Walking calmly over to her daughter, she handed her the baby before leaning her head back against the wall. Looking at Gideon, she said, "Shoot me, let me die so I can be with him." Again, it was Gideon who led the woman back to her daughter and her baby. They had no issue with her, he told her gently, the best thing to do was to attend to her children, they needed her. There was nothing left to do for her husband. It was over . . .

They did not just leave, Josette would repeat again and again to everyone who questioned her—they departed as they had entered—without warning. There was only one significant difference—one less of hers, the same number of theirs . . .

The baby was whimpering, his head resting against Camilla's cheek, eyes wide. Josette pressed the baby's hand to her lips, wiped the tears from her daughter's face and told her that she would be right back, she was going to get help.

Running up the steps to the veranda and off the master bedroom, she flung open the door and stood outside calling for help. But one of the purposeful features of the villa was that it was situated in such a way that unless the wind blew in exactly the right direction nobody could hear sounds—even such as her cries—coming from it. Ironically, it had been intended to insure privacy for the Karami family.

The night was still.

It occurred to her then to telephone for help, but all the phone lines were dead, she discovered. Holding up the hem of her nightgown, she took the stairs two at a time before racing across the foyer floor to the front door. Apparently they had locked it from the outside and it took her a full eight or nine minutes to remember where she had put her keys, run back upstairs to dump out her purse before running back down—key in hand—to unlock the door. At that moment, she never wondered how or where they had gotten a key to enter the house.

Tears running into her mouth, she almost tripped and fell over the two guards who lay sprawled in the driveway, the television producer as well—each with bullets in his head. She turned then to avoid the grisly sight and saw Shwai-shwai, his fur matted with patches of blood, lying under a tree.

Around to the back of the house then, only to discover more bodies, two more dead guards with bullets in the chest and stomach. Around to the front near the gate, which was where she noticed the body of the driver—the back of his head blown out over the seats. She ran until she reached the nearest house, leaned on the bell, and waited perhaps five minutes before someone responded. Another moment or two before she could catch her breath sufficiently to explain what had happened. Reluctantly, the neighbor agreed to lend her his car and driver so she could take her husband to the hospital.

Josette instructed the frightened chauffeur to take the car over to her house and park it inside the courtyard. She would go ahead on foot, the children were waiting for her, her husband. She spoke in disjointed sentences that made little sense.

The body still felt warm, she tried to convince her daughter when she entered the house. There was hope if they could just get him to the doctor. Putting his body into the car was too much for Josette to manage alone, and the borrowed driver refused to go near the death house, as he called it. A weak stomach and a family who needed him alive were muttered excuses for his staying in the car.

Please help, her words ended in a desperate crescendo, *please* . . .

Camilla was too stunned to move.

Lifting the body under its arms, Josette alone dragged it down the rest of the stairs and as far as the front door before whatever self-control she had mustered suddenly left her. Collapsing in a quiet hysteria, she allowed herself to be helped to her feet by her daughter. Placing the baby on the floor near his father's body, the girl held her mother in her arms, somehow now managing to help do what had to be done. Mother and daughter maneuvered the body out of the house, over the pebbles in the driveway and onto the backseat of the car. It would be something that neither would remember. Or forget.

It was a full thirty minutes before they arrived at the hospital somewhere between Sidi Bou Said and Gammarth; another ten minutes to summon help from the night staff; another five minutes to tell the story so the police could be summoned; more time while the doctor examined the body and informed the wife that she was now a widow. And then at least forty minutes before several inefficient and sleepy Tunisian officials arrived.

Again the story took time to tell since Camilla and Josette kept talking, respectively, about the blond woman with the video camera and the killer with the blue eyes.

The police were distracted.

What they should have been concentrating on was how the hit team had arrived in Sidi Bou Said, which would have given a better idea about how they were escaping. As it was, the roadblocks thrown up all around Tunis and the suburbs proved useless.

The Israeli commando unit had already reached the beach. Leaving the car and the two vans parked on the sand, they shoved a ten-dollar bill under each windshield along with a note written in Arabic excusing themselves for any inconvenience they might have caused by not returning the vehicles directly to Avis. Gideon was not amused.

The rafts were inflated and set in the water, this time with eight men in each, with the same two men in each paddling toward the waiting ship six miles off shore. It took only thirty-six minutes to approach and board.

Ronnie had already discarded his black pants and tunic, shoes and wig, and was about to pull on a green jumpsuit and running shoes. Someone whistled.

Forty minutes later Gideon was still standing in the same spot on the deck as the boat made its way toward Haifa. Over. Finished. There was little to say. Still, the pain and anguish were there. He still had no one, Miriam was still dead, and Sasha had become another casualty on the list. Reaching into his pocket, Gideon took out the key to her hotel room and tossed it into the water. That was one appointment he would not be keeping.

Chapter Twenty-six

AT FIVE IN THE MORNING the telephone rang in Sasha's hotel room. She had been dreaming about Carl who became Gideon who became Carl again, the men interchangeable, the plot familiar. Each left her in the dream, walked out with no excuse or warning, no explanation or regret.

Half asleep, she grabbed at the phone, knocking over a glass of water in the process. The voice on the other end seemed to recite words in some sort of bizarre monotone. Someone's husband was dead, murdered, and she was with the body at a clinic called Sidi Sala on Amikar Street and please come quickly please . . .

It wasn't making real sense to Sasha, perhaps she hadn't heard right, maybe it was another dream. But when she sat up in bed her hand brushed against the front of her T-shirt just as her eyes focused on the floor where the glass had broken. She reached over to turn on the light.

Someone gently took the phone from Josette then, when her sobs became too violent for her to continue. There were forms to fill out, a female voice now explained to Sasha, a police report to make, investigations to begin and nothing could happen until Madame Karami surrendered the body to the people who would be conducting the autopsy and the inquiry. Perhaps, Sasha was told, she could convince Madame Karami to cooperate, since the way she was resisting did not make things any easier . . .

Scribbling the name and address of the clinic, directions and telephone number, Sasha heard herself saying that she'd be there in ten minutes, no make it twenty. The children, she hadn't even thought to ask after she hung up, were they there, were they hurt, had they seen what happened? Bernie, what about Bernie, maybe she should call to tell him in case he wanted to get the crew there. God, what a thought. She decided against it, this wasn't about television. A woman had called another woman because her husband had just been murdered, for Christ's sake.

She ripped off the damp T-shirt, pulled on a pair of jeans, rushed into the bathroom to squeeze a glob of toothpaste in her mouth, the toothbrush clenched between her teeth as she searched around for a shirt or sweater. She set the toothbrush on the dresser, pulled on a cotton sweater. She felt a chill as she leaned over the sink to finish brushing her teeth. Why not? She had just seen a man alive, and now he was dead. Shoes. Hunting around on the floor, she found a pair and slipped them on before she began throwing things into a bag—hairbrush, room key, notebook, pen. Should she leave Gideon a message in case he arrived while she was at the clinic? Notebook, pen, hairbrush, she repeated the items again in her head before slamming out of the room and into the hall to run toward the lobby. It was five-fifteen.

There was no need to see the bloody sheet that covered the hulking form on the stretcher to know that Tamir Karami was dead. It was enough to look into the face of his widow. Sitting on a straight-back wooden chair with her hair resting lightly on the covered body, she looked at Sasha as she approached, dead eyes. Camilla was on the floor, her back against the wall, the baby in her arms. Kneeling in front of the chair, Sasha touched the woman's arm. "Josette, I'm here."

"He's dead," was the only response, as if there had been some doubt.

"How?"

"The way we always knew. So many of them, all over the house, shooting at everybody . . ."

"Not at you," Sasha said, "not the children."

Josette shook her head. "No, not us, they didn't hurt us."

The girl had inched forward. "Don't cry," Camilla said, holding her mother's hand. "Are you afraid?"

"No, I'm not afraid," she told her daughter, although the look she gave Sasha said something different.

"Did you see them?" Sasha asked, "did you see . . ." She couldn't bring herself to finish.

Josette nodded. Camilla spoke up. "A blond woman, there was a blond woman with a camera and about five men or maybe more. I don't remember. Just the blond woman, that's all I can remember."

"And my husband's killer," Josette added, pausing to take gulps of air, "with the blue eyes."

There it was. Sasha felt as if she had been stabbed through the heart, as if she was spinning backward and down and couldn't catch her breath. "What can I do?" she asked, trying to push it from her mind—the fear, the fantasy. "How can I help?"—aware that there was no more talk of martyrs or courage or sacrifice or struggle.

Blue eyes.

"Don't let them take him," Josette told her. "Please don't let them touch him. Not yet."

It remained with Sasha, somewhere in her subconscious, the image of the killer with blue eyes. Moving slowly toward the desk, where doctors and police were conferring, where hospital workers milled around, she said, "I'm Sasha Beale and I'm here to help Mrs. Karami." She looked from one to the other. "Someone called me to come help so the body could be released."

They seemed nervous when they answered her. Could she please identify the body, since the passport and driver's license were American? Procedures took longer for a non-Arab foreigner, as she could well imagine.

She shook her head. "What do you mean, American?" she said. "I thought Mr. Karami had a Jordanian passport."

Not Mr. Karami, they told her. Mr. Hernandez, Mr. Bernard Hernandez. They needed her to identify the body so they could remove it to downstairs, where it was cool, until arrangements could be made for transport back to his country of origin.

She slipped down almost to her knees and would have fallen if they hadn't grabbed her under the arms. Seating her gently in a chair, someone put some smelling salts under her nose. It was worse than a nightmare, was the first thought she had when her eyes opened. It was too much, there couldn't be much more, not Bernie, oh my God, no, not Bernie . . .

When she had calmed down they continued their official explanations of what was needed from her. An investigation would begin as soon as each body was accounted for and permission was granted for an autopsy. Would she mind? They would appreciate it if they could deal with the foreigner since that was the most complicated from an official point of view. They hoped she understood. Afterward she could take full responsibility for removing the body as well as hiring an ambulance to transport it to the airport.

She needed a bathroom, she felt as if she would throw up. Two nurses, one on each side, helped her to a foul-smelling toilet down the hall. She refused to use it. Maury. She had to call Maury, she had to find a working phone and call Maury because he would know what to do about permission for an autopsy or refusing permission for an autopsy and about an ambulance for "taking a dead body back to its country of origin," like they said in the damn jargon. Was there a different number to call, she wondered, to make those kind of airline reservations where information like seat assignments or special meals weren't relevant? . . .

They were watching her, the whole lot of them in their blood-stained uniforms were watching her as if she'd come from another planet. Gideon. She didn't leave a message for him at the hotel, she forgot.

Excusing herself so she could think, she walked back to where Josette was still sitting near her husband's bloodied body. Quietly so that no one could hear, she whispered, "Bernie." The woman nodded. "Why?" Sasha mouthed the words. "Everybody, everybody except us. The dog too." The dog. Only someone who knew his name could stop him from attacking. Isn't that what Josette had said? "I've got to call New York. Can you stay here for a few minutes while I find a phone? I promise I won't be long."

Josette nodded, Camilla's head on her lap, the baby in her arms.

"They won't touch him, I promise. Not until I come back." The dog's name flashed through her head— Shwai-shwai. Did she ever tell him? She looked briefly at Josette. Was he tall, this man who killed your husband, was he short, fat, thin, was he graying at the temples and did he have a scar just under his right eye? The unspoken questions stabbed at her as she turned to walk away, wanting to know, not wanting to know. It was crazy. When Gideon came back from his business in Algeria she would introduce him to Josette. The whole thing was absurd, crazy.

* * *

Six in the morning in Tunisia was eleven at night in New York. Maury would either be back at the office working or at home doing other things, which meant that the phone there would be turned off. Of that she was certain, since once she had been one of those ''other things.'' So calling the office meant that at least someone would answer and accept charges and eventually track down Maury even if that meant calling his doorman to ring him on the house phone. Keep a line open, instinct dictated, call the office.

She followed an orderly into a small airless room where there was an archaic dial phone. Her voice sounded as if it belonged to someone else when she picked it up to give the operator the information. She turned to the orderly and asked for a cigarette while she waited for the operator to connect her with New York. Finally she heard ringing, then a female voice answered and the operator announced that there was a collect call from Tunisia.

''He's in edit,'' the voice said.

''Put him on the phone,'' she screamed over the operator's words.

The hostility on the other end was evident, she could hear it. Another desperate broad, another one of Glick's bimbos. ''Who wants him, operator?''

''Sasha Beale,'' Sasha said through clenched teeth.

''You'll have to stop speaking,'' the operator warned, ''until they accept the call or I'll have to disconnect you.''

But Sasha Beale was miles beyond rules and regulations. ''Accept the fucking charges, goddamnit.''

''We can't keep an open line for more than forty-five seconds,'' the operator intoned.

''Please.'' Sasha was begging now, terrified the time was up and she'd be cut off. She heard the receiver slamming and banging and clanking against the side of the metal desk before she heard Maury's voice on the line.

"Sasha, what's the matter? What time is it there?"

"Maury, oh God . . . Maury—"

"Sasha, what's happened?"

"Bernie—Bernie's dead, Karami's dead." She could see the color drain from his face.

"Oh my God, are you all right?"

"Dead." She was crying, out of control now.

"How, Sasha, please, try to tell me how it happened."

"Backgammon . . ." was her seemingly incoherent reply.

"Who, Sasha, who did it?"

How should she know who? If she had played the game she'd know. If she had played the game she'd be dead. "Karami and his bodyguards shot to death. And Bernie, dead."

"The fuckers," he said "goddamn fuckers."

She wasn't sure what fuckers he was talking about.

"I'm on my way," he said.

She was more confused. "Where to?"

"You tell me."

"I don't know, Maury . . ."

Was she alive, was she really standing in this awful place with her nostrils clogged with the sticky odor of fresh blood, her ears filled with sounds of anguish and grief? She wanted to assure Maury that nothing horrible had happened to *her*. Once again, she'd just been caught on the periphery of a catastrophe. A string of bad luck, stand back, hold it right there, this woman seems to attract random acts of violence. A real newshawk, Johnny-on-the-spot.

"What about the funeral?" Maury asked gently.

She didn't know. She didn't know very much. What about the possibility of blue eyes . . . you see, she had this lover who had them and then Josette said the assassin had them too, but then there was the question about the dog because she was pretty sure she had told her lover his name so it couldn't have been him because he could have called off the dog . . .

"Sasha," Maury said. "I want to be there with you now—"

"It's all right," she whispered, "I'm all right."

"Can you find out where Karami's going to be buried?"

Strange, wasn't it, that as prepared for death as Karami was, as fatalistic about living with the inevitable, Sasha somehow was certain that he didn't have a plot in some cemetery somewhere. In his "country of origin," for example. But then, he didn't have a country of origin anymore. Wasn't that his whole point?

Chapter Twenty-seven

WHILE THE KARAMI FAMILY searched for a country that would accept the body for burial, Sasha searched for answers.

Gideon never showed up that night at the hotel or the next night or the night after that. He did not call. There was a part of Sasha that never expected to hear from him again and a part of her that was shocked that she did not. Whatever her feelings, she kept them to herself; there was, after all, no one she could talk to or confide in. And if she had found someone, she would have been taken either for a liar or an accomplice or a woman scorned who preferred to believe that her lover was a cold-blooded killer rather than a routine bastard.

Though there was no victory claimed, no phone call to Agence France Presse as usually happened in these cases, it was generally presumed that it was an Israeli operation. Sasha stayed with the Karami family and so learned firsthand the information about the assassination as it reached the family.

One of the members of the squad had apparently gotten to Saba Khalil, the coffee man's brother, and convinced him that there was a plot against Karami. Less out of loyalty to the PLO than because he had a dying baby, the man was persuaded to deliver his brother, Ali Khalil. In return, it seemed, there was money for the child's operation, doctors, a safe haven for the entire family in some remote part of the Negev

319

and, miraculously, a new identity. Or at least that was the prevailing opinion, since the man and his family had not been seen or heard from since. As for Ali Khalil, the reason he had ended up floating in the wadi of the Yarmuch River was anybody's guess. It was believed, however, that after the Israelis talked to him, they realized they had made a bad choice and decided to cut their losses.

Throughout every hour of every day, while Sasha was taping and interviewing and watching Josette battle the maze of bureaucracy, she thought about Gideon. While she fielded telephone calls and tried to keep the world press at bay outside the villa, she went over her life with him, a history that spanned four weeks and two countries.

She had not been pushed in the Tuileries that morning, she had fallen; she had not been forced to have breakfast, she had been invited; she had not been raped, she had wanted him. Such were her very private admissions. To herself. But then, everything that had to do with her relationship with Gideon remained private, hidden inside her head and her heart.

Josette Karami was another story. There was nothing that resembled privacy when it came to her life. She had become the most important widow of the Palestinian cause, just as once she had been the wife of one of the most important leaders.

King Hussein refused to allow the funeral to take place in his country. Afraid that the masses of Palestinians under his rule would turn the occasion into an excuse to riot and overthrow his already shaken kingdom, he chose not to welcome the remains of the Palestinian leader in Jordan. The family entreaties even enlisted the efforts of one of the speakers of the Jordanian parliament. No use. The little king was adamant, the slain revolutionary would not have a final resting place in Jordan with a view of the West Bank. Josette was bitter.

In the end, all decisions about the funeral were made by a team of Abus who arrived to handle everything that had to do with the Karami family. Fahd, the oldest boy, looking subdued and timid, was brought by one of them from England. As the days passed his behavior changed to overtly aggressive although he seemed confused about how to act as the new head of the family.

Damascus was chosen as the burial city mainly because Syria was the only country that had made an offer. And it was made less as a humanitarian gesture on the part of President Hafez al Assad than as a calculated move to mend the rift between the two Arab entities. At least such was the analysis of the more cynical, who believed that a united Syrian and PLO front would make another push against the Christians in Lebanon successful.

The masses of people that lined the streets in Sidi Bou Said as the family made their way to the airport for the trip to Damascus was remarkable. The scene as the casket was loaded into the belly of the gleaming white airplane that the Saudis had sent was impressive. Third World diplomats and leaders of formerly splintered factions of the PLO acted united in their sorrow. Two other American networks were there, several English and German crews and four French. Clips on Karami's life were broadcast throughout the world, including visuals of his various military actions, or terrorist attacks, take your pick. The first segment of "Family" was the last interview given by the Palestinian and was aired earlier than scheduled, receiving an 11.6 Nielsen share. Controversial, was the verdict. Controversial and barbaric and heartless and dedicated and brave, and all in the name of a revolution that in the end killed him. And still, the Israelis refused to take credit for the act. And still, Gideon didn't call.

* * *

Maury did not come to Syria, after all. Not a good idea, it was decided, not with a name like Glick and random crazies who wanted nothing more than a one-way ticket to Mecca. It was not exactly the time for a Jew to attend a PLO funeral in a hostile Arab country. But what about Sasha? If she told Maury once, she told him a thousand times . . . she was a Jewish girl who knew how to twirl a baton. And anyway, by then she was an accepted member of the Karami entourage.

She interviewed and she taped, she talked and she listened. Damascus was no different than Sidi Bou Said with the same faces and the same speeches and the same threats of reprisal and the same anguish. Through it all she moved as if in a trance, propelled by sporadic surges of adrenaline and by Josette's example of strength in the face of profound sadness. How profound? How could anyone judge the level of someone else's loss? For Josette it had to do only with her past. For Sasha it had to do only with her future.

Maury waited for Sasha in Paris, in the same hotel, he assured her, in the hope that it would keep things simple and uncomplicated. But for her, nothing could ever be simple or uncomplicated again. As she sat on the plane on her way to Paris she decided that this time, Gideon Whoeverhewas, made all those other withholding S.O.B.'s look like rank amateurs. The next time a man expressed a desire or an interest in her, the wisest response would be to disconnect her telephone and call in the movers. *Address unknown. At the customer's request the number has been changed to an unlisted number.*

The possibilities were impossible . . . there was still the little matter of that physical description of one of the killers, and the little matter that Gideon had just happened to disappear from her life.

By the time the plane was making its final approach into Charles de Gaulle, Sasha had accepted the fact that, either way, she had fallen in love with a killer. And either way, she was a loser.

Chapter Twenty-eight

WHEN HE RETURNED to Israel, Gideon went immediately to the cemetery to visit his wife and son. Under a row of young olive trees and several baby spruce, the graves lay unmarked. Dried flowers were strewn on the fresh mound of earth, more flowers were wilting in brown water in glass jars, notes were wedged in between a row of stones that separated mother from son, childish scrawls that had been written by visiting school children. For Avi.

From the first moment that he knelt down to touch the ground, he felt that same assault on his conscience, that same awareness of time in a different context. Time that would never heal those feelings of guilt and impotence, time that would eventually become out of synch with what had once been an earthly order, time when he would be too old to be his wife's husband, too old to be the father of such a small boy.

It was Sunday. As he walked back through the gates and toward his car he wondered if he could ever talk about them again to anyone here without provoking impassioned discussions about war and peace and negotiation. He wondered if they would ever stop being clichés or symbols, already the subject of folk songs performed on the radio and in bars, statistics to the army, incentives for harsher methods by the Likud, conciliation by Labor.

There was something especially mournful about today, more even than on the day that they died, more even than on the day they were buried. Had it been anywhere else but in Israel he would have put to rest what was left in coffins that he would have ordered lowered into flames. At least then he could have breathed them inside instead of anguishing over the totalities of them, without imagining the stages of disintegration from ashes to dust. Dead was dead, wasn't that what Gideon had said as they'd wandered the ruins in Carthage what seemed a lifetime ago? He felt suddenly excluded from everyone he had ever loved, as if he had been left behind and forgotten. Or left behind to forget.

He drove north until he reached the Golan Heights, where he found himself walking among more graves. The bodies of unclaimed Syrian soldiers left over from the 1973 Yom Kippur War. Buried beneath still-active mine fields with white cloth as markers, these were the youth who had been chained by the ankles to their tanks and never reclaimed by their commanding officers.

To the Sea of Galilee, then, where he wandered into a kibbutz near Tiberius. But it could have been an army base with all the tanks and anti-aircraft missiles that were positioned around the fields of vegetables and the orchards of fruit. He thought of Miriam, and felt himself smile. What was it she used to say about pseudo-socialist American women who came to Israel ostensibly to work the soil or teach crafts, but who really came to find husbands? Folk-singing neurotics, she called them, although she always hastened to add that communal living was better than eating a cheese sandwich alone in some dingy apartment in Queens. He wondered what she would have said now, what advice or pithy remark she would have made about how he was supposed to spend the rest of his life.

He drove over miles of unpaved roads and badly paved highways, through villages and newly created settlements. And through every single minute of every single mile, she never left his mind, her voice sounded in his ears, Sasha's face appeared before his eyes. What if she had been there that night? Then what? It was too unthinkable to imagine.

In the early dawn hours Gideon found himself in Eilat, gazing across the Gulf of Aqaba to Jordan. Everything had changed, everything seemed somehow irrelevant to what had once been essential for survival. Mined waters, electrified fences, Bedouin trackers, strategic depth to mobilize an army and an air force or protect against infiltration seemed archaic when long-range technological horrors were now part of the equation. *Kill one man and you are a murderer. Kill millions and you are a conqueror. Kill all and you are God.* It baffled him why the words of Jean Rostand had suddenly entered his head. Something warned him to be careful then, not to confuse political disenchantment with the passion he held for this woman. A part of him believed that it was all the same, there was no difference between his love for her and his love for his country. In each case, what began as duty had turned to obsession had become love had ended in loss.

He got into his car to head back to Herziliah, still not certain who or what was the real cause of his turmoil.

It was no surprise that Rafi came regularly to visit, and it was even less of a surprise that he refused to accept Gideon's resignation. Logical reasons were repeatedly cited: he was acting under enormous strain, his affairs weren't settled, the house should be sold, he should take a leave of absence, a couple of weeks at one of those spas along the Dead Sea. Then they'd talk. Then they'd discuss his resigning.

Eventually Rafi suggested that Gideon move in with him and his wife for a while. Oh, not so much because he was concerned or worried about him but because his wife was driving him crazy. All she did was badger him to know if Gideon was eating properly, sleeping enough, taking care of himself. How was he supposed to assure her that everything was fine if he really wasn't sure himself? So, could Gideon do him a favor and come and stay with them for a while? If nothing else, it would keep Ruthie quiet.

Gideon declined, again and again he declined each time either Rafi or Ruthie brought it up or called or sent notes or dropped by. He made excuses until he couldn't bother anymore and merely explained that he needed time to be alone so he would work things out and make the right decisions. Until one day Gideon called them to announce that he was leaving Israel for a while. Something about an uncle in Toulouse, his father's brother who had real-estate holdings but was getting too old to handle things alone. He was offering Gideon a chance to come in with him and learn the business. Rafi pretended he didn't hear him. Learn the *business* . . . ?

They were running the Karami interview and funeral on the Israeli television tonight, the older man informed him. Apparently they were also airing some of the Palestinian's more violent attacks, and it seemed the Beale girl was hosting the program. So, maybe he'd like to come over, have some dinner and watch a little television with them.

Which, of course, was the last thing Gideon wanted to do. Or was able to face.

Chapter Twenty-nine

SASHA GOT OFF the plane in Paris, rode the movable walkways, cleared passport control—all the time feeling as if she were viewing life from a distance—before walking into Maury's arms.

They had been in touch regularly during those last days in Tunisia, although during the time she spent in Syria they had not talked. There had been no point in making idle conversation, which was all that could be said over the phone from a place like that. Now, waiting for her bags to appear, there was still little to say and hardly any tears, just an unspoken relief to be finally together in a safe place.

Head on his shoulder, arm around his waist, Sasha walked with him toward the waiting car, aware that for the first time in over a month there were no schedules or deadlines. But then, there was no Gideon either, and no Bernie, nothing except Maury and Sasha to rehash what had happened. It did not exactly guarantee an absence of pain. Well, whoever promised her a rose garden?

The first thing she did when she arrived at the hotel was to try the number that Gideon had given her as his home phone in Paris. It rang and it rang, a hollow sound that reverberated in what sounded like an empty apartment. She called the FBN Bureau in Tel Aviv, something that she was unable to do from either Arab country. It took several bad connections before she was put through to the home of the FBN correspondent, who congratulated her on her interview and coverage of the Karami funeral. Unfortunately he had run into a stone wall when it came to any information on those two Israeli victims of the Rome bombing. It was as if they had never existed. Odd, he admitted, but not that odd around there, since there was always the primary concern of security of the state. He'd keep her posted, things would loosen up when all the excitement died down.

She was outraged. She dragged poor Maury into the living room of their suite and sat him down to listen. She told him everything then, from the beginning to the middle to the end, not leaving out a single detail, not leaving out the most minute impression or nuance. She even told him about Gideon, everything, even hauled out the photographs of the woman and the boy after the bombing, even forced herself to tell him her suspicions that he was part of the team that took out Karami. Everything, information she had learned from the Karami family and the PLO and the countless Tunisian officials and other Arabs that she had interviewed along the way. Everyone who was or could have been connected to the story. Except, of course, the Israelis. They were still lying low.

"Am I crazy?" she asked after she had finished. "Maury, what would you do if you were me?"

He stood up, his hands in his pockets as he strolled over to the window. "Unfortunately you got caught in a very ugly mess." He turned around. "Rome." He walked over and sat next to her. "And then you got involved in another ugly mess—Karami. And added to all of that, you got involved with a real prick." He took her hand. "So, if it makes you feel better to believe that he dumped you because he's really a hit man, then be my guest." He leaned forward. "You want my advice?"

She nodded.

"We're in Paris in a beautiful suite in an expensive hotel. The sun's shining and the network's picking up the tab. We're alive and healthy and free to do whatever the fuck we want. So, come on, who wants to sit here and waste all this by speculating about the Middle East or some sonofabitch who was too dumb to know when he had a prize?"

She smiled. "But what about the blue eyes?"

"My Uncle Seymour has blue eyes, and from time to time he disappears and my Aunt Shirley threatens to call Missing Persons. In Seymour's case he's usually with his bimbo bookkeeper." Maury shrugged. "Who knows, he could really be a Mossad hit man." He touched her nose. "He could have been the one who knocked off Karami." He stood. "One thing, did Josette mention if the guy had a Brooklyn accent?"

"All right, all right, Maury," Sasha said. "I get the point." What amazed her then was that Maury was so reassuring and familiar, the sanest person in her life, and even she had to laugh when that thought occurred to her. "Can you imagine what a sorry state my life is in when you're the sanest person in it?"

He looked at her a moment. "So, how come we never made it?"

It was a question of endings, she told him. They set the tone for beginnings. And, let's face it, she told him, I'm an expert on endings. "It ended too well with you to go back to what it was," she said. He was someone she trusted, a friend who had once been a lover and who was still around to be her friend even after the rest of it was over. Maybe she liked S.O.B.s. Maybe she had this thing for men who treated her badly. Gideon.

After dinner that night she asked Maury if she could sleep in his room, in his bed, and then while she happened to be there, if they could make love. At least once in her life, maybe the only time, she wanted to make love with someone and wake up in the morning when the fallout wasn't lethal.

There were no excuses and no ratings. It wasn't great but then neither of them expected it would be. Nor did they particularly care, since the sex part was the least of it. For Sasha it was something she did out of an intense need rather than an intense desire. For Maury—and God how she loved him for being so goddamn sane—it was an expression of concern for someone he cared deeply about. Regardless of the outcome, Sasha made him promise that nothing would ever change between them. Pact, swear to God, cross hearts, fingers, and toes. Never.

"So, what about Bendex?" Sasha asked over breakfast in bed.

Bendex was too young, Maury admitted, too ambitious, too hungry. If he wanted ambitious and hungry he could cover the midwestern markets and have his pick of any of those baby anchors out there. He thought Bendex wanted something more, like a home and children and quiet evenings.

Sasha had to laugh. "As if you want any of those things," she said. "What you want is someone to spend quiet evenings at home with your children while you roam those midwestern markets having your pick of those ambitious and hungry baby anchors out there."

"So, I'm fucked up," he said, "but at least I don't pretend to be something I'm not." He hugged her after he said it because he saw her face and right away realized his mistake.

"What about your fascination with the Middle East?" she said, changing the subject. "Remember, Maury, you promised you'd tell me when I got back from Tunisia."

"I've had it with the Middle East, I told you. Let's

get dressed and get out of here. Let's go shopping and
have a long alcoholic lunch. What do you say? Let's get
your mind off all this bullshit.''

The day was beautiful and things would get back to
normal very soon. He promised. She agreed even if she
didn't believe for an instant that things would ever get
back to the way they once were, as if that was so normal.

Maury left for New York two days later and encouraged her to stay on for a while. To think, to walk, to
have some time alone before everything would begin all
over again in New York. The second segment of the
''Family'' series was scheduled to begin shooting at the
end of the month in Appalachia. This time the location
would be in a migrant laborer's shack in the mountains
of North Carolina. She was ashamed that it sounded so
appealing and so inviting. And so safe.

She went to the street where Gideon's apartment was,
if there had really been a Gideon. No one answered the
intercom and so she rang the concierge. Of course, the
old Portuguese woman knew nothing, never heard of a
Gideon Aitchison, didn't remember seeing a man coming or going out of that apartment. But when Sasha fired
off questions at the woman—who lives there now, could
she go up and take a look, what about the mail, pass-
keys—the guardian simply shut the lobby door in her
face.

She jogged in the Tuileries in the hope that she might
see him there. But even St. Francis of Assisi and the
birds and that photographer were nowhere to be found.
Only the statues and the mime remained, only the Louvre
and the Place de la Concorde and the Eiffel Tower were
still visible. Although had they disappeared as well, she
wouldn't have been surprised.

She walked the streets of Paris looking for him.

Learning Paris like an explorer, she gauged distances, followed maps, memorized various arrondissements, figuring out how one didn't necessarily follow the other. As if her reward for exhausting herself would be Gideon, as if the more she suffered and ached, the greater the chance that he would miraculously appear to offer rational explanations.

She wandered the rue de Vaugirard, discovering that it was the longest street in Paris, beginning at the Porte de Versailles and continuing to the Boulevard Saint Michel, covering at least four major neighborhoods.

Sometimes she would dismiss her suspicions and revert to what was probably the reality, that he was just another bourgeois Frenchman who had picked up an American tourist and got tired of her. Still, she felt compelled to search for him in the tearooms and antique shops along the Avenue Victor Hugo and the Boulevard Haussman, all the while wishing that she had never met Carl Feldhammer, whom she blamed for her trip to Rome in the first place. If only she hadn't gone, if only she hadn't stopped to buy boots. If only, if only, if only.

On the day before she was supposed to fly back to New York she summoned the courage to call Renault.

No one had ever heard of Gideon Aitchison. According to the computerized personnel records there was no one by that name who worked out of either the Paris office or any of the offices in the provinces. And that information went back five years. Longer than that and they would have to call up their dead files.

North Africa, she pressed, feeling like a fool, was it possible that he was on some kind of a consulting basis where he spent most of his time in North Africa?

"For what purpose?" was the baffled reply.

"Why, checking out locations for a new plant."

The voice on the other end of the phone became

amused. "Renault has no plans for expansion, especially in that part of the world." The company's export arrangements, the man went on, were well covered, considering the economy and the potential political instability in North Africa. But when she persisted, when her tone edged into the desperate, the man responded. Was she certain that she had the right name? Would she like to leave a number in case something turned up? Was she sure she wasn't mistaken? Oh, she was mistaken all right, but there was no point in leaving a number. She thanked the man for his trouble before hanging up, before hating herself for allowing the tears to start and to continue off and on for the rest of the afternoon.

There was only one moment when she was granted a reprieve. When she actually had to laugh. She had called for another meeting with that press attaché from the Israeli Embassy to see if he would tell her anything at all. But even as she rode in the taxi for her appointment she wasn't the least bit hopeful. If she had learned anything, it was not to believe anything anybody told her when it came to international terrorism, especially people who came from anywhere in the Middle East.

Seated behind that same paper-strewn desk, the man expressed pleasure at seeing her again, told her how well she looked, that Tunisia must have agreed with her. But before she could ask a question he posed one of his own: who did she think could have done such a terrible deed, killing the Palestinian in front of his whole family like that?

At first she thought it was a joke, certainly after he actually *tisked* twice after asking. But when she realized that he was serious, that he actually thought she would buy his act, she decided to play along. She shrugged, replied that she wondered the same thing, which was one of the reasons why she had come to see him today. There were rumors, of course, but so far nobody had anything that even remotely resembled concrete evi dence. "Although rumor has it that it was the Israelis who killed in revenge. After all, it was reported that Tamir Karami was the last PLO member on Golda Meir's hit list from the seventies."

"If only it was that simple," he said sadly, "if only we were like our enemies and had the mentality to murder in cold blood like that." He stood. "And Golda making a hit list?' He laughed. "She was a grandmother, for goodness sake." He walked around his desk. The appointment was over. But just before he escorted her out the door and down the stairs, she stopped. "By the way, did you happen to see the piece I did on the Karami assassination? I believe it was aired last night."

"Not assassination, Miss Beale. Execution. Tamir Karami was executed."

He then wished her a pleasant stay in Paris and a safe trip back to the States. She said nothing as she stood in the reception area of the Israeli Embassy, wondering if life was nothing more than a series of peculiar euphemisms. "Execution" better than "assassination."

She had already learned that "a coffee" meant breakfast, and "I love you" meant goodbye.

Chapter Thirty

THE SKY WAS GRAY and overcast, the temperatures hovering just above freezing at seven o'clock on a Sunday morning in Central Park. Dressed in layers, sweat pants and shirts, long underwear, socks, gloves and a scarf that covered her head, ears and mouth, Sasha entered the park on West Ninetieth Street.

Walking briskly along the bridle trail, she skirted the piles of horse manure and fallen branches, stopping to wonder how the homeless could stand the cold. Covered with newspaper or cardboard cartons, they slept under the protection of the foot bridge that led to the Metropolitan Museum of Art.

A pair of early-morning riders approached, a man whose habit was more impressive than his horsemanship, suffering from what appeared to be a Roy Rogers complex, yelling "Whoa boy" each time his poor horse picked up his gait. His girlfriend—no wife or close female relative would have suffered the sport in these temperatures—looked so scared and so miserable that Sasha was almost tempted to encourage her to dismount and together they would lead the horse back to the stable.

Climbing the small incline, Sasha stood on the jogging path that surrounded the reservoir and surveyed the clumps of dirty ice that had not yet melted after a week of snow storms and freezing rain that had inundated the city. The path was deserted this morning as far as she could see in either direction. And Sonia the Screamer, who was crouched in her usual spot along the metal fence, was yelling the same words, "You've left me, now you've done it, you're gone," over and over. Once, when Sasha mentioned Sonia to her mother, Caroline claimed that she used to see the woman wandering the aisles at Saks Fifth Avenue, muttering those same words as she shopped. Caroline was convinced that Sonia lived in a duplex on Park Avenue and had more money than she knew what to do with and was obviously the former wife of a multimillionaire who walked out because she was so crazy. Which came first, the insanity or the abandonment? But what difference did it make since dumped was dumped.

Join the club, Sonia, Sasha thought as she passed the woman. "Hi, Sonia," she said, "you're better off without him." It was what Sasha had been saying to Sonia since the first time she'd seen her and asked her name.

The wind was beginning to blow. Sasha took several deep breaths before she began to jog, rubbing her gloved hands together, wondering how crazy she was to run in this weather. Even the pigeons and the rats were not out in their usual numbers this morning.

She approached the first boat house, jumping over several frozen puddles before rounding the first curve leading to the East Side. For some reason she turned around then, which was when she noticed that there was someone gaining on her; a man wearing a face mask and dark glasses. A shiver ran through her, although it had less to do with the temperature than it did with suddenly finding herself on the same side of the reservoir—no one in sight right then—with a man wearing a face mask.

Stay calm, she told herself. It was freezing out. Of course, someone would wear a face mask. In fact, if she had any brains and had thought to buy one, she would be wearing one too. And anyway, she wasn't alone, a couple of joggers were about a quarter of a mile away with Walkmans on their heads. *Dire Straits* they might be hearing, certainly not her screams for help.

More snow began falling, solitary flakes drifting down around her and sticking to the ground. She picked up speed until she reached the only stretch of concrete on the path, after the second small house, almost to the second curve, which meant the beginning of the East Side. Glancing over her shoulder again, she noticed that the man had also picked up speed, the distance between them even more diminished since she first noticed him.

Suppose he was a serial killer who picked on athletic women? Suppose he was a killer who picked on women alone? Suppose he was just another jogger? Run. But that was exactly what he was doing. This was supposed to relax her, her morning jog, allow her to think and reflect and ponder.

Her instinct right then was to stop, even if that meant losing her momentum and lowering her pulse rate. If she stopped, she reasoned, he would pass her. Either pass her or kill her. If he passed her, her anxiety would disappear. If he killed her, her anxiety would disappear. Life was choices. No more, no less. It was ridiculous, considering what she had survived, that her fate might be to die at the hands of a deranged maniac in Central Park. It was anticlimactic, not to mention unfair.

Choices again. It was the point at which she could have cut across the path, over the tree stumps and bushes until she reached the stairs leading to Engineer's Gate and Fifth Avenue. Criminals, perhaps, but usually only muggers. Now. Make a dash for it now.

But she didn't. She kept on running, faster, her reasoning only that she wasn't going to make it easier for this monster. Let him work a little to get what he wanted, she had no intention of forcing a decision on his part. Rape or murder. Her fate appeared before her eyes as headlines on the evening newspapers. It was crazy to have come out this morning. Suicidal, her shrink would have said. Careless, Carl would have judged. Selfish, Caroline would have accused. Dumb, Maury would have lamented. And where would they have all made their observations? Sipping wine after her funeral, no doubt, or driving back from the cemetery in FBN limousines.

The man was directly behind her now, near enough so she could hear his breathing. He was almost on her and slightly to the left, which could have meant that he wanted only to pass. Everyone knew the rules of the track; keep to the right except to pass. So what the hell was he still doing on her left? Her heart pounding, the perspiration dotting her upper lip, she pulled down her scarf so it was around her neck and not covering her mouth. Even Sonia the Screamer wouldn't hear her if she cried for help. Sonia was too busy crying for help herself.

What Sasha did was to stop. Just stopped dead. Stopped without any warning, so that she stumbled into the metal fence that bordered the New York City water supply.

There he was, standing there, not more than two feet from her, the face mask off, the dark glasses pushed on top of his head, backdropped by a sign that advised that dogs and spitting were forbidden on the jogging path. Feeling paralyzed, she could only stare as if he were an apparition. "I thought you were a killer," she said. But that was an old story.

He said nothing, just looked at her with those eyes of his. Which this morning seemed peculiarly moist. "I didn't fall," she said. "Go away," she tried again.

He did not go away. He came closer, took several steps forward until she was in his arms, her face pressed against his jacket. She lifted her head, her hands on his shoulders, and looked squarely at him. What happened to you, she wanted to scream, how could you have done that to me, to them, if you did, and they say you did and where have you been, Gideon whoeveryouare? She said none of those things. "Just tell me," she said, "was it your son in Rome?" If he was surprised he didn't show it. Only nodded slowly.

"Oh my God." Her mouth pressed against his cheek. "Oh my God."

"I love you," he said, as if that covered it. As if that explained how it happened that he disappeared only to turn up again some six thousand or so miles later.

"Why didn't you tell me . . . ?" she began, because it still wasn't enough.

"I did."

"No, about you, about what happened."

He had no answer for it. He held her around her waist, guided her toward the stairs that led to Engineer's Gate and Fifth Avenue, the same route that only minutes before could have been her escape.

"I waited," she managed, stopping in the middle of a clearing between the jogging path and the bridle trail. But she was in his arms again, and he was wiping the tears from her face. Someday he might explain everything, although he wasn't sure that she could ever understand.

"I can't survive this again," she warned.

"Neither can I," he said, gathering her in his arms. "Neither can I," he repeated, kissing her as a pair of joggers passed by. But they hardly glanced in their direction. This was New York. Who cared? Whether it was getting kissed or getting killed, nobody paid attention. And for some reason just then, she was under the impression that she had already done both.

The first hint of a smile played on her lips in what seemed like decades. ''Do you want *a* coffee?'' she asked. Wasn't that how it all began?

''I want a life,'' he said. ''With you.''

Ballantine brings you The Best in Modern Fiction